MUTE SWAN

Chris Eisner

A portion of this book's sale will be donated to K9s for Warriors, a non-profit organization that provides service dogs for veterans with PTSD and TBI. For more information, please see www.k9sforwarriors.org.

About the cover: Samuel Silva has used a variety of mediums, most notably BIC ballpoint pens. He is based in London.

About the editor: Porter Shreve was born and raised in the Washington, DC area. His book, *The Obituary Writer*, was a *New York Times* Notable Book. He resides in San Francisco with his wife and two children. For more information, see www.portershreve.com.

First published by Dog Ear Publishing
4010 W. 86th Street, Ste H
Indianapolis, IN 46268
www.dogearpublishing.net

ISBN: 978-1-4575-2824-8

This book is printed on acid-free paper.

This book is a work of fiction. Places, events, and situations in this book are purely fictional and any resemblance to actual persons, living or dead, is coincidental.

Printed in the United States of America

When a man finds that it is his destiny to suffer, he will have to accept his suffering as his task; his single and unique task. No one can relieve him of his suffering or suffer in his place. His unique opportunity lies in the way in which he bears his burden.

—Viktor Frankl, M.D., Ph.D.

For Susan

1

ull house. Two on deck. Twenty-one in the tank.

Dr. Cassius Stevenson stared at the Emergency Department's digital board, rubbing fresh bruises on his knuckles. Two more names appeared on the board below the Waiting-For-Triage list, blinking in green, their times at 00:00. Two more in the tank.

Where do they come from?

The pneumatic doors at the end of the hall parted, waking the security guard at the desk in the corner. Nearing retirement age, as most of them were, he dozed next to a case with multiple surveillance TVs, their glow turning his white shirt blue. Two EMTs fast-walked in from the night, pushing a gurney with the back propped up to vertical. A toddler wearing nothing but a diaper was sitting with an oxygen mask on and not struggling to pull it off as most toddlers would. Pete Bonley, unit secretary, leaned over and tapped the top of the EMS radio on the shelf above his desk, looking at the lit buttons and knobs. He shrugged at Stevenson, his second chin enveloping his first. His co-pilot, Sister May, smiled behind oversized glasses at Stevenson and stuck her nose back in her book, waiting to be summoned somewhere bedside.

"A warning would've been nice," Stevenson said, pointing the EMTs into Trauma 1. He recognized their faces, their walks, but they were new and he had trouble remembering the names of the new hires. Baltimore City couldn't compete with the county's pay. Turnover meant new names, and Stevenson couldn't keep up.

"Sorry Doc," the EMT pushing from the back said. His partner walked alongside with a hand on the railing, steering. Both in blue short-sleeves, unbuttoned down to acceptable, their foreheads gleamed with sweat. Mid-October weather could revert back to summer temperatures without warning. "We were on our way to General but the traffic lights went out again. Bunch of fools on the road tonight."

Stevenson slid off his stool, looking over his shoulder into the Pit, the main nurse's station. Jenna Rollins, charge nurse, sat a few chairs down from

Bonley and Sister May at Def Con, the computer terminal that controlled all movement in the ED. She stood and called down the hall on the other side of the counter for Odeh, ED tech.

"What's the story?" Stevenson asked, following the EMTs in.

The gurney smacked against the stainless steel table in the center of T-1 and they transferred the child over. Each time he inhaled his belly pulled in as far as it would go and the skin between his ribs concaved. He positioned himself as he was on the gurney, leaning forward with his hands on his knees, concentrating on nothing but breathing. Tripoding.

"13-month-old found by the mother approximately thirty minutes ago with a complaint of breathing funny. When we arrived he was crying and wheezing but his vitals were stable. Started breathing like this about a block away. Pulse ox persistent at eighty-eight percent."

"Asthma?"

"Mom says no." The EMT unhooked the oxygen tube from the tank on the bottom of their gurney and handed it to Jenna. Hissing from the open tank filled the room and he bent over and turned the knob off. "She'll be here shortly. His name is Butch."

"Dart game on his arm?" Jenna asked. She connected the oxygen tube into the hospital's main line in the wall, nodding at four pinpoint drops of blood in the crook of Butch's elbow.

"Couldn't get a vein," the other EMT said, backing out and pulling the gurney with him. "Roads were too damn bumpy." He left before he could get an earful.

Stevenson stood at the side of the bed. Butch's eyes were rolling lazy, lids half open. His soles and knees were blackened and his diaper drooped at the crotch. Straw hair was clumped with stickiness in spots and still too thin to cover his egg-white scalp. Rings of fading yellow and green circled his upper arms.

Stevenson lifted the oxygen mask just enough to see the lips. Blue, getting bluer.

"Pulse is thready," Jenna said, feeling the carotid. She grabbed the lead wires hanging from the overhead monitor and draped them over the table. Odeh attached electrode stickers to Butch's chest, talking softly with a smile about how everything would be okay in that soothing Nigerian tongue, where any word sounded rhythmic. Nurse Kay clamped the pulse oximeter on a big toe, wrapped the blood pressure cuff around the upper arm.

"He's going to crash," Stevenson said. "Draw up some epi. Tell Pete to page radiology for a portable. And get respiratory."

"Don't you want a line first?" Kay asked. She grabbed the child's other arm and whipped it around, inspecting for veins.

2

"We'll give the first dose in the glute," Stevenson said. "Then go intraosseous."

"In his *bone?*" Kay asked.

"They haven't changed the definition of intraosseous, Kay."

She sighed, shaking her head as Jenna handed over the intraosseous line kit. Stevenson glanced at Kay, the first time in weeks. The less he saw of her, the better. Frail as ever, the spots on her lower lip darkened more every month. The only nurse still wearing a cap in all of Saint Catherines Hospital. Always with questions, already knowing the answers. I suffer, therefore all will suffer.

A stick of a woman in jean shorts and tank top sauntered in and took a place in the corner, as far away from the action as possible. Arms crossed, lips straight and pressed together, she watched the staff work. Stevenson asked if she was the mother. She nodded once.

"Has Butch had any previous problems breathing?"

"Nope," she said, looking at the floor, crossing her arms even tighter over a flat chest.

Odeh attached the last of the cardiac monitor's leads and undid Butch's diaper. Jenna lifted under the armpits and Odeh slipped the diaper off. What looked like coal was in the center of a diaper saturated in old and new urine, intertwining with stale cigarette smoke. He had a peeling diaper rash from his cheeks to his testicles. Odeh held the diaper over the red trashcan, pausing until the mother looked his way, seeing what he held.

"When's the—" Jenna started. The monitor went into a tirade of beeps. Butch fell forward, unconscious. Green lines on the screen looked like the tracing of fingertips.

"V-tach," Stevenson said, pulling Butch by the ankles and laying him on his back. He felt for a pulse at the upper arm while taking the oxygen mask off. Blue was overwhelming the boy's face. "No pulse."

Odeh put a hand on the child's chest and started compressions. Jenna leaned over and stuck Butch in the rear with a shot of epinephrine. Butch jerked suddenly, reaching his hands straight up, breathing in. A whistle came from Butch's throat, faint but obvious over the clatter of it all, and then he was unconscious again. Stevenson stepped to the head of the bed, looking at Jenna.

"I heard it too," Jenna said, opening the cart's bottom drawer. She put a laryngoscope into Stevenson's waiting hand. He flipped it open like a switchblade and the light at the base came on.

"Draw up 3 of Etomidate for sedation," he said, stepping sideways back and forth into a crouch. None of the beds were at a comfortable level for his 6'2" frame. "Get ready to shock at 40 joules. Got that line in, Kay?"

3

Kay said nothing, staring Stevenson down while putting on sterile gloves.

Stevenson slipped the blade down the toddler's throat and pulled up against the tongue. The gatekeeper of the airway, the epiglottis, was covered in thick saliva.

"Suction," Stevenson said as he went further down. "What's his rhythm?"

"Tachycardic and regular," Jenna said, handing him the suction wand.

"What're y'all doin' to him?" the mother asked. She stood on tiptoes, bobbing, wrinkling her nose.

The vocal cords appeared at the bottom of a tunnel of pink—vertical flaps in an inverted V, opening and closing over the highway to the lungs. Imbedded in the crease on the left side of the cords was a foreign body. Stevenson manipulated the blade and saw a National Bohemian logo. With each breath, the bottle cap would tilt over, covering the airway partially, sometimes completely, then pull back again. Stevenson stuck the suction wand down and it caught the cap easily. He pulled the wand out slow, then the blade.

"Oh boy, what a beer," Jenna said, humming the logo.

"Give him rescue breaths with the bag," Stevenson said, pulling the cap off the tip of the wand. He pinched it between his thumb and middle finger and snapped. The cap flew by the mother's head and she dodged to the side, her gold hoop earrings dancing about. It bounced off the sliding glass door and she watched it come to a rest on the floor, then looked at Stevenson, brow frowned.

Jenna had the bag-valve mask on Butch's mouth and got two puffs of air in before Butch woke up with a snort and cough. Odeh sat Butch up and the child looked around, bug-eyed, breathing deep as the fuse was lit for one almighty wail.

Butch cried and tears flowed, but he was blue no more.

"Normal rhythm," Jenna said loudly over the crying, looking at the monitor, then to the patient. "Let it all out, little man."

Stevenson watched Butch's color return, watched Odeh pat his back.

"I told you so, my friend," Odeh said. "I told you."

The child had almost no upper lip and the area above where the cupid's bow should have been was flat. Small eyes were spaced too wide to be normal. Button nose, with a hint of a slope.

"Call social," Stevenson said to Kay. "Now."

"Now?" Kay asked. "Like, right now?"

"Social?" the mother asked, stepping forward finally. "You mean a social worker? 'Cause I already got one."

Stevenson said nothing, squeezing the laryngoscope handle like a club, staring at the mother. A crowd was at the door, trying to get a good view. The staff would stand quiet and out of the way, waiting for orders. Techs, nurses, housekeeping—everything stopped for a child. When they saw Butch had come back from the abyss, they dispersed with whispers and speculation.

"Her name is Mrs. Laura," the mother said, crossing her arms again.

Her hair was a darker blonde than her son's, short and slicked back with gel into a hint of a ponytail. Her cheeks were cratered with scabs old and new from picking fingers. Eyeliner and eye shadow had been thrown on in haste or not touched up in days.

Target areas are attacked violently. There are no second chances. Do you hear me, Ranger?

"Do you know what a bedpan baby is?" Stevenson asked, approaching her. The shrill of his ever-present tinnitus worsened, drowning out the surrounding noise.

"No-uh," she said. She jutted her hip and huffed, enough that Stevenson could smell a recent belt of spirits.

"Some women don't know they are pregnant or don't care and will continue their ways, drinking and smoking and whatever other debauchery they can get into. When the big day arrives, it's a surprise for some of these women, especially the obese that are so big they have to use a bedpan. They deliver right there, right in the pan, and set it under the bed as if it were waste that needed to be dumped."

"Butch going to be okay?" she asked, looking past Stevenson.

Stevenson leaned down, a few inches from being nose-to-nose, speaking just above a whisper. "The most important relationship in a child's life is between him and the parent. If that fails, he will fail. Is that what you've wanted all along? For Butch to be a failure like you?"

Her eyes went wide as she stepped back, pointing both hands at Stevenson.

"Fuck you, boy. I take care of my baby."

"You couldn't put the bottle down? Not even when you were pregnant?"

She took her earrings off and spiked them on the floor. "Say it again, bitch." Bitch was said in a hiss, through her teeth.

Kay walked out of the room, eyeing them both as she passed. Jenna stepped between Stevenson and the mother and walked her backward into the corner, hands on her pockmarked shoulders. Stevenson followed Kay out, still squeezing the laryngoscope handle.

*   *   *

When Stevenson came out of T-1, Dr. Larry Coleman was standing in front of the doorway to T-2. He squinted at the ambo bay, vertical furrows between his eyes deepening.

"Hey," Stevenson said, looking back into T-1. Both of Jenna's hands were on the mother's shoulders, wearing the thick smile that came out when someone needed a talking to. "I may be getting a complaint soon."

Coleman didn't respond. Two black men were walking out the pneumatic doors into the ambo bay but one had stopped in the vestibule. Thickset, dressed in ill-fitting black jeans and an ultra white t-shirt, he was staring back at Coleman. One of his hands was bandaged heavily.

"Friends of yours?" Stevenson asked.

"That's Knott's son, Jaris."

Stevenson saw it then, the resemblance. The late Felix Knott, a malingerer of no fixed address and onetime frequent guest of the ED, was the same height as his son but a fraction of the weight. Felix Knott had exited through the same doors over two years ago, never to return.

"He's got some balls," Stevenson said, "I'll give him that."

Coleman had gone into T-2 and slid the door closed behind him. When Stevenson looked back at the vestibule of the ambo bay, Knott was gone.

Jenna came out of T-1, still smiling. Her blackened upper canine tooth had been dead since Stevenson met her when he started as a resident almost a decade before. Her hair had lost the last of its auburn pigment officially last year, now a silver mane always tied back.

"What did you say to her?" she asked, taking her hair out of the ponytail, readjusting it tighter. Sweat had darkened her scrubs around the armpits.

"I said I liked her earrings." Stevenson looked into the room. Odeh was bedside, laughing with the toddler, who slapped his wide palms. The mother was on the other side, watching, face blank. "How's he doing?"

"Fine, but," turning around, looking at Butch, "he doesn't look right."

"Fetal alcohol syndrome."

She sighed, then shut her eyes and turned away. "Listen, can you check on the gomer in 27? She's a drop-off from the Perkins Home."

The Gomer, a medical anomaly, the patient that could not be healed. They couldn't communicate, they would never get better, and, according to legend, would never die.

"I've got that OD in T-4, then I'll be there," Stevenson said. "I don't sup—"

6

"Can somebody help me with this?"

A pale, emaciated man, naked but for a pair of purple tube socks, stood in the center of the Pit. One sock was up, the other at the ankle, and he had an erection that he pointed at with both hands. Sister May set her book down and rocked twice to launch herself out of her chair. She wobbled toward the man, keeping eye contact, her head held high.

"There we are," she said with a hum, whipping off her veil and covering his member. She grabbed his arm and turned him around, pointing the way back from which he came. She teetered, he stumbled, and together they left the Pit and disappeared down the hall.

"Never saw her take that off before," Stevenson said, watching the sister's hair bounce, a dull red, thick and frizzed.

"OD in T-4." Jenna smacked his shoulder. "Then 27?" She was sliding the glass door of T-2 open.

"Got it. What's in there?"

"Rotten gallbladder," she said, shutting the door.

"A priority 2 in a trauma room?"

She shrugged and walked away.

When he entered T-4, Bonley was paging him over the intercom but he slid the door closed. Manuel, ED Tech, scurried around an unconscious patient.

"Doctor," he said with a nod.

The patient, naturally tan and tattooed sporadically in prison ink, had a tube in his nose, black from the charcoal the EMTs administered. A catheter was in, monitor leads on the chest, and he had IV lines in both arms. Manuel sat on a stool next to the bed, pulling out a roll of medical tape from his pocket.

"Mother found him about an hour ago with an empty bottle of Percocet and some liquor. Cocaine too." Manuel fastened the IV line with another strip of tape. "Evan Williams?"

"Cheap whiskey." Stevenson went to the counter, opening the chart. DaSilva, Javier. Age 22. Chief Complaint: OD. "Did they draw labs in the field?"

Manuel pointed to the tray behind the bed where six vials of blood lay next to a box of latex gloves. "They're sending someone to pick it up now," he said.

The door slid open and a woman in a crisp lab coat a size too large entered. Stevenson knew her first name only. Zooey. She was still new in ED time, quick, always found a vein if she was drawing the blood. The fluorescent lights had not gotten to her yet. She still smiled a lot and no wrinkles blemished her face, no shadows darkened her eyes.

"Those for me?" she said to Manuel, pointing at the tray.

"Yeah," Stevenson answered for him. He smelled fruit when she passed. Dark hair swung back and forth across her back, contrasting sharply with the coat.

She said thanks, grabbed the vials, and was gone in a moment, sliding the door shut behind her. He watched after her. Manuel called his name twice.

"I said Mrs. Kay got a second shot of Narcan in him about 20 minutes ago, just to be safe. He was a little bradycardic but now, not so much."

"Urine tox?" Stevenson closed the chart, taking a Phillips 66 penlight from his shirt pocket.

"I don't think they did it."

Stevenson pulled the patient's lower eyelids down and shined the light in both. He checked pulses, auscultated the heart, pushed on the belly. The patient stirred but didn't awaken. He stepped back to the counter and documented orders in the chart.

"What's that?" Manuel asked. He was at the foot of the bed, leaning forward, looking between the man's legs.

"What?" Stevenson came over.

"His...be...hind."

Stevenson reached over and lifted the man's scrotum with his pen. There was a flesh-colored piece of erotic paraphernalia in the man's rear.

"Good eye," Stevenson said, tossing the pen on the floor.

"Just yank it out?" Manuel asked, his hand already reaching in.

Stevenson said go for it and Manuel pulled the plug with a yank. A brief suction followed and the two shivered. Manuel dropped the device and it rolled under the gurney.

Javier DaSilva awoke and bolted upright. His injected eyes looked between Stevenson and Manuel. His chest began heaving, neck craning. He retched a geyser of black and red tar over his legs.

"I knew it," Manuel said, grabbing a stack of bedpads from the counter drawer. "Knew I forgot something."

DaSilva paused for a moment, waiting out the aftershocks, but the retching started again. As Manuel unfolded the pads, DaSilva noticed the catheter and started tugging at it.

"No you don't," Manuel said, grabbing the back of DaSilva's neck and pulling him over the gurney's railing.

DaSilva vomited what little remained, then pulled away from Manuel's grip, swinging a left fist into the side of Manuel's head. Manuel groaned and stepped back, hissing *oh mi cabeza*. DaSilva started sliding toward the foot of the bed but Stevenson grabbed DaSilva by the throat, yanking him back. While holding him down, he pressed his thumb into the corner of DaSilva's left eye.

"Yaaa, sai de cima, sai de cima," DaSilva said, clutching at Stevenson's wrist.

"Vou devorar sua alma," Stevenson said, leaning in, speaking through clenched teeth. He felt a thump under his thumb. DaSilva squealed, letting go of Stevenson's wrists, putting his hands at his sides.

"Por favor." DaSilva was pressing his head into the bed, his words whispered. "Por favor."

Stevenson let go and stepped back. DaSilva cupped his hands over his nose, his red eyes glistening. Manuel was throwing the bedpads on the floor.

"That wasn't Spanish," Manuel said. He threw more pads over DaSilva's legs but the patient didn't notice. He was turning on his side, facing the wall.

"Portuguese. You okay?"

"Yeah, yeah," Manuel said, waving downward at the patient. "Got me when I not looking."

"You want him restrained?"

Manuel said no and went about cleaning up. Stevenson washed his hands in the corner sink and grabbed the chart. "Let me know if he gives you any problems."

"What did you say to him?"

"I told him to knock it off or you were going to put that plug down his throat."

Manuel hunched his shoulders and laughed.

"Do no harm," Stevenson said.

"And take no shit," Manuel said, his index finger pointing to the heavens.

The gomer in 27 was spewing a word salad for all the ED to hear and Stevenson ducked into T-2 before anyone could call him out. Coleman stood on one side of the bed and Odeh the other, doing compressions. A boulder of a black man was laid flat, head to the side, body jerking with Odeh's compressions. An intubation tube stuck out of his mouth. Jenna worked the crash cart.

"Do you see me?" Coleman was crouched over, eye-to-eye with the patient. "There is nothing I can do for you now. We have to stop."

Coleman stood straight. Under the halogen lamp over the bed, beads of sweat glistened under thinning hair. A single stream rolled down his temple and between a few moles like a pachinko ball.

Odeh stopped compressions and the patient kept staring at Coleman but no longer blinked.

"You should have stayed," Coleman said, picking up the chart off the end of the bed. He looked at the clock above the door, then to Stevenson. "He was here about five hours ago with belly pain. Kept going on about how everybody in his family had their gallbladder out at the same age. I told him it may be his heart and he just laughed."

"AMA form signed?"

"Before he had time to button up his shirt. We should combine the against medical advice form with the death packet forms. Would save us a lot of time if the patient filled it all out for us."

"Have them call the morgue too," Stevenson said. "They can do the negotiations about picking up the body."

Coleman mumbled agreement and closed the chart. He handed it to Jenna, then looked at the expired patient. "Asshole," he said, slapping the dead man on the side of the head with the back of his hand. He looked to Odeh. "Are the old folks in Nigeria just as stupid?"

"There are no old folks in Nigeria."

Coleman smiled, breathed in, but stopped short of laughing. He nodded and shuffled to the door, turning the florescent lights out as he left. Only the halogens remained on when a patient expired.

"Two seven," Jenna said, pointing at Stevenson.

He said okay and followed Coleman out. Father Clay was coming in, dressed in his last rites garb, breathing heavily from a sprint. Clay jogged in his off time, his frame lean from marathons and a diet of broiled and baked meats, none red, and vegetables. He heard the deeds of thousands, before the physician even knew the patient was in the building. Never frowned, never smirked. *I'm Father Clay. What can I do for you, friend?*

"Too Late?" Clay asked. He straightened his purple sash, pushed back on the bridge of his silver-rimmed glasses.

"Very," Coleman said, stepping aside, "but be my guest."

Clay went to the foot of the bed and started his chant. Jenna went about her post-code routine but Odeh stopped what he was doing, bowing his head.

"He see you?" Adrian Lotts asked, pushing the Accord's lighter in. It would be his third smoke since they got there. He chewed a hangnail on his thumb, watching for the lighter to pop.

"He saw me," Knott said.

"And it was the same doctor?"

"Same doctor."

"Why you ain't say something?"

"I just wanted him to see me. That's all. I didn't want y'all making noise up in there."

"Still should have said something."

A pearl Escalade pulled into the alley, then whipped around to back in. The reverse lights came on.

"Finally," Adrian said. He reached over and opened the glove compartment, removing a Bowie knife with no sheath. "Can't believe you let this fool drive your truck. You know he probably fucked that up too, right?"

Knott didn't answer, trying and failing at not looking at the blade Adrian had. He got out of the car and a foul breeze off the Harbor's water hit him in the face. The alley ended at a dilapidated pier, where they had been waiting over an hour for Timmy Darrens. Knott's hand throbbed, even with the pain meds, but he kept quiet about it.

Timmy hopped out and fumbled with the keys, trying to find the one for the back door.

"It's open," Knott said, taking his keys from Timmy.

Timmy yanked on the back door handle and it rose slowly, revealing a pile of dead pit bulls, lined up side-by-side with heads pointed out. Streaked with saliva and blood, some had tongues protruding while others were mangled throughout. Timmy had never bothered to roll down the windows.

"I told you," Adrian said, dancing around in circles, throwing his hands in the air. Pebbles scratched the asphalt under his untied Timberlands. "Shit all over the place."

"You got to bag them up before you load them in the truck," Knott said to Timmy, his voice low. "They can still shit after they dead." He nudged Timmy's bony shoulder, offering a smirk, but Timmy didn't seem to notice. He only stared at the carcasses and the unopened box of trash bags next to them. A single fly had already found the stench.

"Sorry, yo," Timmy said, grabbing a dog by the scruff. It landed head first with a hollow thud, stirring up the smell more.

"Goddamn, Timmy," Adrian said, backing away again, pulling his peach polo over his nose. "You some kind of stupid."

"Whachu crying about?" Knott asked. "It's my damn truck."

"You ain't defending this boy, is you?" Adrian asked. "After what he did?"

Headlights lit the alley but the men paid little attention to it. A black Lexus parked in front of the Escalade. RJ Reeves and Tink Whitley got out as the trunk popped open.

"Damn, man," RJ said, walking up to them. His dress shirt was untucked, the tie he had on earlier long gone. "You got to bag them first."

"You ain't got to tell me," Adrian said, pointing to Timmy.

Timmy pulled the remaining dogs out and grabbed the box of trash bags. He went to shut the back door.

"Naw, naw, naw," Adrian said, grabbing the door. "Got to air it out now."

Knott watched Timmy do the bagging. It had been a bad night for the hustler. He had brought a bait dog in at the last minute for the other fighters to practice on before their matches but the dog, a stolen standard poodle, ended up biting the front foot off a fight dog. That fight dog belonged to Markus Kruk, the east side dealer who was outgrowing the east side. Knott, trying to break up the dogs, got bit on the hand by the poodle. A yard boy, weighing about the same as the dog, hit it over the head with a pipe, killing it on the spot, as Timmy stood there watching it all happen. Adrian and RJ took Knott to the hospital and Timmy was left with the most hated task of the operation: Clean up.

With the dogs in the bags, their tops knotted tight, Timmy grabbed four, Adrian two, and Knott one with his uninjured hand. They walked to the end of the alley and over a chain-link fence that, for as long as Knott could remember, had never stood straight. Beyond the fence was the pier that stretched out into the Baltimore Harbor. No lights lit this part of the water on the edge of Fells Point, except for the Domino Sugars sign on the other side, an orange neon billboard atop the factory that overlooked smoke stacks and cargo ships at its dock. Bars for the college kids and a cop on every corner were five blocks over but here, at the end of the cobblestone road flanked by the ghosts of manufacturing, few dared go.

"C'mon, Tink," Knott said, looking back at the ally. "Sun's coming up soon."

Tink emerged from the back of the Lexus, chains in his hands. They were attached by a carabiner to coffee cans filled with cement, each with a hook in the center. In the shadows they looked like maces.

RJ caught up with Knott. "How's your hand?" he asked. They watched where they stepped for missing planks, their gait stop-and-go like hopscotch.

"It's alright. Ain't all that."

"Yeah, okay."

Knott looked over, saw RJ looking at Timmy with a smirk.

They all reached the end and dropped the bags on the planks. When Tink approached, the pier started to sway but they were used to it and did little to brace themselves. His rose tracksuit swished with friction, joining the sound of water slapping the crooked posts. He dropped the anchors and the rattling chains echoed across the water. He pulled free a roll of duct tape that had been around his wrist, set it down, and headed back to the car.

"Go on," RJ said, pointing at Timmy, then the bags. "Drop them in the Brown."

Knott lit a cigarette, the smell of sulfur and fish worse than the last time they dumped dogs. Styrofoam and plastic bobbed on the gentle water. The Brown. Too deep to know what lay at the bottom, too filthy to see beyond the surface.

Timmy grabbed a bag and wrapped a strip of tape around the knot repeatedly. He looped the chain connected to an anchor around the bag multiple times until it was tight against the contents, then hooked the carabiner into one of the links. He rolled it over the edge, getting a face full of the Brown when it hit. He repeated the sequence, each bucket thumping the water, each splashing back. Adrian got closer to Timmy with each bag being thrown in.

"At least you got this right," Adrian said, fidgeting with the back of his waistband.

Tink had come back, this time waddling as he carried a 5-gallon bucket filled with cement, a thick chain dragging behind him. As Timmy pushed the last carcass in, Tink set the bucket down.

"That's all of em'," Timmy said, standing, brushing beads of water off his tired sweatpants. "You done dragged that here for nothin'."

Knott saw it, the drop of Timmy's cheeks, the corners of his mouth turning down. Flat, wide nose, skin dark just on the face from too many days on the hunt for a fix. You just got to give a half-shit about yourself, he would tell Timmy. New clothes, new hair, that'll get you some play.

"I'll carry it back for you," Timmy said in his monotone chuckle. He looked around at everyone until he faced Knott and RJ.

"Sorry, yo," Knott said. "You just—"

Adrian stepped forward and sank the Bowie knife in Timmy's back, down to the guard. Timmy gasped briefly, as if spooked. The tip of the knife poked out of the left side of his chest, then disappeared as Adrian pulled it out. A circle of crimson grew where the tip of the knife once was.

"Jaris," Timmy mouthed, bringing his hand up to his chest. The front of his sweat pants darkened at the crotch.

Adrian grabbed the side of Timmy's neck and ran the knife across the other side, once forward and once back, pushing blade and skin together. He stepped back and Timmy stumbled some, then put his hands up to his new wound, trying to hold the blood in. Tink came from behind with a trash bag and pulled it over Timmy's head, down to the ankles where it could go no further. He grabbed the roll of duct tape and wrapped a strip repeatedly around Timmy's ankles. He had to get on his knees to tear the tape with his teeth. Timmy was poking at the inside of the bag, softly.

"Just die, mutha' fucker," Adrian said, kicking Timmy's legs out from under him.

Tink grabbed the chain on the 5-gallon bucket and wrapped it around the ankles. Timmy's knockoff Air Jordans, with dog shit caked on the bottom, moved circular and Knott closed his eyes at this, thankful that RJ had not asked him to do the deed. Tink pushed the bucket in and the body followed, the bag crinkling as it slid over the planks. Adrian stood at the edge of the pier, watching the bubbles. Tink started back to the cars, his job done.

"We cool?" RJ asked. He lit a cigarette and pulled deep, looking up at the sky. The surrounding buildings were emerging in the dawn's light.

"Yeah," Knott said, still looking where Timmy once was. Damp wood, with a few drops of blood mixed in. "He had to go."

"Got that right," Adrian said, spitting in the water. He tossed the Bowie knife in. "Nigga' got on my last goddamn nerve."

"Guess you can relax now, huh whody?" Knott said, eyeing Adrian.

Adrian looked at Knott but kept quiet. He picked up the roll of duct tape and headed back to the cars.

"He had a grand coming to him tonight," RJ said, walking back. "You can have it, since y'all was close."

"We weren't close," Knott said. "Just felt sorry for him is all."

He and RJ had killed and seen killing before their teens. Through the years he had learned that there was no sense in mourning. Dead was dead. Players played, most lost, and there was no room in the mind for memories of better days.

But he was getting older. His back ached in the morning. Knees stiffened in the rain. Fist fights and stompings, running for miles through alleys and wrecked houses from blue and whites, or running after someone whose time had come. He would lay in bed hours before dawn, awake, thinking back over the years about all the faces of the men looking him in the eye moments before they died.

The Escalade's engine started, then the horn tapped twice. Knott walked back, eyes on the pier, avoiding the Brown.

*   *   *

"Help me, help me. Help me, help me."

Maureen Tuuvey, the gomer in room 27, raised the cry of the demented. Her poisonous piss had driven her past the edge of senility to the point where only pharmaceuticals could silence her.

"Helllllllp me, help me."

"If she just had some rhythm," Jenna said, typing at Def Con.

"Almost done," Stevenson said from the doctor's bar, scribbling orders for Tuuvey. Coleman sat beside him on the end, finishing up the death packet paperwork for the dead man in T-2. The death packet required identity and cause of death in triplicate for all those that died on the ED's watch. The blank toe tag with red string stuck out of the side of the packet. The last identifier, the last piece of paperwork the ED would ever complete for a patient.

Stevenson closed Tuuvey's chart. "Here," he said, holding it over the counter.

"Finally." Jenna stood and grabbed it, heading straight for the Pyxis machine at the edge of the Pit. The Pyxis, resembling a small automated teller machine with a flanking glass refrigerator, held most of the drugs used in the ED. It was meant to keep better track of inventory and deter theft but neither seemed to occur. The Pyxis could be fooled by using ex-employees codes or simply pressing multiple keys at once. The alarm had not sounded in years on the old machine so prying the drawers open was also an option. Stolen pills were replaced with aspirins or acetaminophens and doing a drug screen on employees working during a shift when meds were stolen was pointless, since most of them were already on medications in the same drug class, prescribed by their personal doctors.

Stevenson opened the blue baby's chart, little Butch Shifflet. Both Butch and Mama Shifflet were long gone now, Social Services convinced that Butch was safe within his mother's picked-over arms. Pen in hand, he glanced at the board, the constantly changing directory of who was on deck in triage, who was in-house in one of the rooms, and who sat in the fish tank, waiting to be scooped out, all manipulated by the traffic controller at Def Con.

Twelve in house. One on deck. Two in the tank.

Across the Pit stood rooms 5 through 8 and between 6 and 7, a dry-erase board listed the physicians on for the shift and the two head nurses: Coleman/Stevenson, Jenna/Kay. The patients in room 6 and 7, both men, both too young and disheveled to be anything other than addicts, were staring back at Stevenson. They always stared. Always.

The shape of the ED was one that Lawrence Coleman, Medical Director of Saint Catherines Emergency Department, regretted soon after it was renovated in 1980. He had helped design what, on paper, resembled a square tape measure with a few inches of the tape pulled out. When entering from the ambo bay, an immediate left past the security desk led to a white metal door, the psychiatric pod. Four rooms, two padded, surrounded a nurse's station and though the soundproofing helped muffle the screams, the pounding on the room's doors could be heard throughout the ED. Further down the hall, the fast-track finished out the rest of the tape measure. Ten rooms with a nurse station half the size of the Pit, the fast-track was meant for injuries and ailments a mid-level provider and nurse could move in and out quickly.

In the main ED, rooms fanned around the outside with the Pit in the center, so almost all could see and stare at the department's inner workings. A chest-high counter surrounded the Pit and an office was at its base for the doctors to put their belongings in or finish charts or just hide. In the Pit was Def Con and the unit secretary, where anyone not a physician wandered about. The doctor's bar, the section of counter in front of the trauma rooms, overlooked the Pit.

There had been talk of dropping the T from the names of rooms T-1 through T-4, since Saint Catherines had not had a designated trauma team for five years or any residents or interns in the same amount of time. The hospital suits blamed this on insurance costs, yet the trauma kept coming. Gunshot wounds, stabbings, motor vehicle accidents, assault and batteries, rapes—whatever an ambulance crew could heap onto a gurney and wheel through the pneumatic doors. If the crew's drive was too far to the university hospitals a few miles away, their shifts close to ending, or, most commonly, if the patient requested it, Saint Catherines was the designated drop zone. Saint Catherines, a church long before a hospital, was where criminals claimed their scarlet wristband. Either by ambulance or on foot, they came, bleeding from some temporary or permanent cavity. Their hands still smelling of gunpowder, IV fluids going in as fast as they came out, even the dying still demanded to talk to a priest first, before a doctor. The hospital had consumed the church the day they took in the first patient but a century later, Canon Law still ruled. Whatever the ED patient confessed, the true story of their injuries would go no further than the room and no court of law could say otherwise. Even the charts had to be censored. No Snitching was the rule and Saint Catherines was the only hospital in the city that pledged allegiance to this Code of the Street.

Stevenson finished the documentation on Butch Shifflet's visit and closed the chart. He pushed in on his eyes with the heels of his hands, setting fireworks off on the back of his eyelids. A yawn was coming on, the aura starting a half hour ago. Shift change was near.

"Don't do it," Coleman said, but Stevenson had already started. Coleman did the same, then turned around to the clock.

"Two hours," he said, repeating it twice more.

"Who is coming in?" Stevenson asked.

"Baldanza and Jeller. Bal-I need a consult for a hangnail-Danza."

"She's not that bad."

"Averaging two patients an hour? Bonley could get them out faster."

"I heard that," Bonley said, sipping on a water bottle.

"At least she has pretty handwriting," Stevenson said.

"Has to. She's research. All they do is write."

Coleman had trouble filling the physician schedule with bodies before Stevenson came on as a resident, and it never changed. As murder rates rose, available and trained physicians went down. With the loss of the resident program, Coleman gave up on trying to staff his group with full-time, board certified emergency physicians. All that was left was himself, Stevenson, and Jeller. The rest were part-timers and agency physicians from rent-a-doc companies that skimmed large percentages off the wages of providers often not suitable for emergency medicine, or operating a band-aid.

"I'll be back." Stevenson slid off the stool and put the Shifflet chart into the discharged bin next to the Pyxis machine. He walked out of the Pit, eyeing the board.

Fourteen in house. Zero on deck. One in the tank.

He rounded the corner and stopped at the bulletin board next to the break room. Every week, someone cut the Murder Ink section out of the City Paper and posted it in the lower right-hand corner next to the announcements and memos. Murder Ink was the weekly tally of the homicides with names and causes of death. Nine this week, he read, one a two-month-old infant, strangled and thrown over the 95 overpass at the base of the city. He read it a few times, rubbing the bruises on his fists.

Your hands, Bulldog.

Random thoughts and quotes from yesteryear bounced around his head frequently these days, more so in the ED. They cut in, inserted themselves when the flame brightened, not helping matters at all.

He looked away from the clipping, disgusted with himself again for searching it out, but he would be there next week and the week after. Why he read it, he never knew.

*   *   *

"Tonto," David Folger, physician assistant, said. He sat at the head of the break room table, alone, with a pile of charts on either side of him. "You need a haircut."

"Yeah?" Stevenson looked at the steel paper towel dispenser next to the sink, patting the top of his curled hair. In the summer it would go blonde if he was under the sun enough, but otherwise it stayed chestnut. "Barely an inch."

"Like a brillo pad. Usually you keep it tight."

"I'm just glad to have it."

"Shit, is it getting worse?" Folger put his pen down, feeling the crown of his scalp with his fingertips.

"I wasn't talking about you." Stevenson took a paper cup from the stack next to the coffee maker. "And no, it's not getting worse."

"You sure?"

Stevenson assured him he was sure. He looked at the clock. "Thought you were gone."

"Got hit with a few lacerations. Had to skip dinner."

"Like the post office over there." Stevenson filled the cup with the last bit of coffee and sat at the table. He took a sip. Coffee grinds stuck to his tongue.

"Post office closes on Sundays and holidays," Folger said, taking a chart from the pile on the left. One remained after that. He opened it and started writing.

Folger was hired five years before, straight out of PA school, to run the fast-track department. The previous PA had walked out after being bit by a child while suturing her head, then struck in the face by the mother for hurting the child. Saint Catherines was the only place Folger had sent his resume and Coleman the only one who ever read it. The ED was run by Chesapeake Physicians, the emergency medicine group contracted with the hospital since the ED opened, and Coleman, the founder, did the hiring and firing. The gamble paid off. Folger talked fast, worked faster, and usually ate standing up, if at all.

"Anything good tonight?" Stevenson asked, taking a chart off the top of the larger pile and opening it to the last page. He co-signed next to Folger's signature, a requirement for all patients seen by mid-levels.

"Not really." Folger slapped the completed chart on the pile and opened the last one. "Coleman's buddy made an appearance."

Stevenson asked who, getting into the groove of co-signing. Lacerations, fractures, boils, sore throats, foreign bodies. Never a night without a foreign body.

18

"Jaris Knott. Had a mean dog bite on his hand."

"I saw him leaving. Nobody's killed him yet."

"Not yet. Somebody tried though. I hate closing bites but that thing was totally filleted open. I know it's going to get infected."

"Whose dog?"

"No idea. He never filled out the dog bite form. Declined the rabies shot, too. He'd better hope that dog wasn't sick."

"He give you any trouble?"

"No, he didn't say much of anything. He had an entourage at first but I kicked most of them out. Gotta love security here. They let anybody in." Folger finished the last chart and put it on the pile. "Is Coleman still being sued by that asshole over his father?"

"Think so."

"Stroke, wasn't it?" Folger sat back, stretching.

"Heart."

"That's right. Coleman wouldn't give him morphine for the chest pain until the cardiologist came down for consult so the dumb bastard left. Didn't sign the AMA form."

"He signed it. Records lost it."

"Shit, man. Of all the things to lose."

To lose the Against Medical Advice form was as bad as forgetting to get it signed. To an attorney, this meant the patient was sent home not knowing he would die. Medical negligence. Malpractice. Please pay up or everyone suffers as the case is dragged through the courts for years before ending up at trial where a jury of Felix Knott's peers hands his family the full amount asked for, and twice more for the inconvenience. Doesn't matter that Felix Knott was an ex-con and drug addict and domestic abuser extraordinaire, leaving behind a couple lost kids, numerous battered girlfriends, and a vegetable wife, barely existing in a state hospital he never visited. Bailiff, take the good doctor's belongings please.

"I'm out of here," Folger said, getting up and sliding the chair under the table. He picked up a book bag on the floor covered in the patches of college basketball teams. A Maryland Terps hat was in the loop at the top of the bag and he pulled it out and put it on. "Is it pointless to ask you to come over Thursday to watch the game?"

"Yes."

"C'mon, man. Just for the first half. The kids keep asking about you."

"They met me once."

"You made an impression."

"Good or bad?"

"They're asking for you. Must be good."

Stevenson put the last signed chart on the pile and put the pen down. "Next time," he said, yawning.

"You need to get out of the city once in a while, Cassius. See some real human beings for a change." Folger went to the break room door. "I'll get Karen to invite some of her old sorority friends over." He opened the door but stayed put.

"Yeah?" Stevenson said.

"You walk in and *bam*—panties around the ankles, all of them. I'll be prying them off you with a crowbar."

Sister May had walked silently up to the door but Folger hadn't noticed her. She held a coffee mug with both hands, looking straight at Stevenson with a smile as large as possible without opening her mouth. Her veil, a lighter blue then the previous one, was snugly in place.

"This one chick, Crystal, does this thing with a Kielbasa—"

"Hello, Mr. Folger."

Folger had his head back and mouth open with a fist over it, simulating debauchery, when Sister May spoke up. He froze, looking at Stevenson.

"Please tell your friend with the Kielbasa that Jesus loves her." Sister May passed Folger and went to the sink.

"Will do," Folger said, eyes wide and lower lip pulled down. He waved at Stevenson and trotted away.

"Doctor," Sister May said, taking the coffee pot from the maker, holding it to the light and inspecting it. She set her mug down and went about making another pot. "Did I interrupt?"

"Not at all. You saved me, actually."

"That's what I do." She filled the pot with tap water and dumped it into the coffee maker. "Isn't Mr. Folger married?"

"He is. He was talking about some friends of his wife."

"Well, I guess he means well. Maybe there is one in the lot that would not be so quick with dropping the panties?"

"I would rather catch up on some sleep than try to find out which one."

"Smart man."

Having taken her vows before Stevenson was in grade school, Sister May Dufner was one of a few sisters remaining who helped out in the ED. She had heard more confessions than anyone, even Father Clay, and would occasionally be there to bid farewell to some departing soul in the trauma rooms or listen to the confessions of a bleeding teenager who refused treatment until he talked to a priest or somebody representing a priest. Doughy face with eyes set so deep it was hard to tell their color, she listened with intensity and would offer advice not always kind but without animosity or motive.

"When did you clock in?" She filled the coffee filter and turned the pot on. "You look beat."

"Seven." Stevenson gulped the rest of his coffee down. Grinds remained at the bottom like fleas in muddy water and he swirled the cup around, watching them spin. "Had a couple code blues back to back. Zaps the life right out of you."

"I often wonder how you remember all the things it takes to keep them alive."

"You kind of wing it most of the time. Hopefully they don't figure out we have no idea what we're doing."

"Oh go on." She laughed. The coffee maker chimed and she turned around, picking up her mug. "Do you have anyone in need of guidance?"

"Not at the moment." Stevenson picked up the pile of charts and stood. "But I'll keep an eye out."

Coleman was in the same position, hunched over a pile of charts, scribbling away. The hump in his upper back stretched his lab coat, causing the sleeves to pull back to mid-forearm. He could look Stevenson in the eye before the hump started but now it pushed his head down a little more each year. Soon he would only see his gut and feet.

"The sister is looking for business," Stevenson said, dropping Folger's charts into the discharged bin.

Coleman grunted as he signed his name and closed a chart. "You're off tomorrow?"

"For a couple days. What's up?"

"I was thinking it's been too long since I made chili." Coleman sat back, tucking his pen into his pocket protector. "When was the last time you came over?"

"I don't know. Couple years. I'm still recovering from the last batch."

It had been three years. Coleman's wife, Elaine, had died the month before and he called Stevenson, demanding he come over for chili. With Coleman's son living in New York, the brownstone was too quiet once the phone stopped ringing and people stopped bringing food over.

"Why don't you come over around five?" Coleman asked. "I'll lay off the spice."

"You mean the uranium?"

"That too." Coleman looked at the board, then back to Stevenson. "You want to get out of here? Tank's been empty for an hour."

"You sure?" Stevenson asked. It was an hour before shift change. "I've got the overdose in T-4."

"Mr. Butt Plug? Psych just took him upstairs. I watched a piece of Manuel's innocence die when I told him what that thing was for."

Stevenson slid his chair in, looking around to be sure. It was quiet but he didn't say it. The Q word was never said out loud in the ED.

"And the gomer in 27?" he asked.

"I'll babysit until her ride shows. Go on, before I change my mind."

Stevenson went in the office and took his helmet off the filing cabinet. Two desks in the office faced the hallway leading to the ambo bay and he took his keys out from the drawer of the desk on the right. The mailbox cubbies for the physicians were on the opposite wall and though he had messages waiting to be answered, he walked out and patted Bonley on the shoulder, telling him see you later.

"Bring suds," Coleman called after Stevenson.

"Red Stripe?"

"Twelve of them."

Stevenson waved as he walked out of the ambo bay, nodding to the guard who nodded back, eyes open for a moment only. Never the same face for more than a month at the security desk, this was certain.

"And be careful on that damn thing," Coleman yelled.

Stevenson walked up the concrete ramp on the side of the cafeteria loading dock and went in through the side door, bypassing the open garage. He kept his bike, a '69 BMW, in the hallway with the timecards, out of the elements and in eyesight of Mildred Talmidge, cafeteria supervisor. He booted the kickstand and sat down. The kitchen was full of bodies and activity. Metal spoons stirring, ovens opening and closing, a dropped pan followed by expletives.

"How ya' doing, Doc?"

Mildred stood at the end of the hall, hands on hips and a soiled apron over a round belly. She smiled thick, not at all affected by the activity behind her.

"Sun's not even up yet," Stevenson said. "What are you doing here already?"

"Suits are having a big breakfast meeting today. Can't let them go hungry." She strode up next to him and kissed him on the cheek, leaving the smell of baked bread behind for a moment. "How's business?"

"Non-stop."

"You didn't do what I tol' you, did you?"

"What, lock the door? They'd just find another way in."

She laughed deep, her upper arms rippling. She readjusted her hairnet over hair that never went past her neck.

"How's the baby?" Stevenson asked.

"Wild as ever. Not even two yet and somebody up and taught him a couple of curses."

"No."

"Yeah. Woke up this morning sounding like a pirate's parrot. It was the F word today. Yes it was. Like he's watching some X-rated Sesame Street when I'm not home."

"Patrice been around?" Stevenson started walking the bike forward and she walked beside him.

"Lord, no." Her smile faded. "Lost her to the street."

"She'll figure it out."

Mildred looked at the sky and shook her head, said *maybe*, and Stevenson felt a fool for asking about it. Patrice Talmidge, Mildred's daughter, would never be back. He saw her as a patient occasionally, always for complications from hepatitis C, and anyone could see that heroin had her for keeps. She was suicidal, a passive suicidal where the driver puts on a seatbelt as they're headed for a brick wall.

A flatbed truck pulled up to the loading dock next to a row of oil drums. They were lined end-to-end along the cinderblock wall, each blue and stenciled with the words WASTE COOKING GREASE.

"Doc, I got to go yell at these boys for a minute. They're a week late. You stay out of trouble, ya' hear?"

"Roger that."

He turned the ignition on the bike and leaned over, putting the petcock horizontal. With a couple twists on the throttle, the second kick brought the hum of the two cylinders to life. He strapped his helmet on and drifted down the ramp. Mildred was ranting at the driver of the grease truck who had yet to get out of the cab. At the lot's entrance, he stopped, letting the engine warm. Only the North Star remained as the sky faded to electric blue. He could see the outline of the old American National Brewery roof a few blocks over, looming over the decay. Like a giant samurai Kabuto, it seemed the roof was placed on the head of the

Victorian building as an afterthought. All around stood boarded row-houses, malt liquor billboards, storefront churches, long-abandoned cars.

He revved the throttle and gave a look over his shoulder at the ambo bay. Someone was on the dock, looking in his direction. Under the vestibule's florescent light, he could make out the figure of a man, wavy black hair reaching way down to the middle of his back.

Not a man at all. The lab tech, Zooey something, in the oversized lab coat.

He thought he should wave but she turned around and went back in before the decision was made.

2

"*Y*our hands, Bulldog. Fire. Fuckin' fire."

Stevenson stood in a grand hall, holding his M16 at low-ready. Smoke hovered over his blackened arms and many faces stared. They circled him in a massive huddle, closing in.

"Took out a mosquito on the roof."

A few raps on the door woke him. His arms were fine, the shine of burn scars now mottled and faded. He had sat on the couch when he got home, a mistake this early in the morning. Always wired after a night shift, he would go to Gentleman's Boxing Club before sleeping most of the afternoon, but this night shift had gone beneath the scars. Butch's mother, the overdosed Latino—they woke what should not be for a physician and exhaustion always followed when it made an appearance.

Another series of knocks and he got up, grabbing his gym bag off the coffee table. The knit blanket draped over the back of the couch had fallen down and he draped it over again. He had it since he was boy, this blanket made of patches of multiple colors. Red was his favorite and his mother had knit an extra few squares in, though the blanket was meant for his brother. All this time and the colors were as bright as ever.

More knocking.

"You asleep?"

Taren Fisher stood at the bottom of the stoop, adjusting his backpack on his shoulders. His mother, Kendra, stood in her doorway five rowhouses down, hands crossed tight over her bathrobe. The wind was cool and warned of winter. Stevenson waved and she waved back as she went inside.

"Dozed off," he said, yanking the door shut and locking the deadbolt. "Night shift."

The Fishers, Taren and Kendra, had been his neighbors before Taren was school age, the only neighbors he knew by name on the strip of two- and three-level rowhouses between Pratt and Gough Street. He had lived on Chester Street, a narrow one-way alley, since medical school and not once, up until the Fishers moved in and Taren picked Stevenson's stoop to bounce a basketball, had he seen another person exit one of the other houses. There were scattered seniors and those who inherited the properties from the previous generation but most of them never seemed to leave their homes or even turn the front stoop light on.

"You missed it," Taren said, walking backward, thumbs hooked under the straps of his bookbag. "Helicopters were out last night. Thought they were coming for me."

"Yeah? On the most wanted list again?"

"High roller like me? You know it."

They reached the top of the street and turned left on Pratt. Cars moved fast up and down the main road that stretched from the east side to the west. Twice a week, gym days, he walked Taren to PS 128. He'd been doing this for two years, since Taren started kindergarten, and this was the beginning of the third.

"How's school?" Stevenson asked as they crossed the street. The light turned green for oncoming traffic and he eyed the front car, a convertible Mercedes that was drifting toward them. Taren jogged to the sidewalk, but Stevenson slowed his pace.

"Fine. Not enough desks, though. I gotta share with some girl that don't speak no English." Taren stopped at the corner, waiting, hands in his pockets.

"So teach her."

Stevenson got to the corner and the driver, a headset in his ear and a napkin stuffed in his collar, shook his head as he gunned it, giving Stevenson the finger. Taren checked to see if Stevenson would react, but he kept walking.

Taren said, "She'll be gone in a couple weeks. After the first month don't nobody come back." He kicked at a beer can. "Wish I didn't have to go back."

They crossed Broadway Avenue, the direct route south into Fells Point, and Taren slowed his pace on the other side. A pack of day workers stood outside the convenience store on the corner. A truck pulled up on the curb in front and the passenger rolled the window down, holding up four fingers. The entire pack scrambled for the truck and the first four jumped in back. The others meandered back to the store but two smacked the side of the truck, raising a fist as it took off.

"I don't like it here some days," Taren said, stopping.

"Why not?" Stevenson put his hands in the front pocket of the hooded sweatshirt, adjusting his keys so they stuck out between the fingers of his fist.

"Everybody angryment all the time."

"Angryment?"

Taren nodded, looking up. Plump cheeks. Iris color not much different from the skin. Bottom incisors missing and the remaining teeth well-cared for at the insistence of a parent without dental insurance. A faint horizontal scar crossed the chin, the remnants of a suturing by Stevenson, performed on the Fisher's couch when the boy ran into the front door's knob. *It will fade. I promise.*

Stevenson said, "I got your back so don't worry about it."

"I know but still. Wish we could live somewhere chill."

They shuffled in place, looking around, kicking at the sidewalk. This was as far as he walked Taren, even when he was in kindergarten. Like prison, where inmates wanted only to do their time and attract no attention, nobody wanted to be walked to school by an adult, especially one that looked white from the distance.

"You be home later?" Taren asked, trotting backward. The school was at the end of the block and dozens of children filed into the corner door.

"Maybe."

Taren turned around and jogged the rest of the way. Stevenson readjusted the gym bag on his shoulder and waited until Taren was inside before going back the direction they came. Another pickup truck pulled up and the day workers scrambled again before the hand even appeared out the window.

He began most workouts with six sets on the heavy bag, three minutes each. One-two or one-two-three straight punches, then jabs, then hooks and jabs, each with a minute rest in between. Afterward and without much pause, he'd take on the speed bag for fifteen minutes and finish with another fifteen of jump rope. It had been this way for years, twice a week, when the neon fitness centers could no longer fatigue him enough to distract him from the surroundings. Soft people prayed to the Nautilus machines for a few more years on plaque-streaked vessels and shame had eventually caught up to him. He too told the lie that many physicians did, that pills and pseudo-exercise would save these lemmings from themselves. The boxing club was escape. No neon, no Nautilus machines, no soft people lifting dumbbells while talking on their cell phone.

Some days, most days, when the previous shift was heavy with gore and drama, the rhythmic bappity-bap of the speed bag would hypnotize him. Patients from days or years gone by would creep in and hit the lights of Stevenson Theater. Each would take their place under surgical lamps so bright they washed the faces pure. One act went into dozens and the sets and actors changed endlessly. The burn in his shoulders, the fighters punching bags and bodies and skipping rope, none of it could distract him from the show. Occasionally the owner, Russell Blake, would have to amble out of his office and stand between him and the bag. Short and wide, one ear cauliflowered and the other just a nub, Blake's saddle nose would be whistling by the time he made it to Stevenson. *Go skip some rope, Goldie.*

Today, it was Butch the Blue Baby. *Is Butch going to be OK?* Why yes he is, you urban troglodyte, so have another beer with that shot of whiskey and pebble of meth. I'm paying for it, aren't I?

And Javier DaSilva. *Yaaa, sai de cima, sai de cima.* I'll get off, but you hit one of us. *Vou devorar sua alma.* I'll devour your soul.

And Maureen Tuuvey. *Help me, help me. Help me, Help me.* There is no helping you now, dear. How about a long kiss from a pillowcase?

Target areas are attacked violently. There are no second chances. Do you hear me, Ranger? Yes sir, RI. *What?* Yes sir, Ranger Instructor, sir!

Something hit the back of Stevenson's leg and he turned to see a tennis ball bounce away.

"What's that bag ever done to you, Goldie?"

Blake sat in his office, leaning back from his desk. He tapped his watch, then sat up straight. Everyone who lasted a few months got a nickname. For Stevenson, who paid in cash and never told Blake his name because it was never asked of him, it was Goldie, bastardized from Golden. Blake asked him, after getting paid, why a man twice everybody else's age would want to spend his golden years in a dump like Gentleman's. For a fighter, the golden years was over thirty. Stevenson never gave him an answer.

He walked towards the office, wind-milling his arms. The sweat soaked the long sleeves of his shirt and started to chill. His hands were already aching, the cushioning on the gloves thinned and providing little protection. Bruises would splotch over his knuckles the next day, over top the lemon-lime swirl of older bruises not yet faded. He could get new gloves, could tape his hands before he started, but he never bothered.

Next to the office door were ten hooks lined down the wall but only one had a jump rope. When he reached for it, a hand came from behind and yanked the rope away. A lightweight whom Stevenson had never seen break a sweat or throw hands in the ring trotted away, the rope handles smacking the floor. He was one of the sparring partners for Vince Alfredo, Russell Blake's prized heavyweight. Alfredo stood shirtless at the end of the gym, looking beyond his partner at Stevenson. Tan skin without blemish or tattoo, Alfredo had to bend forward to hear his partner over the noise of the full gym. They eyed Stevenson, their smirks ending in laughter.

"I got one in here," Blake said, briefly poking his head out of the office. A few metal drawers opened and slammed and he came out, a beaded rope in hand. "Brand-new."

"Thanks."

His vocal cords scarred and hardened from decades of barking ringside, Blake's conversation voice was rasp with occasional baritone slipping through. His brow and upper eyelids were thickened from punches he'd absorbed for decades.

"Don't let them get at you," Blake said, waving a hand at the two like shooing flies. They turned around. Alfredo jumped rope and the lightweight clapped his hands to the strike of the rope on the floor.

"Never do."

Stevenson saw a few fighters during his membership who would catch Blake's attention. They would be there every time Stevenson showed up and still there when he left, usually with Blake at their side. Injury, drugs, prison or all these factors combined would take the contender away from Blake just as they started to resemble a pro. Alfredo had been in the club over a year, double the time the last fighter Blake favored. Alfredo was 6-0, five by knockout. Blake was past retirement age, his shuffle slower every year, the words harder to find when he spoke of better days. Alfredo was the condo in Florida, the 401K just starting to ripen.

"He keeps telling me he wants a few rounds with you," Blake said, nodding at Alfredo.

"Yeah? I suppose it doesn't matter that I'm old enough to be his father?"

"He's not in your weight class so there won't be no fighting between you two." Blake leaned against the frame of the office door, crossing his arms. "Don't matter anyway. Not like you ever get in the ring."

"Scary up there," Stevenson said. In the far corner of the floor was the ring. Two fighters slap-sparred with taped hands. "I don't like heights."

"Listen to you." Blake's laugh went into a cough and throat clearing. "You been here long enough to know how it works, right?"

"Four years. And you still haven't taught me a thing."

"You knew what you were doing before you got here. I wouldn't have to teach you much at all." Blake came out of the office, looking Stevenson up and down. "Cruiserweight, maybe light-heavy. We got a few here you could spar with."

"They're kids."

29

"They're over eighteen. They can take it."

Stevenson said thanks anyway and crossed to the corner of the gym and started jumping rope. Blake called after him, saying to think about it, as he went the other direction toward Alfredo.

"Work it, Nacho," Blake said, clapping his hands faster than the lightweight was. "Faster, faster."

Alfredo did just that, his V-shaped back rigid like an arrowhead. He hopped, only his toes touching the floor.

Midday on East Read Street was what Stevenson had always remembered it to be: deserted, except for Coleman's Cadillac Deville in front of 2826. When Coleman bought the four-story brownstone in the center of a row of seven on a dead-end street, each home had been occupied by white-collar families—white collar, apron, and hairnets. Across the street was Sunset Bakery, a one-story cinderblock factory that emanated the scent of baked bread for miles. Stevenson had visited the Coleman family as a child on a few Easter Sundays, when his mother was still alive, and she and the Colemans worked together at Saint Catherines. He remembered none of the visits, despite Coleman trying repeatedly to elicit some memory of it during the slow hours in the ED. Years later, the bakery went bankrupt and all the families moved away, all but the Colemans.

At the end of the street was a guardrail with a dirt embankment behind it. Jones Falls Expressway, the vertical vein into downtown, was on the other side, but the embankment absorbed most of the hum of traffic. Stevenson made a U-turn at the end and rode the bike onto the sidewalk. The roots of the only maple left on the street had lifted two slabs of the walk into a speed bump in front of Coleman's steps. He stopped short of the bump as the double doors of 2826 opened.

"There he is," Coleman said, pushing his Orioles cap back. He wore a t-shirt too small for him now, and stick legs poked out from khaki shorts. Patches of black dirt covered his knees and the skin sagged on his inner thighs. "Bring the beer?"

"Dammit," Stevenson said. He took off his helmet and tossed it to Coleman. "I'll walk down to the store."

"Already did." Coleman put the open-faced helmet on over his cap. "Still fits."

The bike and helmet had been Coleman's once, sold to Stevenson after sitting for years covered by a tarp in the back room off the kitchen. Elaine Coleman, forbidding their only son Blaine from inheriting it, was overjoyed when Stevenson offered to buy it. She struggled to embrace

Stevenson when he came to pick it up, her skin phone-book-yellow, her scalp bare. It would be the last time he saw her alive.

"Should never have sold it to you," Coleman said. "What's it cost to fill it up now?"

"About twenty."

Coleman sighed, shaking his head. "Cost me seventy-five bucks to fill up the Caddy yesterday." He turned around and went inside, mumbling curses about oil prices and presidents. Stevenson followed him in and shut the doors behind him. Coleman rubbed the top of Stevenson's head.

"You need a haircut," he said. "Feels like steel wool."

Stevenson jerked his head away. "I know."

The floorboards protested in creaks and moans as they walked through the foyer and down the hall. On either side were doorways, one to the den, the other to a living room, and along the mahogany-paneled walls were a row of nails where photos and paintings of landscapes used to hang. The stairway ahead ascended to a seeming oblivion, the lights off and curtains drawn on the landing's window.

To the left of the stairs they pushed through the swinging door to the kitchen, where a wave of heat and cumin engulfed them. The AM radio on top of the old Frigidaire refrigerator squawked.

"... but the steep cuts in spending won't get this city on track, not with a deficit close to half a billion. Am I right or am I right, Ron?"

"Let me turn that off." Coleman smacked the radio and it went silent. He yanked the meat locker handle and grabbed two Red Stripes, handing one to Stevenson.

"You ever going to get a new fridge?" Stevenson wiggled his field jacket off and hung it on the back of the chair. Two bowls rested in the center of the round laminate table, each with fork and napkin, no spoon.

"Hell no. Came with the house. Stays with the house."

Coleman popped the top off the beer and took a swig. The helmet slipped off his head and bounced a few times on the floor. His baseball cap went askew but stayed put. A scratching sound came from above, nails on wood. Then galloping. It was faint at first, coming from the front of the house to the back.

"Oops." Coleman grinned. "Woke the baby."

The back staircase into the kitchen was alive in a chorus of snorts and thumps. If not for the perfect cadence of a dog running down familiar steps, one would think a toddler was falling down the stairs. A black and tan Dachshund hit the landing at the bottom of the staircase and its hindquarters whipped around like a hook-and-ladder truck. It ran straight for Stevenson.

"Locked on target," Coleman said, stepping back.

The dog leapt straight for Stevenson's groin but he twisted at his waist a moment before she made contact. Her front paws bounced off his hip and she landed on all fours, dancing around Stevenson with yips and more snorts.

"Aww," Coleman said, "she remembers you."

Stevenson crouched down and scratched her head. "You still got this thing."

"Of course. Best funeral present ever."

Jenna gave the puppy to Coleman a week after Elaine's death. He protested at first, insisting on a trial basis, but the dog slept with him the same night, and every night thereafter. He named her Baby.

"She's going to make somebody impotent one day," Stevenson said, standing up.

"What do you care?" Coleman turned to the stove, pulling the lid off the white enamel pot. "You don't want kids."

"I wouldn't say that." Stevenson pulled a chair out and sat. Baby immediately jumped into his lap as he opened his beer.

"Uh-huh." Coleman stirred the pot and brought the spoon to his mouth, blowing, then sipping. "Whatever happened with Liz?"

"Married. Had a baby."

"That's right, you told me..." Coleman froze, staring at Stevenson. "What?"

"Don't. Move." He put the lid down with the spoon on the counter.

Stevenson looked left and right, then down. Baby was looking up at him too, one side of her lip stuck on her upper fang. Coleman stepped over and put his hand to Stevenson's shoulder.

"You don't want to be in here," Coleman said, in the voice used for sick kids. He pulled his hand back slowly, the index finger out with a butterfly sitting at the tip. Its wings, yellow with black on the edges and vertical stripes on the upper portion, flapped in slow motion.

"Where'd that come from?"

"He's one of mine." Coleman was twisting his wrist slowly, smiling. "I guess it's been a while since you've been here."

"Apparently."

The butterfly took off again, flying over their heads and out of reach.

"C'mon," Coleman said, heading towards the back door at the bottom of the stairs.

Stevenson followed him into the room where the motorcycle was once stored. The windows had been spray-painted black and the clutter of gardening tools was gone, but there were a few bags of topsoil in a wheel-barrow by the back door.

"Keep this to yourself," Coleman said, his hand on the door handle. "Nobody knows I built this, not even Jenna. If it gets out, every asshole I know will want to see it."

Stevenson nodded agreement and Coleman opened the door. The room lit up enough that they both squinted hard.

"Holy shit," Stevenson said.

They entered what looked like a glass chapel, three walls connected to a pitched roof. A slate path went down the center and on either side were semi-organized shrubs and flowers, some taller than both men. Baby ran down the path and Coleman followed, arms out, disturbing the plants. Dozens of butterflies erupted and flew above them erratically in the open air. Most were black and orange but some, like the one in the kitchen, were faint yellow with black outlines and stripes.

"When did this happen?"

"Last year." Coleman stopped, looking up. "Wasn't that hard, really. Like a giant erector set. I tore down the deck next door and used the wood for the beds." He pointed at driftwood-gray 4x4s stacked three high and running along the path, holding the guts of soil and foliage in. "Nobody has lived there for years so I don't think anyone will notice."

"Hot," Stevenson said, flapping the front of his shirt.

"It can get over a hundred." Coleman pointed to a digital thermometer hanging on the side of a wooden shed at the end of the path, the red numbers glowing 86. The shed was painted pine green and mingled well within the surrounding plants. "The heater pops on if it gets too cold in here. It's a 10,000-watt unit so no worries about frost." He pointed at a tan metal box hanging at the end of the center truss above the back door. A screen covered the front, with open vents below it.

"I needed this," Coleman said, sitting down on a bench against the shed. Baby jumped up next to him, panting heavily, tail wagging. He took his cap off and fanned himself with it. "Had too much time on my hands. Too many thoughts I don't want to think about. You know how that goes."

"How big is this thing?" Stevenson sat on the other end of the bench.

"Fifty feet by twenty. The roof was a bitch." Coleman looked up. "Thirty feet at the center. Bolting that heater up there by myself should've killed me. I almost called you for help."

"Should've."

The mist machine at the other end of the center truss hissed in spurts. Coleman closed his eyes as the spray fell upon them both. Across from the bench the butterflies settled on a patch of purple flowers resembling feather dusters.

"How did you catch them all?" Stevenson asked.

"You don't actually catch them. Not the way you're thinking, anyway. You breed them."

"Breed them?"

"It's better to start with the eggs than just going out and catching them one by one. Can you see me dancing around the forest with a net and safari hat?"

"At this point, yes. And who sells butterfly eggs?"

"Depends on the type of butterfly. You can order the exotic ones online. The Monarchs, Tiger Swallowtails, and Checkerspots are all over Maryland so I just walk around Patapsco State Park and look under the leaves of their host plants. The Monarchs lay the eggs on milkweed. I found the Checkerspot eggs by accident on some white turtleheads. I just pick the leaf off and bring it back here and set them up with a nice place to live. Eventually a caterpillar comes out and then you just make sure they have something to eat. As long as you keep the temperature comfortable and the plants healthy, they'll be happy."

Stevenson stood and went to the wall of windows next to the shed. The adjoining rowhouses each had a patch of concrete patio but the grass, although maintained, had grown through the cracks. A brick building twice the height of the houses was at the back of the lot and a 12-foot wall on either side, also brick.

"You're taking care of this all yourself?"

"For now. It's not much, really. It's no mansion in the county."

"I don't take care of the Green. Carminda does."

"I know. Just saying." Coleman stood, stretched. "I think I'm going to shut it down for the winter. Let them all go. The Monarchs migrate south to Mexico when it gets cold. They're the only insect that does that. I didn't know that last year." He picked at a brown leaf on a bush with a single Monarch. It stumbled about on a stalk of purple flowers, poking its proboscis within the confines of the petals. "Sad seeing all of them dead."

Stevenson looked around for a way to let them out. Behind the misting machine was an aluminum rod along the base of a pane of slanted glass. The rod connected to a crank wheel on the wall with a loop of chain that ran down to the floor.

Stevenson asked, "What about the others?"

Coleman looked at him, brow raised.

"The other butterflies. The Checkerspots."

"They don't have the stamina of a Monarch. I suppose they'll keep up for awhile. At least a few people will get to see a parade of them all flying in a place they have no business being."

Baby jumped down and waddled into the foliage, the taller plants parting as she walked in deeper. The mist machine hissed and the water chilled Stevenson's neck.

"Elaine would have loved this," Stevenson said.

Coleman didn't answer. He watched where Baby had gone, waiting for her.

They sat across from one another at the kitchen table, dabbing their foreheads, their mouth's O-shaped. Blowing the hot out was futile, the beer only slightly taking away the pleasant pain of it all.

"This is barely worth it," Stevenson said, tears mixing with sweat at the corners of his eyes.

"Sent away for the peppers," Coleman said, reaching across the table and flipping the switch for the ceiling fan. "Called ghost peppers. I only used a half one for the whole pot."

"A half too much."

"Elaine had a whole one when we were in Bangladesh." Coleman leaned back in his chair, napkin to his mouth as he chuckled. "She jumped in the fountain out in front of the restaurant and had her face right in the spout of the thing. The whole place was in tears, man." He dropped the napkin, gaze locked on the bowl. "That was a great trip. Changed me forever."

Stevenson had heard about most of the places Coleman and Elaine had traveled, but occasionally there would be a forgotten journey remembered. For Coleman, to drag these memories out from under the clutter of medicine and routine, it was lost treasure found.

"Hopkins sent some of the alumni over there for a conference on emergency medicine at the University of Dhaka. The day after the conference Elaine and I went exploring and stumbled into the middle of the biggest damn party I've ever seen. Turns out it was the Bengali New Year. Parades, food, happy people everywhere. From sun up to sun down." Coleman picked at the chili with his spoon, nodding slightly as his smile faded. "Elaine would find me under the bed sometimes before that trip. Every time a helicopter would go by at night, there I went. Big blubbering mess I was."

After medical school, Coleman enlisted before the government had a chance to send him a draft notice. He did a year in a hospital company on the outskirts of Da Nang, close enough to the action that he heard gunshots every day. He triaged mostly, but rounded on soldiers in a medical-surgical unit. He was close, too close, when the Tet Offensive occurred. About this, he never spoke.

Stevenson ate the last of the chili and stood. Baby stretched and followed him to the sink.

"Grab your beer," Coleman said. He dropped his napkin in the half-empty bowl, scooted out, and left the kitchen.

Baby rushed past the two, jumped on one of the oxblood chairs in the den, and settled into the shape of a meatloaf. The room had been emptied of its contents and Stevenson could not remember what was there to begin with. Red velvet wallpaper with gold lilies no longer had paintings or pictures. The fireplace was empty and cleaned, the smell of soot barely noticeable. The two chairs were pointed cockeyed in front of the fireplace, each with its own nightstand, as if an old couple with a book and crochet had recently moved out. The floor-to-ceiling bookcase built into the back wall stood empty of books, and in the corner were two mounds of white sheets for the furniture. The mantle above the fireplace had but a single 8x10 photo, framed, of the Coleman family. Father, mother, son, dressed post-wedding with the men's ties loosened, each flanking the matriarch, and all three with unlit cigars in their mouths. All had color in their skin from summer sun. The red in Coleman's hair was still visible in streaks.

"How's Blaine?" Stevenson asked.

"Good." Coleman pushed Baby to the side as he sat down. He pulled the string on the lamp next to the chair and nothing happened. He peered up into the lampshade. "Still in New York working for Toshiba. They're almost done with this top secret project." He opened the drawer on the nightstand and pulled a single piece of paper out. He held it up to Stevenson. "See that?"

Stevenson squinted at the black and white printout. It had been handled often, wrinkled, and the print dulled. Blaine was looking up at a rectangle of glass the size of a sheet of plywood on the wall. Vertical wires were lined end-to-end inside of it.

"Now," Coleman said, slowly flipping the paper, his face brightening. "Check this out."

The same glass was now a picture of Cal Ripken swinging a bat at home plate. Blaine was grinning, standing in the same location as before.

"That's a TV?"

"Believe that? Thing only weighs three pounds. Bends like plastic. Some kind of organic compound screen. He said he'll get me one a year before it's on the market." Coleman folded the paper up and put it back in the drawer. "Maybe he'll give me two."

"That's okay. I don't watch much TV."

"Truth be told, neither do I, but I wouldn't tell him that."

"Still no grandkids?"

"Nah. Him and Belle are the corporate America types. Couple of ladder climbers."

The men took turns swigging beers. Stevenson looked at the photo again, the only place in the empty room for the eyes to go. Blaine had light blonde hair, curls like a tangled mop, and his face was round, devoid of bony features. He was shorter than Coleman, with a potbelly never shed in his teen years. He's a mother's son, Coleman had told Stevenson at that wedding, a few gin and tonics peppering his breath.

Coleman asked, "So how's it by you?"

"Same old. You would know. I see you more than anybody else these days."

"I hear that. Jenna comes over once a week to straighten up the place so I see a lot of her miserable ass, but other than that, work is it." He stretched his legs out, crossing them at the ankles. He dusted the caked soil off his knees.

"She still comes by?"

"Not to see me, I can assure you." Coleman tussled Baby's head and she huffed, not opening her eyes. "There's really not much to clean, anyway. I packed up most of the stuff because I got tired of looking at it. She just likes the company. She's in the same boat as us, ya' know. No porch light on when she gets home."

"When did her husband die? '95?"

"About then, I think. Stroke. She keeps on truckin' though. Never lets the place get to her." Coleman finished his beer and set it on the nightstand. "Heard about your friend Mr. Butt Plug."

Stevenson kept his gaze at the window, thumb picking at the beer label. "Manuel?"

"Kay, in a roundabout way. Your friend's eye went black and swollen the day after we had him and he told one of the nurses that a doctor in the ED did it. The head of psych called down and asked the charge nurse if we had any record of an altercation. Kay was one of the charge nurses that night, of course, and she cornered Manuel but he said the patient fell. Long story short, it seems that Mr. Plug had some outstanding warrants and somehow the police found out where he was."

"And you wouldn't know anything about that."

Coleman leaned forward, inspecting his feet. He moved his toes back and forth.

Stevenson began to apologize, but Coleman cut him off. "Want another beer?" he asked, getting up with a groan and a pop of his ankles. Stevenson declined and Coleman hobbled to the kitchen. Baby didn't move but kept her eyes on Stevenson until Coleman returned.

"You ask that girl in the lab out yet?" Coleman sat back down.

"What girl?"

"Oh please. Don't gimme that."

He could see her, walking toward him. Hands jammed deep in her lab coat, him doing the same.

"Zooey. Little dark-haired gal. Likes earrings." Coleman motioned the shape of an hourglass, spilling beer when his hands went diagonal for the waist.

"Where is this coming from?"

"Feet don't even touch the ground when she walks."

"Cole."

"Jenna told me she was asking about you a couple weeks ago."

"Shut up."

"Seriously. I wouldn't shit you. You two were trying to get a line on some guy with Parkinsons. He couldn't stay still. Sound familiar?"

"Not really."

She had not tied her hair back when she was drawing the patient's blood, and it drifted strand by strand onto the patient's arm while she was leaning over. Stevenson reached across and tucked it behind her ear, revealing multiple stud earrings, each different from the next. She thanked him without looking at him and walked out, leaving the patient's arm without a band-aid.

"I worry, you know. I don't want you being like your father." Coleman took a swig of beer, his jaw shifting sideways. "Son of a bitch, he was."

His mind on Zooey, Stevenson had no retort. All he could do was look back at the photo on the mantle, the men flanking Elaine, unaware of what was to be.

"Your mother was a hell of a woman. Great nurse. John, on the other hand, was just this machine. Great to his patients but no interest in any-one he couldn't operate on. Emotionally tone deaf in social situations. No surprise he died alone out there in that palace." Coleman picked at the chair's armrest.

Stevenson pieced together in his younger years who his father was from overheard whispers and quick comments from rushed adults. When he started his residency with Coleman, large puzzle pieces fell into place, but never enough to complete the picture. Coleman and his father had been roommates in college, were about the same age, and were accepted to Hopkins at the same time. The similarities stopped there.

"Bet you didn't know that you almost moved in with us."

"No I didn't." Stevenson sat up. "How old was I?"

"Two or three, I think. Elaine asked Sally to move in since she was on her own but Sally wouldn't do it. Stubborn as hell, she was. Her parents were gone. John was out of the picture at that point and she was too proud to ask him for child support. Once she got pregnant with you he just stopped talking to her. He'd see her in the halls when he was rounding on patients and it was as if Sally were invisible. Wouldn't even acknowledge her."

His throat tingled, warmed. The chair became noticeably stiff. *It's getting late. I left my oven on. There's a storm coming.*

Coleman said, "I think I was studying for a pharmacology exam when you were conceived."

"That is just..." Stevenson shook his head, eyes squeezed shut, "creepy."

Coleman laughed and Baby awoke, looking up at him, then Stevenson, then the fireplace.

"Sorry, just trying to lighten the mood."

"You were on Market Street then?"

"Yeah, right downtown. John moved out during his surgical residency and we never saw him again. He had these goals, these milestones that were to be reached by any means necessary. He couldn't let a child get in the way of that." Coleman took a drink and set the beer on the nightstand. One hand planted back on the armrest, the other in his lap, he looked at the picture on the mantle, stayed on it. "The MLK assassination was still fresh on people's minds. The riots too, so I guess it was all for the best. White man and black woman together on that side of town? That would have started another riot."

"Residency for him, 'Nam for you."

"Yep. Camp Pendleton, then Nam. Got back, did my emergency medicine residency at Hopkins, and somehow got sucked back into Saint Cat in the process. They called the ED the Accident Room then. Hospitals never heard of emergency medicine in those days and Saint Catherines was being inundated with trauma and all kinds of shit the internists couldn't handle. They were so desperate they were going to name the ED after me if I stayed." Coleman chuckled, crossing his legs and arms. "Lucky for me Elaine was still there. Your mother, too."

"Must've been a good crew."

"For a couple years, at least. Elaine quit after she got pregnant with Blaine and Sally left soon after. Worked at a clinic down the street."

It was later in the day, the daylight darkening to orange. Stevenson could see the bike parked out front. A grackle perched on the seat, looking left and right and all around, as if deciding where to go, whom to follow.

"I'm so sorry, Cassius."

Coleman was in tears, his trembling hand rubbing his brow, shielding his eyes as if Stevenson was sunlight.

"I—we loved her so much. It wasn't..." Coleman breathed in and the air skipped down his trachea. His lips quivered and he squeezed his eyes shut. "Her and your brother. I can't imagine your pain, son. How you ever became the man you are is beyond me."

"Jesus, Cole, c'mon now." Stevenson reached across and put his hand on Coleman's shoulder. "Why are you bringing that up?"

"It's still there, within you, and I can see it some days. Feel it. The heat." Coleman looked away, choking up. He reached up and clutched Stevenson's hand. "I've seen thousands die but when it's family, when they die in your arms, you carry that to your last day. I don't—"

"Larry!"

Stevenson said it loud and he squeezed Coleman's shoulder as he did, giving him a shove. Coleman stopped abruptly. His mouth closed slowly.

"That's enough. I put that behind me. All of it. I had a roof over my head, food on my plate. He was rarely home and when he was, he avoided me. Carminda raised me well. I made it out just fine."

Coleman nodded slowly. Stevenson tried to take his hand away but Coleman held onto it. He leaned forward, looking at the bruises on Stevenson's knuckles under the sunlight, then the burn scars, poking out from under the shirt's cuff.

"You never told me how you got burned," Coleman said, letting go. "That wasn't there when you were a kid."

Stevenson kept quiet as he tucked his hands out of view. Coleman reached into the nightstand drawer, took out a handkerchief and blew his nose.

Stevenson said, "Don't worry about me being like John Stevenson. We may become our parents when we reach adulthood but the man was never a parent to me. Only my mother was. And Carminda. I'm my own man."

Coleman was tearing up again but smiling. The evening light bathed him, and Stevenson saw an old man looking back on his life, reviewing the memories that remained, both good and horrible.

"You're not dying on me, are you?" Stevenson asked.

Coleman labored to his feet and walked to the window. "No," he said, his back turned. "Not yet, anyway. Funny you mention that, though."

*   *   *

Coleman insisted on adjourning outside for some fresh air. They sat on the stoop, looking over the BMW. Dead leaves blew about at the bottom of the hill. Passing cars on the expressway could be mistaken for a distant beachfront.

"You know you stole it from me," Coleman said.

"This again? I paid you good money for that clunker."

"Clunker?"

"Had to replace the shocks and carburetor. Both tires were cracked."

"Carburetor too?" Coleman asked, not surprised. "I shouldn't have left it out there for so long."

"I'm not complaining. Learned a lot about bike engines." Stevenson patted his front pocket for the keys. "You want to take her for a ride?"

"No thanks." Coleman leaned forward, elbows on top of his knees. "You ever take her up to the palace? Open her up on those back roads?"

"Sometimes."

"When was the last time?" Coleman asked, smirking.

"Can't remember."

"Get out there soon. Before the snow comes."

The branches of the lone maple bent sideways, the underside of the leaves showing. Some came off and joined the others at the bottom of the hill.

Coleman said, "I'm retiring."

Stevenson looked at his beer, then set it down. "I kind of figured."

"I've only told you and the lawyer. You remember Lemmy?"

"Of course."

He had only met Lemmy McPhee a few times. A sweaty mess, with wrinkled clothing and the odor of a few skipped showers hovering over him. And he only wore brown. Brown shirt, pants, socks, shoes. Friendly enough, but Stevenson had difficulty keeping up with his chatter.

"The suits will be the last to know," Coleman said. "Only seems fair. I was the last to know about them closing the residency program. Liability my ass."

"Residents do kill an average of three patients before they're set free. You told me that."

"But you didn't. Not one. That's why I hired you."

"You remember that?"

"I remember too much." Coleman was turning his hands back and forth, studying them. "Too damn much."

"What about Jeller?"

41

Coleman shook his head. "I'll tell him later. I haven't signed off on anything yet. Lemmy is just waiting to get the ball rolling. He needs a name to do that."

"If you're selling the practice, you better notify the docs first. They probably want to put in a bid."

"You think I'm going to sell the practice to one of those assholes? Baldanza will never go beyond part-time and Jeller just hates the place. Besides the few other part-timers we rarely see, everybody else is agency. If I'm going to sign the practice over to somebody, it's going to be you. I'd rather leave it to someone competent than sell to a bunch of half-assed physicians." Coleman looked over at Stevenson. Kept his gaze firm.

"What?"

"It's not all bad. Sure it's Scumbag Med, but the money's good. Even with fifty percent reimbursement on charges, I bet you could make two hundred an hour on average. I outsourced the billing and payroll years ago to an accounting firm out in Towson. Lemmy takes care of all the legal bullshit. All you would need to do is clean house. Throw the slackers overboard, stop using agency docs, and demand more from the staff members who stay. Make Folger a partner and you two could whip the place into shape in no time."

"If it's so simple, why don't you stay a little longer and do it yourself?"

"I'm tired, Cassius. It's been a long time since I didn't have to think about Chesapeake."

The breeze picked up enough that the garage door on the factory across the street rattled. The bottom corner had been kicked in, and only half of the row of windows running along the front sill had their iron grills intact enough to protect the desolation within.

Coleman got up and circled the bike. His foot caught on the seat briefly as he heaved his leg over. He grabbed the handlebars, looked straight ahead.

"You're ambushing me here," Stevenson said.

"Sorry, Tonto. I didn't mean to throw it at you like this. I had planned on staying longer but I want to get a little travel in before somebody decides I'm too old to be on my own. I'll still be around as a consultant. I just won't be practicing anymore."

"What about the lawsuit?"

"That will follow me, not Chesapeake. The practice is listed as one of the defendants but that's the way it works. At first they list everybody involved in a malpractice suit. The doc, the hospital, radiologist. Hell, parking attendants if the lawyer thinks his client's parking stub wasn't stamped fast enough. When the suit moves forward, most of the names are dropped until they have the last man standing."

"Is the hospital helping at all?"

"You're kidding, right? Once they were dropped from the list of litigants I was on my own. We have a department meeting next week just so they can make sure they're no longer liable, but otherwise, no, they're no help at all."

"Will malpractice insurance cover it?"

"They won't get my money, if that's what you're getting at. If they want more than what the malpractice policy provides, they won't find it. I'll live on the streets before they get a dime of my loot." Coleman got off the bike with much effort, then held onto the seat for balance. "It's a weak case. They'll eventually drop it when their attorney runs out of patience."

"When do you need an answer?"

"I'm looking to sign off at the end of the year, after Christmas. How about we meet back here in November and we'll figure out where we are?"

Stevenson leaned forward and rested his forehead on his crossed arms. Ants walked about on the stoop, ignoring one another in their travels.

Coleman said, "Don't stress about it. In fact, why don't you take some time off? You haven't taken a trip in awhile. When was your last conference?"

"Last year. Maui."

"Go back." Coleman sat next to him. Put a hand on his shoulder. "Take the girl from the lab."

Stevenson lifted his head and looked Coleman in the eye.

"I'm serious. You need to get out more. You're a loner, like me, and you're too damn young for that. I know you just go back to that little house after work and stare at the wall or go pound the heavy bags. I hope that's what your pounding, anyway." He pinched Stevenson's thumb, jerking it briefly.

"If you're talking about what happened with Manuel, what was I supposed to do?"

"You did what I would have done. And I don't like that." Coleman picked up the beer on the step and sipped from it. "Make some friends, Cassius. Get the girl. Be the hero."

"What in the hell are you talking about?"

"I don't know. I've had a few."

A ticking came from inside the house, slow at first. The sound of tin warming. It became a rattle, then a thump.

"Damn furnace," Coleman said, then belched. "Needs a tune-up."

*　　*　　*

Stevenson leaned on his chimney, counting planets and constellations. Beyond the tar island rooftops, a schooner was drifting along in the south end of the Inner Harbor, back to the Chesapeake Bay. Its three masts appeared and disappeared between the buildings and the green lights on the tips of each mast dragged from dark to full brightness.

Son of a bitch, he was.

Cassius James Stevenson was eight when he was sent to live with his father, on the estate he would name Fiddler's Green when it became his. On a Halloween night, he stood in the kitchen under a great chandelier that cast shadows over granite and iron. His father and the housekeeper, Carminda Cruz, loomed over him like willow branches.

Blonde hair came loose and hung over his father's forehead and into his eye. Gray was starting at his temples and making its way up the scalp. It would go full white by the time Stevenson left for boot camp.

"A mae do menino esta morto," his father said, not taking his eyes off his son. "Ele mora aqui agora."

Then he turned and left, his riding boots clicking on the granite floor. He slid open the screen door and strode to the horse barn on the lone hill out back. Carminda got on her knees and hugged young Stevenson tight, tight enough that he lost his grip on a secondhand Mickey Mouse suitcase that contained two shirts, two pairs of corduroys, socks, underwear, his brother's knit blanket and some of his mother's belongings—all the things he could call his. She spoke as she cried in Portuguese and it took a few months for Stevenson to learn the basics of broken English, during their morning breakfasts in her basement apartment. Over fried eggs and linguica, he asked her what was said that day.

"He say you Mama die and you live with us now."

"And what did you say to me?"

"I say I can't be your Mama, but I try every day to make you happy."

She had no children or husband, and accepted Stevenson as her own. Together they lived for close to a decade as makeshift mother and son while his father dwelled on the periphery of his life. Conversations with him never lasted more than a minute, and each was separated from the last by weeks and months. His father haunted the halls and rooms of the 14,000-square-foot mansion, giving no warning when he would come or go. With eight bedrooms and nine bathrooms, going unnoticed required little stratagem. Stevenson did not hate his father the way Coleman did, for they never spoke long enough for him to grasp who the man was. In mid-career John Stevenson became a researcher, eventually isolating himself so that his horses saw more of him than anyone else.

Two weeks after high school graduation, Stevenson left for the Army. It was the same as the day he arrived, Carminda crying in Portuguese, his father up at the barn. A staff sergeant had been sent to pick up Stevenson and he stood in the doorway looking all around, scratching a shaved head as the little woman's cries echoed in the foyer.

Two years later Carminda rose at the usual 5 AM to prepare breakfast. She went to the sink and through the window saw the barn doors wide open. She ran out immediately with a pot and wooden spoon, ready to corral any of the escaped Arabians. When she got there, all the horses were in their stalls, all except for Hector, the great black Friesian purchased a year before Stevenson had left. He stood in the doorway, waiting patiently for his master to finish brushing his feathering. John Stevenson sat slumped too far sideways to be comfortable on the bench against the wall, brush still in hand, with Hector's tack next to him.

Carminda called Fort Bragg and left a message for Stevenson to come home because "the man died." No one knew that "the man" was Stevenson's father and the message was not relayed for two days. A corporal in an Airborne regiment preparing for RIP, Ranger Indoctrination Program, rarely left base to go back on the block, home, but a father's death was granted leave post-haste. He made it to the funeral as the casket was lowered into the ground and a smattering of people he didn't know were walking away. Carminda had waited for him and they went back to the house and talked about military life. She put on his Garrison cap, asked about jumping from airplanes and shooting guns. She asked about his patches and ribbons and if he really had to go back. He was showing her how to march when a knocking at the double doors interrupted them.

"Larry Coleman." A large fellow, thick in the chest, stepped forward and shook Stevenson's hand hard. "You got big, son."

His ginger hair, combed with his fingers, had matching stubble and moustache. His biceps stretched his black suit and he looked out of place all dressed up, as if he'd been born for overalls.

They stood eye-to-eye, then made their way into the kitchen.

"Well, it's all yours now," Coleman said, waving his hand over the kitchen's island. "You're all the miserable asshole had left."

The house, the horses, an old convertible Alfa Romeo and a pickup truck were listed on a piece of paper, where Coleman had underlined ASSETS at the top in his now familiar scrawl. A few phone calls by a lawyer friend, Lemmy McPhee, confirmed investments in stocks, bonds, and a life insurance policy. There was no will, and the benefactors of the policy, John's parents, were long dead. Everything would go to the next of kin.

"We're talking millions here," Coleman said, his smile jerky at the corners, waiting to let loose with congratulations and spirits when the last Stevenson jumped for joy.

He didn't jump. There was no joy. Only nausea.

"I don't want it."

The Irishman lost his smile, looking at Carminda. She only shrugged, looking back and forth between the two.

"You're not thinking clearly right—"

"He was no father to me. If anything, I was a tenant. If anyone should get it, it should be Carm."

"I no want it!" She held her hands up in front of her, holding her breath, looking around at the house as if it had heard her.

They talked into the night, Coleman trying to wear the soldier down like he would when he needed an extra body on the ED floor. As the hours went by, Stevenson learned volumes about who his father was.

"Whether you like it or not, it's yours. You're the only blue blood left."

"Blue blood?"

"Your great, great—I don't know how many greats there should be but your grandfather a few times removed was Jonathan Stevenson. He had a brother, Henry. They were doctors." Coleman stroked the stubble of his beard, trying to decipher the soldier. "Your father ever tell you how he made his fortune?"

Before he touched a stethoscope, John waited tables in a cluster of restaurants in the east side's Little Italy. Dollar by dollar he saved his tips and invested in local real estate. By the time he started college, he was a landlord and within a few years owned twenty-six properties, six commercial. The money from rents paid tuition and the leftovers went to stocks and bonds. When the steel and auto plants started closing and unemployment rose, Mayor William Donald Schaefer had to find an alternative source of income for the city's unemployed. The desolate Inner Harbor, once a major port of commerce, now abandoned with the advent of container ships, had vast potential. As the city made its final plans for the renovation, anyone owning property nearby was offered top dollar. Land deemed swampy and useless only a year before was now doubling in value each week, and John's entire portfolio of real estate fell within that target area. By the end of his residency, unemployment declined, the mayor was reelected, and Dr. John Stevenson was a millionaire.

Coleman left after midnight, telling Stevenson to "think about it." Stevenson did just that, getting no sleep at all, and before daybreak, he woke Carminda, after calling a taxi.

"I don't care what they say," he told her, "the house is yours. You can live here forever if you want."

"Will you come back?" She hugged him tight, smelling of menthol, the vapor rub she would put on his chest when he brought a cold home from school. He never answered the question.

As he got in the taxi, she waved goodbye from the doorway. It took her two hands to open and close the doors. When it rained, the oak would swell and the hinges creaked like worn brakes.

"Don't kill nobody," she called as she pushed on the door. It slammed shut, but he kept looking at it until the driver put the car in drive and he could look no more.

He wouldn't stay at Fort Bragg long. He was sent to Fort Benning, Georgia, for RIP and, eventually, Ranger School. Sixty-one days later, with fewer than half the soldiers left, Corporal Stevenson got his black and gold crescent tab. Ranger-qualified they called it. To go on, a spot in one of the Ranger regiments would have to open, which usually wasn't long. He had found his place in life and special operations school was next on the horizon. He was sent to SERE school—Survival, Evasion, Resistance, Escape—then back to his battalion to wait for the letter that never came.

Instead, war came.

Panama. Operation Just Cause.

Your hands, Bulldog. On fire.

Another life, he told himself more and more instead of less and less. Don't mean nothin', right? Yeah, roger that. Keep talking that shit, dogface.

What started as an ED with rooms and patients within its belly was now trenches filled with casualties and armed enemies, waiting to avulse another shard of sanity.

And it was getting worse.

The patients per year had passed 40,000, and there was no sign of slowing. The complexity of wounds worsened and the trauma patients were mostly the ones who refused transport to an actual trauma hospital. When the suits did away with the residency program to save on insurance, the trauma team, made up mostly of residents, was dissolved as well, but the broken and bloody still came, either by the front door or by ambo. EMTs knew that Saint Catherines' ED was level III, not always prepared because there was not always a specialist on-call. No cardiothoracic, orthopedics, neurosurgery. But the patients would insist on it, for their wounds, gunshot or knife or both, would raise suspicion in a hospital not respectful of Canon Law. The overdoses, the beaten children, the gomers—it never stopped.

He had read more than a few times that the average burnout rate of ED physicians was five years and he was well past that. A decade approached and there was nothing to show for the milestone. No family, no children, no life. He marched alone to a ticking clock of routine. Work, gym, read. Repeat cycle next week. Once or twice a year he took a trip to some exotic location for a medical conference in hopes of recharging. With big guts and loud guffaws, his peers' tales of woe and poor reimbursement disgusted him. He avoided the cocktail hours, fleeing through the fire exit to escape to whatever wilderness or tropics lay beyond. They were the Jodies, that parasitic civilian only known to boot camp privates who ran cadence calls over and over, day or night, rain or shine, until their feet felt like stumps.

Ain't no use in going home
Jody's got your girl and gone.

These brought a smile to Stevenson when they blipped on the radar, sometimes a chuckle. There were the quotes, occasional at first, but now they sounded off daily and he didn't smile much about it anymore.

Complete the mission, though I be the lone survivor.

Excerpts from military textbooks, the screams of a Ranger Instructor to stop fucking up the line, dozens and dozens of cadence calls. Sometimes he heard them when he was having a "moment" with a patient, and these moments were increasing. The drunk with a stomachache who cornered Jenna in the bathroom and, somehow, would require a total knee replacement by morning. Or the father who brought his infant son in for a broken femur that required surgery. When Stevenson advised the father that Social Services was called, the father jumped out of his chair and grabbed Stevenson by the throat. Stevenson broke the man's arm with a grab and twist so violent that the feeling in the fourth and fifth fingers would never return. The father didn't press charges because Jenna told him if he did, the doctor would too, and there had already been a few visits from Social Services on record.

There were other minor attitude adjustments but the one from Sunday led to yet another broken bone. He felt Javier DaSilva's nasal bridge snap under his thumb. DaSilva would have sought counsel the moment he left hospital grounds had someone, Coleman, not reported DaSilva to the police. He couldn't continue to depend on the staff to keep quiet about these episodes, and there was only so much he could burn off at Gentleman's Boxing Club.

Exit with Coleman. Get a job outside of the city. Return one of the monthly calls from Paul Nguyen, the old friend from med school who owned a few clinics in the county and needed another doc. Work part-time, even.

"Three months," Stevenson said aloud, not believing his own words. He felt warmth on his neck, felt his shoulders drooping. He would leave the second civilian job of his life. Maybe they were hiring back at Goddard Quarry, his first employer.

He looked at his Timex. 00:30. Zero dark thirty. The numbers glowed green, casting a toxic hue over his skin. He pushed on the tip of the keloid the shape of a wolf's fang poking out from under his sleeve. It blanched, then went dark again, raised and forever inflamed.

"We all die in a state of regret," Detective Fredrico Viterello said. He walked, sometimes hopped, on uneven cobblestones at the end of Thames Street, trying to stay on the balls of his feet. "We all wish we could do it over."

His arches had been aching for months, stinging when he brought his size twelves out of bed and limped to the bathroom. Dotty would see the squinting eyes, hear the hiss of his pain. Don't forget your cholesterol pill, she'd say, with eggs and scrapple cooking on the stovetop.

"Whoever tells you he's satisfied with his life is too weak to admit his mistakes. He'd give anything to do it all over."

Detective Hyacinth Watkins listened, having to slow her pace so Viterello could keep up. A toothless woman, obese and unkempt, had approached their car at a stop light a couple blocks before, holding up a spray bottle and rag. The car, Watkins' own Buick LaSabre, because she refused to use the dilapidated Caprices provided to the Homicide Department, had just been washed the day before. Watkins waved the woman away, mumbling that she bet the old gal wished she could do it all over again. Viterello took off with it, coffee with four sugars just finished.

At the end of the dead-end street, marked cruisers were parked cockeyed on the other side of police tape but there was no need and no uniforms stood guarding the tape. Civilians didn't walk this far down Thames, the bars being a few blocks in the opposite direction.

Watkins and Viterello ducked under the tape and crossed over a toppled chain-link fence.

"Morning," Viterello said to a few uniforms chatting in a circle. They stepped apart, revealing a body in a trash bag a few yards beyond. The Harbor water slapped at the mud shore.

"Possible decomp?" Watkins asked. She opened her aluminum clipboard box. Viterello had one too, still in the wrapping at the bottom of his coat closet.

"Yes ma'am," one of the uniforms said. He pointed to a lone man standing halfway down an end-stage pier. "That fisherman over there found the floater at dawn. The Marine unit responded and called us when they saw it was on shore."

"He's not fishing," Watkins said. "He's crabbing." She nodded at the body and the groove in the mud trailing back to the water. "Did one of you drag it up here?"

"Nope," the same uniform said, taking off his hat. "The crabber did it. He thought it was trash." He had carefully coifed blond hair, parted on the side with a gel that made it shine. The fragrance had a chemical sweetness that almost overtook the water's stench.

Viterello gave him the once over, running fingers through his own Grecian Formula-black hair. Either crew cut or Hawaii Five-0, Jack Lord style. Grow it out or cut it. None of this in-between mess. Who puts Dippity-Doo on a crew cut? Product, Dotty called it. They use product now.

Watkins sketched the scene. Viterello approached the body, taking out a notepad from his trench coat pocket. The breeze was cool, nipping the tip of his nose. If he stayed too long, he knew he would bring the smell home. It got in the clothes, the skin. Two days and he could still smell it in the shower. God help a man if he fell in.

The bag had been duct-taped above the ankles. At the opening, two stumps poked out, two ankles missing their feet. The smooth cartilage at the joint's end glistened and strands of grayish-white flesh met the edge of the stumps. The skin's edges were jagged, with some portions missing in V-shapes. The blonde uniform drifted over to the body but the other two, a lifer sergeant and a rookie who stood as close as possible to him without touching, had seen enough and walked toward the pier.

"Crabs took his feet off," Viterello said. "There was probably something wrapped around the ankles, something heavy. When the feet came off, our friend here came up for air."

The blonde uniform grunted confirmation. Watkins stepped up and handed her clipboard box to him. "I see nobody looked," she said. She took rubber gloves from her blazer pocket, put them on, and fished a multi-tool from her shirt pocket. She stepped over the body, unbuttoned her blazer and rested her elbows on her thighs.

"Just the face?" Viterello asked.

"Yeah. More?"

"That's fine." Viterello looked at the uniform. "Staying or going?"

"Staying."

"Suit yourself. Better have something to help you sleep tonight."

Watkins pulled the blade out of the tool and grabbed the top of the bag, pulling up firmly between her thumb and index finger. She made a vertical incision, her nose wrinkling as the cut got longer.

"Dammit," Watkins said, letting go of the bag and turning away.

"Oops," Viterello said.

The body lay face down.

"Should we wait?" Watkins asked.

"For the ME? Nah." Viterello looked around. "This isn't the primary scene anyway. Flies haven't even shown up yet." He leaned over, prying the opening with a pen. "Stab wound. Left upper back."

Viterello stepped back and Watkins nodded to the uniform. They both grabbed the side of the bag where the shoulder was, flipping it over slowly. The bag peeled away from the mud with a slurp and water ran out of the opening between the stumps.

"Take two," Viterello said.

Watkins made another incision down to the mid-chest area and pried open the bag. What remained of a face looked back.

"Not as bad as I thought," Viterello said.

The face was bloated with various sized blisters on the cheeks and forehead. The irises' color was gone, now only a cloudy black that would soon mesh with the sclera if left in the water. The tongue stuck out halfway, gray and fat with fluid. A vertical plaque of fluorescent green on the right temple contrasted brilliantly with the rest of the face. The streak stopped at the braided hairline.

"What is that?" the uniform asked, stepping back, using his cap as a fan. A tan fluid oozed in clumps out of the nose and ran down either side of the chin. Its smell overtook the original funk of death. A tang of sour sulfur.

Viterello said, "Dead blood and harbor water. Maybe puke. Know what that means?"

The uniform shook his head.

"The vic was still alive when he got thrown in."

"Neck wound," Watkins said. "Cut the carotid."

The neck was neatly cut on the side, the edges white and turned out. The meat within was the same color. Viterello looked at the wound, the face, the hair.

He said, "Christ. I know this asshole."

"Go on." Watkins stood, taking her clipboard back from the uniform. "Never that easy."

"Danny? Donny? We had him as a witness last year for the robbery on Lombard." He looked at the ground, tapped his Tom McCanns. "C'mon, c'mon."

"Why the trash bag?" the uniform asked Watkins.

"When the bottom feeders start eating a weighed-down body, pieces can come off. A hand here, leg there. Sometimes the head. A smart killer will wrap the body in a sack or oil dr—"

"Timmy!" Viterello said, the name bouncing off the water. "Skinny Timmy."

"Yeah?" Watkins said, cocking her head sideways. She smiled at the face as if greeting an old friend. "Had to start from scratch when he got done with us."

Timothy Darrens had been the sole witness to a robbery at Quinlans Grocery on the west side, or so he told the police. The grocer was gunned down during a midday robbery, shot in the back while reaching for a pint bottle of liquor. It all happened while Timmy was on the front stoop of the store, asleep. Timmy had assumed he would get a reward so he told the detectives a short tale of two white men shooting the grocer without saying a word and then running out. The detectives eventually figured Timmy had lied about the whole thing when he not only said they shot the grocer in the face but also another witness had seen one man, not two and not white, run from the scene. The same witness also had seen Timmy asleep during the whole thing. Timmy had disappeared when he found out there was no reward and two pissed off detectives out looking for him.

Viterello shook his head, looking at the rotting stare of Darrens. He tried to identify with all his victims, tried to be a friend to the dead. It was not possible today. "Told your last lie, I see."

A white van pulled up to the end of the street and backed in. The Baltimore City Police logo was on the doors and Crime Lab's on the back. Two women exited, each wearing white onesies, the hoods crumpled behind their necks. Another van pulled in with Medical Examiner stenciled on every side, then another with Underwater Recovery.

"Hey!" the lifer sergeant shouted from the end of the pier, waving the detectives to come over.

"I bet they found the primary scene," the uniform said.

"Why don't you check it out for us?" Watkins said, not looking up as she wrote.

The uniform put on his cap and trotted away. Viterello stepped next to Watkins as they both moved aside for the incoming techs. One of the women carried a camera bag and camera, the other a large duffel bag. Both had credentials dangling around their necks.

"About a week, you think?" Watkins asked.

"If that. Didn't take the critters long to separate him from his feet."

"Motive?"

"Drugs, I guess. He was pretty low-level from what I recall. Probably didn't have any known associates."

"I'll call Vice and see if they have him marching with any crews."

"I give it seventy-two hours before he gets dropped to Cold Cases." Viterello looked at the crabber on the other side of the pier. The man was tugging a string gently. "I'll go talk to this guy. At least make it look like we tried. You tell the divers not to bother suiting up."

Viterello ambled down the shore, his shoes slipping and crunching on frozen patches of sand. Across the water was the Domino Sugars sign, darkened during the day. He remembered his first date with Dotty, walking along the Harbor's promenade, seeing the sign in the distance come alive in the summer evening. Those times were better, when the citizens of the city had better sense than to chuck bodies into the Harbor once the deed was done.

He stepped in a rut in the sand and the memory was gone, his arches feeling as if slivers of broken glass were moving about. He went bow-legged, trying to walk on the outside of his feet.

"Ahoy matey," he said to the crabber. "What ye anglin' fer?"

The crabber, cigarette dangling from the edge of his lips, watched the fat man in a suit and trench coat dance toward the pier.

RJ sat in the back row of the city council chambers, watching his father work.

"A significant portion of the land will be for commercial use, specifically the properties bordering the water which are already zoned for it, but the majority of the plan calls for razing the residential properties present now."

Councilman Lewis Reeves peered over his reading glasses, hand on hip, the other holding a paper from which he read. "That's the motion."

The fourteen other council members nodded their heads, sitting high upon a half-moon shaped bench that overlooked chambers with six pews. The only citizens in attendance were an elderly white couple in the front pew. The woman was asleep, her head slumped forward, mouth agape and tongue tip out between dentures. The man stared straight ahead, chewing air.

A voluptuous woman with valentine-red lips rose from the center chair, gavel in hand. RJ sat up to see her better.

"All in favor of Councilman Reeves' motion to move this proposal to the planning committee?" she asked.

All the members said aye.

"All opposed?"

Silence.

The gavel smacked and the woman, the city council president, asked if there was any other business. There was none.

"Adjourned." She brought down the gavel again and the members gathered up their papers. Reeves stepped down and walked over to the center of the bench. The council president leaned forward, her dark hair cascading before her. The top four buttons of her silk blouse were undone and RJ could see her bosom quiver from where he sat. The elder Reeves whispered to her and she touched his shoulder as he talked. Whatever tale he was telling ended and the woman stood up straight as she laughed, a waxed thigh revealed in the slit of her skirt.

RJ came out of the pew and started walking toward the front. His father turned and, while walking back to his chair, saw his son approaching. He shook his head once and his smile vanished. RJ stopped and stepped back into another pew. Reeves tucked his glasses inside his camel hair jacket and collected his papers, jamming them into an attaché case. He walked out, passing RJ without looking at him. RJ followed him out of the council chambers and down the hallway. His father's clip-clopping Guccis on the marble gave the sound of a man in a hurry. RJ tried to keep up, grasping his sagging pants at the belt buckle. In public, his father kept the pace of a taller man. In private, his pace was slower, pained when storms were in the forecast.

At the end of the hallway they descended the stairwell to the basement. Reeves undid his jacket and it flapped on either side. They went through the doorway on the bottom floor, passing closed doors, each numbered like motel rooms. At door 10, Reeves fished in his pocket and brought out a key ring fit for a janitor.

The office resembled a carpeted holding cell. With concrete block walls painted cream and no windows, it served as a place to gather thoughts, sleep, or avoid the press. A metal desk hunkered at the far end of the room under a framed map of the city; on the near end sat a black leather couch and a throw rug with vertical stripes of green, black, and red.

RJ shut the door and sat on the arm of the couch. His father placed the attaché case on the desk and took the phone off the hook. He shrugged out of his jacket and draped it on the back of the chair.

"How you doing, Pop?"

It had been a few weeks since RJ last saw his father, even though they lived in the same house. He looked RJ over and RJ did the same—looked himself over. Jeans so baggy they could fit two grown men. A puffy white coat that could fit a few more. Nikes, brand-new, untied. Hat sideways, and not the home team. He had forgotten the dress code of City Hall.

"I'm well." Reeves sat and leaned forward on his desk, his hands clasped in front of him. He hung his head and closed his eyes. "I thought you would meet me down here."

"I like watching you work."

Reeves looked up. The busy signal on the phone finally stopped.

RJ said, "Sorry. I'll—"

"Why was one of your associates floating in my harbor?"

When Reeves had called RJ at home and told him to come by City Hall, his throat tightened and clearing it didn't help. His father knew Baltimore better than any veteran journalist or lifer cop. Eyes everywhere.

"Fuck if I know."

"What?"

"I don't know."

"I see. Well." He drummed his fingers on the desk. "Perhaps you can tell me why you were at Saint Catherines the other night?"

"I wasn't at no Saint Catherines."

Reeves slapped his palms on the desk. The receiver popped up and fell on the floor. He pushed out of his chair and in four long strides was in front of RJ.

"Stand up."

RJ shot to his feet, not taking his eyes off his father. Eye contact was a requirement in the Reeves household and you better be groomed like a civilized human being. No beards, no nappy head. Lotion on them elbows, boy. No ash in this house.

"Don't lie to me, son. You know how much that hurts when you do that to me?"

"Yes sir."

"I don't care about none of that mess out there, RJ. Man's gotta make his way." Reeves put his hands on RJ's shoulders, grasping. "But I don't need you involved in no thuggery. Business is one thing, but you need to start distancing yourself from these low-level types. We don't live in the ghetto no more. You're in college now."

RJ kept his gaze firm and couldn't help thinking that he was looking at an older version of himself. Almond eyes with dark rings under sagging eyelids, the skin overlapping with creases. Thick hair on a large head, still free of gray. A potbelly pressing at the buttons of the dress shirt.

"And selling ounces of weed here and there ain't worth it either. They lock you up for good for something as silly as that. Locked up years for nickel and dime transactions. That's how they do us. Put a felony on our backs and we're done for. Zero-tolerance has killed more of our young men than war. Nobody will hire a young brother with a conviction following him for the rest of his life. You know that, right?"

His father had always steered him from trouble, from the age of eighteen months when his mother left him for good on Lewis Reeves' front porch. A few weeks later, she was struck by a city bus while jaywalking on Martin Luther King Boulevard. She spent a month in Maryland General, another month in rehab, and by the time she got out, the Transportation Department was ready to settle out of court. His mother collected her check and nobody had seen her since. Lewis Reeves did what was unheard of in the city. Many of his peers followed tradition and shied from fatherhood, not for fear of the responsibility but because there simply was no logic to it. No one in the game expected to live long enough to be a father. Either the street killed you or the courts held you hostage until the system killed you on the inside. But Reeves, after matching some of his own baby pictures up to the baby from his porch, held no doubt the boy was his. The name was changed. RaShawn Javan Dixon became RJ Reeves.

"Get your house in order," Reeves said, walking back to the desk. He put the case upright, unzipped it, and pulled out a stack of papers as he sat down. "I'm going to need a hand next year from someone with a college degree and a strong mind. And a clean record."

"Aight."

"And drop the hood talk. I need a well-spoken man with clothes that fit."

"Yes sir." RJ scanned his attire again, hiking up his pants. "What's happening next year?"

"Did you see that pretty little thing I was talking to?"

"Ms. Monica?"

"Monica Bretman, yes. I've known her since she was an intern here. She's a good friend."

"Yeah?"

"She was planning on running for mayor next year. It's possible she may win but it would be tight, considering her age. Voters would probably think she's too young for the job. I told her it would be a better bet to be deputy mayor first."

"Aren't there three deputy mayors?"

"My man." Reeves sat back, grinning. "You been paying attention. Yes, there's three, but the first deputy mayor is the one with the most authority. If something were to ever happen to the mayor, the first deputy takes over. It's also common for the deputy mayor to run for the top spot in the next election year if the presiding mayor gives his blessing."

"So if she don't run, who will?"

Reeves stared at his son, thumbs hooked under the suspenders.

"Naw," RJ said, putting his fist over his mouth, thumb on the lower lip. "You running for mayor, Pop?"

"About time, don't you think?"

RJ cackled, his eyes wide. He came around the desk and put his hand out and Reeves took it with a smack and yank, bringing them together shoulder to shoulder. They hit each other's back a few times before separating.

"That's why I want you out of that hoodlum stew. That mess is small time, RJ. Very small, compared to what we could be into. What's the one thing in this city that can make you a lot of fast money?"

RJ cocked his head.

"Yeah, that. That is where the money's at. And I ain't talking a few thousand here and there. I'm talking millions by the time the day is done."

RJ sat down on the couch, mouth agape.

"You feel me now? If I'm running this city I'm running the police department. I got connections up in there that run deep. I went to school with the commander from my district's station. He'll look the other way if I ask." Reeves sat down, arms crossed on the desk. "It's the only economy with no unemployment. Everybody gets a job."

"When did you think this up?" RJ asked.

"I've been planning this back when I was selling cars. Remember when I ran my campaign right out of the sales office?"

RJ said he did. He was in middle school.

"The plan ends with being mayor. Get in, make a lot of money, get out. We'll never have to get up early again if this works. And it will work, if I have the right people with me."

"What do you need?"

"I told you. Whatever small time transactions you have, start closing up shop. Keep in touch with folks you know that do big business. Don't be up in their face. Just stay in touch."

"Anybody in particular?"

"You still friends with that white boy, Markus Kruk?" Reeves reached around and took his reading glasses from his jacket pocket.

"Haven't seen him in a long time but you know, we boys."

"Used to play ball with him?"

"Against him. He played for Overlea High."

"Give him a call. Take him out to dinner or whatever it is you all do these days. We'll need him later." Reeves put his feet up with paperwork in hand. He pointed at RJ. "And do not tell him or anybody else about me running for mayor."

"Yes sir." RJ went to the door, stopped before turning the knob. "You know what Markus is into, right?"

Reeves laughed, not looking up. "I've heard stories."

4

"*S*een Coleman?"

Stevenson sat at the doctor's bar opposite Jenna. She scribbled a note in an encyclopedia-sized chart at the lower counter.

"He called earlier," she said. "He was meeting his lawyer and then having a quick meeting upstairs with admin." She looked at her watch as she stood. "Should be here soon." She plopped the chart in front of Stevenson. "Here, go see Fred in 12. He doesn't look so good."

Six in house. Zero on deck. Zero in the tank.

With himself and Dr. Baldanza, the patient load was manageable but it would change sometime after lunch. It was the end of the month, when the addicts ran out of money and the agony of detoxification began. The welfare and SSI checks had already been burned through and the next weren't available until the first of the following month. With the addicts came gunshot and stabbing victims from the previous weekend, limping into triage requesting stitches and a priest, the home remedies not adequate enough to heal non-lethal wounds.

The inevitable of them all, the sexually assaulted, would present in a variety of states. Angry, tearful, catatonic—some needed a wheelchair to be rolled into room 18, the gyno room to some, rape room to the staff. On summer weekends, they would be lined up and sedatives at maximum dosage would be given right there in the hallway after a social worker squeezed as much information as they could for the police. The nurse would pinch their arms to keep them awake during the pelvic exam and collection of evidence. Once or twice a year, Stevenson would insert the speculum and find two perfect little feet dangling out of the cervix. *Save the unborn child at all costs, Doctor.* This was Saint Catherine's law but rape could encourage miscarriage in the most viable of pregnancies. After all this, after the violence, followed by the clinical coldness of evaluation and treatment, the evidence would be tossed into a red garbage bag by the end of the night because the victim couldn't give an adequate description of the attacker or anything remotely close to a statement worth an arrest.

And during the busy hours, with every room full, Dr. Baldanza would order every lab and every imaging study possible, using fear of litigation rather than common sense to guide care. As the patients piled up in the hall and the waiting room clogged, Coleman would grind his teeth, staring at the board.

"You don't need to poke a patient full of holes," he would tell Stevenson and the other residents years ago. "You don't need to scan their brain and call their family doctor and shoot the shit about what's wrong with ol' Ethel. It's all in the history and sometimes the exam. If Ethel starts to gork out and tries to turn up the volume on the microwave because she can't hear Archie Bunker yelling at Edith, get a cup of her piss first. Most likely it'll be pure poison, full of E. coli. When we get old, some of our old habits come back. Most likely Ethel is wiping back to front and she gave herself a bladder infection, thus putting her into delirium.

"It's all about moving bodies. Your goal is to get them the hell out of your ED the second they walk or ride in. No labs, no scans, no goddamn phone tag with some worthless family doc who doesn't know the patient you're calling about anyway. Treat em' and street em'. Get them in, get them out. It's that simple."

His language was free of medicalese. It was the combat medic in a foxhole, the triage doc in the field hospital. These were lessons learned the hard way, decades ago when dozens of soldiers would be dumped by choppers at his hospital next to an airstrip in Da Nang and he had to choose who lived and who never made it past triage.

Stevenson walked down the hall, opening the chart. At the upper corner of the page was the patient's name, address, and date of birth. Below this, another block of lines with the present date, room number, and the visit number. The visit number went to 999 and he knew from the name and NO KNOWN ADDRESS that the visit number of this patient had turned over many times now. The chief complaint at the top of the page said HEADACHE X 1 DAY and the vital signs underneath were tolerable.

When he got to room 12, the lights were off and the front curtain pulled. He opened the curtain slowly, squinting through the dimness. The bed's headrest was propped up halfway and a body lay fully clothed on it.

"Who's that?" the patient rasped.

"It's me, Vernon." Stevenson walked to where all the chairs were in the non-trauma rooms and set the chart down. "What's up?"

"Headache." Vernon Lamb sighed, uncrossing and crossing his out-stretched legs. A plastic bag rested in his lap and slipped off the bed when he moved. Pill bottles rattled about inside of it. He didn't bother to pick it up.

"Worst one of your life?" Stevenson asked.

"Naw. Not that bad. But bad."

"You been throwing up?"

"Naw. Feel like it, though."

"Chest pain, numbness on one side?"

"Naw."

Stevenson, adjusting to the dark, took his stethoscope out and pulled the otoscope from the wall unit. "Any idea what may have caused it?"

"Happens when I have something I ain't used to."

"Like what?" Stevenson sniffed in the air. "Tequila?"

"*Tequila*?" Lamb squinted at the force of his own words, moaning through pursed lips. He held his head at the temples, rubbing with his fingertips. "Don't touch that mess. Last time I did I woke up in Central Booking. They said I was humping a fire hydrant." He shook his head. "Embarrassed as hell when they read that arrest report in court."

"What did you have last night?"

"Wine coolers. I was entertaining a lady friend."

"Didn't get burned, did you?"

"Couldn't get burned if I tried."

"Good. I didn't want to see your privates."

Lamb chuckled, holding his head again. "Don't make me laugh, Doc."

Stevenson went through the exam, noticing nothing new. Same waxy ear canals, same yellow eyes, same sporadic teeth poking through pale gingiva with stale alcohol emanating from beyond the throat. Purple cappillaries streaked the cheeks and nose. He had been examining Lamb as far back as his residency, almost ten years, and Lamb had been coming to Saint Catherines before that. Stevenson had forgotten the details of the story, for they all had a story, but knew it involved a lost job, dead wife, and estrangement from the rest of the family. A failed patriarch who gave up on being a citizen. He wanted nothing material and had nothing and his body kept going, taking the abuse day by day. Lamb never gave out signs of homelessness. No conversations with himself, no disheveled gait or odor. He never carried an underlying motive, such as for pain meds or just a place to sleep. He presented when he was in pain or sick. Stevenson only knew of Lamb being admitted twice, both times for pneumonia, and he left in two days.

"Unbutton your shirt a little."

As Lamb unbuttoned, Stevenson released the latch on the back of the bed, lowering the headrest. He put the stethoscope on the side of Lamb's ribs and heard more of the same. Lungs crackled slightly like crumbling tissue paper from the fluid backing up from an enlarged heart. The heart pounded with a distant murmur. Woosh-woosh. The murmur was growing louder over the years as the pectoralis muscles atrophied. Stevenson pulled back the cuffs of Vernon's jeans and pressed the ankle. An indentation the shape of his finger slowly filled in again.

"Ankles are still swollen," Stevenson said.

"All the time." Lamb looked down at his legs, hands clasped behind his head. "Used to be just the end of the day."

"Taking your medicine?"

"When I remember."

"This headache, on a scale of one to ten?"

"Seven and a half."

"I can fix that. I'll see about the ankles too but you have to do something about your heart. You need to take your medicine." Stevenson turned the overhead lamp on. Margarine light cast shadows among the valleys on Lamb's face. His hair, like stuffing in an old sofa, had recently been cut, with a few clippings still on his shoulders. He'd had a shave too, white stubble growing back evenly. Jenna called him Frederick Douglass, Fred for short. "You have to take better care of yourself. Start by letting go of the sauce. I've told you this before. They have a detox unit upstairs. Three hots and a cot."

"Yeah?" Lamb turned his head away and closed his eyes.

Stevenson had more to say, but he'd been giving the same warnings and advice for years.

He made his way to the door. "Back in a few," he said.

Lamb was never one to take Stevenson's or anyone else's invitation to the detoxification unit. He would politely refuse or be gone before someone could ask if he had made up his mind. Lamb knew what everyone knew about detox. The average age was twenty-five and almost none of them were there for alcohol. Once the addicts detoxed, they became bored. Their boredom could be dangerous for an old man, as most addicts were also felons, there on court order. A hierarchy reigned in detox, and it was no place for an old roamer.

As Stevenson sat at the doctor's bar, Jenna came up on the other side.

"What does Fred get today?"

"The usual." He scribbled a few orders and handed the chart to Jenna. "Hang a banana bag for starters."

A cocktail of every vitamin an alcoholic was low on, the banana bag refilled a pickled body and nourished every cell. This alone would relieve muscle cramps, cardiac arrhythmias, fatigue.

"And for the headache?" she asked, opening the chart.

"Toradol. Check his blood count and liver function while we're at it."

"Done." Jenna turned around and headed for a group of nurses at the other counter.

Bonley slammed a patient chart into the top slot of the bin. Stevenson didn't look. Picking up charts was like lifting rocks up to see what lived underneath. Could be a worm. Could be a Cobra. He checked the board.

Five in house. Two on deck. Three in the tank.

And the clock.

Seven hours.

He waited a moment for Dr. Baldanza to appear and grab the chart, but she didn't. He crossed the Pit and grabbed it as Coleman rounded the corner.

"Hey," Coleman said. Sweat dampened the armpits of his short-sleeved button-up.

Stevenson said hello, standing back to allow Coleman to pass into the doctor's office.

"Running late," Coleman said.

"No problem," Stevenson said. He followed him into the office.

A vertical stripe of sweat ran down the center of Coleman's back. He dropped his car keys in the side drawer of the left side desk and pulled his lab coat off the back of the door. His pocket protector and its contents fell out of his coat.

"God *fucking* dammit," Coleman said. The door was open and a few nurses paused, looking at the doctors.

Stevenson stooped to pick up the mess. Coleman thanked him and shoved it all in his side pocket. He nodded at the chart in Stevenson's hand as he adjusted his collar.

"Did you see that yet?"

Stevenson said he hadn't and handed over the chart. Coleman took it and walked out. Jenna was across the Pit and she watched Coleman depart, shrugging at Stevenson.

"Two coming," Bonley said, hanging up the EMS phone. "Motorcycle versus little old lady."

"Who won?" Stevenson asked.

"Neither, but they're stable. That's all I got."

"ETA?"

"Now."

The pneumatic doors opened and a rush of thick-soled shoes approached. Stevenson looked down at the floor, closing his eyes. The footsteps stopped and he felt eyes on him, waiting for direction.

*　　*　　*

An agency nurse whose name Stevenson didn't bother learning dropped Vernon Lamb's chart next to a stack of others he was trying to complete before shift change.

"Mr. Lamb is ready to go. Just need you to sign off on the discharge instructions."

"I can discharge him." He put his hand on top of Lamb's chart without looking up.

"Oh, thank you," she said, sing-songing the words.

The MVA had been between an elderly woman and a 16-year-old drug courier on a dirt bike. The woman was scared but fine, but the courier, riding without a helmet, had gone over the roof and landed on the sidewalk hard enough to knock himself out. When he awoke in T-1, he too was scared but not of his wounds. He asked Stevenson if they had found anything on him.

"They?" Stevenson asked, leaning in closer, his tinnitus flaring up.

"The ambulance dudes. They find my shit?"

"They didn't bring anything so I guess not. Like your wallet? Is that what you mean?"

The teen didn't answer. His eyes went glassy and he looked at the ceiling, shaking his head. His face was tan with dust that had caked from riding for hours. A tear rolled down his cheek, clearing a path in the grime. "Fucking fiends, yo. They just picked it off me. Didn't even check if I was alive or not."

Stevenson walked down the hall, writing on the last page of Lamb's chart.

1) **Cease ETOH use. Enter Detox unit as soon as possible.**
2) **Monitor BP regularly and take prescribed medications.**
3) **Have full physical with lab work completed at St. Cat's out-patient clinic.**

He had written the same instructions for so many of the homeless that it was reflex now, his hand knowing what to write without even looking. He prescribed the blood pressure meds with multiple refills, knowing many of them would never have the follow-up care done at any of the free clinics. But sometimes, one of them would surprise him. He would get a phone call from a pharmacy requesting a refill on the blood pressure medication prescribed six months before when the refills on the bottle had run out. It was this rare patient that the physicians remembered when writing the prescriptions for someone else, this nameless face smelling of street, still having the common sense to take the pill prescribed.

Lamb's overhead room light was on and the curtain open. He was getting dressed. Putting on his coat.

"That looks familiar," Stevenson said.

"What?" Lamb asked, holding the lapels of the coat. It was canvas, heavy and reversible. He wore the tan side today.

"I gave it to you last year." Stevenson put the chart on the bed and came behind Lamb. He unfolded the corduroy collar tucked inside.

"Aw yeah, I remember. When it was snowing. I thanked you, right?"

"Yes."

"Okay then."

Stevenson picked up the chart. "Your labs weren't too bad today. About the same as your last visit. Your liver enzymes are mildly elevated so that could be good."

"Yeah? Don't sound good."

"It is and it isn't. Your liver is angry but it can still give off the chemicals that tell us its angry. One day, it won't be able to do that anymore."

"Huh."

"When's the last time we did an ultrasound?"

"The thing the pregnant gals get?"

Stevenson nodded.

"Long time ago."

"You should have another. Lay off the alcohol and maybe your liver wouldn't be so angry."

Lamb was beyond the CAGE questionnaire included in every alcoholic's discharge paperwork. He didn't feel like he had to Cut down on his drinking, he wasn't Annoyed by the criticisms for it, he didn't feel Guilty, and he always used alcohol as an Eye-opener.

Stevenson said, "If I didn't give a damn, I would have the nurse give the instructions." He tore out the carbon copy discharge note and gave it to Lamb with two prescriptions for his blood pressure.

"I know. I appreciate it." Lamb took the paperwork, folded it into a square, and stuffed it into his coat pocket. He grabbed his plastic bags and stood straight, rotating his shoulders. "Think you can help me out? It's the end of the month. Well is dry."

Stevenson reached into his shirt pocket and handed Lamb a ten. "Need a cab voucher? It's supposed to rain."

Lamb took the money, studied it. "A flood to wash away the flesh."

"What's that?"

66

"Nothing, Doc. I'm good." Lamb stuck out his hand and Stevenson shook it, the palm rough from slapping a thousand sidewalks. "I'll see ya'."

"You should button that coat up," Stevenson said, following Lamb to the doorway. "I had a buddy that never did that."

Lamb looked at Stevenson and did a double take, seeing the concern. He put his bags down and buttoned the coat up. "There," he said when he was done, holding his hands out.

"Thank you."

Lamb picked his bags up. "What happened to your buddy?"

"Long story."

"Next time, then."

Stevenson watched until he disappeared out the ambo bay doors.

Collins took it in the chest.

Stevenson followed the path Lamb had taken, walking in long strides, shaking his head as if this would quiet his thoughts.

Why didn't you button your BDU? I fucking told you, private.

He came around the corner and dropped the chart in the discharged bin next to the Pyxis machine. Folger was trotting up the hall, coming straight for him.

"I need you." He stood in Stevenson's path. "Unfortunately."

Folger's thin lips would disappear when he was joking. His shoulders would slump as he waited for an answer to a joke. Now, Stevenson saw full lips, saw a stiff upper torso. Folger was already trying to walk back to fast-track.

Stevenson said, "I'm on my way out. Coleman's here."

"No he's not."

"I just saw him."

"He had to go back upstairs for something. You better take this one. Remember our friend Knott?"

"C'mon, man."

"Sorry but he's back. That hand I sutured is infected."

"Badly?"

"Not really but he doesn't want to see me because I 'jacked him up' the last time."

"What an asshole," Stevenson said, taking his lab coat off. Dr. Jeller was in the doctor's office, putting his lab coat on. "Let me sign out to Jeller and I'll be over."

"Thanks, dude."

Stevenson went into the office and said hello to Jas Jeller, a thin Indian whose array of facial gestures and emotion were at a one count: neutral. Jeller gave him a nod.

"Clean slate," Stevenson said. He hung his coat up and grabbed his helmet. "Just discharged my last one."

"That is good. Dr. Coleman has left me a handful." He yanked the coat's lapel twice, confirming fit, then ran his thumb over each side of his moustache, also twice.

"Maybe he'll be back."

"And maybe he won't." Jeller walked out of the office, the sweet scent of alcohol faint and brief when he brushed past Stevenson.

Folger was standing at the end of the fast-track hall. He held up four fingers before he disappeared into a room and shut the curtain. The fast-track rooms were nothing more than two thick curtains: One curtain followed a track that curved around and acted as the door while the other was attached permanently to a drywall column where the chart bin hung.

Stevenson took the chart from the room 4 bin and stepped into the empty room 5. Knott's vital signs were normal, then and now. No fever. Normal pulse and blood pressure. Stevenson put his helmet on the bed and paged through the procedure note. Two men spoke in room 4.

"Tuesdays are better because if some shit go down, it'll be a long minute before blue and white get there. Ain't like if it were Friday night. Every blue and white be up in there in no time."

Stevenson could see the shadows of body language moving under the curtain. He was about to step around the partition and introduce himself.

"*Sheeiit,*" a higher pitched voice said with a hint of a southern drawl. "RJ got this setup right. We ain't got to worry about no blues. Don't matter what day it is."

As the two talked, the fast rhythm of paper shuffling underscored the conversation. *Swick-swick-swick.*

"He got it set up on Tuesdays for a reason. Fights be when they got the lowest number of blues on the street. That's Tuesdays. Any other day would be asking for a bust."

"I'm saying, if we did the shit on Fridays, we'd get a lot of people up in there. High rollers and shit."

"You ain't getting paid now?" The swicking noise stopped. "Yeah, look at ya'. I'm telling you, you get too many of them roughnecks up in Stillman and shit just might get crazy."

Stevenson closed the chart and stepped around the curtain. Both men jumped visibly.

"Whoa, creeper," the man in the bedside chair said. He jumped up, holding his arms out slightly. His left hand held a wad of bills. "Don't be all running up in here like that."

The man stepped side to side, then forward and back, as if winding up. The gyration was barely noticeable if not for the gold rope chain dangling from his neck. The gold glistened off the florescent lights and bore sharp contrast to his red running suit. His hat was an exact match in color and sat crooked on his head, a white NY on the crown. He was smaller than Knott, both height and weight. A runt, of no significant threat.

"Mr. Knott." Stevenson went to the other side of the bed, ignoring the agitation of the friend. "I'm Dr. Stevenson."

Knott was wide in the chest and shoulders. Rust-colored eyes had a smattering of pinpoint-sized moles below them and they seemed to jiggle when he looked around. He wore black denim, black T-shirt, black boots.

"Your boy fucked me up." Knott held his injured hand out for inspection.

Stevenson put the chart on the bed and grabbed a pair of latex gloves from the glove box on the wall. The agitated friend sat back down slowly, eyeing Stevenson.

"How long has it been swollen like this?" He took Knott's hand, turning it left and right. Jagged lacerations were on both sides, with multiple sutures in each. The wound on the palm had yellowish crusting on the sutures and was warm to the touch, even through a gloved hand. The other side bulged, the skin taut.

"Few days. Hurts, too."

"Have you been taking your antibiotics?"

Knott said he had.

"How many times a day?"

Knott smirked, looking at the opposite wall. "I don't know, like once a day I think."

"You were supposed to take it twice a day." Stevenson stood and opened the closet in the corner. He took out a culture tube and a scalpel. The friend was back to counting his money. His thumb hit each bill in milliseconds, brushing the greenbacks in perfect time. *Swick-swick-swick*, his lips counting without a sound.

"Any fevers or chills?" Stevenson took Knott's hand again and removed a few stitches. Pus emerged in small bubbles where the stitches had been pulled. He put the scalpel in the sharps box and unwrapped the culture tube, rubbing the cotton top on the pus and then sticking it into the tube.

"Just hurts."

"This will need IV antibiotics tonight and possibly tomorrow." Stevenson peeled the gloves off, dropped them on the floor, and picked up the chart. "I'm going to write you another prescription. You need to get it filled this time, and actually take it."

"You calling him a liar, yo?" The friend stood and jammed his money in his pocket. He smiled at Knott, then straight-faced to Stevenson. "Huh?"

Saint Catherines saw the occasional inmate in the ED, always handcuffed to the gurney. Some of them, no matter the statement, took offense to whatever anyone in authority said. Some were inmates who had not been caught yet, pre-prisoners running wild in the free world. Tick-tock, tick-tock.

"He needs to take all of his medicine or this could become a surgical matter. That is what I'm saying."

"Surgical?" Knott's attention was full now, as it was for all patients when surgery was threatened.

"Yes, they would have to take the rest of the stitches out, clean the wound, and leave it open until it healed from the bottom up."

"What if it don't heal?"

"Sepsis may set in. It would probably need to be amputated if that occurred."

"*Amp*-utated?" Knott sat up, looking at his hand, then his friend.

"Fucking glad he dead," the friend muttered as he sat down.

"*Shut the fuck up, Adrian.*" Knott leaned back, squinting hard at him.

"It will be fine, Mr. Knott." Stevenson shut the chart. "Just take the medicine and come back tomorrow if there is no change or you get a fever. Otherwise have the rest of the stitches removed in six days." Stevenson walked to the doorway and stopped, his back to the two. "The nurse will be in to cover the hand and get the IV going."

"I don't know why I keep coming back here. They killed my Pops and now they trying to cut my hand off. But that's cool." Knott pointed with the wounded hand at Stevenson. "Tell your boy Dr. Coleman he's going to pay up real soon."

Stevenson remembered his last encounter with Jaris Knott's father, Felix Knott. Felix complained of every pain there was, demanding "that one pill that starts with a D" between his nodding out. Addicts clawed their skin, trying to quell the unreachable itch, and for Felix, it was the left side of his neck that had the scars and hyperpigmented spots of a picker.

"Hey Doctor?"

Adrian slumped back, head cocked with one eye closed.

"You got some brother in you, huh?"

Your mother would know. How many have you had in you?

"The nurse will be here shortly." Stevenson grabbed his helmet off the room 5 bed and crossed the hall to the fast-track nurse station. The only nurse in the hospital known to still wear a nurse cap sat there, watching him approach.

"What are you doing over here, Kay?" Stevenson handed the chart over.

"Short staffed." She opened the chart and read the orders, her lips moving in a whisper, and Stevenson saw another dark spot on her lower lip, this one forming in the corner. A smirk appeared when she was done reading. An IV meant she would have to get up.

"Tell Dave to write another prescription for antibiotics. Mr. Knott apparently lost his previous one."

Kay stood and disappeared into the supply closet behind the station. He thought of warning her about Knott and the agitated friend, Adrian, but Kay was not a friend or a trusted coworker. She routinely wrote up complaints on new nurses when they left a single glove on the floor or were a minute late clocking in. She wrote a complaint about Stevenson once when he came on as a resident. He had accidentally left a capped syringe on top of the sharps box rather than dropping it inside. Never mind that a patient had fallen out of the bed after he gave the shot and he was trying to save him from more injury. No, Kay left that out of the report, and Coleman had to bring it up over a couple of Pabsts after the evening shift.

"Good night," Stevenson said. He walked down the hall and out the double doors leading into the main hospital.

The swept and mopped floor of the cafeteria was wide-open space, the tables and chairs folded up against the walls. Only the kitchen lights in back were on, along with one of the buffet case lights. A few wrapped sandwiches were left for night shift employees, that is until Leon, kitchen maintenance man, turned off the ball game blaring from the back office and closed up shop. Stevenson walked across the darkened floor, toward someone hunched over the buffet case, checking out the sandwiches. She had a lab coat on and her hair spilled halfway down her back.

"Good night," Stevenson said. He went around the side of the counter and headed for his bike in back.

"Hey, do you know which one of these don't have salmonella?"

She rotated back and forth at the waist, hands jammed in her coat, studying the sandwiches. The cases' light illuminated only her face. Her hair was tucked behind one ear, revealing all those earrings.

"That's the main ingredient from what I've been told." The case came up to his chest and it was odd, seeing the view from the server's side.

"Oh great." She laughed, taking a few steps back and crossing her arms. She was out of the light from the buffet case and the cafeteria's darkness would swallow her if she stepped back once more. He doubted for a moment that this was the same woman from the lab. She had never smiled at him, never looked him in the eye longer than a glance. She wore aqua scrubs, which nearly matched her pool-blue irises. Her right eye was rounded, her left slightly oval and drifty. She had stopped laughing but the smile remained, and Stevenson could not look away.

He said, "I know the lady that makes them. Always wears gloves."

"Are you sure?"

"Promise."

She picked up an egg salad sandwich and studied the contents, while Stevenson searched for something to say. Her scrub top was a V-neck and when she bent forward, a silver necklace with a cross dangled and beyond it he saw a lilac lace strap. Leon's radio played a commercial for an auto parts store and all Stevenson could think of was the chorus, sung by a woman who sang the last word operatic. *If you want it, we got it, for pennies!* No words formed, and he turned for the door, once again abandoning the idea of speaking to her longer than a moment. He was about to say goodnight again when the creak of an old chair broke the silence, followed by farting and whispered curse words.

Zooey laughed through her nose and covered her mouth.

"Lovely," Stevenson said. He turned back around, no recourse available now.

"Ehh," Leon yelled. "Who's out there?" The office was close, down a short hall and beyond eyesight from the buffet cases.

"It's me, Leon. Getting my bike."

"Okay, Doc."

"Your bike?" Zooey asked. "You keep it in the cafeteria?" She dropped the sandwich in her coat pocket.

"Sort of." He put the helmet on top of the buffet case.

"I've seen you riding before. Aren't you worried about getting hit?"

"Not really."

"I would be."

She looked at the helmet and he thought she would pick it up but she didn't.

"I heard you discharge the man in 12," she said. "I was next door drawing blood."

"Mr. Lamb?"

"You gave him money."

He crossed his arms, looked inside the case. Nothing there he would eat.

"That was really nice of you. Do you do that a lot?"

"Actually, he was robbing me. He had a spork to my jugular."

"Really? Just a spork?"

"I'm not much of a fighter."

"How much did he get?"

"Whatever was in my change purse. A few buttons. Expired condom."

She laughed, tucked her hair back again. "I knew there was something wrong with you." She stepped as close as she could, kneecaps against the case. She was looking his face over from top to bottom, then back again to the eyes. Her hair fell from behind the ear once more, cascading one strand at a time over her arms. He wanted to put it back.

Drawers were being closed. Shuffling feet. Leon was locking up.

I don't want you being like your father.

"So, what's your deal?" Stevenson asked. His cheeks warmed.

"My deal? With what?"

"With tomorrow."

"What *about* tomorrow?"

"Are you off?"

"Yes, but I have class in the morning."

It had been over five years since he asked a woman out. Liz Fine had made it difficult for him. After he asked, Liz had pulled out an appointment book, paging through day after day for an opening before penciling him in weeks later between a Spin class and a dentist appointment.

"Why?" Zooey asked. "Did you want to hang out?"

"Yeah, I guess. Dinner or something. Lunch maybe."

"How about Friday? I'm off then and don't have class."

"Okay." He started backing away. Leave before she changes her mind, he thought. "I can pick you up."

"I'm not getting on that thing." She was backing away now, and they both were just short of shouting. "I live in the middle of downtown. There's lots of good restaurants there."

"Where?"

"Mount Vernon."

He nodded. Stopped walking. He'd not been to Mount Vernon since he was a child and never had the desire to go back. She asked if seven was good for him and he heard himself say sure and he would call her when he found a restaurant. She said bye and disappeared in the cafeteria darkness, appearing again when she opened the entrance door and the hallway's sterile light lit her up. She looked back, smiled, and let the door close.

For the rest of his days he would watch that night play over and over in Stevenson Theater. Her hair, Leon's radio, the rapid back and forth. The more she spoke, the closer she came to him. It was moving along fine when she mentioned a place from long ago.

Mount Vernon.

Please wake up.

5

$\mathcal{T}$he uniform standing at the door nodded as Watkins and Viterello climbed the short stoop of the rowhouse.

"Upstairs," he said, looking at his watch. "6:50." He took a leather notepad from inside his coat and wrote down the time of arrival for the detectives.

Watkins pulled her sleeve back, looking at her watch. "That'll work."

The home was sandwiched between abandonment. Most of the rowhouses were rotting from the roof down, and sheets of gray plywood were nailed over all windows and doors with the real estate kiss of death spray painted on each one: PROPERTY OF BALTIMORE CITY. Plaid couch, wooden coffee table, a few gold-framed photos of family alive and dead on a wall painted with primer. Some homes had carpet but this one had dark planks scarred with deep divots and splinters.

"Hear that?" Watkins said, stopping at the foot of the steps. She turned around and looked up to Viterello. They listened to the footsteps and voices on the upper level.

"What's she doing here?" Viterello asked.

Viterello bounced left and right as he ascended, his shoulders crunching against the plaster walls. On the upper levels of these homes made for people a century ago, they would find king-sized beds, entertainment centers, 100-gallon aquariums, car engines. When he was a younger man who saw letters and numbers clearly, retired beat cops told him about finding goats and chickens, even a donkey, roaming about in the upper levels. Farmers who had moved into the city for work and could not let go of their roots brought the farm with them.

The top floor was a short hallway with a door on either side. A small woman with a buzzcut, wearing a satin jacket with BPD on the back, stood in the doorway of the room on the left. Camera flashes illuminated her frame intermittently.

"Sergeant," Watkins said. She stood on tiptoes, looking over Bentley's shoulder.

"I was on my way in," Bentley said. She stepped inside and to the right. "Heard this over the can while I was taking the boys to school. Thought I'd stop by."

Viterello followed Watkins in and smelled copper, then the contents of an emptied bowel. The single window was open and the shade blew back occasionally from the breeze. A crime lab technician in a disposable onesie was taking pictures of the floor on the other side of a full-size mattress. He had the hood pulled over and cinched and steam trickled from his nose.

"Anonymous call about a sick person at this address a couple hours ago," Bentley said. "Medics found our friend here."

The bed was made with black silk sheets that had lost their shine and on top of this lay a small man curled in a fetal position, his back to the door. He was fully dressed with his shoes tied, as if he'd just settled down for an after-work nap. He had a hole in his temple, the edges of the wound blackened. His head rested in a circle of blood, which had trickled onto the floor and between the planks, gelatinizing. A revolver hung on the tip of his finger, and Viterello removed it.

"Loaded?" Bentley asked.

Viterello set the gun at the foot of the bed. "Yeah."

"Sorry. I should have done that."

Viterello pinched the man's flannel shirt at the forearm and pulled up. It bent easily at the elbow. "Two hours if that," he said. He stood and stepped back, his eyes scanning left to right. He was splitting the room into five grids. He would evaluate each one, then sketch the room entirely, measuring distances by marching heel-toe.

"I can take this," Bentley said.

Watkins, standing at the far end of the room, stopped sketching the scene in her notebook, looking up at Viterello.

"You sure? Viterello asked. "We can give it to a Junior. Not like they have anything to do."

Bentley said no problem and lifted her jacket above her waist, removing a small notepad fluffed at the edges from her back pocket. She readjusted the jacket over her holster.

"How's the Darrens case?" she asked.

"Routine," Viterello said. "Got time of death and mode but no witnesses. Family doesn't want to talk. Or can't."

"We got one call," Watkins said. She pulled the shade back from the window, peeking out.

"Not really." Viterello went to the door. "Just a name. Guy had no record and, honestly, I didn't believe it anyway. Just some asshole trying to get another asshole in trouble."

"You gave it enough time," Bentley said. "You can drop it downstairs if you want. I'll call IT today and we'll purge him off the active case screen."

No longer was there a chalk or dry erase board in the Homicide Department with the names of the victims, time and mode of death, detective assigned, and status of case. Now, with government grants, there were flat screen TVs with color coding. Timmy Darrens' name had changed from green to yellow to red, and now it blinked. Detectives were given seven days before the color change, another seven before the blinking started. The only way to remove the dead was to lock up a credible suspect or have the squad supervisor call the IT Department to have it purged. From there, all files were transferred downstairs to the second floor, the Cold Case Unit. When the budget was being crunched there were proposals of combining Cold Cases and Missing Persons, since none of the missing were alive, none of them were made missing by their own hand, and most of them, even if they did turn up, would have no one to claim their murder. Government grants had prevented the consolidation. New desks and computers. Same missing persons and their paperwork.

Viterello patted his belly as he looked at Watkins, then the victim. Always the same face, no matter the color or level of decomposition. Mouth open, wide or slight, eyes glazed and far off as if the mystery of life had finally been answered just before they died and the simple logic struck them dumb.

Someone ran up the stairs, without the jingle of a uniform's belt. Bentley and Watkins put their hands on the butts of their guns. The technician stepped to the corner of the room. Viterello looked around, no gun on him, and spotted the revolver he had just taken off the victim's finger.

A woman appeared in the doorway and a young boy ran up behind her and hugged her leg. "What the—" was all she managed to say. Watkins stepped forward and got her hands on the woman's shoulders.

"Oh my." She brought her hands to her mouth and buckled at the knees. "Shicky!"

More running came with familiar jingling and leather creaking. The uniform that was playing doorman appeared as Watkins bear-hugged the woman. The child started crying. The uniform put a hand on the back of the woman's shoulder, the other on the child's.

"She came in from the back," he said.

Watkins let go and reached out for the child. She scooped him up and he started to struggle.

"No," she said sternly. The child stopped and Watkins followed the uniform and woman out of the room.

"There's your ID," Viterello said.

Bentley nodded. She was drawing grids in her notepad.

"Why the hell did you tell her about the call?" Viterello looked in the rearview mirror. The uniform was trying to calm the woman down on the sidewalk in front of the house. The child held her leg, looking up at the adults.

"I don't want her thinking we're not working it," Watkins said. She put her seat belt on.

"She knows we are."

"Did you really look into the name?"

Viterello stared at her until she finally looked back.

She said, "Happened before."

"By accident. You know that." Viterello started the car and put it in drive. "Why are you picking at me today?"

"Freddie." She hummed his name and leaned her head back on the headrest, closing her eyes. "Too early for this."

"Knott, Jaris. Black male, age 28, approximately 5'10", 200 pounds. No current address in the system and does not have a driver's license. There, you happy?" Viterello stomped the accelerator. "I'm not searching all over town for somebody who probably isn't a real person."

"He's real. Just got to get up off your ass and look for him."

"Woman, I swear." He pulled up to the stop sign of the neighborhood intersection, one foot on the brake, the other on the accelerator—a habit from his teens that appeared when he wanted to leave faster than his car allowed. "One day."

"What? Shoot me? How you going to do that when you can't remember where you put your gun half the time?"

"I'll find it," he said, stomping the accelerator again. "You'll be the first to know." Watkins had her hands clasped in her lap and Viterello grabbed her left hand, pinching her ring finger. "Speaking of which. Missing something?"

"Left it on the soap dish," she said, pulling her hand away and crossing her arms.

"Don't be getting shit all over my seat," Knott said to Tink through cupped hands. He watched the big man from the metal lawn chair on the porch. Tink, window down on the Escalade and biting into a lake trout sandwich, ignored him. Tink ate alone, or at least tried.

Bean Street was tucked deep within the west side, far off the main vessels leading in and out of the district. It was a blue collar neighborhood decades before and the workers were employed by the surrounding factories. Like all manufacturing in Baltimore, the jobs left when the factories closed and so too the workers. Present-day Bean Street was one of the many former neighborhoods with no street lamps or residents in row after row of shuttered houses, all wearing the PROPERTY OF BALTIMORE CITY tag. Bean was another dead-end, shaped in a J. It stopped at a guardrail, then a fence, then beyond that, train tracks. On the left stood a row of houses, most crumbling or on the verge of, and on the right a square of green the size of a basketball court, now overgrown with weeds and tree stumps. The weeds had spread up and out, now encroaching on the blacktop from the top of the street down. The occasional commuter train flew by too fast for the riders to notice the decay.

RJ had brought Knott to Bean Street a few years ago after finding the property in his father's paperwork. The city's Real Estate and Acquisition Department owned and ignored it and scavengers had stolen the copper pipes and aluminum gutters years ago. 8012 was on the end and the only semi-functional house in the former neighborhood, the rest either collapsed or missing vital appendages. The front door was still attached and most of the windows were intact. Knott cleaned out the upstairs and furnished the rooms with benches and chairs that same day. They had their clubhouse.

"How's your hand?" RJ asked. He spit a sunflower seed on the porch, where it landed among thousands of others. It was difficult to see what color the floorboards were.

"Little better now." Knott held the bandaged hand up, rotating it. "Ain't swolled no more." He stuck his good hand out and RJ dumped seeds into it. He shook the hand like it held dice and dropped all the seeds in his mouth.

"Good. Looked tore up before."

Knott's phone rang. He looked at the number and pushed the button on the side. The ring stopped and he tucked it away. RJ was looking at him.

Knott said, "Lawyer. I'll call back."

"Going to get paid soon?"

"Any day now from what he tells me."

"Been two years. Better be soon." RJ spit a seed out. "How much you think you going to get? I remember you saying a million."

"That was two years ago. Now I don't know. Something close to that I hope."

"You hope? Shit." RJ rested his arms on the back of the couch. "Any less and that mother fucker ain't doing his job."

"He got it handled."

"Yeah, aight."

The lawyer, recommended by a cousin after her payout from a slip-and-fall at a grocery store, was Knott's age and he ended his sentences with *my brother* or *you feel me?* He had told Knott up front that malpractice cases took time but the payout would be worth it, *my brother*. He had three offices in the city and spoke like he was talking to a judge, his language clean and every word annunciated properly. Knott let the man work, rarely checking in. Only recently had the lawyer been calling and Knott was growing tired of the questions about his father. His sister was getting the calls too and she'd call Knott soon after the lawyer would. First she'd yell, then she'd cry without tears about how she missed her daddy, a man she never lived with past the age of five. Minutes later it was all laughs about the new car she was going to get and furs and Timberlands for all the kids. He knew she would waste it on Keno and scratch-off cards. She couldn't pass a party and keep walking.

"You call Kruk?" Knott asked.

"Last night. Said he had to put that dog down. Leg got infected."

"For real?" Knott held his hand up again. The bandage was spotless and fresh, without spots of pus mixed with blood where the bite was underneath. He was taking his medicine this time. Can't be legit with a missing hand.

"Surprised that poodle didn't have the rabies," RJ said.

"I'd be dead too if it did. Y'all would've dragged me down to the Brown and just thrown me in."

"Shit, I ain't dragging you all that way. Just do you right there."

The train whistle warned in the distance, then the rumble of the pistons soon after. The MARC train went by full speed, the wheels snapping like snare drums. When it passed, Knott stood, taking a smoke out. He spit the seeds out, tired of the taste, then lit up. He pulled deep and sat on the railing.

"We ain't did nobody like that in a long time," he said. He picked at flakes of paint.

RJ nodded slow, looking up at the gray sky. "Had to be done. He was a liability."

Knott agreed with as little sound as possible. He took another drag, looking over the old park. The stumps poking out through the weeds and brush were still yellow from moisture. The city left the houses to rot but cut the trees down if they grew too tall.

"Had to," RJ said again.

"You ever think about any of them?" Knott turned to RJ, waiting until RJ met his gaze before going on. "Dream about them?"

"Nope."

"Never?"

"Never." RJ shrugged, resting his elbows on his knees. He put a loose shoelace back through the upper loop of his boot. "Got no time for that."

Knott nodded, not in agreement but in recognition. Compared to others they knew, the city's hustlers and dealers, he and RJ and the rest of the crew weren't killers, but they knew when killing was called for. The summer before high school started was his and RJ's first.

"Remember that one boy that stole your bike?" Knott asked. "Pushed you and that white girl off and just went on with it?"

RJ laughed. "She was from church. Some girl from the county. Pop was trying to get some business done with her father."

"We went over to Tep's house."

Tep Langer, the eventual kingpin of the west side and most of the southern. Langer was an understudy to an uncle, the soldier being groomed for the upper ranks. Knott looked up to Langer and Langer took to him, more so than RJ. There was a place in the next generation for Knott. Langer had said so.

"He was like, 'time for y'all to take care your own.' Gave us that gun and said 'hurry up.'" RJ crossed his arms. "Can't even remember that—"

"Demetrius Pope." Knott stopped picking at the railing. He repeated the name.

"Yeah, Pope. That's it. Broke-ass nigger that lived up in the high-rises. He was older than we thought."

"Heavier too."

RJ laughed loud at this but Knott only chuckled, turning away. Tink was finishing the last of his sandwich.

RJ said, "In the Brown he went."

"Off the middle of the train bridge." Knott shook his head, spit through his incisors. "Stupid ass shorties, weren't we?"

"Remember we were looking in the paper every day? Seeing if he was in there?"

"Do I remember? I looked for a whole year. Never read a thing about it. No obituary or nothing. Like he was never born." Knott stood and flicked his cigarette into the front yard in a high arc. It disappeared in the weeds. "Never did get your bike back."

Tink got out of the Escalade and slammed the door. He brushed the front of his jacket with both hands, then lumbered up the broken sidewalk, thick arms swinging back and forth at the sides. He looked at Knott and RJ, his cheeks rising in laughter.

"Y'all look like couple of old folks," he said. He grabbed the railing and it creaked and bent as he came up. "Playing checkers?"

"Get enough to eat?" Knott asked.

"Fuck you." Tink got to the top of the steps, heaving a little, his steps crunching the sunflower shells. "When you... going to get them tumors burnt... off your face? Look like fleas crawling out your eyes."

RJ laughed and clapped his hands. Knott formed a retort but his phone rang again. He stood, taking it out and looking at the number.

"Lawyer?" RJ asked.

"Sister."

6

"*S*ix. Five. Four."

Stevenson paused, his arms starting to quiver. He laid flat on the bench press in his basement, holding three hundred fifteen pounds over his chest. He counted backward rather than the other way. Don't run to the other fighter, Russell Blake would tell those in the ring. Make them come to you. Control the fight.

He tried yoga, transcendental meditation, had even read Maharishi Mahesh Yogi's book and practiced the teachings for as long as his thoughts allowed—a couple months. It was the ringing combined with stillness, the concentration on breathing and focusing on nothingness—this was not possible. Gentleman's and his basement weight set were the only safe havens but even these places could not always drown out the distraction. Awake or asleep, days gone would replay with fine detail, be it from a day ago or a year. Decades sometimes. The lights of Stevenson Theater were always on. The actors never slept. Sometimes they acted the scenes true to life. Sometimes it was far from reality. Demented.

Last night it was the golden elevator. Water up to his ankles, sloshing left and right as the elevator ascended. His reflection on the gold doors was dull but he could see he was wearing a khaki suit and royal blue tie, like his father's. Someone stood next to him, dressed in jungle fatigues, holding an M16. The soldier was watching him, pointing at him, and the reflection on the doors was not what was true. Both of Stevenson's arms were on fire up to the elbow and the skin dripped off like wax. He awoke then and sat up and looked at them in the moonlight coming in from the upper window. Scars now, the flames long gone.

Someone tapped rhythmically at the tilt-in window. Only one person did this when the basement light bulb was on. He walked over and undid the latch.

"Hey," Taren said, squatting down. He held a basketball under his arm. "Whachu doing?"

"Laundry."

"Come out." Taren stood and walked into the street, bouncing the ball.

Stevenson went upstairs and sat on the couch, putting on a pair of Puma Clydes. He opened the front door and the phone in the kitchen rang when he stepped onto the stoop. An Arabber was coming down the street, calling out his wares, the bells on his trolley and horse all going at once. *Mango, ba-nan-na, toe-mate-oh.*

He picked up the receiver and sat at the pine breakfast table, listening, waiting.

"Hello?" The caller asked. Coleman.

Stevenson said hi.

"Do you ever answer your phone with hello?"

"Never."

"I've asked you why but you won't give me a straight answer."

Taren appeared at the doorstep and Stevenson gave him a nod. Taren did the same, coming in and sitting on the couch. The Arabber passed by, ringing the bell dangling above rows of produce. A chestnut mare pulled the cart, a red plume bobbing above her head with each clop.

"I got some good news," Coleman said.

"Yeah?"

Taren threw the ball up, trying to spin it on his finger. Every time he leaned forward, the knit blanket hanging on the back of the couch slid down a little.

"The lawsuit has been dropped."

"Really?" Stevenson sat up, switching the phone to his better ear. "That's great."

"The AMA form was found. It got stuck in another patient's chart before we switched over to scanning them all. A damn miracle somebody found it."

Taren dropped the ball and it bounced off the coffee table and hit the old 19-inch TV sitting on an even older aluminum stand. Taren's eyes went wide, his mouth O-shaped. As the ball went out the door, Stevenson gave a half-smile, shaking his head. He didn't know if the TV even worked anymore. Taren said sorry without sound and ran out the door.

Coleman said, "I was thinking of telling everyone next week. About my retirement too. Just get it all out there at once."

"I guess it's time."

"Yeah. Yeah it is."

Taren bounced the ball out in the street. Coleman asked what Stevenson was up to.

"I took your advice," Stevenson said.

"About what?"

"The girl in the lab."

"You asked her out?"

Stevenson said he did and Coleman laughed, called him a scoundrel. Stevenson heard him smacking the kitchen table a couple of times.

"It's just a date."

"Yeah, I know. Still proud of you, though."

Taren stood at the top of the stoop again. He faked like he was throwing the ball to Stevenson.

Coleman said, "You're a good kid, Cassius. The best."

The only thing he could think to say, thanks, came out, and Coleman said he would see him in the Pit and hung up. Stevenson put the phone back and stood.

"Damn, man," Taren said. "'Bout time."

Stevenson walked through the living room, stopping at the couch. He put the blanket back up evenly. Stared a moment.

The restaurant, recommended by Mildred Talmidge, was exactly as she described—a corner café on the verge of something more. On the cusp of the Mount Vernon zip code, it was a narrow but long four-story brick building with tinted windows lining the side. The name above the door, in thin alloy letters, spelled Violet, but someone had scrawled an N in chalk between the E and the T.

The hostess stood at what looked to be a conductor's stand wearing a sleeveless blouse with a loosened tie and slacks. A single bulb inside the stand cast her shadow on the red velvet curtain behind her. To her right was a stainless steel door, shined recently, with a few dings at its base.

Before he could say his name she grabbed two menus and waved for him to follow beyond the curtain. She led him into a darkened room with twelve booths on the left and the tinted windows looking over the street on the right. Only a few of the booths were taken and each by couples seated across from one another with a votive candle between them.

Her heels clicked in the cadence of a runway walker on the black marble. She stopped a few booths before the end of the row, but Stevenson kept going to the end. He slid in and around in the corner booth made for a party of at least eight, back to the wall.

"There's just two of us," he said as the hostess placed the other menu opposite him.

"I know." She lit the candle with a flick of a butane lighter. "I was told to take care of you."

"Mildred?"

"Who else?" She laughed and touched Stevenson's shoulder and butane and patchouli oil engulfed him. She went back to her stand in the same manner she had left it.

The day's traffic was dying down and random cars already had their headlights on. The one-way sign on the corner wept rust at the bolts and the white lines in the street were bare in the innards. Someone's belongings were heaped outside an apartment building across the street under a tree past its prime. Two upside down chairs sat on a few trash bags with a floor lamp next to it all, its cord strung out over the curb.

Mount Vernon. Masonry and asphalt wherever one looked, with random deciduous hardwoods that eventually undermined the sidewalks. Quarry stone churches stood out from the businesses and residences. He and his mother had never gone to church, but affiliation was no concern to the young explorer. He had snuck into a Methodist church that took up a city block on a weekday morning as his mother shopped at the corner grocery store across the street with his baby brother Hank. The pews went front to back in a nave that could host hundreds; organ pipes flanked a stained glass window that overlooked the altar. He had taken only a few steps down the center aisle, looking at the balconies, when the organ suddenly billowed. He left in a rush but had hoped to try another expedition when the chance arose. It never did.

He rolled his shoulders a few times. Cracked his neck. Years of routine broken by a trip to the other side of the edge.

A waiter took orders two tables down. He was describing something with his hands while gyrating his hips, his leather trousers tight on legs crossed at the ankles. He wore an orange feathered boa and a tank top that would be tight on most people. A hefty white couple nodded and smiled, stealing glances at one another. Stevenson checked his Timex, then out the window just in time to see Zooey fast-walking up the sidewalk. A moment later the hostess was leading her down the runway to the table. Zooey also wore heels, and the footsteps of the two clicked simultaneously. Her sundress, white and covered in lilacs, came to her knees and a passing car with its headlights on made the dress transparent for a moment only to him.

"Look what I found," the hostess said, clutching the stack of menus on her chest with both arms.

"Wow, cool booth." Zooey set a clutch purse on the table and wiggled out of a busy suede jacket with tassels on the arms. The waitress traded the menus for her jacket and left.

"I'm late," she said, moving down until she was directly across from him. She leaned down to read the menu with what little light the candle gave.

"I thought I was being stood up." Stevenson read his menu. There were no prices next to the dishes.

"Expensive," she said.

"Gimme that." Stevenson exchanged hers for his.

"I had the mantown menu?"

"Yes. Now you have the children's menu so order away."

"Don't tell me that. I have a deep lust for tater tots."

She wore another silver necklace, this one with a sapphire pendant which swung as she leaned forward.

"Thirsty," he said.

"Me too. Has the waiter been by yet?"

"He's coming now," Stevenson said, looking over her shoulder. "Brace yourself."

"For what?" She looked over her shoulder as the waiter jumped into place at the head of the table.

"Hi. I'm Birdie." Hands on hips, he looked to Zooey and Stevenson, back and forth, as if waiting for applause.

"Of course you are," Stevenson said.

"My real name is Jonah."

"I love that name," Zooey said.

"Thank you," Jonah said. He jutted his hip and whipped the boa over his shoulder. "It was my father's idea. He said I looked so relieved when I was born. Like I had just escaped from the belly of a whale. My mother never did like being the whale in that story but she's a bitch so who cares, right?"

Stevenson looked to Zooey, hoping she would take over the conversation. She only laughed, her neck craned forward, eyes wide.

"Anyway, I knew this man was not eating alone. Lucky you came when you did, honey." He put his hands on the table's edge, leaning in. "Because I'm back on the market." He stood up again and did a spin with a hoot, then another hip jut, hands outstretched in display. His hair was cut short and dyed orange like the boa, making his neck movements forceful.

"Oh my god," Zooey said. "He's adorable."

"We can't keep him," Stevenson said.

Jonah and Zooey laughed. A few other diners turned and smiled.

"I guess I should take your order." Jonah took out a pad from his back pocket.

"Let's see," Zooey said. She looked over the menu. "Are you ready?"

"I can order for the both of us," Stevenson said. "I heard some good things about a couple dishes here."

Stevenson pulled his sleeve back and read the writing on his wrist, then ordered the Sicilian pasta with eggplant, with water to drink, and Zooey added sangria. Jonah thanked them, took the menus, and skipped away.

"He's nice," Stevenson said.

"What's on your arm?"

"What?"

"That. There." She reached across the table and grabbed his hand. She pulled back the cuff.

"Who wrote that?"

"I did."

She turned his hand over, pulled up his sleeve, and he didn't catch on to what else her eyes saw. He pondered the amount of force it would take to pull her closer.

He said, "Someone at work told me what their best dishes were. I didn't want to forget."

"It wouldn't happen to be a certain cook, would it?" She let go but looked at his arm a moment longer.

"One and only."

"Milly. I love her."

She had a tattoo on her right wrist, covered mostly by a wide silver bracelet that looked to be made from an aluminum stirrup. He thought of Hector then, his father's Fresian, still alive and alone on the estate, the rest of the barn empty.

"What happened there?" she asked, pointing.

He looked down and back up, eyebrows high.

"Your arms."

The cuff of his shirt was pulled back, revealing the network of scars on the dorsal side. He pulled the cuff down and rested his arms in his lap. "Old injury," he said.

"Burns?"

He nodded. She said nothing, looking him in the eye.

"Chemical burn. Long time ago."

He looked out the window. The chairs on the pile of evicted goods had fallen over.

"What's on your arm?" he asked.

"This?" She pushed her bracelet forward. "Decoration, I guess. Kind of a cross between the Vitruvian man and the Silver Surfer." She held her arm next to the candle.

The man, a metallic black, stood within a ring of marble, holding the arch over him, or tearing it down. Stevenson couldn't tell. Beyond, space and stars reached into infinity. Words were engraved in the marble but all he could see in the single candle's light was FINEM.

"What does that mean?" he asked. "The writing?"

"I don't remember."

"It's Latin. I know that."

She nodded and took her arm away from the light. "Ari, my old boyfriend, he came up with the design. He was a tattoo artist." She rested her hands in her lap. "Long time ago."

Before he even opened a patient's chart he could figure age, weight, socioeconomic status and personality type from the introductions. Body language and muscle tone, clothing color and manner of dress, it all made up who a person was. He had trouble figuring Zooey out, but he saw what the tattoo meant to her, saw why she always wore long sleeves.

She asked, "How about you? Any tattoos?"

"Almost, when I was in the military. I sobered up by the time we got to the parlor."

The hostess came clicking down to them and set the drinks down without a word, then walked away.

"My brother was in the Marines," Zooey said. She sipped her sangria, bypassing the striped straw. "Not long, though."

"Even a month feels like a lifetime."

"When did you join?"

"Right out of high school."

"Marines?"

"Army."

"A grunt?"

"Executive grunt."

She asked about high school and he told her Towson. She said Churchill, in Potomac, and he told her about the mansions he saw there once when he got lost driving home from an internship in DC.

She said, "I lived in the next town over, in Rockville."

"Oh. Your parents live there?"

"I think so."

She looked over her shoulder, out the window. "How about your parents?" she asked. She took a gulp of the sangria this time.

"My father died a couple years after I graduated high school and my mother when I was young."

"I'm sorry. How old were you?"

89

He told her, and she leaned in enough so the candle could catch her in the light. Eyes like Maui water, not a red vessel anywhere, with eyeliner accentuating. She had no rhytids, no blemishes on a face he could not turn from. She reached across the table and stopped short of touching his hand.

"I can't imagine," she said.

He mumbled that it was alright, said again that it was a long time ago. He sipped his water but left his other hand on the table. She had mentioned having a brother, and he thought of telling her about Hank, but his death would only raise more questions.

Stevenson said, "C'mon, I don't want to start like this."

"You're right." She put both her hands palm down on the table, breathing deep. "Okay. So. I. Am. A Taurus."

He told her his sign and his birthday, August 1st. She said June 1st. She sipped her drink and tucked her hair behind her right ear. Every piercing had an earring tonight.

"Have you ever been married?" she asked.

"No. Came close."

"Sobered up before you got to the parlor?"

"Something like that. You?"

"Never. When I was younger I thought that's what I was supposed to do. Have kids and a husband but the older I got, the more I realized I wasn't marriage material."

"You weren't or Ari wasn't?"

"He was. Definitely was. Just not with me." She was turning the glass around and the ice cubes stayed still. "I just couldn't give him what he wanted. I had already lived in a microcosm of empty people for nineteen years. I didn't want to repeat my parents' mistakes." She took another sip. "What's your excuse?"

"I never wanted kids, so I didn't see the point of marriage. Liz didn't agree."

"She wanted kids?"

"Two."

"Why don't you?"

"I don't want to screw some human being up before they even have a chance. Adults have a tendency to do that without even trying."

She nodded. "That's my name, by the way. Liz. Elizabeth."

"No it's not."

"Yeah, it is. My brother Joe called me Zooey since we were young so it just stuck. He was younger than me. Learning his Z words when he was trying to pronounce Elizabeth just evolved into Zooey."

"He's back in Rockville?"

She shook her head. More sipping. He thought of asking if the brother had been wounded but talking about family was better if only skimming the surface. She went silent when questions descended deeper.

"So why did you ask me out?" she asked.

"I don't know. Seemed like the right thing to do, I guess."

"That sounds terrible. You felt sorry for me?"

"Yes. Yes I did."

"Shut up. Really, why?"

"Why are you asking?"

"Because you're like a doctor and I'm just me. Zooey Briggs, lab tech."

"That's deep."

"Seriously, I'm a nobody in that lousy job."

"You don't like your job?"

"I hate it. And you're avoiding the question." She smacked the top of his hand lightly.

"I wanted to hear you talk. I never hear more than a few words from you, then you're gone."

"We're told to get in and get out of the rooms. Pretend it's a crime scene. Don't hang around." She finished her sangria. "So that's it?"

Stevenson shrugged, stepping on his own foot.

"I guess that's okay." She put her arms on top of one another on the table and leaned forward. "I really don't know much about you, though."

"That's the point of a date, don't you think?"

"I think you're kind of a smart ass."

"Uh-huh. Just curious, who's paying for that drink?"

"You asked me out. You pay." She sank in her chair and kicked his shin hard enough for him to wince.

"Well then," he said.

It was Mount Vernon, a place he never wanted to see again but never wandered too far from. Now, he wanted to be no place else in the world.

They talked through dinner and he couldn't recall later what the food tasted like or what had been written on his arm. She was in her last year of grad school for city planning and hoped to move to California when she was done. San Francisco, maybe. Her parents were casual Catholics, both teachers, retired. She had not spoken to them in years but didn't say why or anything more about them. She moved out at nineteen with the tattoo artist, Ari, and got a degree in medical technology. After four years of hovering over humming metal boxes that deciphered bodily fluids, she realized the lab was not her place in life. Around that time she broke things off with Ari and moved to the city.

She asked "What about you?" a few times but Stevenson ended the queries with one and two word answers. Gym. Work. Home. Repeat cycle until retirement. She pinned him down on his parents, fascinated that he worked where they once did and that Coleman knew them both.

"What was your mother's name?"

"Sally Tipton."

"They never married?"

"Broke up before I was born. I didn't meet him until I was eight."

"After she died."

He nodded.

She poked her lip with the straw as she brought the glass up and it tapped the table twice when she set it down. It was her third drink.

"They would be proud of you," she said.

"Perhaps."

Jonah was saying goodbye to the last couple. A man scooted out of the booth while handing over a wad of cash. As soon as he stood, Jonah hugged him. When they were gone, he skipped down to his last table.

"How was it?" he asked. He picked up the plates and utensils, piling them on his forearm.

Zooey handed her glass to him. "Really, really good. Can I have a water?"

"And the check," Stevenson said.

"No dessert?" Jonah looked to Zooey, then Stevenson.

"Next time," Zooey said.

"Okay," Jonah said. He turned around and backed up to Stevenson. "Check's in the back."

The check was tucked in Jonah's waistband and Stevenson yanked it free.

"Back in a sec," Jonah said. He trotted away but didn't lift his feet and his shoes slid on the marble.

"I think he likes you," Zooey said. She was turning a stud earring around, watching for his reply.

Stevenson held the bill under the table, looking at the amount. He took his money clip out and counted out cash.

Swick-swick-swick

Zooey said, "The things you've seen over the past ten years. You should write about it."

"I'd like to forget it all most of the time."

"Really? All of it?"

He tucked the cash into the check holder and put it on the table. She was waiting for an answer and he looked out the window instead. Evening had settled and the passing cars illuminated the evicted furniture. The chairs that had toppled over were gone now, scavenged, but the lamp remained without its shade. If he were at home he'd be reading something by now. Lifting weights and counting down, not up, despite the nausea and burn.

Your hands, Bulldog.

She said, "You could work anywhere you want and you decided to stay on with Dr. Coleman. You save people every day. Give them your money and the clothes off your back. All seems pretty honorable to me."

"If you say so."

"I'm saying so. You're helping those in great need."

"They're not all like that," he said. He scratched at his hand, his arm. The smooth keloids itched deeper than he could reach. "The majority of them don't need to be there and the ones that should are usually too late."

"The kids? Vernon Lamb?"

"The young and the old, I'll give you that. The rest?" He shook his head.

"They're human beings, Cassius. With hearts and souls. We all start out the same."

Contact Front. Frag out. One. Two.

"They're fucking parasites," he said, sitting up, leaning across. He was stabbing the table with his index finger. "I help the worst of the worst and when they die, I help their children live long enough to repeat the same mistakes. All they know is to take and I do nothing to change that, to alter their destiny. I'm an enabler. There's nothing honorable about it. Or me."

She was sitting straight up, as if trying to get out of his reach without being obvious. She was out of the candle's light, staring at him with a blank expression. Jonah came back to the table without shoes on and his steps were silent. When he appeared, Zooey jumped.

"Here's your water," he said, putting it in front of Zooey. "If you—"

"We're fucking fine," Stevenson said.

Jonah stepped back, started to bring his hands up defensively. He looked at Zooey, mouth open, and stumbled into a jog. She reached out for him but he was gone.

She said, "That was not cool," then shot out of the booth. She grabbed her purse and marched down the walkway.

Stevenson followed behind her. She pushed the front door open and the breeze grabbed it, slamming it back in his face. He leaned into it, forcing it open. The cold was immediate on his nose and ears, much more than when he had arrived.

"Zooey!" A few drops of rain smacked his forehead. "Your jacket."

She stopped, not turning around, tapping her chest once. "Dammit."

"I'll get it. Promise to stay there?"

She stepped backward to the building and leaned against it, looking the opposite direction down the street, arms crossed. Her dress blew about but she made no effort to settle it down.

Stevenson walked back in to see the hostess coming out of the kitchen. Zooey's jacket was in her hand.

"Is he in there?" Stevenson asked.

"Leave him be," the hostess said. She shut the kitchen door but Stevenson caught a glimpse of Jonah sitting on a bar stool against the wall, staring down at the terra-cotta tiles. Bent forward with both elbows on his knees, he held a phone to his ear with one hand and the side of his head with the other.

"He's sensitive," she said. She handed the jacket over as she flipped the lights on. Sudden florescence.

"Tell him I'm sorry. He just caught me at a bad time."

"Please go."

It was after eleven and Stevenson insisted on walking her home. He tried to help her with her jacket but she only yanked it from him and tucked it under her arm. A few steps into the trek, the wind eased and a drizzle began.

"Where do you live?" he asked. The street, the sidewalk, everything was familiar. Smaller.

"On Charles," she said. "Two blocks up."

It rained harder. Zooey took her heels off and trotted on the balls of her feet. Tree roots had raised the sidewalk in some sections and she knew all the imperfections but Stevenson lagged behind, dodging, barely able to see them. The streetlights, ancient Novaluxes, their stanchions covered in peeling black paint over army green, glowed like fireflies.

They rounded the corner and Zooey stopped under a crimson awning in front of an apartment building taller than all the others. She started up the stairs, fishing in her purse for her keys. Stevenson stayed beyond the awning, his back to her.

"This is me," she said.

Washington Place, a strip of grass and trees with benches along the sidewalk, bifurcated Charles Street in the center of Mount Vernon. At the edge of the grass where the separated streets met again was a bronze statue of a colonial era soldier riding a horse, sitting upon a block of marble. Rain splashed off the rider's bicorne hat and the water streaming down the horse's haunches glistened. No cars passed. No horns or gunshots.

"Do they still have those iron folding doors on the elevators?" Stevenson asked.

"They're just sliding doors," she said. "Tan." She found her keys and had the right one between thumb and index finger. "You've been here before?"

"That's John Eager Howard," he said, pointing across the street. "Did you know that?"

She said she did.

He peered south at the Washington Monument. The lights at its base flickered and the marble shaft was nothing more than a darker shadow in the night. North, beyond the statue, on the corner of the other side of the street was a bookstore. The door was the same as he remembered but an awning had been added over the half-moon step. The windows had posters of book covers and a sign hung above the door that he couldn't make out.

The wet asphalt smell was gone, overpowered by gunpowder and orange juice. He could taste it, could feel the adhesiveness of drying blood on his right hand, the weight of a limp infant in the crook of the other.

Please wake up.

Stevenson said, "Yes, I've been here before." He turned around. She'd stepped down off the steps and stood in the middle of the sidewalk, hugging her jacket. Her hair clung to her cheeks, and a few strands curled up at the corner of her mouth. She was shivering and he wanted to hold her but he had killed what chance he had. "I used to live here."

She started to talk but Stevenson was walking away.

"See you at work," he said, not turning around.

This boy here says what you do you become, Bulldog.

When he rounded the corner, he started jogging. He went in the street and the jog became a sprint. Traffic came at him slowly and he ran between the cars. One of the drivers leaned on the horn. His thighs burned from the pace, his pants soaked and constricting, but he continued on one block past where he had parked the bike. The rain pelted his eyes and he kept them shut when they started to sting. After a taxi swerved out of his path and brushed a parked car, he slowed, hopping onto the sidewalk and under an empty bus stop shelter.

He had not seen John Eager Howard or his horse in over thirty years.

7

*K*nott turned onto Bean Street, the tires squealing. Ahead, Adrian stood in front of the clubhouse, on the sidewalk. Adrian hated it there, especially by himself, and told anybody who would listen that the lost neighborhood was haunted. No kids playing ball, no cars driving by, not even gunshots, day or night. When Knott told Adrian to be at Bean in an hour, he hung up immediately, not wanting to hear the whining.

"'Sup," Adrian said. He sauntered closer, looking up and down the street. His jeans drooped in the seat and he held his belt with one hand, his phone in the other. "Why you drag my ass out here?"

Knott opened the door and got out, not bothering to park. A cigarette dangled in the corner of his mouth. He wore the clothes from the day before.

"Call your cousin," he said.

"Apollo?"

"Call him. I got work for him."

"Damn, man. Now what's going on?"

"Call him, goddammit."

Adrian shook his head as he poked at his phone. He paged through the numbers with his counting thumb. "Can't RJ get somebody here?"

"He's your cousin. Why you talk like that?" Knott looked up and down the street. Always keep an eye out. One of the few lessons his father taught him.

"'Cause he's crazy as hell, yo. We blood and all but that's it."

Knott pulled off his cigarette and paced. Adrian held the phone closer to his eyes, scrolling, smirking.

"Find it?" Knott asked.

"What's up with you? Why you can't stand still?" Adrian lowered the phone. He tilted his head downward. "RJ don't know about this, do he?"

Knott stopped pacing. Smoke wafted from his mouth and nose as he stared Adrian down. His tone was low. "This ain't his concern. You feel me?"

"Yeah, aight." Adrian went back to scrolling. "Need some details, though, if you want the boy to come all the way down here."

Knott sat on the curb. The sun was setting beyond the former park and the moisture from the rain twinkled on the wider blades of grass.

He said, "I been fucked, A. Hard. I was going to go to school. Get legit. Be a citizen." He cupped his ankles and looked over the hairline cracks in the asphalt.

"What the fuck you talking about, yo?"

A train horn sounded far off. Its pistons thundered.

"It's a doctor. I want him dead." Knott stood, brushing the seat of his pants. "I'll tell Apollo the rest when he get here."

"You talking some green right there," Adrian said. He followed Knott to the Escalade. Knott got in and shut the door. "A lot."

"I'll pay it. Just get him down here. Tonight."

Knott turned the Escalade around and drove away. In the rearview mirror, he saw Adrian in the street, phone to ear.

"Look at this bastard right here," Lewis Reeves said, getting up from his desk. "I swear, every damn time I'm up here, there he is." He put a hand on the window, the other on his hip.

Major Charlie Lincoln stood, his half-full tumbler of Hennessy sloshing as he came around the desk. He shifted his unlit miniature cigar to the corner of his mouth.

"Where?" Lincoln asked, bumping into Reeves at the shoulder, a habit from high school. They were defensive lineman then, both junior varsity and varsity.

Fourteen floors below was the flat blackness of the Inner Harbor. The moonlight was hidden by clouds and the two had to squint to see. Only the surrounding brick promenade and the shops that ran alongside it were lit but no one was walking about.

"Right in front of us," Reeves said. "That boat towing that heap of shit there. See?" Reeves pointed a finger straight down.

A green Jon boat drifted along the edge of the walkway, towing a fishing boat with no motor and full of trash. A man scuttled about on the lead boat, scooping garbage out of the water with a net and dropping it on the mound. He would use the net to rearrange the heap each time, trying to consolidate it as it grew.

"Oh, him. Forgot about him." Lincoln crossed his arms, the tumbler against his bicep. "He comes out to the south end sometimes. Cleans up Smith Cove and Gwynns Falls. He's ex-coast guard."

"You know him?"

"I know of him. He's been brought to the attention of the brass from time to time. The Marine unit lets him be."

"I thought small craft weren't allowed in there after dark."

"They're not." Lincoln turned and strode back to the paisley guest chair and sat down. "And he doesn't even have runner lights. But, he cleans that Harbor better than Solid Waste ever did, even when they had a multi-million dollar budget, and he does it for free."

"Don't they have a special boat? Has a conveyor belt on it and drags the water?"

Lincoln snorted. "The Harbor Dragon? That thing sank three years ago."

Reeves, defeated, sat down. He leaned back, thumbs in his suspenders. He could smell Lincoln's breath from where he sat. Mouth breather. Filled the room with his air.

"I gotta get going," Lincoln said. He looked at his watch. "She's up my ass all the time now."

"Commander of the Western District, caught fucking around by his ninety-pound wife."

Lincoln chuckled, leaning forward. He stroked the lower half of his black tie, the upper half held in by a gold tie clip. "How was I supposed to know she'd be home early?"

"Damn, Charlie. Just. Damn."

Lincoln downed the remaining Hennessey and stood, placing the glass on the desk and the cigar in the glass. Reeves picked it up, looking for scratches on the desk. He dumped the cigar in the trashcan.

"So you think your boy can put this together?" Lincoln asked. He stretched his arms over his head, yawning. The front of his dress shirt came untucked and the buttons were pulled taut over a mound of a belly.

"I know he can," Reeves said. He put the glass on the desk calendar and stood. "He goes way back with Kruk. They played ball together in high school."

Lincoln crept towards the door. Reeves followed.

"Ain't getting my hands dirty on this, Lou." Lincoln took an officer's jacket off the pedestal coat rack and put it on, rolling his shoulders. A few rows of ribbons decorated the right breast, flanked by a gold badge on the left. "Don't need a Hustlers Row in my district."

"My thoughts exactly." Reeves reached in his pocket and took out a starlight peppermint. He handed it over and Lincoln unwrapped it, popped it in his mouth, and handed the wrapper back.

"Just give me the drop spots," Lincoln said. "I'll see what I can do."

"*What you can do*? Did you forget about how much money we're talking about? Just for you to keep your people out of certain sectors of the district for a few hours once a week?"

"I remember."

"Damn right you do. That's what you make in a month."

"Don't remind me." Lincoln tucked his shirt in.

"Listen, Charlie." Reeves put his hands on Lincoln's shoulders, shaking him a few times lightly. "It's that easy. Just tell your boys there are special operations going on and they need to stay away."

Lincoln breathed deep, buttoning his coat but keeping eye contact. "What about complaints?" he said. "We get the retirees calling the hotline every day now. That whole 'see something, say something' ties up the whole damn department. We got to send officers out, you know. Don't want our Councilman thinking we're not looking after his people."

"The Councilman knows the department in his district is doing a fine job."

"I'm serious."

"There won't be any complaints. These boys are just part of the wholesale side of things. Taking it to the streets? That's for them young hoppers."

Lincoln nodded, in thought, and Reeves gave him a moment. In high school, Reeves never worried when Lincoln stood next to them, on or off the field. The girls called him Big. The complexion of gravel, they loved him for his size and both men benefitted from it.

"I'll get it done," Lincoln said.

"My man," Reeves said, hugging him. "In a few years there will be a retired cop in the Cayman Islands. Walking the beach, not knowing what to do with himself."

"That'd be nice." Lincoln stared at the door, seeming to conjure the image of what Reeves predicted, then took his cap off the top of the rack. He put it on snug and opened the door. "Let me know when you want to start."

Reeves said he would. Lincoln walked out of the only occupied office on the fourteenth floor and over to the elevators a few feet away. He hit the button and looked back at Reeves.

Lincoln said, "How am I supposed to hide that kind of money?"

"Offshore accounts. Why do you think your retiring in the Cayman Islands?"

Lincoln grinned and pointed at Reeves, then his temple. The elevator bell chimed and the doors opened. He waved as he stepped in.

Reeves shut the office door and walked back to the window. The trash collector was making his way out of the Harbor, the fishing boat over-flowing.

"And don't come back."

8

A pipe in the bathroom had burst at Gentleman's, flooding the locker room and most of the heavy bag area. Stevenson found Blake stomping around in the puddles, loafers waterlogged and squishing. The mats were draped over the top rope of the ring and Blake was mopping but it wasn't helping much. The place was empty, the sign on the door saying "closed/pipe bust," and nobody had come up to check it out. Stevenson offered to help but Blake wasn't having it. The pipe "could go for goddamn days before I get a plumber up in here."

The walk back through Patterson Park, a square mass of ball fields and jogging paths separating the east side's Highlandtown from Upper Fells Point, was without distraction from his thoughts. Morning fog erased everything beyond a few yards and tan and yellow leaves blew about. Over and over, on a loop, the night out with Zooey played uninterrupted. He destroyed any chance with the girl from the lab by letting his id consume the conversation. Without the gym to smother his thoughts with exhaustion, the loop would play on, the projector's bulb never burning out. Through the years he had been in the occasional scuffles on the way home when the workout wasn't enough and his fists didn't ache the way they should have. Last summer a group of teens walked in the center of the path and purposely tried to bump his shoulder. None of them were standing when he was done.

He picked up his pace, head down. No more fighting, he promised himself. Again.

You've been here before?

A shift had occurred in his chest when she'd asked. Something awoke, turned over and looked around some. When he said the name of the statue and his gaze fell to the corner, where Kwan Grocery once was, it rose, uncoiled. For a moment, he was no longer Dr. Cassius Stevenson. He was what had awakened.

This boy here says what you do you become, Bulldog.

He ran when he heard the words. It was closing in on twenty years since Collins whispered this in the dark, reading it from *The Short-Timers*, a book about the Vietnam War. Collins found it in the streets of El Chorrillo, Panama, across from a burned-down library. They were lying on cots in a tarp hooch among a cluster of others, surrounded in the remnants of a city. The sun was just rising, and pig shit still lingered among the snoring troops, despite all of them taking cold showers.

He outran Collins and the stench, but they would catch up one day, find him again.

Zooey from the Lab. She joined a growing list of people that awoke what he'd hoped would hibernate forever—a slithering entity in his chest with no name. If awoken again, Stevenson would be the organism shifted to dormancy.

When he got home he walked down the back alley to his house's patch of backyard where the shed was and the BMW inside it. No amount of reading or exercise within the four walls could suppress his thoughts. His day empty of plans, he had to go somewhere other than home.

He kept the speedometer's dial dancing around eighty the entire way, until the last exit before the Jones Falls Expressway merged with the beltway. Most of the expressway within city limits was nothing more than a ten-mile overpass. The city had built it high above the rot so no neighborhood would be razed, but also so football and baseball fans from the county did not see what made up the core. With no emergency lanes, it was impossible to set up radar. Cars ignored the speed limit and when one broke down, it became an obstacle course for the motorcyclist.

On the back roads, crowded by dense forest known to consume the unfamiliar driver, the frequency of cars would decrease with each mile passed. The double yellow lines became a single white line, tapering a few miles later to no line at all. He geared down and turned left into the only existing residence within the last mile, the one that owned the end of the road.

The driveway zigzagged through the thickets and the bike whined in second, the engine warming Stevenson's calves beneath his jeans. Left and right he leaned until he approached the entrance and the drive straightened. Between the wrought iron gate attached to eight-foot setters quartzite piers, bought with soldier's pay after his return from Panama, swung a sign.

FIDDLER'S GREEN

*   *   *

"Carminda!"

Stevenson knocked a few times more on the double doors, even used the knocker. He had lost his only key to the house when he was a teen and never asked for another.

Cupping his hand above his forehead, he peered through the side-lights. No light shone from the hallway between the double grand stair-cases or the walkway upstairs that connected the upper wings. He walked around to the four-car garage on the side of the house where he had parked. Only the Alfa Romeo sat inside, covered in tarp, and the work truck next to it, a mustard colored '69 Chevy.

The house and horse pasture sat upon a patch of bare land, the remainder of the parcel surrounded in trees. The northwest corner sloped down and up again in hills of grass, abutting a wall of forest. Directly behind the house on a lone knoll stood the barn. A doublewide with three stalls on each side, only one was used now. The slate roof was missing a few shingles but the stone walls, from the same cut as the house, were unchanged. He caught pine sap and manure in the breeze.

"Hector!" Stevenson yelled. He stuck his index finger and thumb under his tongue and whistled. The barn door would stay open until the first frost, the only inhabitant a creature of routine.

When he whistled a second time, a horse poked its head out of the barn doorway, its ears working independent of one another.

"Hey, big man!"

The horse walked out and stood pointed toward the house. He lowered his head, then raised it again, his black mane hanging past his neck, some of it covering his forehead and eye. When Stevenson called once more, Hector started down the hill, feet crunching the gravel path, head bobbing with each step. His walk was slower than it used to be as a stallion, before his father made him a gelding out of fear that the unregistered Friesian would mount one of the Arabians and create some kind of undesirable.

Stevenson met him at the rail fence gate.

"Big man," Stevenson said. He rested his arms on the top rail. "Long time no see."

Hector came up sideways to the fence. His breath hot on Steven-son's hands, Hector's white chin whiskers irritated Stevenson's scars. Hector nibbled with his lips on the jacket's cuff and left bits of alfalfa and barley on it. Stevenson reached up and scratched his neck and smelled the sandalwood from a recent bath and brushing. Every hoof was draped with black feathering. His tail hovered just above his ankles, the tips blond and white.

"They treating you right?"

The horse snorted, stomped his foot. Stevenson moved strands of the mane away from Hector's eye and wiped the discharge from the canthus, revealing streaks of gray.

A distant beeping from earth-moving machinery came from over the trees in the northwest corner, followed by metal scraping rock. Within the forest was a trail leading to Goddard Quarry, a trail only Stevenson's feet had made. He could see the trailhead from where he stood.

"Go for a walk, old man?"

Stevenson walked down the dirt road to the quarry and Hector followed behind, his nylon bridle on and a short lead dangling from the bottom rung. Seeing the gray in his face and the pause between his steps, Stevenson stopped short of tacking him up the rest of the way. Older horses had to be ridden occasionally, to keep their minds sharp, but not today. Another time, he told him.

At the bottom, as they rounded the berm, there was a short path on the other side of the road. Grass was overgrown and bending over the path that led to a brick building the size of a lawn mower shed. Its doors were steel and at one time all yellow, but the rust was bleeding through and the hinges had no yellow at all. There were DANGER/PELIGRO stickers on the double doors and stenciled below in white was EXPLO-SIVES. Most of the letters were missing pieces.

In the quarry's pit, an excavator was driving the bucket down on top of a wall of setters quartzite. Mostly rubble with some table-sized sheets came down, forming a pile at the base. To the side of the operation was a haul truck half full of the rubble. A driver would take this to a sorting pile two and three times a day. Many hours of his life, devoted to finding rock suitable for construction.

A man in a hard hat stood to the side, watching the excavator. Stevenson picked up a stone and threw it side-armed. It landed at the man's feet and bounced on. The man three-point turned around, brow down in annoyance. When he saw Stevenson and Hector, he shook his head and smacked his thigh, then went to the side of the excavator, waving both hands until the operator killed the engine.

"Hey now," Sal Goddard said, voice alone and echoing. The operator hopped down. Raul Ortiz.

"Hey now!" Raul said. He pulled his goggles down around his neck and came at Stevenson, arms wide open. He bear-hugged him, growling deep as he lifted. He came up to Stevenson's chest and was a fraction the weight, but he'd been lifting rocks since his teens.

"Okay," Stevenson said, trying to catch his breath. Raul dropped him, and the two laughed, taking a few jabs at one another.

"Coupla' faggots," Sal said. He shook hands with Stevenson. "Where you been? Impregnating nurses?"

"Using ten dollar words now? Impressive."

"Somebody got me that word of the day calendar for my birthday," Sal said.

"Yesterday was benevolent," Raul said. He took his hard hat off and ran his hand over the top of his head, working the dust out. "He say, 'you shou' bow to my benevolence.'"

"What'd you say?" Stevenson asked.

"He shou' go fuck a goat."

Their laughter echoed. Hector was digging at a small patch of grass, then munching it, ignoring the noise.

"Biggest damn dog I've ever seen," Sal said, nodding at Hector.

Stevenson pointed at the pit. "Not much deeper than last time I was here. Where is everybody?"

"Ahh, you know," Raul said. He took out a pack of Winstons from his shirt pocket and offered one to Sal. "Business not so good."

"Proctor Quarry closed last year," Sal said. He took a smoke out of the pack. Raul lit it as Sal took off his hard hat. There was a sharp border between the quarry dust on his face and the pale skin on his forehead. The black hair from a decade before was almost gone now, only white strands remaining and slicked back with the body's oils. His hand trembled as he took the cigarette from his mouth after it was lit. "No new houses anymore. Either big government contracts or small renovations now. I can't compete with these low-balling bastards selling stone for half of my proposals."

"Gas prices are tough on deliveries I bet," Stevenson said.

"We stopped delivering last year. The insurance, commercial drivers license fees, maintenance on the trucks. Yeah, gas. Shit, you're lucky to break even."

They shook their heads in unison. Raul offered the pack to Stevenson as Sal tugged on the cigarette and coughed up a mucous plug that smacked the dirt audibly. Stevenson had picked up the habit in the quarry, carried it long after the Army, and quit a few months into his gross anatomy class.

Seeing the black lungs of elderly cadavers being picked over by fledglings of science made him quit that very day. It was the living patients that spooked him, with the trach tubes and the death gurgles and the periorbital blackness of creeping death. "It's like trying to quit a beauty queen with the clap," a patient had told him, oxygen feeding what viable lung tissue he had left. They would eventually need a ventilator before their oxygen-starved brain went delirious and then only death was relief.

"No thanks," Stevenson said.

Beyond the trees a loon cried. Dust kicked up around them as the tops of the trees bent in the breeze.

"Day is done," Sal said. He coughed and spit again. "Let's head up. We'll sort tomorrow."

The shop, a metal building resembling a hangar with a wide dust-caked garage door, capped the top of the hill. The tattered entrance door next to it gave a scream when Raul yanked it open. He flipped the light switch.

"Where the hell is everything?" Stevenson asked. He walked to the center of the empty building as the halogens overhead blinked out of slumber. A Mack boom truck, an oversized flatbed with a small crane bolted on the side for lifting slabs of stone, was retired in the corner. It had no license plates and the front tires were half full. STONED was painted in cursive above the grill. A manual hoist loomed above him, its chains hanging over where the cutting machine once was. "Where's the guillotine?"

"Sold it. Haven't cut any marble or granite for a couple years now."

"Just the quarry?"

"Just quartzite and rubble. Sometimes fill dirt. Course, you need a trommel that actually works to get proper dirt."

"Screen broke off?"

"Every other week. Some things never change, huh?"

Raul walked to the other side of the garage door and hung his hard hat on the wall in a line of a dozen other hard hats. In the opposite corner sat a desk and a couple chairs. Sal plopped down in the cushioned chair and plumes of dust shot out the sides. The walls around the desk were covered in random framed pictures, with newspaper clippings tacked between them or stuck in the frame's edges. To the side stretched shelves with Caterpillar and McMaster Carr catalogs.

"Look here," Sal said. He pointed up to a stack of papers with a thumbtack through the middle. "See that? Those fines?"

SURFACE MINE SAFETY AND HEALTH REPORT ran the header of the top paper, the quarry's address, citation number, and date underneath it. In the center was an open space with "Condition or Practice" as the heading of a bracket. Stevenson took it down.

"Readily visible no smoking signs were not posted throughout the hydraulic cutting room area," he read. He turned around, looking at the bare floor that used to be a cutting area, then to Sal.

"This ain't a cutting room if we ain't got anything to cut it with, don't you think?" Sal asked.

There were half a dozen reports in the pile. *Miner using compressed air to clean clothes. Fire extinguisher located beyond 25 yards allowable distance from the pit. 55-gallon burning drum of wood located in the pit.* Stevenson had seen inspectors back when he dug by shovel. Some Sal paid, others would just allow business as usual. None of them fined him then.

"Those bastards just driving down here cost me $1000. The last one was for $2400 because they said the dynamite magazine was not in compliance with current building codes. Not properly secured, they said."

"It's made of brick." Stevenson tacked the papers back on the wall.

Sal smacked the desk. "That's what I said." He put his feet up, crossing them. "And when the insurance company finds out about the fines, they jack the rate up some more."

"And the water," Raul said. He was looking out the door, watching Hector.

"The water, oh man. The quarry has been retaining water like a pregnant camel whenever it rains, so pumping that out takes all day."

A cell phone rang in Raul's jean pocket and he stepped outside to answer it. Stevenson caught a glimpse of Hector milling about, eating the hedges along the berms surrounding the building.

Sal rocked in his chair, hands clasped on top of his head. "So this is it. Fifty-one years." His eyes searched the rafters, between the lights, the water stains. "When I started I was broke and I'll probably finish that way, too."

Stevenson sat on the foldout chair next to the desk. Leaned back and looked up, like Sal, as if answers were written there in the stains and cobwebs.

Sal said, "Last year I made about a third of what I made ten years ago. And that's after I laid everybody off. Raul hasn't gotten a raise in I don't know how long."

Raul came back in, and Sal shook his head quick before Stevenson could reply.

"She's calling already?" Sal asked. "Barely afternoon."

"She doing a double. I have to pick up the boys."

"Boys?" Stevenson asked. "You got another one?"

"Ricky has a brother now. Ronaldo."

"Get out," Stevenson said.

"He started daycare last week." Raul took his wallet out and opened it to a family picture. They were sitting in front of a lit hearth and Raul stood next to the teenaged Ricky. The teen was taller than his father. Raul's wife sat in front of them with a toddler in her lap.

"Grew like a weed," Stevenson said. "I don't even want to know how old he is."

"Eighteen. He graduates next year."

"*Eighteen*? Damn. I remember when you just started dating Marisa. She was playing hard to get."

Raul said, "Still does."

"Where does she work?"

"Chalcos Restaurant. In Federal Hill."

"Don't get the salad," Sal said.

Raul shook his head, putting a hand up to the side of his mouth. "He thinks it gave him diarrhea," he whispered.

"For a week. I do believe I passed one of my kidneys."

"Go on," Raul said, waving his hand like shooing a fly.

"That could kill somebody my age," Sal said.

"And anyone within twenty yards," Stevenson said.

Raul laughed, clapping his hands a couple of times. Sal threw a rag at him, missing widely.

Sal said to Stevenson, "Hey, do you remember that time the port-a-potty got tipped over? We were talking about that the other day."

"When the Viking was in there?" Stevenson said. "Ward?"

"Ward, that's it," Sal said. He smacked the desk and Raul said the name too. "We could not remember his name. Never called him anything but Leif or Viking."

"You know you did that on purpose," Stevenson said to Raul. "Picking on the new guy."

Raul raised his hands high. "How I know it was going to happen?"

"You should have watched where the hell you were going," Sal said.

"All these years and you still give me shit about that."

Raul was using the forklift to raise a pallet of stone for a customer. A 2x4 had been placed in the pallet opening and it extended out just slightly under the port-a-potty. When Raul lifted the pallet, the 2x4 went with it, catching the edge of the port-a-potty just enough to tip it. It was closing time, so the whole crew had been in the building when the shouts started. They ran out to see Sal yelling at a disgraced Raul as Ward clawed his way back up the embankment, covered in blue deodorizer fluid and clumps of toilet paper.

"How's his mother doing?" Stevenson asked

"She's good. I see her up at the A&P every now and then. I used to talk to her, but now we just wave. The conversation always came back to the Viking whether we meant it to or not. I think we both just got tired of the topic so we avoid each other now."

"Buried him in Crownsville?" Stevenson asked.

Sal nodded. "I suppose I should visit one day while I'm still around. The boy did die in my pit."

The men went silent, sniffing congestion, shuffling feet. The wind whistled through the garage door.

"Good seeing you," Raul said. He reached a hand over and Stevenson shook it. "You come back soon, okay?"

"Will do. Say hi to Marisa."

Raul said he would. He gave a wave and passed through the open door.

"We need Sanka," Sal called out, leaning over the chair. Raul answered okay, his crunching footsteps fading.

Sal opened the deep drawer to his right and pulled out a wine jug and a couple of paper cups.

"For special occasions," he said. He poured wine to the top of both cups. "At least Julio Gallo hasn't gone up in price."

"No surprise there."

Sal took a sip and looked around the shop.

He said, "C'mon, it's depressing in here." He stood with a groan and the two walked out just as Raul's truck turned the bend. Hector ignored it, still chomping on long grass.

They walked over to the embankment of mud and rubble overlooking the pit below. The pit wall, mostly tan and ivory with faded clay streaks, was over fifty feet. The quartzite broke in sheets, and ledges a few inches wide remained from where they fell away. The opposite side had foliage growing from the cracks and some had progressed to small trees.

"I don't know what I'll do with him," Sal said. He sipped his wine. "He's been here the longest."

"He'll be fine."

"He's almost fifty. Nobody is looking for a stoneman in his fifties. They all want young bucks. Little shits they can train their way."

"Like me."

"Like you." Sal leaned back, to look up at Stevenson. "You worked out fine, though. Stoneman to soldier to doctor."

"I was fine with stoneman." Stevenson gulped the wine. He crumpled the cup and tossed it over the edge.

"It's a hard life. I've been doing this since I was barely a teenager, when my father bought it from the old man who owned it before him. Pop died in that pit moving a big old rock he should've let the boys move. I think the Viking got crushed right in the same place Pop died, actually."

"You never told me your father died here."

"Yep. Sixty-two. Heart just exploded, they said. Mom didn't last too much longer after him. They go together, you know."

The breeze picked up the faint scent of stale urine. Stevenson looked him over from the corner of his eye. Dust was encrusted in horizontal wrinkles on blue Dickies that barely held on, even with a leather belt on the last hole. Sal's hand trembled when he raised the cup for a drink, a hand with a congregation of scaling moles and freckles and scars. The tips of his fingers were stained with nicotine.

"I can loan you some scratch, Sal. Keep the place going until things pick back up."

"Yeah?" Sal's head jerked back once, as if he were going to laugh. "Got some mad money to spend?"

"I have some to invest."

"This isn't an investment that would pay out. Hell, what would your father think? He hated you working for me."

"He hated you. He didn't care where I worked."

"That he did. I remember when he bought that place. Came riding down here on one of those pretty horses. We're all behind the berms up here, backs to the dirt, ready to blast, and here he comes down the drive." Sal stooped down and bounced on the balls of his feet left to right. What remained of his wine spilled out. "*Clippity-cloppity, clippity-cloppity*—pardon me, but what are you bloody blokes up to?" He stood straight again, knees popping. "He was a pisser, that one. Insisted I call him a week before I was going to blast."

"You never did."

"Nope."

A bird squawked from down the hill, repeatedly and loud, enough to make Hector look up. Another one overlapped.

"Crows," Sal said. He started down the hill, pointing at a sediment trap behind the building. It was a circular wall of mud taller than the berms by a few feet, a miniature meteor crater. When the water in the pit was too high, they would pump it into the trap where it would gradually drain into a creek bed through a filtration system.

Sal dropped his cup and climbed to the top diagonally. Stevenson walked behind him, hands out to catch the man if need be.

"I knew it," Sal said at the top. He picked up a rock and chucked it into the trap. Two crows flew up and over them, beyond the pit, disappearing into the trees.

"They mess with this poor thing and he doesn't say a word."

The trap was half-full of clay mud water the consistency of oil. In the center was a swan, looking up at Sal, rotating slowly. The tip of its bill faded from red to orange, and black feathers coned out from its eyes, adjoined to a black polyp overlapping the upper bill. The feathers around its breast and side were stained from the water, but its wings were untouched, sugar white and folded up tight on its back.

Sal said, "He was here last year. Or she, I don't know the difference."

"Don't they travel in pairs?"

"Got me. Probably lives around here on one of the estates. Just comes here to hang out sometimes. I never see it come or go. Just appears." Sal turned around to face Stevenson. "Remember that little fawn you found in here?"

Stevenson said he did, watching the bird. It had drifted to the other end of the trap, no longer caring about its audience.

"You would feed her from a baby bottle. The thing followed you around like you were her mama." Sal chuckled and watched Stevenson, waiting for him to do the same, but Stevenson kept quiet.

"You don't want anything to do with this place, Cassius. Trust me." Sal turned and went back down the way he came, at half the speed.

"I wish I never left sometimes." Stevenson followed close behind.

"What, this dump? You're too smart for this place. I would have fired you for your own good."

Hector stood at the top of the hill, watching the men come toward him. Stevenson whistled in crescendo and Hector nodded a few times, snorting, his mane dancing. Sal laughed and called the horse a knucklehead, before going into a coughing fit.

At the top of the hill they stood next to Hector and, in his shadow, Sal reached up and slapped Stevenson's shoulder like so many times before, at the end of a long week of digging and sorting. It would be brief then, along with the *see you Monday* farewell and an extra $20 in his paystub envelope if it was a good week. Now it was a gaze and a smile from an old man with nothing but memories. He left his hand in place and it was a struggle for him to keep it there, Stevenson could see.

"Come around more often. Give us a hand now and then. That'll get your mind off things."

Stevenson said he would and they shook hands on it. The crows squawked at them from the edge of the forest. Hector was walking back up the road on his own.

9

RJ read the question a third time.

I think, therefore I am. Explain.

"Stupid," he said. He dropped his pen in the book and leaned back in the chair as far as he could, closing his eyes.

Footsteps above the dining room marched back and forth. His father hummed and sang, sometimes whistled, some old song RJ never heard on the radio. The man knew hundreds of them.

"Ain't no sunshine when she's gone."

In church his father could overpower a full congregation when they sang hymns. The ladies ran up and down the aisle, arms overhead, tears streaming as they called out to precious Jesus. The band would play and the choir would clap and Lewis Reeves could be heard above it all, weeks before election day, singing between baritone and tenor before his voice danced in vibrato at the conclusion.

"Only darkness ev'rah day."

His father came down the steps and went to the adjoining kitchen. He looked at the counter, then to RJ.

"Made coffee," he said. "My man." He grabbed a mug from the cabinet and filled it. "What are you doing up so early?"

"Gotta finish this up before class."

"When's class?"

"Couple hours."

Reeves nodded, mug held in both hands. He leaned back on the counter. RJ pretended to read the book.

"Met up with Kruk yet?" Reeves asked.

"Not yet. Talked to him a couple times on the phone."

More silence. Nodding.

"He's busy, Pop. I'll get with him." RJ shut the book.

"I didn't say a thing, son. Relax."

"I am relaxed." RJ crossed his arms. Head back, he looked to his father. "I been meaning to ask you something."

"Yeah?" Reeves downed the coffee and put the mug in the sink. He took his fedora off the peg behind the back door and manipulated the dents on the sides. "About what?"

"What am I supposed to say when I see Kruk?"

"Nothing much for now. Just get in tight and give him your number. Try to play ball every week with him or something. Try to be on the regular with your visits."

"Visits?"

"Yeah, you know. Like we used to with Uncle Chappy."

"Chappy was in a nursing home. He was crazy as hell."

"Alzheimer's ain't crazy, son. It's a disease. You going to call me crazy if I forget who I am one day?"

RJ said he wouldn't.

"Yeah, okay. You're going to put me in the cheapest home you can find the second I forget to put the cap on the toothpaste. Just going to dump me right at Church Home on Broadway with a sign around my neck. Free to good home. Housetrained."

"The state home has a better chance of keeping you locked up than Church Home do."

"Is that so?" Reeves came into the dining room as he put his hat on, smiling. He repeated the question, gently grabbing RJ around the neck. RJ laughed, pulled away, and Reeves let him go. He sat at the head of the table.

Reeves said, "We need that connection, though. Only way our side of things will work."

"What side is that?"

RJ knew the gaze well, the pause before a long speech. His father didn't look at him. He looked *in* him, looked around in there, tried to find a hint of doubt or deceit. But now, it went a step further. Now the man switched between father and businessman, and RJ never knew who Lewis Reeves the Businessman was up until a few weeks ago. It was awkward calling him Pop, this new persona that was all about the money.

"Look here," Reeves said. He pulled his chair closer and put an elbow on the table, one fist against his cheek, the other on his hip. "We'll be middlemen in the whole thing. Pick up and drop off service. That's it. Won't never get our hands dirty."

"Suppliers? I'm sure he's got plenty of them already."

"Not for long."

"Whachu mean?"

"Don't worry about it. All that has to be done is to get him a better deal on product and make the environment a little safer for his transactions."

"That's what I'm supposed to say?"

"Eventually." Reeves stood and walked back into the kitchen. He put his coat on and took his keys out of the pocket. "For now, y'all are just going to get tight."

RJ and Knott had tried the drug game twice, once in high school and then after graduation. They never made money. They lost it. Corner boys would lie and say they were robbed. The stash would get stolen or it would get tossed and never found when police gave chase. Somebody in a crew always got shot at or did the shooting. It was a business of no gain, all loss, and only those with money actually made money.

And his father had money.

"Studying philosophy?" Reeves asked. He was brushing the front of his coat flat.

"Yeah. Boring as hell."

"In that book, there's probably a story about a man named Zongyaun. He was a government employee of the Tang Dynasty. A governor at one point, I think."

RJ opened the book as if he were on the hunt for the man's work.

"A poet too," Reeves said. "I had to memorize one for school." He looked at the ceiling, closed his eyes.

"I had so long been troubled by official hat and robe
that I am glad to be an exile here in this wild Southland.
I am a neighbor now of planters and reapers.
I am a guest of the mountains and woods.
I plow in the morning, turning dewy grasses,
and at evening tie my fisher boat, breaking the quiet stream.
Back and forth I go, scarcely meeting anyone,
and sing a long poem and gaze at the blue sky."

When he finished and opened his eyes, RJ had nothing to say.

"Read up on him," Reeves said. "Smart man."

Reeves went out the back door, warning RJ not to be late to class, and RJ said he wouldn't. The car started and its engine faded down the street.

RJ reached in his pocket and took out his cell phone. He called Knott a few times last night and the night before and only got voicemail. Same with Adrian. He thumbed through the phone numbers and found Tink.

Voicemail.

"It's me. Call me." He hung up and put it on the open book.

"Where everybody at?"

10

*T*he kitchen phone rang while Stevenson was in the shower and he ignored it. He was typing his resignation in his mind, thinking of the right words. *To Whom it May Concern* was as far as he could get, saying it out loud even, but nothing respectful followed. *Thanks for the memories? May the sun set low over your buffalo? Fuck you and your families too?* He'd hand it over to whomever was taking over the practice, once Coleman made retirement official.

When he stepped out of the shower the phone in the kitchen stopped and his cell phone started. It was on the bed next to his scrubs but he took his time drying off. He could see the word PIT on the LCD screen, the second pit in his employment history. The one he didn't miss.

He picked up the phone. Listened.

"Cassius?"

Jenna.

"I have two hours," Stevenson said, sitting down on the bed. "Can't I have that at least?"

The commotion in the background was not the usual for the Pit, especially for the middle of the week. He heard a siren echo in the ambo bay, persistent and rapid, unlike the slow wail of an ambulance, and ambulances shut them off before they reached the bay. When it did shut off, there were many voices, too many for the Pit. Someone was asking for gloves right now.

"I need you," Jenna said. Her words went to rasp and whisper. "Something happened."

"What's the matter?"

"Please. Now."

She hesitated, took a deep breath. Then she was sobbing, saying, "Oh God," and sobbing some more. Stevenson had seen tears in her eyes over dead children but never an all-out crying spell.

"On my way," Stevenson said.

*   *   *

There had been a roadblock two streets up from the hospital and the policeman who let Stevenson through after asking for his hospital ID said he didn't know what was going on. The ambo bay was filled with police cruisers and there were more parked around the traffic island. Two policemen guarded the walk-in entrance, another in front of the ambo bay entrance. A helicopter was circling a few blocks over, its spotlight striping the old brewery's roof.

Stevenson parked the bike in the center of the island next to the bare flagpole. As he trotted up to the bay, weaving between the cruisers, the policeman approached, his movement triggering the pneumatic doors. The entrance and hallway were clogged with more people in uniform and suits. Not hospital suits.

Stevenson tapped his nametag. The policeman craned his neck, squinting at the ID.

"They're waiting for you," he said. He turned around, walking back slower than he had come.

The doors opened again and Pete Bonley came out. He was looking at the ground as he walked on. He didn't have his Ravens lunch pail in hand or his jacket on.

"Pete," Stevenson said. "What the hell?"

Bonley stopped but didn't look up. His hands didn't seem to know what to do. He brought them up halfway, then let them fall, one farther down than the other. He fidgeted with his pockets.

"What happened?" Stevenson bent forward, trying to get in Bonley's line of sight.

Bonley's eyes cast about, as if looking for a place to rest, anywhere but on Stevenson.

"Pete?"

Bonley brushed past, walking sideways between the cruisers.

"Petey?"

He walked across the lot and around the corner, never turning around.

Inside, strangers chatted in huddles. Men in suits were crowded around the security desk at the door, all looking at the monitors. They didn't notice Stevenson walking in, walking among them. The doctors' bar was hosting unknown men, two in suits and one in a white coverall, each scribbling away on their own charts. The T-1 door was closed and flash bulbs went off every few seconds. The board had three patients on it, two of which were in discharge status, the other with identifiers he had never seen.

ROOM	ID	CC	AGE	S	TIME IN
T1	X	Trauma	67	M	X

In the Pit, Kay was talking in a circle of techs next to Bonley's desk and she stopped when she saw Stevenson. He bypassed her for Jenna who was sitting at Def Con, the two screens blackened. A wide-backed man in a tweed suit jacket sat on the edge of an adjacent chair, elbows on knees, crowding her.

"Hey," Stevenson said. He eyed the man as Jenna stood. A silver badge hung around his olive-skin neck.

"Hi," he said. He pushed off his knees as he stood. "I'm Detective Viterello." He stuck out his hand and Stevenson gripped it hard. The badge glinted, and Stevenson thought of tearing it off the man's neck.

"Cassius Stevenson."

Jenna had stepped closer, her shoulder pressed into his ribs. Some of the wiry gray had come loose from her hair tie.

"What's all this?" Stevenson said to Jenna, looking around. She rested her forehead on his upper arm.

Viterello said, "One of your coworkers was killed tonight, doctor."

"Who?"

"Dr. Coleman."

Jenna put an arm around Stevenson's waist and sobbed when the name was said. Stevenson watched the detective, could feel the expectant eyes, bracing for the response of such news. The detective wanted tears, questions, drama. He expected weakness, and Stevenson's breathing slowed, muscles tightened.

Are you weak, Ranger? Can you take this?

Detective Viterello said, "I'm very sorry. I understand you worked with him for a long time."

The flashes had stopped in T-1. Between the men at the doctors' bar—his bar—he could see more people in white coveralls walking around slowly, stepping over things that shouldn't have been on the floor. The surgical lamp was on but pulled high and pointed the wrong way. The fluorescents were on too, and Stevenson thought it a waste, all that light for a corpse.

"I know this is a lot to digest right now but we should—"

"What happened?" Stevenson grabbed Jenna's shoulders and gently turned her to face him. "Jenna?"

She looked down, shaking her head. "I'm sorry," she said. It was all she had. Sorry.

Sister May came from behind them and put a hand on Jenna's shoulder, standing between Stevenson and Viterello. The two parted and May guided Jenna out of the Pit and down the hall.

"Is there somewhere private we can talk?" Viterello asked.

As they walked into the office, the flash bulbs started again. Father Clay was standing with Odeh in front of T-3. Their heads were bowed. Clay was praying.

"The cameras are wired upstairs," Viterello said. "We're trying to get somebody in here that can make a tape."

Stevenson sat at the desk on the right and Viterello at the other, thumbing through a small notepad. The blinds were all down but cracked slightly. The security desk had cleared and the six monitors, color but of poor cathode ray quality, showed empty halls in all but the ambo bay entrance.

Stevenson looked the detective over. Round chest that probably protruded more than the belly at one time. Meat and potatoes man. Triglyceride levels double what they should be. Doesn't take his meds but swears he does. Misses appointments. A living liability for primary care.

"Where is the guard?" Stevenson asked. "Was he here when it happened?"

"Called in sick. By the time security from the main building got down here, the first units had already arrived."

He visualized the security desk's chair being empty, the monitors unwatched. He reached up and twisted the blind wand for the side window until the blind was closed.

You're a good kid, Cassius. The best.

"We have quite a few witnesses, which is unusual in this line of work." Viterello flipped the pages, glancing up at Stevenson and getting no response. "So, sometime after eight o'clock, the suspects arrived in a city ambulance. Two people dressed as EMTs, a man and a woman, wheeled a male patient into that first room there. Dr. Coleman was the first in, followed by Rollins, Jenna."

They were starting to filter out of T-1, uniforms and suits with ID tags and badges dangling from their necks, looking uninterested. The man in the white coveralls who had been at the bar walked past the office talking on a phone, a duffel bag slung over his shoulder. He carried a few brown bags, each taped at the top with red EVIDENCE stickers.

Viterello said, "The EMTs didn't stay long, said very little, and left their gurney."

"Left their gurney?"

"They weren't EMTs. My partner got a call a few minutes ago from a unit in the southern district. A fire department in Cherry Hill responded to a torched ambulance in Branch Park. No occupants. It was probably stolen from one of the garages that works on city vehicles."

The florescent lights went out in T-1 and only the halogen lamp lit the room. Stevenson smelled peanuts and vomit and rubbed his nose but it was still there, and for a moment his hands were covered in jungle grease paint.

"The driver and passenger left the way they came, and Dr. Coleman attempted to evaluate the patient who was covered in a blanket. When the doctor introduced himself, the suspect asked his name again. Dr. Coleman said it and the suspect pulled the blanket off and stabbed the doctor in the chest twice with a large knife. The suspect then fled through the entrance." Viterello shut the memo pad and sat up. "Efforts to revive the doctor were unsuccessful."

He could see every staff member in there, working Coleman, as if he were a child. Everything stopped for a child in T-1. Pushing drugs, pumping the chest, writing down all the efforts attempted to bring him back. Everybody taking a role.

"What did they look like?" Stevenson asked.

"The female was average height, thin, possibly a light-skinned black, but this was debated among the witnesses. Maybe Hispanic. They wore caps but the female possibly had a blonde, braided wig. The other one was apparently a big fellow, definitely black. Your nurse said he looked up at the door frame as he came in and out, so that tells me he's hit his head more than once on smaller doorways. He had dreadlocks and his cap was stuffed like ten pounds of potatoes in a five-pound bag." Viterello put his hands up on either side of his head for emphasis.

"The killer?"

"Short, possibly shorter than the female, small build. For some reason they couldn't tell me too much about him. The mind does that. Makes you forget the horrors. We'll get a better description from the security tape."

"Black?"

"Yes. He had a gold front tooth. People did remember that."

"And he stabbed him?"

"Twice."

"No gun?"

"Gunshots bring attention. They're loud, and they didn't want that. The suspect had a gun but used it just for show."

"Who was the attending?"

"How's that?"

"The doctor who treated him. Tried to revive him."

Viterello took out his notepad. "Tall fellow. Indian."

"Jeller."

"That's him."

"Stabbed twice and he couldn't handle that?" Stevenson said it out loud, but it was meant for him only. Viterello stared at him.

Stevenson said, "A couple stab wounds usually isn't that bad. We see them all the time. We can get them stabilized long enough for transfer to a trauma center."

"Ms. Rollins said the doctor had already bled out before they even got an IV in him." Viterello crossed his arms, sighed. "Never had a chance."

Most of the non-hospital staff had left and Stevenson had a clear view of T-1. On the floor rested a hand with a wedding ring but this was all he could see of Coleman, the rest of him covered with a sheet. Just out of reach of the hand was a butcher knife and a two-faced yellow card with the letter A next to it. Trash littered the floor—wrappers, used gloves, bloody gauze. The debris of a code.

"Hate to ask you this Doc, but where were you a few hours ago?"

"Getting ready to come here. I was due in at eleven."

"Can anyone at home confirm that?"

"No. Why?"

"Someone called emergency dispatch approximately fifteen minutes before the suspects arrived. They told them the ED was not taking any more ambulances tonight."

"A code yellow. Who made the call?"

Viterello said nothing, and Stevenson shook his head and turned away.

Viterello said, "I may need a recorded statement for forensics to use."

"Fine."

"I know it wasn't you. I figured that out about ten seconds after you walked in. It's just protocol. You're not a suspect."

A svelte black woman in khakis and a sweatshirt walked by from the ambo bay, a badge around her neck. She was tapping her watch, looking into the office. Viterello mouthed okay.

Stevenson pulled down on the blind.

"Why is he still on the fucking floor?" he asked.

"There was concern for a spinal cord injury. I think he was—"

Stevenson shot out the door.

In T-1, a photographer was putting his camera back into his bag. He too wore coveralls, complete with the hood pulled over.

"You done here?" Stevenson asked. On the table was a translucent body bag and he pushed it off.

"I'm done," the photographer said. "You gotta put some shoe slippers on. The ME hasn't been here yet."

"Fuck off."

Stevenson knelt down next to Coleman's body and scooped his hands under the torso and legs. Gelatinized blood coated his forearms and the coolness of the linoleum was comforting on his scars.

"Hey wait," the photographer said. "You can't do that." He was backing toward the door, motioning at someone outside the room.

Stevenson stood from a squat with a grunt, lifting Coleman up. The resistance angered him, and he gave it his all, bouncing to a standing position. The body was stiffening.

Two uniforms came inside and approached him.

"You can't be doing that!" a uniform said, grabbing Stevenson's arm. Her grip was without strength enough to bother his balance and Stevenson jerked his arm away. The other uniform grabbed Stevenson's shoulder and squeezed a handful of his scrub top but this did nothing.

"It's okay," Viterello said, trotting in. Odeh and Father Clay came to the door and Viterello swung around, giving them the hit-the-road thumb.

"Detective, he can't be moving my body around like that." The uniform, a young woman with bulbous eyes and a throbbing vessel on her temple, stood her ground. "The ME will report me for not securing the scene."

"I'll take care of it," Viterello said. He nodded at the door and the uniform's body relaxed. She turned slowly and with a huff, shot a look at her partner. They left, shaking their heads.

Stevenson set Coleman down on the table and adjusted the extremities, tucking the stiffening arm to the side the best he could. There were saturated bedpads all over, some stuck to Coleman's leg, the blood clotting, sticky. The blanket had pulled back enough to reveal Coleman's scalp. Within the copper and antiseptic, Stevenson smelled the remnants of Old Spice and he pulled the blanket down just enough to reveal the rest of the face. The remnants of an intubation tube barely poked out of his mentor's mouth. Hazel eyes stared forever, with a grin so subtle only a friend could see it.

"Just wanted him off the ground," Stevenson said. He pulled the sheet back over.

Viterello stepped over to the other side. "I can't think of a worse time for me to be asking you this. Forgive me."

Stevenson told him it was fine. Go ahead.

"Do you know anyone that may have wanted to cause Dr. Coleman any harm?"

"No."

"Hold on now. Think about it. This was planned. Nothing random about it."

"Okay, yes. About half our clientele. We turn away about ten addicts a day. Toward the end of the month it's even worse. They get upset when we don't give them their fix. They make a lot of threats."

"Anyone recently? One that stands out?"

Stevenson shifted on his feet. Coleman's belly gurgled, but neither man flinched. Death and its sounds were familiar to them both.

"No."

Viterello reached into his jacket as the door slid open. Jeller crept in, his steps apprehensive. Folger was behind him.

"If you can think of anything, call me. Anytime. My home number is on the back."

Stevenson took the card, leaving a bloody thumbprint on it as he shoved it in his breast pocket. He turned to the sink behind him and smacked the soap dispenser. He told Viterello he would call.

"I'll end up calling you first or stopping by. I have your number and address."

Viterello walked out, turning right down the hallway.

"Cassius," Jeller said. His voice was barely audible, quick. Folger slid the door shut.

Stevenson dried his arms and hands. The water in the sink went down the drain but the porcelain still had a circular film of blood.

"How you doing?" Folger asked. He was staring at the body.

Jeller approached the other side of the table and rested his fingertips on the edge. He stared where the head was.

"Were they regulars?" Stevenson asked. "Anybody we've seen before?"

Folger shook his head. "I asked Jenna and Odeh the same thing."

Jeller reached up for the lamp, turning it right side down. The body glowed under the sheet, except at the spots of blood.

"I have to fill out a death packet on him," Jeller said. "Tie a toe tag." He looked at Coleman's feet. Battered Puma Clydes on. Black.

A woman in a trench coat and glasses walked up to the window and cupped her hand, peering in. She'd pulled her blonde hair up as if in haste, and she wore no jewelry or makeup. A uniform stepped up to her and she reached inside her coat, pulling out a hospital badge from around her neck. A man appeared behind her in a festive sweater and jeans. Hospital suits.

"Pull the curtain," Stevenson said to Folger.

Folger turned around and saw the suits and yanked the curtain across.

"What shall we do?" Jeller asked. He had his hands on the table now, one over Coleman's. He took a deep breath and blew out and Stevenson smelled liquor, with no mint to disguise.

"We'll re-open at nine. That should give the police plenty of time to wrap up. Call dispatch and tell them we're on yellow. Priority ones only, meaning the patient is truly near death. Refer all walk-ins to another hospital and have a couple local fire departments park a unit out front for transfers." Stevenson looked at Folger. "You want to handle the suits? The PR department should be down here soon. They'll need an accurate description of the events."

Folger nodded slowly, stepping closer to the head of the table.

"I have a couple calls to make," Stevenson said. He went to the door and slid it open. He looked back. "We square, gentleman?"

They both nodded, didn't look at him.

He stepped out and slid the door closed. Viterello was talking with the woman that had walked by the office, the watch tapper. Viterello gave him a nod.

Farther down the hallway beyond Viterello under a recessed light stood Vernon Lamb. He wore Stevensons old coat, unbuttoned. He raised his hand, holding it there a few seconds but not waving. Stevenson did the same. Lamb's cheeks were wet and Stevenson turned from this, smacking his pocket for his keys. Someone called his name but he ignored it. He looked at the ambo bay doors, then the office, back and forth, his keys in hand.

Knott watched the I-95 overpass looming overhead. Every few years the winds would carry an empty tractor-trailer over the side, spiraling the ten stories down into a heap of scrap metal.

"How's your hand?" Adrian asked. He gazed out the window into total darkness. No streetlights were under the overpass.

"Good." Knott held his hand up, inspecting the crusting over the scars. He stopped wearing a bandage days before. Took his own stitches out.

Knott said, "Here, you give it to him." He pulled a tight block of twenties from inside his coat and dropped it in Adrian's lap.

"You know I was worried, right?" Adrian took the money and held it up. He hooted in relief and put it under his seat.

"If I'm here, you know I got it. Ain't going to front like that. The last person I want on my ass is that little voodoo doll." Knott reached under his seat and took out his .45. He tucked it behind him, in his waistband.

"You should have lived with him."

Apollo Benshaw, Adrian's cousin, came up from Atlanta every summer for two weeks and would take over Adrian's room and friends and life when they were kids. Apollo was smoking by 11 and, the summer after sixth grade, chasing neighborhood girls nightly, his smooth delivery wearing even the meanest of the girls down. He would sneak back in the house late at night and turn the bedroom light on, showing Adrian his member, covered in the blood of another massacred hymen.

During the day when no girls could be found, he'd light fires and kill animals. Pigeons and cats at first, then dogs when he got older, and what little innocence of youth he had became memory. A mutt made the mistake of walking into Adrian's yard on July 4th when they were in their mid-teens. Apollo tied it to a telephone pole in the alley behind some vacant houses and when the sun went down and fireworks illuminated the sky over the Harbor, he stoned the dog to death, its howls muted by the explosions overhead. That was the last summer Apollo visited, as he quit high school and moved to New York, and Adrian was thankful for it. Knott had met him a few times in the neighborhood when they were growing up. He remembered a small kid that could not say a sentence without a curse word. Adrian, always animated, would turn inward when Apollo was around. He was an assistant in the Apollo Show, waiting in the wings to be beckoned.

"He didn't waste any time," Knott said.

"You said you needed it done."

Headlights shook them both. Straight ahead a car pulled into the empty lot and was coming fast toward them. Adrian put his hand on the door handle when the red bubble light went on above the headlights.

"Oh shit," Adrian said, frozen.

"God*damn* these mother fuckers." Knott reached for the .45 but the car, a white Crown Victoria, was already upon them. "They everywhere." Adrian said, "Five-O going to take that money if they find it."

The car braked and skidded, whipping to the left. It stopped a few feet from broadsiding the front of the Escalade and the interior light went on. Apollo was in the passenger seat pointing at Knott and Adrian through the open window, laughing. Dust consumed the surroundings.

"Crazy ass," Knott said. He opened his door and Adrian was already out, leaving the money. Knott reached under the seat for the block. He didn't want to be the payer. He didn't want to shake Apollo's hand or look at him or say his name.

"Y'all shit yourselves?" Apollo asked. He took the red light off the car and dropped it inside.

"Naw," Adrian said, waving the dust from his path. His pimp walk was hurried and silly. He stuck out his hand and slapped Apollo's hard, touching shoulder-to-shoulder. "'Sup, Cuz. How you doing?"

"Same shit, man. Different day." Apollo leaned back on the car as his associates got out.

"Where RJ at?" a woman asked, stepping out of the back. She came around the door, her heels grinding in the gravel. She wore a patent leather jacket with a yellow skirt and gold braids dangled over her chest and back. She was bathed in cocoa butter, and her legs glistened.

"How you doing?" Adrian asked, his words high-pitched.

The woman groaned and, while turning, spied Knott in the shadows. She cocked her head for a moment, looked him up and down, then went around to the trunk. She leaned against it and fidgeted with her cell phone.

Knott was watching the driver walk around the car. He shifted his stance just to feel the .45, to know it was there.

Adrian leaned into Apollo, not taking his eyes off her. "What's her name again, yo?"

"Sierra. It's his sister."

"Whose sister?"

Apollo nodded over Adrian's shoulder and Adrian turned to a wall of a man with thick dreads to his chest. Arms crossed, his short sleeves strangled his biceps.

"Ho-goddamn!" Adrian said, jumping back against the car.

Apollo put his arm around Adrian. "You never met Bwell," he said, laughing.

"Bwell? He look like the damn Predator."

Apollo laughed harder. Bwell stepped closer, looking over at Knott.

"Who's that?" Bwell asked.

"My boy J," Adrian said.

Knott came over, nodding at Bwell. "'Sup."

"I remember you," Apollo said. He put his hand out. "RJ's boy. From back in the day. Where he at?"

"Don't know." Knott handed the brick of cash to Apollo, rather than his hand. Apollo turned his hand over, taking the brick.

"That twenty?" Bwell asked.

"Wouldn't have called you if I ain't had it."

Apollo looked over Knott, dropping the money in the front seat. "Heard about it then?"

"They shut down the whole west side," Adrian said. "Helicopters and shit."

"Little late."

"How you do it?" Knott asked.

"Do what?" Apollo stood, stepping into Knott's space abruptly. "I didn't do shit. You feel me?"

The interior light lit half of Apollo's face. He was smiling, and Knott could see the gold incisor. There was a champagne glass on it, tilted, with bubbles spilling over the top. Knott nodded, not backing away but not looking down on Apollo either. Apollo stepped back against the car next to Adrian and put his arm around his cousin.

Apollo said, "I loved coming up here back in the day. Baltimore girls don't take no work. White girls too, yo. I got so many shorties running around here I lost track."

Adrian laughed, crossing his arms. He looked to Knott for rescue but Knott was eyeing Bwell. The man was a statue among the shadows. One word from Apollo and he would kill Knott, and Knott knew it. Another shift in stance. The .45 was snug.

"You ever see any those girls from back in the day?" Apollo asked.

"I don't live over there no more," Adrian said.

"Well if you do, you ain't seen me." Apollo turned, yawned. "Alright, we out." He stepped around Adrian and opened the door. "Come up some time. Take you to Manhattan."

"Soon," Adrian said.

Apollo got in the car, as did Sierra and Bwell. Knott stepped back, knowing Bwell would punch it. He did, kicking up dust in the blackness. The car bounced out of the lot and turned onto the ramp to the highway a block up. Tension rolled off Knott's shoulders and he wasn't sure he had breathed at all toward the end of the meet.

"I'm never calling him again," Adrian said. He went around to the passenger side of the Escalade. "And you know what? I wasn't here tonight."

They got in. Adrian's arms were crossed tight and he was slumped low in his seat. Knott tried not to laugh. His oldest, LeSean, did this, pouted when he didn't get his way. Nine-years-old and he'd give Knott the silent treatment like a girlfriend close to expiration.

"You know I appreciate this," Knott said. He turned the ignition, put the lights on. Dust clouds hovered over the tire marks. "If RJ asks, I called him myself."

"You fucking right you did. Now take my ass home."

11

*S*tevenson lay in his bed, soaked, trying twice to shower off everything Saint Cat. He had sat in the office of the ED for an hour, phone to his ear, trying to clear his head long enough to call Blaine Coleman. The dial tone died after a minute but not his thoughts. It didn't matter.

He didn't know Blaine's number.

Your hands, Bulldog.

Without any patients in-house and the staff roaming the halls like lost children, the silence scrambled his mind. Jeller sat at the bar, filling out Coleman's death packet, occasionally having to grab hold of the bar to steady himself after a few belts of spirits in the office. Kay had tied the toe tag on Coleman and when the Medical Examiner techs stuffed the body into the translucent body bag and wheeled the package out, the staff followed in a mute cortège. Stevenson gave up then and fled, failing at the last step in completing the bureaucracy of death: Notify the family.

Please wake up.

He had seen death more times than he could remember but when it was someone familiar, loved, the dread became viral, forming symptoms that could be mistaken for nothing else. His movements felt as though he were underwater. Breathing was a task itself. The flashbacks from another life awoke and traveled with his blood like antigens, circulating through every organ and some settling in the brain like embers. They were spiked, lacerating the walls of the vessels as they drifted along, searching for a nook to go dormant in again. There were no antibodies to search them out and kill them off, no antibiotics to dissolve them. They arose on their own initiative, agitated the host, and hid again when the system denied them further control.

Hank, his brother, was the first one he ever saw. Hank and his colic, crying day and night. Stevenson and his mother took turns rocking the cradle or walking Hank around the Charles Street apartment, bundled in the blanket now on Stevenson's couch. Stevenson would look down on the park from the fifth floor apartment window, watching the John Eager Howard statue. It would tease his fatigue and he would swear it was trotting in place when a passing car's headlights lit up the haunches. Hank would let out a good belch or a gob of spitup and finally pass out, his stomach uncurling and losing tone. Plump cheeks, a tuft of dark hair over the center of his head that never did flatten out. "He looks just like you when you were a baby," his mother told him.

The colic would be Hank's demise, and his mother's too.

Why don't that baby shut the fuck up?

Though it was August, the gunman wore an antifreeze-green ski mask and spoke in a high-pitched voice that couldn't hide his worry. His partner, in a red mask, stood at the door of Kwan Grocery. The doorman moved with precision and never spoke but his tongue flickered within the mouth hole as if he were chewing it. He changed gun hands often and looked out the window every few seconds, up and down the sidewalk.

He going to shut up right now!

Stevenson sat up, stood and crossed the room to the dresser. He took out the walnut jewelry box from the bottom drawer and set it down and opened it. A folded nurse's cap lay on top and he took it out, unfolded it. A few wiry black hairs clung to the inside crease, and old sweat stains yellowed the corners.

There were old photos, baseball cards, his mother's silver Claddagh ring he had slipped off her bloodied finger by accident the last time he ever saw her. An Airborne patch with a Ranger tab stuck to the back and a basic parachutist badge, awarded for passing Airborne school; a Combat Infantry Badge, stuck in the blue velvet lining the box's bottom.

All trinkets now, the honor erased.

Next to the Combat Infantry Badge was a folded camouflage beret with a red patch on the front. MACHO DE MONTE lined the top in an arc around a skull with two swords crossed behind it—The Mountain Men, an infantry unit within Noriega's Panamanian Defense Force. Bearded, wearing black shirts, the unit was not supposed to be at the El Chorrillo barrio where La Comandancia, Noriega's headquarters, was. But Stevenson found one shooting from a storefront and killed him with one shot and took the beret off the dead soldier before the permanent cavity in the eye socket stained it.

His first kill, and far from his last.

December 21st, 1989, D-Day+1, the day after death engulfed the El Chorrillo barrio and La Comandancia was taken, squads were formed to clear the streets and alleys around the compound. The sensitive area was being picked over for intelligence by American Spooks who came only at night in Mosquitoes, the unmarked bubble-front AH-6 helicopters. Corporal Stevenson, team leader and the only one who'd completed Ranger School, was assembled with seven other Airborne infantry troops to patrol the area. The team called him Bulldog, the identifying call someone had overheard Rangers use when parachuting into Rio Hato Airport, the Panamanian Defense Base. Their orders were to seek out citizens and get them back to base camp for transport to a nearby airport hangar. They handed out fliers that said *ES TU DEBER*—It's Your Duty—with a graphic of a woman holding a baby and pointing out some atrocity in the distance to a US soldier, all with a menu of weapons and the amount paid if turned in. Panamanian Defense Forces and Dignity Battalion soldiers were to be taken prisoner if they surrendered, killed if not. Most surrendered, and it was obvious who they were. EPWs, Enemy Prisoners of War, were the only ones in their underwear with their hands above their head, having stripped their uniforms off before surrendering.

Throughout the barrio most of the hovels were empty and burnt to some extent but the taller mortar buildings held random holdouts. A few PDF soldiers either hiding or waiting for rescue or both were found every night. With no power or running water, the streets reeked of all kinds of trash and waste in the heat of the smoldering buildings. Alleyways were littered with the dead. Their tongues would grow plump and protrude, splitting down the middle when there was no more tissue for the rot to invade. Eyes were black with a cream film and looking at this seemed to violate the corpse's privacy, seeing them in such a poor state. The bodies bloated after a few days like feeding ticks and sunlight roasted them so thoroughly that certain places were impassable due to the hovering putridity no breeze could remove. His team had seen commandeered backhoes digging holes in a field several blocks from La Comandancia on the second night. A Sherman tank and a few squads stood guard while the work was done behind their backs. A pile of bodies was off to the side of the backhoe, and Panamanians yelled as they hid in burned-out buildings. *Soez Demonios*, on and on. Further into the patrol they had seen infantry teams of three and four flushing out refugees from clusters of hovels. When his team came back at daybreak the hovels were either burnt to the ground or halfway there.

They patrolled weapons tight, only fire when fired upon, but they ignored this after the first night when Jarrito bottles and bricks and furniture came flying at them from rooftops and balconies. The assailants, angry civilians or holdout PDF troops out of ammo, fled to other buildings like lost dogs. On the third night buckets of feces and pig entrails hit every man in the team when they passed an office building ten minutes into their patrol. By the time they got back to base camp, they were streaked in dried blood and shit and sweat. Their weapons would need multiple field strips for cleaning and some in the team would bring only the minimum after that, not wanting to scrub out every piece of their gear and clothing after a night patrolling.

"Just pig shit," Private Wayne Collins reassured everyone in the showers. "It ain't nothin'. Ain't that right, Bulldog?"

Collins, a big Georgia redbone with no time for the G of present participles, was on the field trip of his life. He was the breacher of the team, in charge of breaking into or sealing up entries. A shotgun, sledgehammer, portable blowtorch, a few blocks of C4 explosive—all tucked neatly into his rucksack. Preferring the Vietnam-era flak jacket to the heavy body armor vests, Collins always left his jacket open, his helmet strap dangling. A worthless BDU, Battle Dress Uniform, that no drill sergeant or officer would tolerate stateside. He was of little value in a firefight but Collins could gain entry into a bank vault if needed.

"Don't much care for shootin' folks," he told Stevenson while the team weeded through a burned-out hovel. Collins would stay at the door. "What you do, you become. Know what I mean?"

Collins would talk to anyone before they could say hello, regardless of rank, and listen intently as the other party replied. He watched their lips, repeating their words in a whisper the moment they spoke them. Big eyes that held no deceit, Chiclet teeth with vertical coffee stains, block chin and a badly healed S-shaped scar on his forehead Stevenson never got to ask about. Collins held a library of stories and Stevenson, never a talker, appreciated the tales of West Georgia when sleep was in the far off. He'd fall asleep with a cigarette between his fingers and when it singed his skin and he awoke, Collins would still be talking.

When a grenade was dropped from an apartment balcony into the middle of the team, the moon was the only light and no one but Collins, on point at the time, could see it.

"Contact front!" he said and jumped on the grenade. "Frag out! One. Two."

It detonated when he got to the beginning of three.

"Collins took it in the chest," someone screamed in the dark. The team hugged the apartment building wall while the heavy gunner crossed the alley and took post behind a cinder block partition. When Stevenson signaled to light the building up, another grenade fell a few feet ahead from where Collins lay.

"Medic!"

Stevenson dragged him to the curb by his collar. He had taken it to the chest and face, and neither his jacket or helmet had been secured. His chin was gone, now strips of dangling meat, his tongue floppy in dying laughter. His chest was a crater of concaved flesh and stained camo, singed and smoking, smelling of gunpowder.

"Why didn't you button your BDU?" Stevenson yelled over the gunfire of the heavy gunner's belt-fed M240B machine gun. The others fired on the building and bullets bit the masonry and blew out the windows where the grenade had come from. Falling bits of cement rained down on them both. "I fucking told you, private. Zip your fucking gear."

Collins sucked air through an exposed trachea and was trying to say something, raising a hand. He gurgled from the open carotids flowing heavily over his neck, and was gone before the medic got to him.

The radio man stumbled upon Stevenson in darkness and flashes of gunfire.

"Bulldog, we should—"

He never heard the rest. He charged the building, on his own. Whatever grasp he had of the hazards within was gone. Collins was dead in a street flowing with trash and human waste. Sally Tipton and Hank Tipton were there with him, their lives spat upon. These people who never hurt anybody. Killed for being in a place they should not have been.

On fire, on fucking fire.

He put the contents of the box back in place and put the box back in the dresser but stared at it. Contemplating. His quest for distraction had only made his thoughts louder. Maybe it was time to burn this box and all its contents. Nothing good ever came of his poking around in it.

He was wondering where the matches might be when unfamiliar knocking erupted at the front door.

"Oh," Zooey said in mid-knock. She stepped back on Stevenson's stoop, a few inches from the edge, staring at his bare chest. He had managed to put on jeans. "Hi."

Her peacoat hung on her like on a hanger, the shoulders square and wide. The large buttons with anchors on them seemed too big for her hands to manipulate. She wore a lab coat underneath and it hung below the pea coat like a slip. Stevenson looked up and down the street, then went to the kitchen. He heard her come in, shut the door, walk through the living room.

"I have to go," he said. He bent down and grabbed his shoes from under the table and when he stood she was upon him. She wrapped her arms around him fast, her face resting on his chest.

Her coat itched but he didn't complain. He felt moisture roll down his belly. He brought an arm around her shoulders and she clutched tighter. He tilted his head and smelled the scent from their date. Strawberry.

The slamming of metal and the hum of hydraulics broke the moment and he pulled back, looking at the trashcan.

"Damn," he said.

"Didn't put the trash out?"

He shook his head.

"There's a dumpster behind my building." She stepped back, wiped at her eyes with hands covered by purple mittens.

"Only one bag." He flipped the light switch and the stained glass lampshade hanging over the center of the kitchen came on. He wiped her tears off his belly and felt a fool for not having a shirt on.

She walked past him, looking around as if in a showroom. Half the main floor was kitchen, the other living room, and he had renovated what little square footage there was. She ran a finger over the stainless steel refrigerator door, to the black granite countertop and backsplash. She turned one of the knobs on the stove. The front burner came on.

"It works," she said.

Stevenson grabbed a shirt and pair of socks from the hamper behind the couch and finished dressing. Hearing someone else's voice in his home, a female voice, was foreign.

"Did you do all this?"

He nodded. "I used to work at a quarry. Got a discount on the countertops."

"The floor too?" She bent down, hands flat on the stone.

"Pennsylvania Bluestone." He sat on the couch and tied his shoes. "That floor won't budge."

"When did you work at a quarry?" She sat at the kitchen table.

"During high school. It's behind where I used to live."

She nodded a few times, keeping her gaze on him. Her brow relaxed and she smiled. The inside of his head was quiet, except for the ringing. Always the ringing.

"I was supposed to work the 10 to 10 shift," she said. "They wouldn't let me in. There were news people there. A cameraman told me what happened." She bowed her head, the last words cracking. "I don't want to go back."

"I have to get his dog," Stevenson said. He grabbed his keys off the coffee table and when he stood, the blanket slid down. He put it back on top of the couch, spying on her from the corner of his eye. A tear fell on her coat, beaded, then ran down the side and disintegrated on the Bluestone. He looked at the door, to her, then the old TV, at his reflection.

"What kind of dog?" she asked.

"A spoiled one." He went to her, stood next to her. "Dachshund."

"What's its name?"

"Baby." He turned the light off. "Why don't you come meet her?"

She tilted her head all the way back to look him in the eye and he felt it starting again, the peace her presence brought. He tucked her hair behind one ear and she closed her eyes.

"Okay," she said, standing. "But I'm driving."

"That's good. I only have one helmet."

"Can't find it," Stevenson said. He closed another kitchen drawer. The great chili pot was on the stove, empty and clean, with the wooden spoon still in it.

"Does he have a study?" Zooey asked.

She was in the hallway, not making it past the front door where she met Baby. She sat on the floor, letting Baby crawl into her lap and writhe around.

He climbed the back stairwell and passed by the master bedroom. Coleman had told him he'd never again used it after Elaine's death, not even for company. In the bathroom, a red towel was draped over the commode. Water tapped in the sink basin, dripping from the faucet every few seconds. In Blaine's old room, where Coleman had slept when the machines keeping Elaine alive eventually crowded him out, the twin bed was unmade and newspapers littered the floor next to a pair of penny loafers and a dog bed. The blue wallpaper had sailboats riding squiggle lines of waves.

The last door across from the master bedroom was the study. Stevenson hit the light and the ceiling fan lazily came on. A walnut desk sat in the center and to the left books lined the floor in tall and short stacks under a double-pane window facing the street. There was only one chair other than the desk chair, a fold-out, and it was filled with more books. The opposite wall had the closet and, like the rest of the house, a few nails stuck out naked, the pictures packed away.

He stepped around and sat in the desk's chair. Saint Catherine's memos, Emergency Medicine Times magazines, bills, letters with Lemmy McPhee's letterhead at the top. They were cockeyed in their own organized piles. A bone white rotary phone sat in the far left corner with a small horn next to it, laid on its side, dark with shades of patina on the base and edges where the horn widened. The oval plaque on top said Cunningham Air Whistle, Seattle Washington, along with a patent number and serial number.

Stevenson brought the papers together in neater piles, uncovering a yellow 8x14 notepad. It was blank but half the pad's paper was gone and there were indentations of the same two words in rows and columns covering the whole page. He held it to his face, turning it left and right, recognizing the lettering as cursive, before the light caught the indentation enough to be legible.

Felix Knott Felix Knott Felix Knott Felix Knott Felix Knott

He tore the page out, ripping it into many pieces. The indentation was still visible on the next sheet and he did the same for that and a few more. He took the scraps of squares to the bathroom and took the red towel off the toilet. He flushed them all, and when he washed his hands and dried them out of habit, he felt dampness on the towel from the person that had used it before.

He found the address book where Zooey said it might be—in the study, top drawer on the right. A small red leather thing, stuffed with slips of paper with numbers and names. The actual pages held few numbers. It was more of a holder of the scraps than a phone book. Blaine's number was not there, nor on the slips of paper.

The phone rang, leaving a ting in the air when it paused. He picked it up during the third ring.

"Hello?" A male voice said.

"Who's this?"

"Blaine." Breathing in the phone. Someone in the background cleared her throat, and sobbed. "Cassius?"

"Yeah."

"Some...person called this morning. A detective."

"I'm sorry, Blaine. I was about to call you. I couldn't find your number."

"He said Dad was dead. He was asking me a bunch of questions."

Stevenson apologized again. He leaned back in the chair and it creaked.

"You're in Dad's office."

Stevenson said yes. He looked at the bare walls, the nails each with its own pencil thin shadow underneath. The closet door was open a crack.

Felix Knott Felix Knott Felix Knott

"He's still got that rotary phone, I bet."

"Still works."

Blaine sighed when he should have laughed.

"I'll take care of this, Blaine. I'll call his lawyer today."

"So soon?"

"Better now than later. The more time that passes, the more things get complicated."

"It happened the way the detective said?"

"I wish I could say no."

Blaine cursed under his breath. A glass broke on his end and someone told him to stop it. Stevenson let it play out.

Blaine said, "We'll fly down tomorrow. I have to get a few things situated in the morning but we should be there by late afternoon."

"I'll get the place cleaned up for you."

"We'll stay at the Hilton, Cassius. I can't. We can't."

The sobs in the background went to crying and Blaine moved closer to that person.

"We're pregnant," Blaine said.

"Congratulations," Stevenson said, feeling clumsy saying it. "How far along?"

"Twelve weeks. I was going to call Dad this weekend."

The crying worsened and then faded as footsteps ran away. Blaine called out *Belle* but she didn't come back. Stevenson pushed down the corner of the address book with his fingertip and the book popped open. There was a combination on the first page. 44-6-36.

"I'm sure there's some lame Zen thing I could say that has some significance here," Blaine said. His breathing picked up and a door opened and closed. "Did you see him, Cassius? Is it true?"

Stevenson said he did and it was, and he said he was sure when Blaine asked him if he was sure. He closed his eyes, exhaustion starting to ooze over him. The image of Kay tying the toe tag without a bit of anything human in her face was bright on the back of his eyelids.

Stevenson said, "He showed me that project you guys were working on. That's really something."

Blaine mustered what sounded like a chuckle. "You didn't tell anybody about that, I hope?"

"No, no. He made me swear."

"He better have. Yeah, we're pretty much done with the R&D." Blaine's voice fluctuated, the monotone gaining life. "The great thing is the manufacturing will be done in the states because they don't have the right machines overseas to make the organic light-emitting diode screens."

"I didn't think anything was manufactured here anymore."

"It's not, really."

Felix Knott Felix Knott Felix Knott

Stevenson stood and pushed the chair in and came around to the front of the desk. The fan was clacking with every turn and the pull chain was within reach but he let it be.

Blaine said, "I hated it there, Cassius. I couldn't wait to get out." He went flat again, hushed.

"Here? Your parents' house?"

"Baltimore. So glad when I left for college. I promised myself I would never spend more than a week there on visits home. The hate. It's in the water. The air." His words were straining. "I told him to leave." Another glass broke on Blaine's end. No one told him to stop this time.

Stevenson thought of telling him it's like that in any city, but he couldn't get the lie out.

Blaine cleared his throat. "Are you still living downtown?"

"Upper Fells Point."

"You have to get out of there. Move to the county or out of state altogether. Plenty of houses to buy now, especially with all the foreclosures."

He expected Blaine to mention Fiddler's Green here. His father would. *Your house, Tonto. Live it up.*

"Sorry," Blaine said. "None of my business."

"Not a problem. I've been thinking about it for months now, actually."

They exchanged numbers and said goodbye but not before Blaine warned once more for Stevenson to leave the city. Stevenson put the phone in the cradle and opened the address book and read the combination. He stepped over and opened the closet. Numerous suits and coats; on the shelf, magazines and folded t-shirts, flanking a black doctor's bag with small gold initials inscribed on one side: LTC. On the floor a few pairs of dress shoes sat in a row next to a floor safe the size of a milk crate. Stevenson got on his hands and knees.

It opened on the first try.

Upon a small stack of papers rested a revolver in a leather holster and a box of bullets next to it with a tin cigarette case on top. When he took the revolver out some of the papers clung to the grip, including a newspaper clipping. He peeled them off and put them back. The barrel was longer than expected and said 500 S&W MAGNUM along the side. All five cylinders were empty and it was heavier than he remembered a revolver should be. It was the first time he'd handled a firearm since Panama.

When he put the revolver back it clinked against something solid, so he took it back out again along with the papers and bullets. The bottom of the box opened and bullets scattered throughout the inside of the closet. The cigarette case slipped from his hands and it popped open when it hit the floor. POKE was inscribed on the inside in cursive and it was empty.

At the bottom of the safe lay an 8x10 framed photo, taken sometime before he was born. A young Coleman and his girlfriend Elaine stood to the left, smiling, holding hands, dressed for a night out. On the right stood Jonathan Stevenson, arms at his sides, his widow's peak forming a heart-shaped face with no expression at all. Sally Tipton stood next to him, almost as tall. The flashbulb caught her mid-laugh and she was holding onto her pillbox hat. The men wore suits, the women dresses, all of them in long coats. The lower edges were faded white with pale orange in streaks that looked like ECG waves and he realized then that every photo he ever saw from that time seemed to be taken in the Fall.

The back door was open. Stevenson found Zooey sitting cross-legged in the middle of the greenhouse, watching butterflies dart about in the unobstructed sunlight. Baby inspected the foliage farther on. The digital thermometer on the shed read 68 and a fine mist sprayed from the spigots above the far corner. The heater hummed quietly at the opposite end, like Coleman said it would when the temperature dropped too low.

"This is..." She shook her head. "I was going to let the dog out. I didn't know this was back here."

He stood next to her. She had taken her coats off and draped them across her lap. Her scrub top was like the coat—oversized.

"How long has he had this?"

"Couple years. I just found out about it myself."

"Couple years? He never told you?"

"Never told anybody. I don't think it was meant to be talked about."

Baby walked down the path to Zooey and climbed into her lap. Stevenson sat down next to them. There were fewer butterflies than his previous visit but enough for the newcomer to be dazzled. Primarily Monarchs, but a few Checkerspots and Swallowtails appeared sporadically.

"I heard the phone ring," she said.

"Blaine. His son. One of the detectives already called him."

"Only son?"

Stevenson said yes. There was no one else.

The words were a pinch and Zooey's lower lip pulled in slightly. "It's so sad," she said.

He didn't want her to cry again. It angered him, that someone committed an act that brought her sorrow. He looked up at the heater, thankful for its noise. Something else besides the ringing.

"What's that?" Zooey said, pointing at the picture.

"Found it upstairs." He handed it to her. "That's Larry and Elaine, before they were married. My parents are on the right."

"That's your mother?" She brought the picture closer to her face, then looked at Stevenson. Eyes, then mouth, then neck. "She was beautiful." She handed it back and he set it to the side, within the shrubbery.

They watched the butterflies until the heater turned off. Baby was snoring.

"Do you know anything about butterflies?" Stevenson asked. He stood, dusting off his rear. "Like, what they eat?"

"I took two semesters of zoology," she said. She scooped up Baby in one arm and grabbed her coats off her lap with the other. Stevenson reached his hand to her but she leaned back, then rocked forward to a squat position, standing straight up. "Most flying insects consume the same thing. And butterflies don't eat. They drink."

They walked to the shed and Zooey set her coat on the bench in front of it. Stevenson opened the door and pulled the light string dangling in the middle. A wooden table screwed to the wall had been constructed from 2x4s and plywood. Remnants of clumped soil were on one end and a few one-gallon jugs of water on the other. Multiple tools of a home gardener were hanging on the opposite wall, the largest an ax. Under the table were a few sacks of oranges and apples and a smaller one with seeds.

"You have to cut the fruit in half and lay it out. He has plenty of plants for the Monarchs but the fruit would be good too." She leaned out of the shed door, looking up, repositioning the panting Baby. "There are about three dozen of them I'm guessing but they won't last long."

"He said they don't have much of a life span. That and the Monarchs migrate south in the winter."

Zooey nodded, coming back in. "I forgot about that. Should we release them?"

"Not yet."

They stepped out of the shed and Zooey put Baby down on the bench. "This took a long time to put together. A lot of money, too. Do the neighbors mind?"

"He has no neighbors."

"They're all empty?" She walked over to the side, looking out.

"The bread factory across the street closed thirty-some years ago so everybody left. I guess nobody wants to live by the expressway."

"What a comfort zone he had." She sat on the bench, leaning back and yawning. She scratched the dog's head and Baby's eyes rolled, her eyelids heavy.

"We better get going." Stevenson shut the shed door. "I have to call his lawyer."

"Are you coming back tonight?"

"Yeah. I'll cut the fruit up then."

She looked around, watching the butterflies. Pigeons perched at the top of the building, balancing on the cross beam. Zooey made no gesture to leave and Stevenson sat down next to her.

Reeves sat at his desk in the basement of City Hall, reading glasses on the tip of his nose, going over the agenda for the Council meeting while snacking on cashews and cream soda. In a few minutes the meeting would start and he looked for his name in each of the eleven proposals to be introduced. He was a co-sponsor on most, along with the majority of the Council. A handshake and signature were all that was required to be a co-sponsor and the more co-sponsors there were, the better the odds the proposal would slide through committee review without a request for additional information. His own bills and proposals for municipal code amendments, zoning matters, licensing requirements and whatever else he found himself tangled up in the previous week had not been rejected in years, if ever.

The phone on the desk rang and he whispered expletives at himself for forgetting to take it off the hook.

"Reeves."

"You hear about that doctor?" Charlie Lincoln asked on the other end.

"I got a council meeting in ten minutes." Reeves took the glasses off. "I don't have—"

"So you didn't hear?"

Reeves sat back, pinching the bridge of his nose. "What doctor?"

"At Saint Catherines. Forgot his name. Stabbed to death right there in the emergency department."

"That's a shame, Charlie."

"It's your district, Lou."

"And when the paper calls, I'll tell them I've spoken with our police department and they have assured me they are doing everything they can. Hear how easy that was?"

"You got to do better than that on this one."

"Where you calling me from?"

"Across the street. We had the commanders meeting and—"

"The station? Charlie, come on, goddammit. You know better."

"I tried your cell. No answer."

Reeves reached into his jacket pocket, took the phone out and pushed the on button.

"It was off," Reeves said. "Call me back."

Reeves hung up. The cell phone vibrated moments later.

"So, yeah," Lincoln said. "That's the news for today."

"What's the doctor's name?"

Papers were shuffled. The phone was dropped.

"Sorry," Lincoln said. "Here we go. Lawrence Coleman. Did you know him?"

"No," Reeves said immediately. He looked at the doorknob. Locked.

"This is going to be around for a long time. A doctor, a *white* doctor, killed right in the hospital like that. You better prepare a statement. Get with the public affairs officer and call a press conference with the Mayor. The whole thing."

Reeves sat back and brushed the cashew crumbs off his lap. "They have a suspect?"

"Not yet. They have a lead but that's—"

"Who?"

"You really want to know?"

"Charlie."

More shuffling paper. "Homicide's case file is thin at the moment but they have a person of interest logged in the system. He was suing the doctor for malpractice. Here it is. Jaris Knott. Know him?"

"No," he said again, quick. He stood, other hand clenched as he bit his lip and turned his head as far right as it would go.

"Brass is going to be up my ass when I get upstairs."

"About what?"

"Have you read the stats? We have these meetings every month and every month the numbers are the same or worse than the last. Don't a day go by without at least one body hitting the ground. The weekends are a damn warzone and now they're walking into the hospitals and killing doctors. And here I am, walking in with a handful of 95 memos. Know what that is? That's when a patrol officer writes an apology to his commander for not making any arrests for a whole month."

"You're doing the best you can, officer."

"And that ain't shit. I see these tactical units looking like they're going into Baghdad and I got uniforms driving Caprices with two hundred thousand miles on the odometer. I'm telling you, Lou. I don't know about all this."

"All what?"

Lincoln didn't reply. Cleared his throat, but didn't reply.

"A doctor gets killed and you think that's going to affect us? Charlie, you serious? You going to pull this sapling out the ground before the first leaf show?"

"I'm not saying that."

"I didn't think so. This has nothing to do with us." Reeves sat down. "I'll put the fires out just to make you feel better, alright?"

"We don't need the attention right now."

"No, we don't."

Lincoln was grunting like he was standing. Then footsteps. "I got to get upstairs," he said. "I'll get with you tonight."

Reeves nodded rather than said goodbye and turned the phone off. He looked at the front, turned it around to the back, and to the front again. There would be problems. That was a given. But not from within the organization. Won't make it past the planning stage with fools marching behind you.

"Not taking this from me," he said. He turned the phone on and dialed his son's number. "No you ain't."

Viterello twirled the golden bullet between his index and middle finger, cradling the phone against his neck the way his doctor told him not to after the migraines started.

"You want apple sauce or carrots?"

"Carrots?" Viterello asked. "With Shake 'N Bake? Dotty, I could have you arrested for that."

"Just asking, Fred. You know you don't need the sugar."

"Apples don't have sugar." He smiled, expecting a diatribe on his blood sugar and cholesterol and belly girth. Metabolic Syndrome, Dr. Bergman told him. Sounds like I won't make it out of your office alive, he said, trying to shake the doctor's hand. Dr. Bergman didn't laugh and didn't shake his hand. They didn't do that anymore, because of the germs.

"I'll make both," she said.

"Okay, hon. Love ya'."

"Love ya'. Hurry up."

Viterello hung up and sat back, inspecting the bullet. The slug had been worn down at the tip over the years from his rubbing and picking. Gold, a soft metal, was never meant to be shot. This bullet, a .38 round, was meant for the Smith and Wesson issued to uniforms decades ago before the 9mm took precedence. The Boy gave it to him for Christmas '95. The Boy had bought a truck and plow that summer after reading the Farmer's Almanac and Viterello told him he shouldn't have spent all that money. Don't worry, Papa. It's coming. White gold. Days later, the city was crushed in the white.

The bullet slipped from his fingers and it landed on Lawrence Coleman's hospital ID, a mugshot from the hospital HR Department. It was too old to be used in court, the picture dating back to Reagan's second term. A healthy looking man then, content, almost smirking, his upper incisors slightly visible. Auburn hair parted on the side fell slightly over his forehead and past his eyebrow. He looked less like the head of an emergency department than a part-timer or nurse. A custodian, maybe.

Video from the hospital showed decipherable shapes of humans within shadows, nothing more. Neither the race nor the gender of the three suspects could be identified. The ambulance had pulled into the ambo bay, not backed in, and both suspects got out, rather than the passenger climbing through the cab to the patient in back like EMTs do. When they entered the ED the suspect on the stretcher was wrapped completely in a sheet. Thirty-nine seconds later the first two suspects were leaving the way they came, minus their gurney. They drove away and one minute twenty-two seconds later, the third suspect appeared, running backward in the hall, pointing a pistol at people off camera. The ambulance had indeed been stolen hours before from a city garage and there was nothing salvageable for forensics in the burned out remains. The weapon, an Old Hickory ten-inch kitchen knife, had no prints, and witnesses confirmed the suspect was wearing gloves.

The call placed to the dispatch center that night informing them the ED was not taking patients by ambulance was made by a woman, so Dr. Stevenson would not have to come in for a voice sample after all. Viterello tried to ignore it, the relief of not having to see the doctor. Stevenson was the calm type, his voice even, low, his hands at his side when he spoke, rather than waving about to add weight to his words. He was white from a distance but up close, there was faint color in his skin, from bloodline more than sunlight. His hair was cropped and it was an odd hue, as if a dye job going for blonde settled at butternut. He had enough height that Viterello only had to look up with his eyes more than his neck but, though Stevenson's scrubs were baggy, there was some bulk covered by the sleeves, and wide shoulders that could not be hidden no matter how over-sized the scrubs were.

It was the eyes, Viterello concluded, feral eyes that kept contact always, that betrayed the rest of the physician's demeanor. There was no fear in them for the badge, like most civilians had, no sorrow when the news of a friend perishing was delivered. Of all the hospitals in the city, Viterello had been to Saint Catherines the least, but the few times he was there over the years, he couldn't remember meeting Dr. Stevenson, couldn't remember those feral eyes that looked within and deciphered without consent. There was something familiar about him and Viterello dwelled on it afterward, in the car, when that same feeling of relief came once he was down the road a few blocks. *Who are you to me?*

All Viterello had were witnesses and a body. The ME told Viterello the unofficial, and obvious, mode of death, before the final report was typed up. Lawrence Coleman had many years left. Good heart, minus the puncture wounds to the center of the aorta and right ventricle. Good brain and good colon. What else did a body need? The witnesses that saw everything, two nurses, an emergency technician, and an x-ray technologist, gave the opposite of the usual fodder made up at a moment's notice by Baltimore's Best and Brightest. These folks wanted justice, now, and would do all they could to help. Three of the four were leaving voicemail messages already, before the media or brass even had their first bite of him. They gave excellent descriptions and came to the station that morning to meet with the sketch artist.

The older nurse, Jenna Rollins, had been standing at arm's length from the doctor when he was stabbed. Though shaken, she gave the best details of the suspect. Short, black, spindly but muscular. A front gold tooth with an inscription or design on it. When Viterello asked about anyone who may have wanted to see Dr. Coleman dead, she thought long on it.

"There's a lawsuit," she had said finally, "or was one. A malpractice suit. It was dropped a couple days ago."

"Why?" Viterello asked her.

"Dr. Coleman didn't say."

"Who was suing him?"

"The family of Felix Knott."

Knott. There was another Knott spoken of days before and again at the commander's meeting, the name uttered softly by Sergeant Bentley before the party was crashed by the commissioner and his laser pointer that went squirrely over slides of graph after graph after goddamn graph of how crime across the board was not where it should be, gentlemen. Jaris Knott, Felix Knott's son, the ghost. Watkins had gone out looking for the man that afternoon after Viterello opened a new case file in the database, adding Knott's name to the otherwise blank list of People of Interest. Not a suspect yet, just an interesting person pertaining to a specific case. There wasn't enough evidence to write up a warrant for a suspect's arrest and to present to a judge to sign, but even if there was, adding Knott to the Warrant Apprehension Task Force's wish list would get him into an interrogation room sometime after the case was dropped to Cold Cases, if they ever found him at all. With body armor and weaponry and vehicles more suited for war, the tactical teams still had trouble finding their targets.

Instead, Watkins, never one to ask for help or a hand to hold, decided to track the man herself and invite him down to the station for a chat with a tap-tap on her badge and a flash of the butt of her Glock. Viterello had statement forms ready and brand new pens but Watkins had not called or shown. After seven hours of searching, she had probably called it a night, he concluded, without calling the office, a habit of hers he begrudgingly got use to. Went home to her bean counting husband and a poodle named Honey, because having kids means they'd have to inherit the mess we made, Freddie.

Viterello shut the computer off and filed the manila folder in his desk in the ACTIVE tabbed file, closing it and locking it, so no one could see a habit he couldn't let go of: hard copy. There were seven files presently in the desk drawer for which he was the primary investigator and a dozen more floating around the department with him listed as secondary. With six of his cases over a month old without a suspect, they would soon be handed down to the Cold Cases Unit after a verbal request was mumbled to the shift commander or squad supervisor. More cases would come and room would have to be made in his single drawer. His requests were never denied by any of the past two shift commanders and though rare five years before, they had become a weekly ritual. He'd hand a slip of paper with the case number to Bentley like they were passing notes in high school algebra. No explanation needed, not even a nod and thanks. Just strangers passing by, passing notes.

He stood, looking down on the metal desk made for a kindergarten teacher, grabbed his keys and his golden bullet and pushed the chair in. His trench coat lay on the burlap loveseat against the wall, lifted during a Thanksgiving graveyard shift when the neck pain from sleeping at his desk was making his arms go numb. The federal grants well had run dry then, so the couch was commandeered, like most materials needed before another grant check cleared.

He grabbed his coat, turned out the desk lamp, and exited, keeping to the outside of the squad room. An open office space cluttered with carpeted cubicles, the squad room had random Juniors typing and chatting on the phone or just staring at their computer screen, waiting for something to happen. The Senior detective offices, drywall boxes the same size as the cubicles, were along the back wall, along with the interrogation room. At the center of it all was a common area consisting of two half-moon couches surrounding a round coffee table. It seemed more a telemarketing operation than a homicide department and it didn't help morale among the Seniors seeing cube dwellers walking around without shoes on, the new carpeting gentle on their perfectly shaped feet that didn't ache in the mornings. Senior detectives could no longer respond to all the non-homicide calls and had needed the extra staff for years. Each district had its own detectives but that wasn't enough.

Overdoses, drownings, sudden infant death syndromes, suicides, stabbings, shootings where the shooter was of poor aim—they all required a visit from someone with a badge and a tie. Despite protest from the Seniors, a grant from Homeland Security made it official and the Junior squads were created, increasing the squad number from four to six. The same grant also afforded more military-grade weapons, body armor, office renovations, cell phones, and new computer programs that took a year to figure out. The Juniors, young men and women with college degrees and averaging less than two years beat experience, were given the detective badge and a carpeted cube if they passed the agility test and a written exam. The department lost them all eventually to the county, where the clearance rates were twice that of the city, the pay better, and homicides averaged one every ten days, not ten hours. Closing a case and upping the clearance rate depended on solid charges. It didn't matter if a grand jury didn't want to indict or the prosecutor dropped the case or placed it on the inactive docket where it rotted and was forgotten. Evidence *and* competent witnesses were a required relationship to get a suspect arrested and in custody— a closed and cleared case for Homicide at that point. But when even the churches taught the mantra "don't snitch," no amount of grant money would increase the city's clearance rates.

Viterello passed the two flat-screen televisions, knowing most of his cases blinked red. Only one was solid green now, the Coleman case. It would change to yellow within a week, red within two. Where was the nonintrusive blackboard, manned then by squad commander Sgt. Clindacle, a limping old

Mick who did not care of the rules and regs in his last year? The TV boards were installed during Clindacle's tenure but he refused to learn how to use them. After his retirement, the blackboard was taken down and IT set up their user-friendly program with multicolored lights, reminding all those who passed that the red blinking dead were not getting their retribution.

Viterello was out the door and halfway down the hall when, at the other end, the elevator opened. Watkins stepped out, her hand around the bicep of a stout black man who stood a head above her. He was not hand-cuffed but he looked to the floor like someone in custody.

"Told you he was real," Watkins said.

Tink and Adrian stood at the top of the blacktop path, watching the basketball players run up and down the court. The bottom of the path emptied into the street that cut through Monroe Park and the two didn't hear RJ pull up in a skid. He hopped out, keeping one foot in the car, yelling their names and smacking the roof of the Lexus.

"'Sup," Adrian said, coming down the hill, holding his jeans up by the belt buckle. He rested his forearms on the other side of the Lexus' roof, looking left and right. Tink walked up behind him.

"Where J at?" RJ said.

Adrian shook his head. "Ain't seen him." He turned to Tink and Tink said the same.

"Dammit." RJ smacked the roof again and stepped out of the car com-pletely, leaving the door open. He paced, slowly, studying the ground. He knew these would be the first answers he would get. *Don't know. Ain't seen him.* Nobody knew anything when he needed them to.

"What's up with you?" Tink asked.

"You hear about that doctor?" RJ came around and leaned back on the front wheel well. "At Saint Cat?"

Tink said he heard something about it. Got attacked or some shit.

"Got cut," RJ said. "Died right there."

"Damn," Tink said, shaking his head. "Shit getting crazy around here."

Adrian had turned around and slid down the car, leaning on the rear wheel well. He pulled a pack of smokes from his coat.

RJ said, "They think J did it." He watched Adrian as he spoke.

"Stop playing," Tink said.

"Serious. Just got a call."

"He ain't kill nobody," Adrian said, not looking at the two. He lit his smoke.

"How you know?" RJ asked.

"I know."

RJ stepped over to him.

"It was the doctor that J and his family were suing," RJ said. "One that killed his pops."

Adrian nodded.

RJ smacked the cigarette out of Adrian's mouth and it spiraled high, the cherry bursting and the remnants leaving a brief trail of reddish-orange. RJ stepped off the curb but was still taller than Adrian. He grabbed Adrian's jacket at the lapels.

"Who you fucking with, huh?" RJ jerked his grip. "Why you play me like a bitch?"

Adrian tried to stand up straight, his face contorted as he looked RJ's face up and down but RJ kept his grip, jerking him again. Tink said nothing, did nothing.

Adrian said, "Man, get the—"

"What?" RJ bent him backward over the trunk. "Whachu goin' do? Huh?"

"RJ, I'm saying. I know."

RJ let him go and stepped back. Adrian. Always the first one to give him problems, to give him and everybody else lip, just because he could.

RJ said, "You better tell me what you know right now, yo."

When Adrian stood straight, he started to talk but stopped, nodding over RJ's shoulder. A young boy was running toward them, the friction of his nylon black jacket getting louder as he approached. Pup, a kid they employed to help with the dogs on fight night or to act as lookout.

"The fuck he want," RJ said.

Tink met him, told him to go on, but Pup was already talking, pointing back the way he came. When he was done he stared up at Tink and Tink nodded and told him the same as before, to go on. This time he did.

"They got J," Tink said.

RJ turned to Adrian, stepping close but not touching him. He spoke through his teeth, low and emphasizing every word. "What. The fuck. Happened?"

"The lawsuit didn't work out. He wasn't trying to let it go down like that."

"So you don't know anything about it?"

"No."

An hour had passed and Viterello had yet to establish personality type, the first task of interrogation. Was Jaris Knott an introvert or an extrovert? Mentally deficient or intelligent? Psychopath or pacifist? He rubbed the back of his neck. A headache was coming.

Only with type revealed could a detective tailor the questions along the path to confession. Denial, anger, depression, bargaining, and, finally, acceptance, each suspect had his own way of exhibiting these emotions. They were the stages of grief, for guilt was pain, and confession deliverance, and every human, demented or not, had at least a hint of its existence. The interrogator was to know his suspect and how they would emote at each stage within the short minutes of entering the interrogation room—a soundproof cube the color of cigarette ash. The Toaster, they called it. Hot in the winter and hotter in the summer, and no HVAC tech could ever tell them why.

They all started in denial and ended in acceptance but the in-between was the actor's choice. They would yell and cuss and spit, stare and huff and cry. They touched their lips, picked their nose, bit fingernails to the matrix and bit some more. The fatigue of denial brought yawn upon yawn and they dug their knuckles in their eyes as if blinding themselves from the truth. Their arms and legs would betray them, all but blurting *I Did It*. Legs spasmed, feet tapped, arms crossed and crossed again higher and tighter until the wrists were millimeters from touching the underside of a quivering chin. Spittle gathered at the corners of their mouth as deceit dehydrated even the seasoned liar. Their cracking voices lied on and on, but their bodies told only truth. To conceal truth was to torture every cell of the guilty and Viterello had witnessed the relief of hundreds, thousands maybe, when the real story was finally set free.

But Jaris Knott never passed denial. His tone was even, his voice calm. He didn't touch his face, rub his nose, or dig in his eyes. He didn't cross his arms or legs. Didn't stare or look away. His head was neither bowed nor looking at the ceiling. His arms rested, apart and palms up, on the aluminum plank separating interrogator from suspect. The plank, an inch thick and attached to the wall by three hinges, could fold into the wall like an ironing board in a '50s kitchen. When bargaining started, the interrogator would fold the plank into the wall and move his chair to within inches of the suspect. With no barrier to hide behind, all defenses would fall. Interview became interrogation and soon the guilty accepted the accusations, to live with for the rest of their days. Knott, however, claimed nothing. Without a warrant, even if he did confess, there was a chance they would have to let him go briefly, but it was rare that this occurred.

Most that killed had IQs hovering around 100 and they knew little of their rights. Many couldn't recite the alphabet.

"Besides your girlfriend, can anyone else verify where you were the night the doctor was murdered?" Viterello asked.

"My kids, I guess. They ain't but three and four but you can go on and ask them if you need to."

"This girlfriend's name?"

Knott repeated it, like he did the other two times, and still without a raised voice or v-shaped brow.

"Can I get a smoke?" Knott asked, looking to where Watkins stood, leaning on the wall cattycorner to the door.

Viterello shrugged and Watkins tossed a pack on the plank. Smoking was not allowed, but denying those in the Toaster of anything was dirty pool.

"Mr. Knott," Watkins said. She was smiling, eyes content. She had not spoken to him since they started. "I hear voices sometimes. You hear voices?"

"No." He pulled deep after lighting up and the overhead air filled with thin smoke.

"I do. When I get the man I'm looking for, the dead, they talk to me. They tell me, that's your man, Hyacinth. That's who you want."

"You should see somebody about that, sister." Another drag. "Ain't right."

Watkins stepped up to the plank. Lawrence Coleman's photocopied name badge from the hospital sat next to a blank statement sheet and Watkins slid it in front of Knott. "I got this guy in one ear and somebody else in the other, both whispering your name."

Viterello watched Knott, studied the brown eyes, the little moles underneath both, waiting for something. A blink, maybe a single word to hang his hat on and start shaping a confession. He had stood on the pier with the crabber at the Timmy Darrens scene, watching the man dangle a piece of raw chicken in front of a crab. The crab refused, holding tight to the pillar of the pier, its legs intertwined within the algae. The crabber was stooped over, net in water, waiting for something, anything from the crab. Viterello watched too, watched the lone crustacean as the world turned. He was also an expert in the waiting game. Decades spent in the Toaster, watching and waiting.

"The name is Timothy Darrens," she said.

Knott crinkled his nose, sniffed. Smoke thickened above them. Viterello counted the moles.

"You know him?" Watkins asked.

"No."

"Sure?"

"I'm sure."

"Because I have people that say otherwise."

"Let 'em. Don't matter none."

Reasonable deception, the interrogators last chance. Judges frowned upon it but Knott didn't bite anyway. Viterello jumped up, sucking in air, his stomach groaning. He stretched his arms overhead, wanting to strike the man who was keeping him from dinner. He drifted to where Watkins had been standing and, as he started to say let's call it a night, she picked up everything on the plank and dropped the pile on the floor. She folded the plank into place and sat down, moving the chair closer to Knott.

"I checked up on you," Watkins said, elbows on her knees. She was still eye-to-eye with Knott, looking up. "Your sheet is clean."

"Sheet?"

"BPI sheet. Baltimore Police Identification. Nothing there. Same with the state police. I even checked the National Crime Information Center's database and they don't know you either." Watkins slid forward on the chair, sitting on the edge. "But I did find you in the state court database."

Knott looked down, then at the folded plank, seeming to recognize his barrier was gone.

"Your mother had a stroke when you were in grade school and she's been in hospice ever since. You lived with your aunt until you were thirteen but she died, so you moved in with your father. Now, your father? He had a sheet."

Knott studied his cigarette, turning his wrist and watching the shapes the smoke would take. Flakes of ash drifted to the charcoal carpet. He crossed his right leg over the other tight and unnatural for a a man with his frame. He bent forward, crisscrossing his arms at the wrist.

"He did time in Jessup. Then some rehab. The courts let little Jaris Knott slip into the cracks where nobody could watch over him. Living but not raised. Dropped into the middle of it all without a roadmap. When did you quit school?"

Knott looked at Watkins, glanced at Viterello, then to Watkins again before dropping his head slow. He was blinking every few seconds, biting his lower lip.

"Eleventh grade," Knott said.

"I bet you look back and think damn, I should have stayed."

Knott barely nodded. His cigarette fell from between his fingers and before he could pick it up, Watkins stretched her foot over, stamping it out.

"Doesn't have to be like this," she said, putting her hand on his knee. "You don't have to be what this city says you have to be."

"I don't know nothing about no Darrens."

"I won't bother with that and neither will anybody else. Nobody gives a damn about it anyway."

Knott mumbled, looked away as he did, and Viterello thought he heard *ain't like that* but couldn't be sure.

Knott looked over Watkins' shoulder, then leaned in. "What happens to the man responsible?"

"The judge always goes easy on a first timer, especially if they help get the case closed."

"Yeah?"

"Happens all the time. And look here, you can go back to school. College even."

The rap on the door was like gunshots. They all jumped and Viterello pulled the door open. He raised his other arm up halfway, palm up, eyes wide. A uniform with an overbite and peroxide perm stepped into the doorway.

"Got a Mr. Hooper looking for your man," she said, pointing at Knott. "His attorney."

"He didn't call an attorney," Viterello said, shutting the door as she stepped out fast.

"My attorney?" Knott stood. "What she say?"

As quickly as Watkins had cleaned the debris from the path to confession, it was covered over again in a fraction of the time.

Knott walked to the door just as it closed. "She said *my attorney*."

"Yes she did." Viterello stepped back, leaning on the wall.

"You know what? Y'all never read me my rights." Knott was nodding his head vigorously. He crossed his arms, looking between the two detectives. "I guess I'm not arrested then?"

Watkins stood and also leaned on the wall on the other side of the room. Both watched Knott. Now he ran the Toaster.

"I can go, right?"

Viterello opened the door. Knott took a long look at Watkins, up and down, reassessing, his mouth pulled down at the corners.

"Bullshit," he whispered, exiting.

Viterello slammed the door. "Did he call his lawyer when you picked him up?"

"Couldn't have," Watkins said. "He was on the front stoop when I pulled up. Him and some child."

"You know what just happened here?"

"That uniform is fifty bucks heavier. That I know."

Attorneys could not request to see their client. A client could request an attorney, but not the other way around. Knott had no idea who a Mr. Hooper was, but when the word *attorney* was released into the Toaster, it didn't matter how far along they were in the interview or if it progressed to interrogation. There was no warrant. Once Knott knew there was someone on his side, everything crumbled.

"Goddamn hump," Viterello said. He opened the door. "Where is she?"

"Freddie," Watkins said.

"Fuck it, Hy. It was pork chop night and now they're going to be like rawhide when I get home."

Watkins put her hand over her mouth, hiding a smile.

"It's not funny," Viterello said. "Apple sauce and everything."

12

*T*he preacher, holding an open bible, spoke in a strong baritone used to not having a microphone. The wind blew uncomfortably at times across the cemetery but all could hear him under the canopy.

"Save me Oh Lord, for the waters have come unto my soul. They that hate without cause are more than the hairs of mine head. They that would destroy are mighty. Deliver me out of the mire and let me not sink. Let me be delivered from them that hate, out of these deep waters. Their reproach hath broken my heart and I am full of heaviness. Oh Lord, save me. Take me home."

Stevenson, sitting on the edge of the last row with Zooey next to him, looked about at surroundings he had seen many times before, during his youth. Nothing had changed and he was surprised there was enough room for another body among the sea of common headstones. In the front row sat Blaine and his wife but he could only see a partial profile of the younger Coleman. Blaine stared at the mahogany coffin, set upon a green tarp and surrounded by flower arrangements of all types and colors. His wife, in a black pillbox hat and veil, with red curls escaping all around, leaned her head on his shoulder. Father Clay and Sister May were behind them, along with Jenna, Mildred and Odeh. Jeller was alone in the next row, his stick legs crossed. He watched the preacher like he would when a patient droned on about their last colonoscopy and urine smelling like cabbage.

Stevenson couldn't place some of the other faces but one in the second to last row, on the other end, he did remember. Ben Denholm, CEO of the hospital, sat attentively with hands in formfitting leather gloves clasped on his lap. He was bundled in black, his scarf wrapped neatly around and tucked into his overcoat like an oversized ascot. Almond and gray hair parted on the side paid no heed to the wind. The sun glinted off the gold frames of his glasses whenever he nodded at the preacher's words.

"It isn't fair," the preacher said, closing the Bible. He was pacing, his path a short back and forth. He smacked the Bible on his thigh. "To take a man in such a way, it isn't fair. The good doctor spent a lifetime helping others see another day. He saved my life and I know he saved a few others under this tent."

A smattering of *yes sirs* and *hallelujahs* erupted, intermingled with Catholic calm.

"What reason, Lord? What reason do you have for turning your back and letting this happen?"

To Stevenson's right, someone had been in and out of the corner of his eye. He turned around to see the detective from the other night. Viterello.

Zooey put her hand on top of Stevenson's, and he jerked it away in reflex.

"Sorry," she said in a whisper. She looked back at the coffin, lips pursed.

She had on the peacoat from the other day and a wool pencil skirt that clung to her bare legs, halfway covering her kneecaps. Her shoes were a heel and boot combo with battered laces.

Stevenson took his gloves off. "Here, before they fall off."

She half-smiled and took them. They looked like mittens on her.

"My friends, this is of no use, these questions of faith. We cannot possibly understand the Almighty plan and the intricacies it contains. Though these inequities anger us, we will one day find out the purpose of it all, for there is a purpose. We will be made aware of why the Lord does what he does, but that is for another time, far and away from this place. I ask that, on this day, this hour, this minute during which we are all present and alive, I ask that we all remember this time of sorrow as a time for change. Call upon thy neighbor, thy friends, thy family, call upon those we have not spoken with nor seen in far too long. Tell them, make them aware, hold them tight and make sure they know that while some of us have moved on, you are still here. You still love them and you always will." The preacher raised both hands above his head and nodded once. Everyone stood, bowing their heads.

Stevenson spied Viterello again. Hands jammed in an unbuttoned trench coat, the man rocked on his feet, head tilted down but eyes open. On the doorstep of sixty, Stevenson thought.

When the preacher finished, he ambled around until he was facing the coffin. The crowd stood still, silent, waiting for instruction. The grave was in the middle of a row, next to Elaine Coleman, and at the end was a narrow blacktop road where a pickup truck was parked in front of a line of cars. Two men dressed for labor sat in the cab.

"Rest in peace," the preacher said. He took a houndstooth cap from inside a corduroy jacket and put it on his bald brown head. He patted the coffin and walked away, down the row of headstones, singing to himself.

Everyone turned to one another, their voices hushed.

"Is everyone going back to Dr. Coleman's?" Zooey asked. She looked around, her eyes fixing on someone approaching from behind Stevenson.

"Dr. Stevenson?" Detective Viterello smiled with a nod to Zooey. "Got a minute?"

Zooey stared the detective down. She had no expression for the man, no greeting. "I'll go see what's up," she said to Stevenson. She looped around to the next row and walked over to the hospital staff. They were crowded around Blaine and his wife. Jenna had her hands on the woman's baby bump. She was of small build, wearing oversized sunglasses, and the enlarged belly looked cumbersome on her frame.

"Sorry about this," Viterello said. "Bad timing, I know."

"It's fine," Stevenson said. Beyond them, Denholm was walking away with another suit from the hospital. The suit had a cell phone out. Stevenson shook his head. "Can't even wait until they're gone."

Viterello turned around, then back. "Friends of yours?"

"Management. From the hospital."

"We have those. We don't call them management, though."

Viterello smiled. Stevenson tucked his hands in his field jacket, peered at the coffin. Viterello sniffed a few times, rubbed his nose.

"Not many people here," Viterello said. "He was a veteran, right?"

Stevenson nodded.

"No honor guard?" Viterello looked around.

"He didn't much care for his days in uniform."

Viterello shrugged. "Thought there would be more people than this, at least."

"Why would you think that?"

"Well, you know. The man was a doctor."

"Emergency medicine doctor. We tend not to be people persons."

"That's an odd thing to say."

"Other than the policeman's ball, do you go out every Saturday night for cocktails at the country club?"

Viterello snorted. "Got me there."

Mildred had broken from the small crowd around Blaine and his wife. Over the center of the coffin fanned a spray of black-eyed susans and red gerberas with stalks of butterfly bush like Coleman had in the greenhouse. She was adjusting the flowers evenly, though they looked perfect as they were. She wore a floppy black hat that had a matching black-eyed susan on the side.

"I just wanted to let you know we're getting a lot of solid leads," Viterello said. "The video wasn't as good as we hoped but the witnesses have helped immensely."

"Did you still need me to come down to the station?"

"No. It was obviously a woman that made the code yellow call."

"Have you arrested anyone?"

"Not yet, but we did bring a person of interest in for questioning."

"How'd it go?"

"Good. Good."

The detective looked away as he said the words, shifting on his feet left and right. The bottom of the trench coat swayed like a theater curtain closing abruptly.

"Who was it?"

"Have to keep that confidential. For investigative purposes. If he was a suspect or charged, I could tell you. The process is still in a delicate stage right now."

Stevenson nodded, turning to see Jenna introducing Zooey to Blaine and his wife. He should have been the one doing the introductions but he was stuck in back, hearing a whole lot of nothing about Coleman's case. No suspect, no charges, no clue.

"Thank you for coming by," Stevenson said. He stuck his hand out and Viterello took it.

"I did have one question for you. There was a malpractice suit dropped shortly before the doctor's death. Is Dr. Coleman's attorney here now?"

"I don't think so," Stevenson said, looking around. "He may be at the house if you want to try there."

"That's okay. I have his number. I was hoping to run into him here but it can wait." Viterello yanked one side of the coat over the other but didn't button it. "I'll be in touch."

"Did you want to talk to his son?"

Viterello was already walking away. He shook his head as he waved. Stevenson watched him walk among the headstones to the blacktop road where a battered Ford Taurus was parked. On the other side of the road was a bench at the entrance of a sidewalk leading into more headstones.

Vernon Lamb sat there, paying no attention to the people leaving and the cars driving by. He held his plastic grocery bag in his lap, head cocked back and a hand shading his forehead, looking at the sky.

*   *   *

"Hey Vernon."

Lamb dropped his hand and leaned forward, eyes squinting. His purple ski cap clung tight, coming down to his eyebrows. "Doc?"

"How you doing?" Stevenson asked. He sat down and Lamb looked him up and down, eyes recognizing.

"Not a cloud in the sky," Lamb said, looking up again. "My wife wouldn't step out the house if there weren't no clouds."

"Why not?" Stevenson looked up.

"Said a sky without clouds ain't worth trusting." He took his hand away and leaned in to Stevenson. "She had to take nervous pills sometimes."

The gravediggers were sitting on the back bumper of the pickup. Elbows propped on the tailgate, they were in no hurry.

"Never seen you in a tie," Stevenson said.

Lamb studied it, turned it up. It was striped with the colors of a barber's pole. "Been awhile," he said.

"You could have come up and sat with us. You knew him better than most of the people that came."

"*Shoot.*" Lamb leaned the other way. His laughter stumbled. "Come on, now."

"Why don't you come back to the house? Get something to eat."

Lamb was shaking his head. "Naw, that's not me. Just here to pay my respects." He leaned forward and rubbed his right calf. He let out a whispered hoot when he pressed deep.

Stevenson didn't pursue it. He often thought the reason Lamb didn't go to the detox unit, besides the danger, was because it was too public and lacked space. What little privacy existed in homelessness, the man sought out and cherished. There was no privacy in therapy. No quiet places in a hospital. No place to hide.

"Uh-oh," Lamb said. "Whachu got here?"

Zooey was walking toward them, still wearing Stevenson's gloves. Her hair swept sideways in the breeze, revealing only one earring in each ear. Lamb mumbled but Stevenson couldn't hear it all. Something about an angel. The men rose, Lamb groaning as he did.

"Hi," she said.

Stevenson said, "Zooey Briggs, Vernon Lamb."

She took a glove off and put her hand out. Lamb's hand enveloped hers.

"Think I've seen you at Saint Cat once or twice," Lamb said.

The last of the attendees made their way to the cars. The gravediggers saw them coming and walked around the other side of the truck, shovels in hand.

"Got a couple friends buried in here somewhere," Lamb said. "Maybe I'll make a day of it if my feet hold up."

"Sure you don't want to come with us?" Stevenson asked. "Getting a little cold out."

"Naw, naw," Lamb said, his voice gruff. He looked at the sky, then took a few steps forward and stopped again. "Always thought this was a potter's field," he said. He walked on, waving at the two. Like the gravediggers, he avoided those leaving by flanking left and around the gravedigger's truck. The diggers were pulling the tarp off the dirt mound.

"Is he going to be okay?" Zooey asked.

"Always is," Stevenson said. He loosened his tie and undid the top button. "I wish he had a place of his own. Especially in the winter."

She hooked her arm around his at the elbow and they watched the last of the cars leave and the canopy being taken down. Lamb stood where the preacher once was, hat off and head bowed.

"I didn't know this place was here," she said. "It's really tucked away from it all."

They walked down the side of the road and around the corner to the car. They were parked close to the entrance where stone walls met two octagonal towers on either side. Barbicans for the dead. As a child he was disappointed to find a graveyard on the other side of the walls, where he expected a castle's ward with medieval folk and jugglers and peasants. Where were the king and queen, prince and princess? Where were the knights? The ward of the court, a man more interested in the grip of Stevenson's hand than sightseeing, had no answers.

When they approached Zooey's Escort, she let go of his arm and jogged the rest of the way. The sun was in the middle of the sky but did nothing against a breeze that pinched at the ears. She got in and started the car but he paused, standing in the middle of the road.

In the other direction at the corner of the cemetery was a small plot bordered in crooked white stones that were almost level with the ground. The two headstones were older and though they were cut from the same granite and stood the same height, one had a veiled woman holding a baby on the top, the other a cross.

"What's the matter?" Zooey asked. She stood next to the car, looking at Stevenson, then in the direction of his gaze.

Stevenson turned around and trotted to the car. They got in and she handed his gloves over. The heat was blasting.

"What were you looking at?" she asked.

"Nothing."

"Uh-huh." She put the car in drive. "Seriously, what?"

He didn't answer and they drove on and out of the cemetary. A lone police cruiser sat at one end of the entrance and a news van at the other. The cameraman was loading up equipment. They passed pawnshops, corner liquor stores, storefront churches. Jaywalkers dodged traffic between intersections.

After crossing a few intersections, she put her hand on top of his. "Hey."

"My mother and brother are buried there."

She kept her hand on his, showing no hint of anything dramatic, and he appreciated it. The longer she was quiet, the more he knew he had to try again with the girl from the lab.

"We can go back if you want."

He said it was okay. Another time.

At the next stoplight she squeezed his hand and looked at him. He squeezed back.

"I saw you running away that night," she said. "I was going to tell you to come back but when I went around the corner you were running down the middle of the road. That taxi almost hit you."

The car behind them honked. The light had turned green. Without turning away from him, she pushed the button on the console for the hazard lights.

Stevenson said, "We can go."

"They'll go around."

Just as she said it, traffic started to pass them on the right. She turned her body toward him completely.

Stevenson said, "The bookstore across from your building. It used to be a grocery store. I—we were in it one day when it was robbed."

No questions. No deep breaths or bug eyes. She only listened.

"They were about to close. Flour and orange juice, that was all we needed. I got the juice from the refrigerator in back and when I came up to the counter these two guys are robbing the place. Ski masks, guns, gloves. The whole bit. Mom's got her hands up. The clerk behind the counter too, Mr. Kwan. And Hank's crying like he always did. He had colic something fierce. The gunman at the counter was nervous, sweaty, asking Mom why Hank won't shut up and he's going to shut him up for her. He was sticking his head in the stroller, yelling." Stevenson shook his head, chuckled. "I look over at Mr. Kwan and he's calm as can be. Smiling at me. He'd sneak me Chunky bars on the side of the counter and his wife would catch him half the time. Gave him hell. He'd just blow his cheeks out and cross his eyes at her. Pissed her off even more."

The light was red again. An old woman with an empty shopping cart ambled across the crosswalk. She looked at the two as she passed, as if they would run her down if they had the chance.

"Adults are so loud," Stevenson continued. "To a kid, the shouting, it's painful. Doesn't matter if it's nonsense. It scares them." He looked out the window, breathed deep. "I lost my grip on the juice bottle and dropped it. That scared Hank. The gunman too. He jumped and yelled at me, and Hank cried twice as loud. He wasn't having that. Picked up Hank's carriage by the handle," swinging arm in an arc, "and swung it over his head. Big carriage, too. Spoke wheels and blue lace. I'm sure the guy was on something, as jumpy as he was. It folded up like an accordion when it hit the ground."

A horn tapped behind them and Zooey ignored it but Stevenson turned to see a police cruiser. He waved, and Zooey looked then. She put the car in drive and pulled over. The cruiser drove on.

"Go on," she said. Her eyes had pooled, but no tears fell.

"Mom went nuts. She grabbed the guy by the throat and he's pushing her away, trying to protect himself. She was clawing at him. Screaming. She never saw it coming."

Please wake up.

"The guy that's watching the door puts one in the back of her head. She goes down and the other guy takes off. Mr. Kwan pulls a revolver out and lets a shot go and the other guy returns fire, but they got away in the end. I get Hank out of his carriage. His head is in pretty bad shape. The fontanelles are overlapped. Mouth opening and closing. Fish out of water. Agonal breaths. I grab Mom by the arm and I'm seven and she's too heavy for me but I'm pulling, telling her to please wake up. Hank and his blanket in one hand, dragging Mom through orange juice and blood with the other. Maybe if we get home it won't be so bad. We're halfway to the door when a cop shows up and grabs us, Hank and me. Runs right out of there with Mr. Kwan behind us. Right over to the John Eager Howard statue."

She reached across and put her arms around him. It was uncomfortable on his neck, the force she applied, but he let her be, her breath warm in his ear. She heaved air in once but if she was weeping, he couldn't tell.

*   *   *

The Coleman residence hummed with conversation, intertwining with the aroma of light fare and coffee. It had been chilly in the house, the thermostat on fifty-five. When Stevenson turned it up to sixty-seven, it took half a minute for the furnace to come on with a boom that halted all the voices for a moment.

"What was that?" Zooey asked. She was petting Baby in the front hallway.

"It's an old furnace," Stevenson said. He had the same in his house. When the fuel didn't light when it should, it built up in the combustion chamber, causing a small explosion when fire finally did come. With time, it would get worse if the transformer wasn't replaced.

He took her coat and was headed up the front stairwell when Folger came out of the kitchen, a glass of red wine sloshing in his hand. He was still in scrubs, his name tag hanging around his neck.

"Hey dude," he said, coming up the stairs. He tripped on the third step, bracing his fall on the railing but spilling half the glass onto the stair's runner. He turned around and sat, gulping the rest. "Let's put the fun back in funeral."

"How long have you been here?" Stevenson asked. He sat down one step above him, coats on his lap.

"Couple hours. The attending let me off early."

Folger seemed to want to say more. His mouth opened again and he raised a hand to gesture, but no words came out. He looked at Zooey and Baby in the hallway below and let the moment go, his head sinking toward his knees. He studied the empty glass.

"You didn't miss anything," Stevenson said.

"Nice casket?"

"Mahogany. Lots of flowers."

Folger nodded, and Stevenson noticed the hair loss at Folger's crown was worsening after all. He had kept it long for his first few years at Saint Cat, and often wore it in a ponytail, until the bald spot appeared.

"I need a refill," he said. He got up and grabbed the railing and was slow to rise, waiting for the house to stop spinning.

"No you don't," Stevenson said. He stepped down next to him, took the glass, and told him to come up. They walked side by side to the second floor.

The office door was open a crack and the light on. The ceiling fan whirred full speed, clacking away. They entered Coleman's bedroom and

Folger sat down on the bed, releasing Old Spice and the musk of unwashed hair.

"You'd think he'd have a nicer house," Folger said, looking around the room. He laid back and onto his side.

Stevenson set the wine glass on the dresser and hung Zooey's coat on the closet doorknob, with his overtop. He watched Folger for a minute until there was snoring. He turned the light out and left the door open a crack. A few steps down, he stopped at the office door.

"Who's that?" A man asked.

Stevenson pushed the door open. A pasty fellow sat at the desk, reading glasses on the tip of his rosy nose. The once neat stack of papers now lay scattered about.

"Cassius," Lemmy McPhee said. He stood, taking his glasses off. "Good Lord, look at you."

He came around the desk in a swaying waddle, saying *look-at-you* again, stretching the words out. He was rounder than the last time they saw each other, at the ED Christmas party five years before. His head had strands of black and gray combed over a shining scalp with divots and freckles. Black hair blocked the ear canal like bamboo and looked about to overtake the auricle.

Stevenson said hello and stuck out his hand and Lemmy took it, then hugged him. The lawyer's face was at Stevenson's chest and he couldn't recall if Lemmy was that short until he saw the man was without shoes, wearing brown socks, with brown pants and tan button-up shirt. Shoe lifts. All this time.

Lemmy smacked Stevenson twice on the back before letting go. He went back and sat at Coleman's place. The metal folding chair was positioned in front of the desk and Stevenson sat in it, expecting cold. But it was warm.

"Ain't this a pickle?" Lemmy said. He was looking over the desk. "Thank God he let me handle the paperwork."

"Didn't see you at the funeral."

"I left before everyone got there. Made sure everything was in place, then came back here to set up. I'm no good to anybody at those things." McPhee took a handkerchief from his pocket and blew his nose, checking the cloth before stuffing it back in his pocket. "The guy in the scrubs, Mr. Folger? He was sitting on the stoop when I got here. He's nice. Helped me set up."

Stevenson told him who Folger was and how long he had been working at the ED. The topic faded, and they sat there looking over the papers again. The sweetness of tinea circulated through the room.

164

"I was just asking Larry about you the other day," McPhee said. "He told me you don't go up to the estate much."

"I was just there not too long ago. But before that, yeah. Been too long."

"Busted my ass getting you all official on that place. Never even got paid."

"You're kidding?"

"Not a cent. That lawyer your father had was going to screw you out of the whole deal. Rat bastard. He died in a plane crash. Flew his Cessna right into a corn silo." Lemmy pointed at Stevenson, squinting. "You have a will?"

"No."

"Dammit, come on." McPhee threw his pen on the desk and tilted his head back, shaking it. "Damn doctors. Pain in my ass."

"Do I look that bad?"

"You look great. That doesn't mean death isn't waiting outside for you. You still riding that motorcycle?"

Stevenson said he was and McPhee cursed again, then asked for Stevenson's address and phone number. Stevenson recited it, taking a newspaper off the edge of the desk as he did. The Baltimore Sun's headline read WATER MAIN BREAK FLOODS DOWNTOWN RUSH HOUR AGAIN, with a color picture of bumper-to-bumper cars, water halfway up the hubcaps. A side column read No Suspects in West Baltimore Hospital Murder.

"The detective was looking for you at the funeral," Stevenson said, putting the paper back. "He was asking about the malpractice case."

"He's left me a couple messages. I'll call him today."

"I'm assuming he thinks there is a connection."

"I wouldn't doubt it. The Knotts were barking up that tree for two years trying to get a payday. Thank God they dropped it. I haven't been in a courtroom in years."

The yellow notepad was under the disordered papers, Stevenson was sure of it. He looked at the desktop up and down, side to side. Papers everywhere. Lemmy seemed to notice him scanning and started tidying up.

"Why was it dropped?" Stevenson asked.

"Hospital records department found the AMA form. Apparently it was misfiled for two years but Larry knew all along it had to be somewhere. I called their attorney myself. Even faxed a copy over." McPhee sat back, hands behind his head. "You would have thought the hospital would have been happy about it."

"What do you mean?"

"You know, the contract and all. You'd think the board would have changed their minds about renewing."

Stevenson stared, tilted his head sideways.

"He didn't tell you?" Lemmy asked.

"I guess not. I haven't a clue what you're talking about."

Lemmy sighed deeply. "Did he procrastinate at work too?"

"Daily."

"The hospital decided a few months ago not to renew their contract with Chesapeake at the end of the year. Larry was supposed to have told you that but I guess he was holding out. Hoping he could change their minds."

Stevenson leaned forward in the chair. "He told me he was going to retire at the end of the year. Nothing about the hospital not renewing."

"They never did give a reason, other than they wanted to go in a new direction. That means they hired a new group."

"Who?"

"I don't know but there was a rumor that the new group would hire most of the doctors from Chesapeake once the break was made."

Stevenson stood but wasn't sure where to go. He eyed the door but went to the window. Across the street, Zooey had Baby on a leash. The dog was squatting on a square patch of grass that had a stump in the middle. Zooey had one arm over her chest, gripping her opposite shoulder. Her blouse was sleeveless and he could see the tattoo on her other arm. Just a smudge from far away. When the dog was done they trotted back toward the house.

"I'm sorry, Cassius. You weren't supposed to find out like this."

"You said they were going to hire most of the doctors."

"As far as I know, yes. And Mr. Folger, I believe."

"Who were they leaving out?"

"Larry assumed he was one of them but I'm not sure who else. Maybe it was just him. I don't know." Lemmy stared at his clasped hands on the desk, said he was sorry again.

"I'm going to take off." Stevenson went to the door. "Good seeing you."

"Hold on a second."

McPhee got up and came around, shutting the door. He faced Stevenson, reaching up and grabbing his shoulders.

"There had to be a reason for him not telling you. I'm sure it was a good one."

"Doesn't matter now. I'm quitting at the end of the year."

"I don't blame you, but you are the best doctor they have. Larry said it all the time." McPhee let go. "Which leads me to the next topic. His will."

"What about it?"

"You're in it." Lemmy walked back around the desk but didn't sit down. "Blaine is all he had left. Blaine and you."

"Me?"

"He's known you since you were a baby. He's always considered you family."

Stevenson sat down.

McPhee did the same.

"Larry wasn't the best planner but he did manage to save a few bucks. He had some property too. And a boat."

"The Catalina," Stevenson said.

"He sold LaShonda and bought another one. Don't ask me why. When somebody says boat I think Break Out Another Thousand." He shifted some of the papers around. "It's docked in the Harbor, off Clinton Street in Canton."

"Are you saying it's mine?"

"Yes. He left you some property and money as well."

"I don't need any money."

"Oh, I know that. I made sure of that when you were off at Camp Granada. I remember how much you ended up with, too. I bet you haven't spent a dime. Just been sitting exactly where it's always been. Getting fatter every year."

"The dividends take care of the Green."

"I bet they do. Pays the housekeeper too?"

Stevenson said it did. McPhee leaned back, looking at the paperwork on the desk.

"Millions, Cassius. He left you millions. And a property down in the Shenandoah Valley. See why I'm getting on you about a will? Your estate combined with what you're getting, you need to—"

"I don't want it."

McPhee chuckled. "I heard you said that the last time somebody tried to give you money."

"What about Blaine?"

"He's taken care of, don't worry. The only thing not going to you or Blaine is this block of houses. This goes to the hospital."

"I'll just give Blaine my half."

"He won't take it. Don't even bother."

Stevenson stood and opened the door. Folgers's snoring filled the hallway.

"I'll have some things for you to sign when it's official," Lemmy said. "After that we'll talk about dissolving the company and writing up your will as well."

Stevenson walked away. His throat went hot and he tried to cough it out. He descended the back stairs, hearing voices in the kitchen as he approached, and stopped abruptly. Couldn't go up or down.

Jenna had been in the kitchen, crying in Mildred's arms, the weight of it all catching up with her. She had been pondering aloud how odd it was that she had given Baby to Coleman after Elaine's funeral and now she was taking Baby back, like Coleman always said she would. Zooey was there at her side and Blaine at the kitchen door, looking on with an empty glass of wine and not sure if he should leave or approach. Stevenson, standing at the bottom of the steps the whole time, grabbed the greenhouse keys above the refrigerator and waved for Blaine to follow him.

"Whoa," Blaine said, looking all around. "When did this happen?"

"Not too long ago. I just found out about it myself."

The greenhouse was bright and the overhead heater buzzed. The thermometer on the shed read 71 but sweating was immediate. Stevenson rolled up his sleeves and Blaine took off his blazer. Stevenson ran his hand along the flowers and bushes, disturbing the butterfly's feeding. Most flew overhead, then drifted back down in a circular flight pattern, settling on stalks of mauve petals. Some joined others fanning their wings on the roof of the shed.

"Belle would love this," Blaine said. He walked backward. "I didn't even know he liked gardening."

They sat on the bench and Stevenson gave him a few minutes. It was overload, the tropical aquarium encased in a concrete jungle, the contrast between inside and out.

His face was the same, pale and without blemish. Only when Blaine smiled could his facial bones be discerned but otherwise his cheeks were flat and his nose straight. Brown hair was short on the sides and tousled on top. There were holes in each ear lobe where earrings once were.

"I knew he stopped sailing after mom died. He said it wasn't possible to man a vessel that size by himself but I knew that wasn't true. I'm glad he was doing this instead." Blaine waved his hand diagonally just as a checkerspot flew by. It danced about in tight figure eights straight upwards, then glided down over the shed.

"Who the hell names their boat LaShonda?" Blaine asked.

"Only one person I know."

"I mean, come on, that thing was what, forty feet?"

"Forty-seven."

"Forty-seven foot yacht and that's the only name he could come up with."

"He said it was the name of his first girlfriend."

"Get out of here," Blaine said, laughing. He clapped his hands once and the jacket he had draped over his leg slid off. He looked at it, left it lay. "Dad said that?"

"I think he was kidding but with him, who knows."

Blaine leaned back and crossed his arms, resting his head against the shed wall. "I couldn't do it," he said. "I couldn't sit there and, not more than an hour after Dad was in the ground, listen to what Lemmy had to say. He started rambling about the circle of life and Belle being pregnant. I used to play in there when I was a kid. I couldn't do it."

"I think he wanted to get everything squared away before you headed back to New York. Easier with you here."

"You talked to him?"

Stevenson nodded and looked away. A hummingbird moth floated around the butterfly bush in front of them, working its proboscis like a whip.

"Did he leave you anything?" Blaine asked.

Stevenson was about to answer but Blaine stood fast, hands on top of his head.

Blaine said, "Sorry, sorry. That's none of my business. Sorry."

"No problem."

The heater turned off and trickling water cooed from behind them. Baby came through the open screen door, wagging her tail. She went to Stevenson and lay on her side, driving her shoulder into the ground as she rolled around. Blaine was at the side of the greenhouse, looking out.

"I haven't seen you since mom's funeral."

"Your hair was longer," Stevenson said. He scratched Baby behind the ears and rubbed her belly. "You were just starting to date Belle, I think."

Blaine nodded and turned around, watching Baby's antics.

Stevenson said, "Thought of a name?"

"Ramsey if it's a girl. Lawrence if the other." Blaine nodded towards the house. "How long have you been with, uhh—"

"Zooey. She's just a friend."

"What happened to Liz?"

"Didn't work out."

Blaine sat down again, picking up his jacket and dusting it off. "People come and go. There will be others."

"I heard that probably from the same person you did."

Baby hopped up on the bench between the two and Blaine reached out, touching her head gently. She leaned into him and he scratched behind her ear.

Blaine said, "Who was that man you were talking to after the service?"

"The detective. He said they are progressing on your father's case."

"And you believe him?"

"Don't have a choice."

"I was on the FBI's website yesterday. You should see the crime rates for the city and the unsolved murder rate. Atrocious."

Blaine stopped petting Baby, his head shaking slowly, eyes vacant. He cupped his hands in his lap, turning a plain wedding band with his middle finger and thumb in a way that seemed habitual.

"They have the guys that did it on camera," Stevenson said. "Everybody who was working that night is more than willing to help identify the suspects."

"They reach a certain point and that will be it. It'll just dry up and be forgotten. All he's done for that place." Blaine made a fist, covering it with his other hand. "He was in the middle of a hospital. Why couldn't they save him?"

His face reddened, but he exhaled and regained control. Stevenson watched the curious pigeons above. Their claws scratched the glass.

Blaine said, "I was going to tell him to retire and move up by us. Be there before the baby was born. I knew he was lonely down here but I dragged my ass. Sometimes I'd call him and I wouldn't know what to say. Now I've got plenty to say but nobody to say it to." He stood, walked back to the windows again. He picked at a streak of green that had gotten on the window when the shed was painted. "I used to hate you."

"What? When?"

"When we were kids. You came over for Easter a couple times. Found more eggs than me. He talked about you a lot. He would call your house sometimes to check up on you. Talk to the housekeeper."

"I didn't know that."

"I thought he liked you more."

"Blaine."

"I know, I know." Blaine held a hand up, waved it in a hushing manner. He took a few steps down the path toward the house. "What do you think happens to the butterflies?"

"They have to be let go."

Blaine nodded. Kicked at gravel.

"Talk to Lemmy again, Blaine. Before you leave."

"Do I have to?"

"Get it over with. You don't want to come back down here next month just to sign paperwork."

"True."

Blaine said he was going to check on Belle and left Stevenson there with the dog. Stevenson stood, looked around. The crank for the roof windows was greased in clumps and he thought of opening it. Next time, he thought, walking on, with Baby following. She bounded past him and her feet kicked up gravel, some of it making a clicking noise as it landed in the shrubs. Stevenson stooped down and reached in where the clicking came from.

The picture of Stevenson's parents with Coleman and bride-to-be, Elaine, lay within the stalks of the shrubs. He had forgotten it on the last visit.

Ash clouds scudded across the evening sky, threatening a storm. The lights were off in Stevenson's bedroom and he lay supine, staring up at the ceiling, the previous days replaying in his head. Baby initially curled up on the floor in the corner, but couldn't settle, groaning to her feet every few minutes and lumbering into the short hallway, her nails clicking the floorboards. A pause filled the air when she would peer down the stairwell for someone familiar, who never came. She returned and headed to the corner, laying next to, but never in, the dog bed from Coleman's room. She repeated this for hours before she finally settled at the top of the stairs sometime after two in the morning.

You're dying.

He exercised five days a week, never ate fast food, never drank alcohol, slept plenty, but he was dying and he realized it at the funeral. Passing the patch of crooked headstones under which his mother and brother lay made him realize what he'd ignored for so long. Routine was strangling him and simultaneously feeding what lie beneath, waiting for release— what wouldn't die no matter how many times he punched a speed bag until he bled.

Your hands, Bulldog.

Thoughts strobed through his mind and closing his eyes only made the images sharper.

To take a man in such a way, it isn't fair.

The preacher, so earnest.

We're getting a lot of solid leads.

The detective, with his words holding no merit. Numbers didn't lie and the city had little chance of bringing anyone in.

You should see the crime rates for the city.

No need in that, sole son. The hospital provided all the facts.

Tell your boy he's going to pay up real soon.

Knott, with his henchman counting bills.

Swick-swick-swick

Dirty money.

I'm telling you, you get too many of them roughnecks up in Stillman and shit just might get crazy.

There was only one Stillman Stevenson knew of.

He got it set up on Tuesdays for a reason. Fights be when they got the lowest number of blues on the street. That's Tuesdays.

Stevenson sat upright. In the darkness he opened his eyes and saw all there was without the aid of light. Every fiber was alive, every cell with their mitochondria working at full capacity.

Within his chest, movement.

13

*K*nott was walking through the door of Reeves Motor Company when someone grabbed the back of his collar and spun him around. He was slammed into the door, the impact shaking the front window.

"What the fuck, yo?" RJ said, letting go and stepping back. His arms were raised at his sides as if he were going to shove again. "Huh?"

"RJ, c'mon man."

"Fuck you, J!" RJ pointed his hand like a gun. "Did me like a punk, yo."

Knott said nothing and RJ backed away to the other side of the brick box that was once the sales office for Reeves Motor Company, his father's used car business. Against the far wall sat a pine desk with two cushioned chairs for customers, cockeyed and facing what used to be the sales manager's post. The chair's wooden frames were scarred with initials carved on the armrest and the cloth back cushion was shorter than the seat cushion. A makeshift lounge, consisting of a matching couch and coffee table with two more chairs, took up the rest of the space. A corner floor lamp, gold and arched with a timeworn hemisphere shade, cast the only light in the room.

"How much the lawyer cost?" Knott asked, sitting on the corner of the couch. The cushion released the smell of stale cigar smoke, reminding him of his grandparents' basement, where his grandfather roamed most of the day. Pappy, the only male in his family that he ever respected.

"I don't know," RJ snapped. "Pop's got him on retainer." He flopped into a leather executive chair behind the desk, new and out of place with the decor. "He was yelling at me like I was a shorty. Shit's embarrassing."

"I didn't say nothing to the police, RJ."

"Why you didn't tell me you were going to do this?"

"I knew you'd try to change my mind."

"Damn right I would've. You killed a doctor."

"I didn't kill nobody."

"Fuck you. You know what I mean."

RJ brought his arms up to the desk, resting them on open textbooks. He fidgeted with an orange wristband, grinding his jaw and cursing under his breath. His white Ralph Lauren Polo was the kind Knott avoided. The shorties—his children—always found a way to stain anything white.

"You couldn't get nobody here to do it?" RJ asked. "You had to get Apollo?"

"I'd be booked and charged if I got somebody here. You know how trigger boys are. Po-Po tell them thirty years with a chance of parole and they jump on it. Sign a confession before they even make a phone call." Knott couldn't look at him when he said this. The detective that picked him up, Watkins, had almost pulled him in. It doesn't have to be like this, she had said. Put her hand on his knee, even.

RJ mumbled some more, shaking his head. Knott stood and came over to the desk but RJ ignored him.

Knott said, "It was my father, yo. What would you have done it if it were yours? You would've just let it go?"

RJ smirked and sat back. He looked at the door, the ceiling, then the wall. Knott leaned forward, putting his hands flat and wide on the desk.

"That money was going to get my mother into a nursing home. I wanted to get her out of the state hospital, into somewhere nice where the sheets are clean and the nurses smile. Ain't like nobody else in the family going to do it. They all forgot about her, just wrote her ass off like she was dead." Knott leaned forward more, craning his neck and getting into RJ's gaze. "I'm tired of it, RJ. Tired of being shit on all the time. The mother fucker killed my pops so I got him done. I know he wasn't much but he was my pops. Fucking mines." Knott smacked his chest. "Wasn't going to let him go out like that. You feel me?"

RJ, head down but eyes looking up now, barely nodded. RJ had no scars on his face, no moles or crooked teeth. Hair cut a half-inch from the scalp, trimmed every week by a barber in the county. Knott could smell the lotion shining on RJ's arms and he looked at his own. They were cracked and scaling on the hands, between the fingers and along the knuckles.

Knott stood straight, crossing his arms. "I didn't mean no disrespect by it, going behind your back and all. It's just that, for all these years, running together, working the streets, putting bodies in the Brown." Knott turned, looked at the couch. "I put in a lot of time to find something that would get me paid and somebody up and takes it from me."

"We doing just fine. We getting paid."

Knott sat back on the couch, in the center this time. He leaned his head back, looked at the ceiling. "But where's it all going at?"

The two sat for a few minutes, listening to the west side's breathing. Cars passed the empty lot, empty now since Lewis Reeves became Councilman Reeves and left the title of small businessman behind forever. Through the sheer curtains, the decal of Reeves Motor Company on the bay window cast a shadow on the linoleum floor, its letters stretched and backward.

"So the police ain't been by since?" RJ asked.

"Nope. Mr. Hooper said they got nothing on me so we good."

"I wouldn't say that."

"Why not?"

RJ stood and came around and sat on the edge of the desk. "We have to stop with the dogs."

"What?" Knott's head jerked, brow high. "Stop the fights? RJ, that's a lot of money, yo. I told you we good. The shit will pass."

"It ain't that. I mean, this situation didn't help us none but the fights are getting too big. Too many people know about it."

"I took home twenty-five large last time." Knott sat up. The fights paid for his lifestyle. Bought the Escalade, with his money and his grandmother's signature. The fight took care of his children and their mothers. "What am I going to do?"

"We'll do one more," RJ said. "Double our money. That'll take care of you until the other thing gets going."

"Are you getting back at me?" Knott asked, his voice short of whining.

RJ walked over to the window and pulled the curtain back. Sunlight lit their faces and they both squinted.

"If I tell you something, you gotta be cool with it." RJ smiled, nodding. "Sit on it until everything gets moving."

Knott said that he would.

"You know how Kruk has been coming to the fights and doing his thing?"

"What, sitting up in the bleachers and making that green? Probably make more than us."

"Definitely more than us. And that's good. We want that. We want him to make money when we're around."

"I always said we should be getting some of that. Getting some of everything. It's our damn house."

"And I'm going to be talking to him at the next fights about that."

"With Kruk? He don't run with no black folk."

"We're not trying to run with him. We just trying to get paid. You know he has to get his shit driven up from Florida or down from New York, right?"

"No."

"Well he do, and sometimes it ain't that good or he don't get all the shit he paid for. Ain't like you can load a car up full of weight and expect it to have every ounce it had when it left."

"Aww, is he in a bad way?" Knott leaned back, shook his head and murmured curses.

"That's our way in, yo. What if we had a better way of getting product to him?"

"What better way?"

"At the Point."

"Boats and shit?"

RJ shrugged. "Maybe."

"Who we know that's got a boat?"

"Nobody, but that ain't our problem." RJ came over and sat on the couch's armrest. "We increase Kruk's shipment size. Make sure he don't lose any of it."

Knott only stared and RJ held his hands up, neck jutted out. "Middlemen, fool. You know, wholesalers."

RJ slid down the armrest and sat, clasping his hands behind his head. In the pale light his smile was full bloom.

Knott said, "You know you talking foolishness, right? Don't nobody get away with that for long. Even if you got people on the inside it always gets fucked up. Somebody always runs they mouth."

"Won't happen. Not if we're connected."

"Yeah? And who we gonna connect to?"

RJ sat up, looked Knott in the eye. Knott asked again.

"My pop is running for mayor next year." RJ smacked Knott on the chest. "How's that for a connection?"

"Stop playing. For real?"

"He's connected, too. He's been planning this for years. Already got it worked out." RJ reached his hand out. "No more of this dog fight shit. This is big time."

Knott put his hand out and RJ grabbed it, yanked it. Then the two were laughing.

A car pulled up to the front. RJ stood when the engine cut off.

"Damn," RJ said, listening more than looking. "It's him."

"Hello killa', how you been?"

Knott was headed for the back door in long strides when Reeves came through the front. RJ stood in front of the couch, looking between the two. His son was dressed respectably, but Knott was in all black, pants sagged at the seat. Reeves stopped yelling at youths in the city to pull their damn pants up years ago.

"I didn't kill nobody," Knott said, standing still. He didn't turn around.

"Uh-huh." Reeves unbuttoned his blazer and put a hand on one hip, scanning his old office. The door was still open and cars rode by with booming systems. "Go on then, backdoor man."

Knott continued on but in a creep and he shut the door behind him without a sound.

"And you're welcome for use of my counsel." Reeves reached around and slammed the front door, then looked to RJ. "Hooper's a real estate attorney, you know. Man's got no idea what goes on in a court room."

RJ sat down, studied his shoes.

Reeves said, "Talk."

"About what?"

"Don't play with me, boy. I had to stand in front of that hospital with the mayor and the commissioner, in front of all those cameras, shucking and jiving about all the killing in my district, how we're going to put an end to it because killing this doctor was too much." Reeves went to the desk and sat, looking at the armrests, appreciating them. He bounced back a few times against the back support. "Those reporters are goddamn snakes. Take your words and strangle you with them."

RJ said, "He didn't do it."

Reeves leaned the chair back, sighing deeply. "I was going to school full-time when I was running this place. Always had a full lot. Twenty-one spots, twenty-one cars. Sold a car, replaced it in an hour. Never caught nobody's attention. You remember coming in here, playing with your Tonka trucks? Making all kinds of noise."

"Yes sir."

"Raised you up on a used car lot. I knew I didn't want you in this business. That's why I closed it up when I became a council member, before you got the idea of taking it over."

"You don't think I could do it?"

"I'm sure you could. I just have bigger plans for you." Reeves thumbed through one of RJ's textbook. "That doctor. I knew that man."

"Pop, I didn't—"

"Have anything to do with it? Yeah I've heard that before."

Reeves stood, spying the pictures on the opposite wall he had seen a thousand times. He walked over to them, studying one in particular. He was sitting on the hood of a red El Dorado parked in front of the building. He wore a wide black belt, black shoes and tie, with pants and shirt matching the car. Hair thicker, taller on top. The El Dorado was sold the same day.

"I'd tell you stay away from that boy but I know his situation," Reeves said. "I knew his father. Stupid ass junkie. Used to beat that boy all the time."

"Jaris?"

"West side is a small village. Everybody know everybody's business. His father was on disability because he had liver problems. Felix was the one that *caused* the liver problems but the taxpayers had to pay for it. And you know what? He didn't give a dime of that money to his family. People like that, they're not meant to go any further than the corner. It's all they know and all they want to know."

He was killing time with his son, dragging it out until the boy spilled everything. When RJ was 8 he found a pair of bolt cutters in the alley. Cut up the neighbor's chain-link fence, their dog's chain, their garden hose. RJ knew nothing about it of course, so Reeves bought a few garden hoses and put them in various rooms, telling his son they had to keep an eye on them because there was somebody cutting up hoses in all the neighborhoods and the hardware store stopped selling them because they were scared. RJ couldn't go out for weeks, not because he was grounded, but because he had to keep watch on the hoses. They were placed everywhere—the kitchen, the bathtub, the hallway; in RJ's bed toward the end, before his confession.

"J didn't kill that man," RJ said, standing.

"Trying your damndest to convince me, ain't you? Well stop, 'cause I know he didn't. The boy's not stupid. He got somebody else to do it when he found out he wasn't going to get any money out of that lawsuit." Reeves turned around and faced RJ. "I bet you know who cut that man, don't you?"

"I didn't have anything to do with it. I swear."

Reeves walked over and sat next to RJ. He crossed his leg, threw his arm up along the back cushion. "This kind of garbage can screw us up right here. This can come back and burn us if certain people thought you were involved. That means we can say goodbye to a lot of money."

"I wasn't involved, Pop."

"Missing the point, son. Whether you were or not, it don't matter. This type of activity," Reeves pointed at the back door where Knott exited, "can scare our partners. People we need. Scare them, they walk away. You hear?"

"Yeah."

"What?"

"Yes sir."

"You need to keep away from the thuggery, starting now. I meant it when I said you got to cut ties with the low-level business dealings. Killing that doctor, that was one low-level thing there. Low like a catfish. Eating garbage from out the mud. There was no point to it other than revenge and revenge makes you sloppy. You need to separate yourself from that life."

RJ said he would. Reeves stood and stretched.

"How'd you know that doctor?" RJ asked.

"Him and me went way back."

"High school?"

"Business partner. I did some work for him. He did some work for me. Smart man."

"Business partner? With a doctor?"

"Aw yeah. We were young men then. Hungry, too."

"What kind of business?"

Reeves' smile faded as he looked far off in thought. "Can't even remember, so damn long ago."

RJ spoke but Reeves cleared his throat excessively. He went to the door and opened it, looking out at the empty lot.

"How's our man Kruk?" Reeves asked.

"Good. Going to play ball with him soon."

"My man." Reeves, hands in his pockets, jingled his keys and change. "My main man."

14

*H*is Clydes were silent in the hallway but each step felt as though he was stomping on live wires. His spine buzzed, scalped tingled, like electric lice had burrowed into the follocles. Eyes assessed all things, both alive and inanimate, before his brain recognized the action. A retired symbiont had returned, put back into service, and organic turbines within blackened mitochondria spun like they did on their first day.

The parking lot had been full when he rode in and the ambo bay had two ambulances docked and two more waiting their turn. Every room would have a patient, some standing at their doors, their paper gowns wrinkled and untied in the back. *When's the doctor coming? Where's my medicine? What's wrong with that man that keeps yelling?*

When he opened the door to fast-track, the smell of flowers consumed him, along with the chatter of TVs and too many people. Two baskets rested on the nurse station counter, each a different color of carnations and roses and lilies and more. Folger was sitting behind the counter, writing in a chart.

"Hey," Stevenson said as he passed.

Folger didn't look up. Stevenson said it again but no response again. He kept on walking, late as it was already.

In the Pit, someone had put a massive bouquet of pink roses at Coleman's place at the bar. At various spots on both counters, asymmetrically, were smaller bunches. Someone pounded on one of the doors in the psych pod and the soundproof door let out just the faintest of fist on metal. Kay sat at Def Con while bodies in scrubs walked around her. The trauma rooms were full and two ambulance crews waited in the hallway, lined up like planes ready for takeoff. He checked the board.

Full house. Two on deck. Twenty-four in the tank.

"Dr. Stevenson?"

Jeller. Coming down the hall from the break room. Stevenson gave him a nod and stepped into the office. More flowers. On the desk. On the filing cabinet. A few on the floor lining the wall.

Jeller followed him in and shut the door.

"Let me get some coffee, Jas. Long night."

"Did you know about this?"

Jeller pointed to the cubbies on the wall. Each, even Coleman's, had an 8x10 manila folder, bent in half and stuffed all the way in. Stevenson took the folder out of his and a While You Were Out note fell to the floor. He picked it up and stuck it in the pocket of his scrubs without looking at it. He opened the folder and removed the single letter.

"Dear Chesapeake Physician. After careful review it is the decision of the board of trustees for Saint Catherines Hospital not to renew the contract with your employer, Chesapeake Physicians. We thank you..." Stevenson shoved the folder and letter back in his box, looking at Coleman's as he did. "They didn't waste any time."

"Well?"

"Did I know? Yes."

"How long?"

"Found out after the funeral."

Stevenson sat at the second desk, dropping his keys in the drawer. He picked the two vases of flowers off the desk and put them on the floor with the others. Jeller crossed his arms, readjusted his stance. A gold Ulysse Nardin watch with a diamond for the number 12 dangled off his wrist. Stevenson looked at his own bare wrist. He reached up and tapped the top of his head with both hands.

"I find that hard to swallow," Jeller said.

"Forgot my helmet."

"What?"

"My helmet. Never even put it on. Watch too."

"Did you not hear me?" Jeller stepped closer.

"I fucking heard you, Jas. I heard you, and I don't care. You can't swallow it? Fucking choke then."

Jeller dropped his arms to the side. "You don't speak at me like that, boy."

"Really?" Stevenson shot up into Jeller's space with a single step. Jeller had height, a couple inches over him, but nothing else. The Indian's respirations increased and his mouth tightened. Air whistled through his nostrils and over his plump mustache, the scent of mint in overkill.

The door opened and Father Clay had a hand on Jeller's shoulder, the other on Stevenson's.

"Gentlemen," Clay said, looking between them both. "How are we today?"

"Father," Stevenson said. His eyes were locked on Jeller. "Doing well."

Jeller nodded, breaking from the stare. He mumbled a greeting and stepped back.

"If you two don't mind, I'd prefer we not pollute the hospital with more rage. He was a good man. His death was tragedy enough."

Stevenson nodded at Jeller once and Jeller did the same. Clay let go of their shoulders and opened the door. As he shut it, Stevenson caught a glimpse of the staff. Odeh, Manuel, and Kay, freeze-framed, all looking in.

"Displacing," Jeller said. He pulled the other chair out and sat down. "Excuse my shrapnel. I just don't like surprises."

Stevenson tucked his legs under the desk and looked through the blinds. A cachectic gomer with a resting tremor was peering out the door of T-1. She wore a heavy housecoat, a patriotic debacle covered in stars and stripes, unbuttoned halfway with lead wires snaking up and over her shoulder. The floor was waxed and clean. No evidence of what had happened.

"Death or retirement," Jeller said. "They were waiting for either."

"They're suits, Jas. What do you expect? One suit makes a deal with another and a lot of people lose their jobs."

"Not necessarily. Mr. Denholm called me this morning when I was driving in. He warned me about this letter. He said they were going in a new direction with the ED but I was not to worry about my position."

"What a swell guy."

"I'm assuming you did not get a call."

Stevenson said no. Odeh was adjusting the gomer's IV and talking to someone out of sight at the T-1 counter. The gomer paid no attention to him. Spittle gathered at the corners of her mouth. She gave a toothless yawn, her dentures still in a glass of water on a nightstand somewhere.

Jeller said, "They will be signing contracts with a new group this week. SEP. I don't know what that stands for. The business of medicine would not be complete without obscure abbreviations."

"So you're staying? Is that what you're getting at?"

"And a few others."

Stevenson stood. "Good luck."

"Wait. Cassius."

The man rarely said Stevenson's first name and it did make him wait. Jeller got up and pushed the chair under the desk.

"I'm not close with anyone here, despite being an employee for more years than I care to remember. That is no one else's fault but my own. Lawrence was fond of you, more so than anyone else here. He told me little, but what I do know, I respect greatly. If you do not stay, I will not either."

"You don't have to do that," Stevenson said. "I'll be fine."

"That is not the point, now is it?"

"I don't think they want me here."

"I highly doubt that."

"Was I one of the doctors he mentioned they wanted to keep?"

Jeller was quiet, looking at Stevenson's forehead, then his eyes again.

Stevenson said, "That's what I thought." He grabbed his lab coat off the back of the door and put it on. "I had too much history with the man. They know I don't have an interest in moving toward their new direction. Whatever that means."

"Talk. That's all it is. There is no new direction to take. It will never change, no matter who is cracking the whip."

"Never thought of it like that. Why would I ever want to leave?"

Jeller opened the door and told Stevenson to think about it, told him he would talk to Denholm. Stevenson followed him out and grabbed the chart for T-1. Odeh and an EMT were talking at the counter. The gomer, from a distance, was sleeping or dead now. A few steps in, Stevenson saw the blip of a pulse on the monitor. He opened the chart.

"Ms. Zelinski?" Stevenson said, touching her skeletal hand. Veins bulged like blue licorice under tissue paper. Her eyes opened and her lower lids everted, showing pale red tissue at the union of eye with skin.

"I'm Dr. Stevenson."

She opened her mouth and he thought she was smiling but her jaw clenched. Her lips spread apart, revealing pink gums specked with white plaque. She filled her chest full of air and, jaw still clenched, hissed.

Stevenson sipped from a paper cup of coffee, watching Folger eat a gyro. Folger bit more than a mouthful, mayonnaise splattering beyond the wax paper and onto the break room table.

"Sorry about the silent treatment, Tonto," Folger said, dabbing a napkin at his lips as he talked and chewed. "I thought you were in on it."

"First day back and you think I'm a turncoat. Thanks a lot."

"Don't mention it."

Stevenson yawned enough that tears came to his eyes.

"Don't do that," Folger said and then yawned too, mouth full of mangled bread and meat.

"Couldn't sleep," Stevenson said. "I was getting used to the dog being there. Now it's too quiet."

"Jenna took her?"

Stevenson said she did.

"Kelly kept me up half the night. She's on my ass about me getting out of here. Won't hush until she gets her way."

The lights flickered and went off. A few gasps and a brief scream came from beyond the break room. They flickered on again a moment later.

"Doing that since I got here," Folger said. "Going back and forth between grid power and the generators."

"Lines down?"

"Who knows? The substation down the road was built by the Mayans."

His coffee gone, Stevenson picked at the cup's rim. The new unit secretary, a temp not old enough to drink, was paging Dr. Jeller, her southeast dialect a concoction of West Virginia ancestors and inner-city slang. *DoK-er Jell-ir, 'stension one-Oa-ite.*

Folger said, "So yeah, she's been on me for the last year, actually."

"About leaving?"

"She wants another baby. I only stay because of you and the old man. Now that he's gone, I don't know. It's just all going to go to hell, I think."

"It is hell."

"Didn't used to be. I've heard stories about the good old days, when docs and priests ran everything. Reimbursements for services averaged eighty percent and the place rarely saw over a hundred patients a day. Now, with half the staff, we're lucky to see less than double that and for a fraction of the pay. What happened?"

Stevenson only shook his head. Folger put his gyro down and wiped his hands on another napkin. He pointed at the door.

"And they think getting a new group to run the show will help. They have no idea. They don't know shit about how it works here. First yo-boy that comes in bleeding like a stuck pig, telling them he wants to see the priest first, there's going to be a lot of deer in the headlights around here. I don't want to stick around for that."

Stevenson said, "Jas thinks it will be fine."

"He does?" Folger leaned forward, pushing his food away and crossing his forearms on the table. "Coleman is in the ground less than a week and they're already chopping heads. Does Jas know who he's dealing with? They have no souls, Cassius. Just hollow vessels in suits, walking the walk, talking the talk. And all this time, the police still don't know who killed him. I know. You know. But *they* don't seem to know. Think the hospital gives a shit? After all he did for this place?"

The cup was shredded and Stevenson dropped what remained. He looked Folger in the eye.

Swick-swick-swick

Folger said, "The choir, I know." He leaned back, crossed his arms. "I just had to put it out there."

"He was going to retire," Stevenson said.

"Really? When?"

"End of the year. He asked me if I wanted to take over the practice. He wanted to make you partner."

"What did you tell him?"

"Never had a chance to give him an answer."

Folger looked away, nodding. The break room was quiet and Stevenson heard nothing but his ringing. He thought of many things to say, none sounding better than the silence.

Folger picked up his lunch and stood and went to the trashcan. He dropped it in and stood there for a moment, looking at the contents.

"I'll stick around until the end of the year," Folger said. With that, he picked up the trashcan and slammed it against the wall cabinets. The innards shot out of the other side and covered the counter and floor, barely missing Stevenson. He opened the door gently and exited.

Stevenson reached in his pocket and took out the pink While You Were Out note.

Call Paul Nguyen at office.

It was marked urgent, like all the rest Paul had left over the past year.

They had met on their obstetrics internship at a small hospital on the east side. The first day, Paul, with Stevenson assisting, was trying to free a baby from a 16-year-old mother's womb as a gaggle of hardened nurses watched, not helping or lending advice. She was two weeks past due and not quite a hundred pounds. Paul made the episiotomy incision after reading the surgical anatomy and technique reference guide once. The book said the body released natural chemicals during childbirth, making the pelvic floor numb, but it was a lie. The teen screamed from beginning to end. When the newborn girl finally came out, or, rather, shot out, a week's worth of feces came with her. "Take her," Paul said, handing her to Stevenson. Paul then collapsed into the woman's crotch.

Coleman's death was a blurb on national news and was fading fast from local, but Stevenson knew why Paul was calling. The murder would be used against him in a way, to get him out of Saint Cat and into the county.

After a half ring, the phone picked up.

"We Care Urgent Care. This is Jessica, how may I assist you?"

"This is Dr. Nguyen's urologist. I have his STD results. I was won—"

185

"Oh my goodness. Hold please."

Stevenson glanced out of the blinds of the office. Housekeeping was cleaning up T-1. Ms. Zelinski, having no changes to an otherwise three-page list of chronic ailments, was discharged.

The line was alive again. "Who is this?"

"Paully."

"You rat," Paul said, laughing. "You know how hard it is to find receptionists these days?"

"With unemployment at nineteen percent? I'd think rather easy."

"You'd think wrong. How you doing?"

They talked for a few minutes about the murder and the city and the world not what it used to be, when they were interns and nothing existed outside of the hospital. Overhead intercoms on both ends paged each doctor but they ignored it.

"It's too crazy down there now," Paul said. "You know that."

"Been crazy for years."

"A doctor stabbed in his place of work? That's unheard of. Vile is what it is."

Paul went on. Zooey walked by, coming in from the ambo bay. She tapped on the glass and waved and Stevenson got lost in everything that was her. She was just getting to work, her peacoat still buttoned. He watched her until she was out of sight and kept watching, hoping she would come back. As his eyes tracked backward, they caught Coleman's chair at the bar. His lab coat was still draped over the back.

"You know the spiel, Cassius. Ninety-five an hour and eighteen percent of net billings. Malpractice paid, three and half weeks vay-kay. Medical directors get an extra week for meetings every year down in the Keys."

"Continuing education?"

"Five thousand dollar stipend." The chair creaked on Paul's end. "Hey, is something happening here?"

An ambulance crew passed through the ambo bay and went in T-1 just as housekeeping was leaving. A couple IV lines were in and the patient, a bald black man, eyes wide and an oxygen mask in place, jerked his head with every turn of the gurney. He was shirtless and, when he started kicking his legs, the sheet slid down, revealing only boxer shorts. A catheter was in the slit of the shorts.

Stevenson said, "I've been thinking about leaving lately. Getting tired of the graveyard shifts."

"We close at nine. You would be home by ten. Cassius, I can't see you working for an organization like SEP."

"How did you hear about that?"

"Friend of a friend. They're pure agency. Probably run out of some-body's kitchen. All it takes is a desk calendar and a phone. They send these glossy 4x5 mailers to hospital execs every month with," radio DJ voice, "Up your profits, increase productivity and patient satisfaction within weeks."

"Christ."

"They called me once. Wine and dine types, all smiley-glad hands. They'll give you a couple A-list physicians for half the year, then it's all foreign grads after that, guys with malpractice suits chasing them in every other state. By the time Johnny Law comes for them, they've already moved back to Tai-Pakis-Kraine."

Kay had walked into T-1 with Odeh and, as she got the report from the EMT, Odeh rifled through the drawer of the supply cart. The patient suddenly seemed to notice the catheter and smacked it like it was a wasp.

Paul said, "Get out of there, Cassius. I don't want to see your name in the obits."

Paul sang his contact numbers, the ones Stevenson already had. Stevenson said he would call him next week and hung up. He stood, looked on top of the filing cabinet where his helmet should have been.

Pedro doesn't give a shit if you're hungry or tired or out of ammo. He only cares about one thing: you being dead.

The Commander, a man who was supposed to retire that year if not for the war, lectured his battalion at Fort Sherman, the training grounds the troops were dropped at a month before Operation Just Cause was launched. The day before D-Day, December 19, the Commander assembled them in the chow hall.

Are you going to give Pedro the satisfaction?

Stevenson jerked his head, trying to clear the memory, and walked out of the office.

"Dr. Stevenson," Kay called from T-1. "Doctor?"

He was out of the Pit and down the hall. He turned the corner and went to what he had been ignoring.

In the lower corner of the bulletin board was the Murder Ink clipping from the previous week. The date was listed, along with the address of the scene of the crime.

9:38 pm: Officers were called to a stabbing at a unique location: Saint Catherines Emergency Room. 67-year-old Dr.
Lawrence Coleman had been stabbed in the chest by a man
brought in minutes before by ambulance. The staff was

unable to revive Dr. Coleman and he was pronounced dead at his place of work. City detectives later recovered the ambulance used to transport the suspect of the murder. It was stolen earlier in the week from a city vehicle garage and the driver and passenger, dressed as paramedics, are also suspects. The case is active and there have been no arrests.

When Stevenson came back, another ambulance crew was wheeling in a young man holding bloodied gauze on his cheek, his other hand gesturing at the wound. The headrest sat vertical and the gurney elevated him as high as he could go. Two uniforms trailed behind.

"Can't feel my face." He garbled his words, looking around, telling anyone in sight. Staff members emptied the Pit to gawk or aid. Stevenson went to Def Con and sat, grabbing the mouse. On the menu bar he clicked the Patients tab and went to search.

KNOTT, JARIS

The screen returned three Jaris Knott's along with dates of birth. One was born in the sixties, the other a few years before. The last, late seventies. Stevenson clicked on it and the visit history page came up on the left, home addresses, previous and current, on the right. There were two listed but one was a homeless shelter on the southside. Vernon Lamb had used the same address for correspondence for years. The other, 2013 Perry Boulevard, was unknown to him. Used weeks ago on the last visit.

His arm itched sharply and he pulled his sleeve up, scratching.

"Dr. Stevenson," Kay called from the doorway of T-1.

He got it set up for Tuesdays.

"Hello?" Kay said, in three parts.

Swick-swick-swick

"Dammit." She was walking toward him, stomping. "Hey, I'm talking to—"

Stevenson stood fast and the chair shot out, hitting the opposite counter hard. Kay stepped back. He looked her in the eye.

"We need you," Kay said. She held a pen at her side, like a dagger.

Stevenson walked the opposite direction out of the Pit, passing Coleman's chair to T-1. The ID badge was gone but the pocket protector was full of pens and the gold nametag from a time when they referred to the place as the Accident Room was still pinned under it, the edges chipped.

Lawrence Coleman, MD

15

*A*fter the fifth ring, someone picked up the phone, dropped it, and picked it up again.

"Hello?" A female voice answered in a huff.

"Hello," Viterello said. "Is Ms. Darrens home?"

"Yeah. Who's this?"

"Detective Viterello from Baltimore City Police."

The woman dropped the phone again. Viterello could hear her in the background yelling for her mother that some detective was on the phone. Eventually, slippered footsteps approached. The voice was raspy. Woken up.

"Yes, what is it?"

"Hello Ms. Darrens. This is Detective Viterello. How are you today?"

"Fine. I told you everything I know three times now."

"I know but we forgot to ask you about an associate of Timmy's, a fellow by the name of Jaris Knott. Sound familiar?"

"No."

"Are you sure? Stocky, 5'10", weighs around 200 pounds. Bad complexion."

"Never heard of him."

Viterello squinted at the computer screen. He fumbled around for reading glasses that were not in his pocket. "Have you thought about any of the other names we asked about?"

"Yes I did and I never heard of any of them either."

The woman who had answered the phone was yelling in the background about there being too much water. Ms. Darrens yelled for her to hold on without holding the phone away from her mouth.

"Are we done, sir?"

"For now. Thank you for—"

She hung up.

As he began typing he saw that his reading glasses sat next to the keyboard. He put them on and entered a note into the case report, in the communications section.

14:05: Contacted mother, Ms. Darrens. No recollection of any of victim's possible associates. FV

The phone rang and he pushed the ignore tab, not recognizing the number. A few media outlets had called relentlessly the first few days, bypassing the public affairs office. The calls about the Saint Cat murder were starting to dwindle but he still didn't answer unidentified numbers. He never spoke to the media personally. Never. Media kept the public informed, including suspects. They destroyed cases. Kept killers in the game.

Watkins walked in and stood in front of the desk, watching Viterello with a half-smile. "Circus bear riding a tricycle, right?" she asked.

"Shut up woman." Viterello looked over the top of his glasses, reading what he typed. "You'd think they would make keyboards for thick-fingered guys like me."

Watkins craned her head around to see the monitor, almost having to put her knee up on the desk for balance. She always wore unisex dress shirts, leaving only the top button undone, but today a few were undone and a gold necklace was visible from where Viterello sat.

"I thought you sent that down to Cold Cases?" she asked.

"I did." Viterello leaned back and took his glasses off. "I just wanted to throw one more name at the mother. What's new?"

"Nada." Watkins sat down on the couch. "Guess who's upstairs getting her ass handed to her?"

"I don't have to ask what about, do I?" Viterello sat up and rubbed his temples, closing his eyes tight. Using reading glasses caused his eyes to ache. From there, neck stiffness, then a migraine if he ignored it too long.

"No you don't."

"Dropping the Darrens case downstairs left nineteen opens on my plate, seven of which I'm primary." Viterello turned in his chair and looked out the tinted window. "If somebody ever finds a suspect for Darrens, I'm going to teach him how to bag a corpse the right way. None of this trashbag shit. Canvas bags, like the post office uses. Only way."

In the squad room they could hear Sergeant Bentley coming down the hall, telling someone she'll get with them later. She knocked on Viterello's open door.

"Ladies," she said. She sat on the couch next to Watkins. Her forehead shined and the cropped hair on the left side of her head was askew. "What a day."

"I saw you on TV," Viterello said.

"Don't remind me." She pulled her empty holster forward while sitting back, then closed her eyes. "Need a shower after that."

The press conference at Saint Catherines was all of six minutes and only a few media outlets showed. Councilmen, the state's attorney, the commissioner, the public affairs director—they all flanked the mayor and a priest from the hospital. The mayor reassured the city that the killer of the Saint Catherines' doctor would be arrested soon but to please call Homicide detectives with any information. Bentley stood behind them all with no badge to identify her affiliation with the speakers. Viterello thanked the Almighty it wasn't him in front of those cameras.

"How did it go upstairs?" Watkins asked.

"You'd think our beloved shift commander would help me out a little. Maybe point out the barrel of cases we've closed lately. No, not the lieutenant, not if it could blemish his record. He just sat there, staring like the rest of them. Like a firing squad up there. Quoting statistics, throwing around the idea of yet another task force. And nobody's asking for my opinion." She sat up and forward, looking at her watch, then to Viterello. "What are you working on?"

"The Darrens case. It's already downstairs but I wanted to try one more name on the mother."

"I signed off on that last week, Fred. Darrens is an NFC. Let it go. He was barely human to begin with."

Nobody Fucking Cares cases were the hardest to find a claimant for and the least worried about at night after the lights were off and the kids in bed. Almost all of these were due to drugs or some other low to intermediate-level crime and no one, not even family members, would utter a single sentence to benefit a detective's case.

"Do I even want to know about the progress on the Saint Cat case?"

"Probably not," Watkins said. She had her phone out, reading and poking buttons.

"We have a person of interest," Viterello said. "We have video. And a motive."

"I saw you had a little chat with a POI. So did the brass. Love how anybody can poke around in an investigation now." Bentley pointed at the computer, thumb up and index finger out. She let the hammer drop. "So where is he?"

"Under the watchful eye of counsel."

"Lawyered up?"

"Yes ma'am."

"And we don't have enough for warrants," Watkins said, putting her phone away.

"Not even a search?"

"Still have to figure out where he actually lives first," Viterello said.

"Does he have a car?" Bentley asked.

"Not that I know of," Viterello said. "Not in his name anyway."

"Married? Kids? Girlfriend?"

Viterello rattled off what little he knew of Knott's family situation.

Bentley stood, scratched her chin. "Forensics?"

Watkins said, "They pulled a few hairs from the scene but no matches as of yet. Considering it was a hospital, could be anybody. The weapon was a dollar-store kitchen knife. Made in China. No prints."

"On the plus side," Viterello said, "the media has backed off."

"Until next Friday, neither of you are to go out on calls. Focus on the Coleman case only. I'd rather it not be sent downstairs. Nor would the Commissioner."

Viterello and Watkins both nodded, looking at each other.

"Make sure you're updating the file daily. When upstairs logs in, I want them to see dicks on the beat. Maybe grab a Junior to follow up on leads."

The detectives said they would and Bentley bid them farewell and left. A moment later someone called out to her in the squad room.

"That's a load off my mind," Viterello said.

"One case for two weeks," Watkins said, standing. She put her hands in her pockets and rocked back and forth. "I can live with that." She turned for the door. "Hope you get a Junior with a strong stomach."

"No shit," Viterello said. He stood and rolled the chair under his desk.

The last Junior to assist him was on a murder-suicide. The murder victim was on the couch, slumped, with a shotgun blast to the belly and a lap full of soot-colored organ meat. The victim's long hair covered her face and when the Junior pulled it back, she saw that the victim's eyes had been gouged out and the pulp strung out on the cheeks. The Junior vomited on the victim explosively, long before the Medical Examiner Techs had time to set up and collect evidence.

"Where do you want to start?" Watkins asked.

"Not here. Let's go, before she changes her mind."

"Hungry?"

"I could eat."

They walked out of the office and along the perimeter toward the exit, both eyeing up the dayshift Junior squad in the center of the room. Four of them sat at the edge of their cubicles, facing one another in a circle, kicking a hacky sack around. A lone Junior with a shaved head stood at the window, his emerald dress shirt stretched tight over a wide back. He was watching the street below.

"The future," Watkins said.

"Ain't it bright."

16

R J and Knott stepped out of the elevator and looked over the top floor of the Stillman Point building. Knott lit a cigarette and offered one to RJ but RJ ignored him. Dirty dog and feces offended the senses. Cigarette butts studded the ground, each with its own circle of ash. RJ kicked at an empty glassine bag with the bottom torn off.

"The shorties gotta clean up a little, J. Get on them. This is nasty."

The Point, a seven-floor L-shaped remnant of the manufacturing industry, sat at the edge of a thirty-one-acre parcel of commercially zoned property. Once the beacon building of Stillman Grain Company, its sandy tan concrete shell, along with six concrete silos flanking the side, crumbled grain by grain with each rain drop and breeze.

RJ reached back in the service elevator and jiggled the key in the panel a few times until it gave way and clicked into the lock position. They walked on, their voices and footsteps echoing throughout the 6000 square feet. Afternoon sunlight blazed through the wire mesh windows and they each shaded their eyes against it.

"Gotta piss," Knott said, kicking a beer can as he rounded the corner. A scale hung from one of the trusses with a dog harness hooked on the under hook, and he pushed it from his path. A trio of port-a-potties lined the back wall and he stepped into the middle one.

At the end of the floor were aluminium bleachers with six rows, overlooking a miniature arena. A jail cell balustrade, waist high, encircled a square strip of cream-colored carpet that left half-circle segments of concrete floor exposed on either side. Light and dark stains marred the carpet, including a large crimson and black one in the middle, thick enough to mat the tufts of carpet yarn flat. The scratch marks, spray painted lines for which dogmen dropped their warriors behind, were barely visible.

"Stank bad up in here," RJ said, unzipping his coat and pulling the collar of his t-shirt over his nose. The arena and bleachers had been there since before he was born. His father brought him there when he was a teen, hoping to purchase the property at an auction, but only the city had the funds, eventually buying the entire parcel. Years later, it fell back under the eye of newly elected Councilman Lewis Reeves.

"What's that for, Pop?" RJ had asked him while touring the facility. "Boxing?"

"Cock fights. Had them here back in the day after the grain company closed down."

A few years after high school, RJ and Knott would be in the basement of an abandoned rowhouse on the east side thick with people of all races, all of them throwing wads of money at one another. They poked and prodded for a view of the pathetic arena made of three sheets of plywood held by mean looking brothers with bulges in their front waistband. Pit bulls were tossed in, immediately mauling themselves to pulps, and the wads were thrown again once the victor was pulled from the ring. The loser was taken in the back lot and, if still alive, hung on a noose so it died in silence. Then and there RJ thought of Stillman Point and, as he and Knott left, dodging the hanging dogs like laundry hung out to dry, the plan was devised. A month later they had their first fight. The introduction to the spoils of an underground economy smelled of shit and death but they walked away from the Point that night, and every fight night, with pockets full of money. Word spread, and not long after dogmen from as far as Atlanta and Chicago and Boston would come to the Point, looking for success with their prospects. Pit Bulls Only was the rule and they came, bulging at the chest and legs, their hindquarters speckled with spots of pinpoint bleeding from steroid injections. Every month a bigger bull came, claiming the title of champion after three fights won consecutively. Rarely did one make it to grand champion—five wins in a row—before being taken out by another chemically insane bull.

"Not too bad in here," Knott called from inside the port-a-potty. "We'll have to empty it soon, though."

"Whachu mean *we*?"

RJ tugged his shirt down and walked behind the bleachers. A floor-to-ceiling sliding door hung on a metal track, its planks splintered and red paint chipped at the bottom and throughout. He pulled the handle with all he had and a few sparks popped from the track, grinding and squealing. The breeze struck him like an ocean wave. At the base of the building were rusted train tracks off a main line miles away and on the other side was Cherry Cove, with cockeyed pillars from a collapsed pier poking out of its murk. In the distance, far enough where only a hum of motors could be heard, stacks of interchanges connecting the city to I-95 loomed over calm waters and if not for the cars moving at highway speeds back and forth, the eye would deem it mirage.

Across the Cove were deeper waters where cargo ships and cruise liners were docked at the industrial port. Further up were the yachts and the Inner Harbor, with their dockside restaurants and million-dollar apartments overlooking the Brown.

"The hell you doing?" Knott asked. He stood next to the bleachers and no closer.

"Taking a last look. Won't be seeing this again for a long time. Maybe forever." RJ turned, wanting to laugh at Knott's apprehension of getting any closer. Thick bastard, killer of many, and scared as hell of any height past one floor. "You going to miss it?"

Knott climbed the bleachers and sat at the top, where high rollers like Kruk sat. He draped his arms over the railing and took in the view. "Won't miss seeing broke-ass niggas coming up in here with more money than me. Believe that."

"We did get paid up in here."

"Forty at the door and ten percent of every fight." Knott shrugged. "Could've done better."

"Yeah? How?"

"Check it. You see these hoes taking people downstairs? Soon as they win, dogmen tie they dogs up in back and take a ho downstairs. Spend all their money on some pussy and we don't see none of that. The hoes do that shit all night, too."

"We ain't pimps, J."

"And don't want to be one, neither." Knott slid to the side of bleachers, pointing at the floor, where empty glassine bags and crushed vials littered the corner. "You see all the drugs up in here, right?"

RJ said he did.

Knott threw his hands up, neck jutted, mouth downturned at the corners.

RJ said, "Adrian gets some play off that."

"C'mon, man. Kruk gets his cousin to give him that homegrown weed just to be nice. Kruk knows he making bank up in here. We giving him a safe place to do business and what do we get? Not a goddamn thing. I'm telling you, this could have been run a lot better." Knott stood, walked down the bleachers and to the ring. "Co-branding. That's what they call it in business. Two or more companies working together."

RJ laughed. "Listen to you," he said. "You been reading about that shit?"

Knott turned, leaned against the balustrade, hands jammed in his puffer coat pockets. "Live and learn, man. My grand pappy would say that."

"We'll do better, J. Next thing we do, we'll do better."

"You know I got a couple dogs of my own now, right?"

"J, look, this here?" RJ sidestepped, pointing at the ring. "This ghetto as hell right here. I'm done with this stank-ass place and these dirty people. We got fiends showing up now. Shooting their arms up in the bathrooms and shit. Know what I'm saying?"

Knott didn't answer. RJ asked him again.

"Saw a couple needles in that middle one." Knott jerked his head toward the port-a-potties.

"And you want to keep this going? C'mon, yo. We better than this."

Knott came over to where RJ stood, standing behind him, and the two looked over the Cove. The horn of a cargo ship sounded in the distance but no ship was visible.

Knott said, "I'll miss it, though. Not just the money. This was our thing. Nobody ran it like we did. Nobody in this whole city. The coast, really."

"Yeah, you right, but we should leave out while we on top. You ain't out of trouble yet, know what I'm saying? Police still watching you. You don't need to get busted for this, too."

Knott nodded. RJ shut the sliding door and latched it. He started for the elevators and Knott followed.

"I bet I don't even want to go back there," RJ said, pointing at the other side of the room. An L-shaped drywall partition with paneled doors at either end abutted the concrete block that housed the elevator shaft.

They got in the elevator and RJ wrestled with the key, finally getting it to turn in the panel's keyhole.

Knott said, "So Kruk get another dog? I know that last one died."

"I think. Haven't talked to him about it." RJ looked up at where lit numbers would be if it weren't a service elevator. It moved at half the speed of a normal elevator.

"If Tep were still here, he'd be all up in this game."

"It ain't the same game. Shit's changed. He wouldn't know how to run this."

RJ pushed the button again, as if it would speed it up, then said, "Why you keep talking about dead people?"

"I don't know. Just been thinking about it lately. Timmy—"

"We didn't kill Timmy. Timmy killed Timmy. Stupid motherfucker was dead already. He burned half the people we know. Did his ass a favor."

RJ spit through his incisors, then turned and faced Knott. "Why you care anyway? You all about getting people took out now."

"Fuck you, yo."

RJ stared at Knott, smiling. He leaned in close but Knott ignored him. "When you going to get those moles burnt off?" RJ asked.

"When your Mama gonna suck my dick?"

"Shit, let me know if you find her. She owe me some birthday cake."

The elevator reached the bottom and the two stepped out. The door shut and RJ put the key in the exterior control panel, shutting it down. They walked to the exit where a row of four electrical panels were lined up on the wall. Only one of the handles was in the on position and RJ pulled it down. They stepped outside and the metal fire door slammed shut behind them.

"Get them shorties out here to clean up," RJ said. He scanned the building's empty lot. "Pup and them. Only got a week."

Knott walked down the short concrete staircase, lighting a cigarette. RJ looked into the dumpster that was at the bottom of a vinyl trash chute attached to the side of the building. In the setting sun he could see the splatter marks of blood and waste on the dumpster's floor. Sometimes they tossed the dogs down the chute but the yardboys, kids that watched the dogs in back and brought them out when it was time to fight, were supposed to keep everything clean, even the dumpster. After the last fight, Timmy Darrens was assigned to cleanup. The last task of his life, he failed.

"Lazy bitches," RJ said.

The Escalade battled the potholes in the lot with precision and Stevenson watched from the side of the building, just then realizing he had not brought a weapon. A chain-link fence surrounded most of the perimeter and someone got out of the passenger side after the Escalade passed through the gate, shutting it and chaining it up. Knott maybe, or the other person he heard. They were too far off to see. Stevenson stood and walked into the lot when the Escalade left.

None of the buildings within Stillman Point were in use and city road crews had long forgotten the roads leading to them. The desolation outdid anything surrounding the hospital. He had parked the BMW a few factories down between rotting stacks of pallets and followed the train tracks separating the buildings from the Cove's water. They ended next to the building he stood before, at a red caboose. Streams of rust had dried over the white B & O lettering on both sides of the railcar and all the windows were boarded. A circular seal was below the lettering with the Washington Capitol building in the center, sitting upon a smaller B & O insignia. The words LINKING 13 GREAT STATES WITH THE NATION circled the seal, reminding him of Zooey's tattoo. Her seal had its own words and he had yet to figure out what it meant.

FINEM

Coming around the dumpster, he climbed the steps and pulled on the door. Locked. A garage door fit for two tractor trailers was adjacent to the staircase and smelled of piss when he walked by. He didn't bother with it. He walked around the side where a sidewalk once was, now repossessed by weeds and piles of trash blown in from the water. Windows started at the second floor, too high to reach, and farther on a double door entrance was boarded over with plywood and 2x6 planks. The silos on the other side had no ladders and looked to be minutes from collapsing. Two conveyer belts started at the train tracks and led to sliding doors he assumed were locked. Seeing the other belts that had collapsed, he declined testing their stability and kept on until he was back at the dumpster. A square cage with metal bars encased a vinyl trash chute torn in multiple places, with faded yellow strands waving in the wind. At the top of the chute was an opening, and he looked around. Hearing only the traffic on the interchanges, he started the climb.

Halfway up, he came to a sliding door and gave it a yank but it didn't budge, locked long ago with rust sealing it for good. At the top, the chute's mouth was set back from where another sliding door had been. Strips of plastic separated inside from out and he stepped in slowly, listening. The hood of his sweatshirt caught on a wayward bolt and he reached around and yanked it. The cloth ripping was a knife in his heart and he froze, waiting for footsteps, voices. For lights to turn on.

Darkness and silence. He crouched behind what felt like a box and waited for his eyes to adjust. The stench of canine was thick to breathe. It wouldn't be easy, he had thought. He wouldn't find it, or there would be people. He would be spotted, or the bike wouldn't make the trek over the pothole-infested back road.

He stood, Achilles tendons popping. It was a narrow room and a flat panel door was cracked at the end, enough for daylight to cut in. He could see that the boxes were cages, some stainless steel and others gnarled plastic, stacked two and three high along the entire wall. Ropes hung from metal trusses behind him, across from another door, closed.

On the balls of his boots he crept along to the open door, peering through. A fire door with multiple dead bolts stood to the left and a rectangular steel mesh window straight across. To the right, another flat panel door, open wide. He looked out the window as he passed, seeing boarded factories flanking one another. Row upon row of retired industry.

199

More cages lined the left side of the next room, steel only and piled one atop another two high, six across. Past this a chicken wire enclosure, circular with a few sheets of gouged and stained plywood underneath and squares of soiled carpet samples nailed into it. The unpainted drywall was brushed with blood and scuff of all colors. The drywall abutted a concrete wall and another door, across from the chicken wire, was shut.

Glass crunched under his feet and he stooped and picked up the remnants of a vial. Dexamethasone Sodium Phosphate 4mg/mL. It would be sometime before he deduced its use for rapid wound care and edema, possibly for an injured fighter with some heart left. Another vial said Winstrol V. Anabolic steroid.

Behind the makeshift ring was an old diesel generator covered in dust, and on either side of it on the wall, multiple electrical panels large and small. The largest had newer, up to code wiring that led to numerous metal conduits. One supplied a single light in the room while others passed beyond the drywall partition. Above the generator, a manual hoist attached to a truss, its chains hanging to the floor and a hook snug at the top. An iron ladder bolted into the wall's corner led to a roof access door. A few rags hung on the ladder rungs and higher up a t-shirt smeared with blood hung on the end of a pipe coming through the roof.

He took the rags off the ladder and climbed up, yanking the t-shirt off as well. It had been hanging over a red gate valve the size of a hubcap, its paint peeling and the threading rusted. The vertical pipe was a 10-incher but a slightly smaller one elbowed on the other side of it and buddied along the trusses through the drywall partition. Across from the ladder was another gate valve, the same size and color, only its elbowed pipe went horizontally into the concrete wall. Feeder pipes.

The Ranger will evaluate all tactical options within urban terrain, both natural and man-made.

He thought on it, these pipes and what they were for. It was a grain operation in the beginning, when the railroad built it, but later they used it for textile manufacturing. There was no electricity then and the generator only looked decades-old, but the wiring from the current generation.

Textile manufacturing in the late 1800s. People smoked as they worked. Used lanterns if working at night.

He passed through the door and crept along the concrete wall, passing the elevator into the main area. It was empty of people and growing dim in the orange light of evening.

When he saw it, the arena and the comfortable seating with accommodating facilities, it grabbed him, held him in place. He had seen and smelled this before, in Panama, behind a cluster of burning hovels. Square rather than round, with wooden bleachers and barbed wire enclosing a dirt pit, it had been built under a tin roof with no walls. Clumps of bloody mud and dog hair were littered throughout. Private Collins knew what it was, for they did it in the south too. "Never had that in me," he had said, his back to it all the whole time, "to watch such a thing."

After a few attempts at trying to focus on why he was there—recon—his eyes would fall back on the arena. He took the camera out of the inside pocket of his field jacket and snapped pictures. The bleachers, the ring, the elevator, port-a-potties, the pipes overhead within the trusses.

The pipes.

On the other side of the wall where the gate valve was, the feeder pipe came out over the port-a-potties, stopping short of the end of the room. Six smaller and rusted pipes branched off of it evenly apart and ran over the arena, stopping just above the bleachers. The other gate valve's feeder pipe was the same, only its six pipes ran over the area between the bleachers and the elevator. These smaller pipes had half-inch holes about a foot apart. He focused the camera on this, walking backward toward the port-a-potties.

The bottom was cut out in the back of all three and a plastic tub inserted to catch waste. He came around and opened the door of the one on the end, snapping a picture before the smell got out. He shut the door slowly, then opened it again. The lid was up and the hole dark, but his eye had caught something when the flash went off, something that glistened in a way it shouldn't have at the bottom of a cesspool. He took another picture and shut the door again. As he switched the camera to view mode, he walked past the arena and behind the bleachers. The weathered sliding door clacked from the outside breeze. It swayed inward near the grooves in the floor where a bottom track had been. He yanked it open just enough to squeeze his head out. Below, next to the train tracks and caboose, stretched a field of tangled weeds and train parts mixed with the collapsed conveyor belts. The two belts still standing were at the opposite end of the building close to where he had watched the previous party depart. No railing. No net. A fall of thirteen feet or higher earned a full-body CAT scan. This fall would see a physician but not in a hospital.

He slid the door closed, came around the bleachers, and sat on the bottom bench.

The Ranger will know the type of attack required once intelligence is gathered.

There were three ways in and out but he doubted anyone would make the climb down what would be his insertion and exit platform, the trash chute. There would be external security, a few in the lot and at the door most likely. Once he'd taken out communication, the interior security would need to be neutralized, and the exterior prevented from getting in. A mass of people, too many for one aggressor, would all try to leave the kill zone at once. He was after one, but the rest would need to be distracted, wounded.

Collateral damage.

Guerrilla combat operations are to be at unexpected times and places. Low visibility and adverse conditions are to be used to the Ranger's advantage.

The stairwell would have to be cut off to block reinforcements and escape, leaving one way out and easing the ability to find the target.

Raid, with a frontal attack.

The camera beeped and the lens retracted. He turned it on again and scrolled the pictures, finding the one of the port-a-potty's innards. Grainy, it still confirmed what he thought he saw. He tucked the camera away and walked back to the port-a-potty, opening the door wide. He had the Phillips 66 penlight in his back pocket, and he took it out and shined it in the hole.

Among toilet paper dumplings and indecipherable foulness were two puppies, their skin shrunken around atrophied frames. The light glistened off the bare jawbones and the razor teeth implanted within. They lay muzzle to muzzle forming a V. One was black and white, the other all white, both from the same litter it seemed and dumped weeks into their life.

He let the door slam and stared until external light fell below the rim of the earth and his shadow became one with the Point's darkness.

17

"It's really...curvy," Zooey said, yanking the car's steering wheel around a patch of thicket encroaching the driveway.

"It'll open up to a straightway in about fifty meters," Stevenson said.

"How far is that?"

"Half a football field."

The Escort revved high and jerked in second gear around the turns. Stevenson leaned with the car, then grabbed the dashboard with both hands.

"Oh shut up," she said.

The driveway widened as they approached the open gate. She leaned forward, looked up at the sign.

"Wow, that's cool."

Stevenson nodded, not looking at it. The sign needed painting again and he dreaded the task. An ironsmith from Western Maryland, a Vietnam Vet, had put months into the job when Stevenson told him what he wanted. The words were cursive, and the letters with four sides. Spray painting it was not feasible. It had to be taken down, painted with a brush and greased when it was dry, and he trusted no one else to do it.

"How much land is there?"

"A hundred acres, mostly wooded. It backs to the quarry I was telling you about and that's another dozen acres at least."

Ahead a few yards, a doe popped her head out from the thicket and Zooey gasped, slammed on the brakes. They rocked forward, even though she was driving at walking speed.

"Don't see that downtown," Stevenson said.

The doe came out and stopped in the center of the drive, her tail flittering as she looked at the car, then behind her. Another nose poked out, lower to the ground, then a head. A fawn.

"Look at that," Zooey said, most of her words a whisper. She smiled, mouth closed.

The doe and fawn took their time crossing and eventually disappeared on the other side into dense green. Zooey let off the brake and let the car drift, looking into where the two had disappeared.

"I found a fawn once," Stevenson said. "It fell in one of the sediment traps at the quarry. Happens a lot down there. Baby foxes, too."

"Really?"

"I had just started working there. One night I left my keys to the house in the office so I had to go back. It's pitch black down there at night, and I hear this crying echoing in the pit. Sounded like a lamb. I couldn't see what it was until I was knee-deep in the mud. It would just scream when I put it down. I couldn't leave it and the doe was nowhere to be found."

"And?"

"My keys? Never found them."

She smacked his arm.

"She stayed at the quarry, up until we closed for Christmas. I brought her home and kept her in the tool shed behind the barn. Fed her goat's milk, grape vine leaves. I'd let her out when my father went to work. Hector didn't know what to think of her." Stevenson laughed at this, the monstrosity stooping its head down to smell the little being, then getting spooked when the fawn felt a sudden urge to hop.

"Hector?"

"You'll meet him."

The thickets widened and stopped abruptly when the drive became a straightaway. Birch trees lined either side and the house stood at the end. A square of frontage flanked the blacktop driveway, flat and mowed and without a single dead leaf.

"Oh my," Zooey said, stopping the car. "God." She put it in park and got out, leaving her door open. Stevenson got out as well.

"It's a toilet, I know," he said. "They should pave this place over. Put in a parking garage or something."

She ignored him, walking a few paces down the drive. A breeze bent the upper branches of the birch trees. Her quilted jacket danced at the hem.

"It's a Georgian mansion," she said. She raised a hand and pointed, her index finger bobbing. "Six chimneys?" She turned, hands on hips. "This place has six fireplaces?"

"Not enough?" Now he looked at the house. It seemed almost new to him, as if he was seeing it for the first time in many years. He never actually looked at the entire house—the front door, the interior, but never the whole thing.

"Well," she said, turning around, "I guess it'll do. But I'm slumming it here." She walked back to the car and put one foot on the floorboard, arms draped over the door. "It's all stone. Like a castle."

"Setters quartzite. It's all from Goddard Quarry. I—what?"

She was laughing, getting in the car. "You're a dork," she said.

They walked up the front stairs and Zooey held the railing, looking up at the awning.

"Not everybody can identify mansions," Stevenson said.

"I saw a lot of them when I was a kid. Rich friends. Does that work?" She pointed at the iron chandelier. "All twelve lights?"

"Better."

He gave the knocker a few light taps and the sound of it bounced down the halls on the other side. The double oak doors each had a speakeasy with an iron grill but the lone occupant of the house was too short to use them.

"I shouldn't have parked there," Zooey said, looking at the Escort. She had parked on the circular cobblestone, rather than driving around to the garage.

"Why? It's not in the way."

"I know but parking that thing next to this?" Hands outstretched. "It's like somebody pooped on the White House lawn."

Feet were approaching from the inside, sliding on the floor.

Swick-swick-swick

Stevenson stepped back, his fists clenched. The locks turned. Both doors opened.

"Menino Bonito," the little woman said, still in pajamas and an untied robe. She came at Stevenson and put her arms around his waist. "Onde osteve?" She swayed back and forth, hugging tight.

"Trabalho, trabalho, trabalho," Stevenson said. He leaned down to hug back. Zooey smiled at this.

"Carminda," Stevenson said, "this is Zooey."

Carminda let go, turning to Zooey and closing her robe as she did. She ran a hand down the side of semi-brushed hair, dark with random silver strands. The two shook hands, said hello at the same time.

Carminda stepped next to Stevenson, looking over Zooey. "Aqueles olhos."

"What?" Zooey asked, looking at Carminda, then Stevenson.

"It's cold," Carminda said, stepping inside. The two followed and Stevenson shut the doors behind them. He flipped the light switch, looking up at the chandelier outside through the transom window. All twelve lights came on.

"Did you get my card?" Carminda asked, her voice booming in the foyer.

"Yes. Thank you."

"He was a nice man. I sorry I didn't go to the funeral. I didn't know."

"I should have called you sooner. Sinto muito."

"It's okay."

Zooey, hands in her jacket pockets, wandered in small steps of no direction. She put a hand on the end of the curved banister, looking at the other staircase as she did. She tapped the coffee marble floor with her toe, eyes going to each of the black diamonds that connected the junction of four pieces.

"Are you hungry?" Carminda said to Stevenson.

"A little. Zooey?"

"I'm fine."

"That doesn't translate," Stevenson said.

"Oh. Um, yes?"

"That's better."

Carminda locked elbows with Zooey. "You like waffles?"

"Yes, ma'am."

"Okay then."

They started down the center of the foyer to the back of the house, passing under the walkway overhead.

"I have to call somebody," Stevenson said. "Be right there."

They were around the corner and gone, chatting away. To the right of the staircase were sliding doors, dark and tall like the entryway. He separated them and stepped in, closing them again.

He turned the wheel of the wall safe and yanked the handle. Inside were gold coins in plastic rolls, stacks of twenties bound haphazardly, so many he had forgotten. Underneath the money was a pile of paperwork, and he thought it strange then, the similarity to Coleman's safe. He lifted the papers but there was no framed picture, cigarette tin or gun—just paperwork linking him to the estate and the accounts it held. He took out four stacks of cash, closed it and re-hung the painting of a white stallion outrunning an approaching storm.

He sat at the cherry pedestal desk, with five drawers on either side and one between them. An accountant's light, a pushbutton desktop phone, and a crystal paper weight were all that sat on top. He put the money in the desk drawer and dug in his pocket while grabbing the phone receiver.

"Good Shepherd," a woman answered on the other end.

"Hi, I'm Dr. Stevenson. I'm looking for one of my patients. Vernon Lamb."

"Let me check the list."

He could hear the shuffling of papers, a clipboard's spring clip snapping. He sat back, turned the chair around. The built-in bookcase behind the desk took up the whole wall. Most of the books were leather but a few paperbacks were scattered about, all on lower shelves and out of sight. *The Odyssey. To Have and Have Not. The Great Gatsby. On Booze. Green Eggs and Ham. General Surgery.*

"Here he is. Signed in at six last night. He's probably eating. Is it an emergency?"

"It could be, eventually."

"Good enough for me. Hold on."

Stevenson thanked her but she had already put the phone down. He opened the top drawer. Pens and pencils with the old Johns Hopkins logo. A red marble. Paperclips. Nothing of value or shine.

Someone, Lamb, approached the phone, saying something about not having a doctor.

"I got no doctor so who the hell is this?"

"It's me, Vernon. Dr. Stevenson. From Saint Cat."

Pause. A sniff.

"Young buck?"

"You got it. How you doing?"

"My in trouble?"

"No, no. Everything's fine. Sorry to bother you like this but I need a favor."

"A favor? From me?"

"Yes sir. It's short notice but I'll need to cash it in soon."

Lamb mumbled a groan and a chair's cushion blew in the background. "Well, you know I owe you plenty. Whachu need?"

"A motorcycle."

"*Motorcycle* you said?"

"Yes, sir."

The chair creaked and whisker's scraped the phone's mouthpiece.

"Doc," Vernon whispered, "you been drinkin'?"

*　　*　　*

Zooey walked backward up the gravel path to the barn, hands deep in her pockets and shoulders hunched. A shiver ran across her face and upper body. Evening was settling in.

"Chilly," she said.

"It's colder up here," Stevenson said. He looked around the forest, expecting lightning bugs to blink in the blackness like green-eyed Cyclopes, what he thought was there as a boy after he read The Odyssey. But there were no blinking eyes. Summer was gone.

They spent the day talking and eating. Carminda spoke of a younger Stevenson and his exploits, all behind the back of "homem senor," his father, Lord of the estate. He showed her the innards of 14,000 square feet. Most of the upstairs bedrooms were empty and their vents closed off. One bedroom, the master, was kept available in case of guests and the linens on the bed were as old as the house. Carminda's apartment was in the basement, where they ate and talked, bypassing the main kitchen with all its overabundance of culinary machinery. The woman cooked with a skillet only but had an oven just in case.

"Mind if I ask a personal question?" Zooey asked, turning around. "About money?"

"Go for it."

"Does your job really pay that well?"

"To keep this place going? Not really but I don't pay a thing for upkeep. Dividends, interest. That takes care of it all. Carminda too. It's all wrapped up in the estate."

"But it's your house?"

"Depends on who you ask."

"Why do you speak in riddles?"

Stevenson stopped, looking back. Again, a sight not seen in years, despite walking by it numerous times. Only the great room light was on, the glass chandelier sparkling through the two story window.

"It's mine if you ask the state of Maryland. But if you ask me, it's Carminda's. Her relatives are in Brazil but she doesn't want to go back, and there's no sense in her having her own house if she can stay here as the caretaker. It's worked out fine so far."

"You don't want to sell it?"

"Where would she live then?"

They walked on.

"So what does a kid do by himself out here?" Zooey asked.

"I read a lot. Walked around the woods and the quarry." Stevenson pointed off to the left down the hill where it rose again and met the forest. "About a click through those woods there is Goddard's."

"Click?"

"Half a mile, give or take."

"So no kids around?"

"No. I had school friends. Acquaintances, actually. Lots of those."

"One of those background kids. The ones that were never in the front row of a yearbook picture."

"You got it."

She looked him over. Waiting.

Stevenson said, "I didn't know where I fit in. Was I black? White? Nobody picked on me about it but I didn't hang out that much with other kids. Summertime, I was mostly on my own."

"Did you think about her? And your brother?"

She took a step over when she said this and he thought she was expecting something, a tirade maybe.

"When I first moved here, yes. When you've no one to talk to but the horses and trees, sooner or later your mind starts to fill in the quiet with memories. Bad or good, doesn't matter."

"Who was Hank's father? I'm guessing it wasn't your father?"

"No, not him. The birth certificate was blank under the father's name so I never found out. I don't think anyone knew, except my mother."

He could see her looking at him from the corner of his eye. Formulating questions.

Stevenson said, "What about you? Old friends still around?"

"Some, but once I graduated, forget it. Only a handful were around at first but I haven't seen any of them in years. They either moved away or became professional parents. That's okay. I've always been a bit of a loner. I was always happy with reading or listening to music in my room all day."

"What did you listen to?"

"Everything. You?"

"Let's see. Beatles, Johnny Paycheck, Bad Brains, Marvin Gaye, Zeppelin, Floyd."

Zooey said, "Cream, Billie Holiday, Wham, Iron Maiden."

"You just said Wham and Iron Maiden in the same breath. I believe that's punishable by death in certain countries."

She laughed, and the vapors of the chill consumed her head.

"I never got past the mid-nineties with music," Stevenson said. "Once Cobain died, everything after felt ototoxic."

"Hard to disagree with that."

They came upon the barn. The weathercock on the cupola was bent slightly and frozen in the breeze. Both doors were open, and the light above them did little to illuminate the inside. He looked at the doors, the track it hung on.

Zooey sniffed, cleared her throat.

"You like horses?" Stevenson asked.

She said she did.

"Big horses?"

"They're all big."

He smiled, stepping into the darkness of the barn. The alfalfa and barley were light on the senses, the premises cleaned recently. At the last stall he opened the gate and walked back out, with the clip-clop of perfect cadence following.

"You should step aside," Stevenson said.

Zooey did just as Hector appeared from the barn and she stepped back some more. Under the light his haunches were rounded, solid. His head bobbed and his mane rippled with each step.

"Uhh," she stammered, looking behind her and taking her hands out of her pockets.

"Hey old man," Stevenson said. "C'mon."

Hector bowed slightly to smell Stevenson's hand. He sniffed and blew out his nostrils, then shook his head. His exhales billowed, and the steam rose above like snow clouds.

"He's huge," Zooey said.

"Almost nineteen hands tall."

She came around Stevenson, reaching her hand past him as if she would push him in for sacrifice if the horse went wild. Hector sniffed her, chin whiskers tickling her pale hand, his lips nibbling. She giggled, pulling her hand back. "Hector?"

"The previous owner named him. I don't think my father wanted him but I guess the price was right. He's a Friesian, but there's no paperwork to prove it. No record of registration or who he's the offspring of."

"Is he the only one?"

"Used to have Arabians in every stall but we sold them when my father died. They were too much for Carminda to take care of."

"I bet he gets lonely."

"There's an equestrian center down the road. They come by twice a week and check him over. Sometimes they bring his girlfriend."

"Girlfriend?"

"Don't feel sorry for him. Trust me, he's got the life. All this land, warm stall. He doesn't look that old, does he?"

"No."

Hector grew bored of them and wandered around the side of the barn. The grass was taller here and his bites sounded like the seam of someone's pants giving way. Beyond the barn sat the tool shed, a fraction of the size and built with the same stone. Next to it was a horse trailer with a tarp overtop.

"What happened to the fawn you rescued?" Zooey said.

With nowhere to go, nothing to call her attention to, he looked at the moon, the barn, the dipping hills and surrounding forest. Hector urinated like a garden hose opened full blast.

"My father found her one day when I was in school. He told Carminda they carry Lyme disease, rabies."

"I don't want to know," Zooey said. She approached Hector and stroked his neck. He paid her no mind. "This was no place for a child."

Honking rose up from the distance, one, then another, some in unison. Soon a skein flew overhead, their calls bouncing over the hills.

"It wasn't that bad," Stevenson said. "I had Carminda. I grew up in a mansion." His tone was that of someone listing positives but there was nothing more to list.

"I'd rather be in a shack with loved ones than a mansion with no one."

Stevenson nodded, saying nothing. Her hand stopped mid-stroke on Hector's neck.

"I didn't mean that," she said.

"Sure you did."

"It was rude."

"No it wasn't."

She tucked her hands in her coat but stayed next to Hector, watching Stevenson.

"What are we doing?" she asked. "Us, I mean."

"Hanging out. Forming a. Something. I don't know, why?"

"I don't want to keep making an ass of myself in front of a stranger."

"That's the best audience you could have. That way it doesn't matter."

"You matter."

"So I'm not a stranger?"

"I guess not."

He caught her smile before she turned to the horse.

"I better get him inside. They're creatures of habit. Throw them off schedule and they get weird. Or diarrhea."

"Yikes."

Stevenson clapped his hands and whistled and Hector's head popped up, ears independently turning and twitching. He turned and trotted back into the barn, leaving Zooey alone in the tall grass.

"I don't think it's possible for you to make an ass of yourself," Stevenson said when he came out of the barn. "Not to me."

She didn't answer. Nodded, looked at her shoes. Smiled. But didn't answer.

After Hector settled in his stall, Stevenson pulled on the door handle, looking up at the tracks. The bottom of the door swung upward when he gave it a yank.

There are three techniques of breach a squad can use. Explosive.

"Ready?" Zooey said, walking down the path.

Ballistic.

"Yeah." Stevenson let the door down gently, walking backward. Deep within, the turbines whirred, overpowering the ringing.

And mechanical.

18

"Where Pup at?" Knott asked.

"Front room," Adrian said, scrolling through his phone. He leaned forward, turning his head to the door. "Hey Pup!"

They were in the back room of the Bean Street house, waiting. Once a master bedroom, the stripped down box had no resemblance to a place of rest now. A church pew lined the entire wall on the left of the corner entrance and another, where Adrian sat, ran catty-corner to it. Between them stood a doorway with no door, a former bathroom, now with holes in the floor where pipes had been ripped out and sold at the scrap yard. An old two-person school desk sat at the front of the room and to the side a wicker rocking chair where Knott rocked, pulling on a half-spent Kool. A single 60-watt mechanics light hung from the center of the peeling ceiling, connected to an extension cord that passed through one of the two boarded windows. Tags of graffiti swirled all over the boarded windows, but the plaster walls were bare.

The front door opened and closed and footsteps stomped up the stairs. Tink appeared in the doorway. His sunshine warm-up suit hissed with each stride.

"'Sup, short bus," Adrian said.

Tink mumbled expletives and sat at the other end of the bench, jolting Adrian.

"*Boy*," Adrian said, standing. "Careful."

"Cold as hell up here," Tink said. He crossed his arms over his belly.

"You ain't never been cold in your life."

"Serious, Adrian. Fuck you, aight?"

Knott laughed himself into a coughing fit. Pup walked in and sat next to Tink. Half the size of the others, his feet dangled.

"Whachu up to, shorty?" Knott asked him.

Pup shrugged. "There's a rat up in here. I saw him."

"Why you ain't kill it?" Tink asked, looking at the floor around him. "Hate rats."

"Too fast," Pup said. His feet swung and he gripped the edges of the bench, looking up at Tink, smiling. Two front teeth were missing. "You afraid of rats."

"No I ain't."

Pup accused Tink again and they bickered back and forth. Adrian laughed, his fist to his mouth as if trying to keep his hand warm. Tink jerked forward and Pup jumped down, ready for flight. Tink stayed put.

"Faggot," Tink said in a sigh.

"Yo mama is."

"What?"

"You heard me."

Tink rose this time.

"Sit your ass down," Knott said. "He ain't nothin' but a shorty."

Tink flopped down, rattling Adrian's seat. "Why er'body on me?"

"'Cause there ain't nowhere else to be," Knott said. "Everywhere I look, there you is."

This set Adrian and Pup off in guffaws and choking giggles. Knott controlled himself, feeling sorry for the big man. It had been this way for decades, when they were all shorties. Knott had been the one that insisted everyone call Tink by his name, not KFC or The Sit Down or just Fat Boy. The order stuck, but they still teased him, usually without the nicknames.

The front door opened and closed. Someone took the steps by two.

"'Sup," RJ said. He sat on the table. "This it?"

"All we need," Knott said.

RJ took a pack from inside his coat and lit up. "Point look like shit, y'all. You get on 'em, J?"

Knott said he did. RJ would repeat everything Knott had told the crew already, like always.

"Pup, you and some boys got to get up there and clean your yard. The pit needs a new carpet. Got to sweep up."

Pup nodded, spitting through the gap in his teeth.

"I got carpet," Knott said. "I'll bring it up tomorrow."

"Spray some scratch lines on it," RJ said. He pulled from the cigarette, looking up at the light. Smoke drifted from his nostrils.

He said, "Just got off the phone with Georgia. This one going to be big. He got dogmen coming from north and south. Three grand champion fights and a whole bunch of others."

"How many you think?" Knott asked.

"At least fifteen."

The room gasped. Tink hooted.

"One of them fights is at a hundred large. Might go up more."

Everyone hooted this time. Adrian slapped his hands together. Knott leaned forward on the rocking chair.

RJ stood, arms wide open. "See what I'm saying? Y'all feel me now? We gotta be ready."

The three on benches spoke at once to each other, not listening, just talking with smiles and wide eyes. RJ waved at them to settle down.

"Georgia ain't going to fall out this time?" Knott asked.

"Had a long talk about that. He said he ain't drinking until the show's over. Too many matches going down."

"How old is that man?" Tink asked.

RJ said, "Too old." He took a last pull on the cigarette and crushed it with wheat Timberlands, the laces loose and untied. "You doing the upstairs door again, Tink. $60 a head. You ain't no change machine, neither. They got exact or they got to go."

Tink nodded, eyebrows raised. The entry fee had gone up.

"Adrian, you the usual, too. Scale and moneyman. Any them dogs overweight, you get that penalty money if they still want to get their dog in the pit. Don't want to hear nobody's bullshit about the scale being wrong. Either they pay the penalty or get the fuck out, you hear? J will back you up."

Knott the Enforcer. His whole life. In adulthood, it was a .45 that was the backup to the backup, but he rarely needed it.

RJ stepped over to Tink. "Your cousins want in?"

"Who? Bing Bing and them?"

RJ frowned, jutted his neck.

Tink said, "Yeah, I guess. They watching the downstairs door and the parking lot, right?"

"You know it."

"Same pay?"

"Little more."

"I'll get on 'em."

RJ nodded and stepped over to Pup. "You get your boys, too. You'll need help."

"I can do it," Pup said, voice high in defense.

"You got the fight dogs so that's what, like thirty at least. Then you got dogmen bringing some to sell. Few baits, too. It's going to be busy back there. Dogs, dogmen, yard boys. Lot of traffic."

"They roll out when the matches start," Pup said. Dry snot rings circled his nostrils and Knott wanted to wipe them off.

"Why you play with me?" RJ said. "Do what I say."

Knott said to Pup, "It ain't wrong getting some help, shorty. Ain't nobody thinking you can't run the yard. Just going to be a big night is all."

"I'll be right there," Tink said. "Anybody cause problems I'll—"

"You asleep half the time on the stool," Pup said. "How you going to help me?"

RJ turned to Tink as Adrian laughed.

"No stool," RJ said. "You trying to get robbed?"

Tink stared at Pup. Pup smiled wide, eyes closed.

"And look here," RJ said. "J and me been talking. Them hoes wanting you to let them in one of the other floors so they can get business done? Naw. First floor only. That way Bing Bing can keep an eye on them. You make sure Bing gets a cut. They coming up there to get work from our crowd, they got to pay some rent."

Tink nodded. RJ went back to the desk and sat down. He looked at Knott.

"Anything else?"

"Yeah. Adrian."

"What?" Adrian asked.

Knott said, "Get as much homegrown from Kruk's boy Rogo as you can. Whatever he got to give, get it. We'll turn it around the next night."

"Get that cake baked," Adrian said.

"Kruk coming?" Tink asked.

"You know he is. Been to the last three fights. Georgia said he got two matches set up this time."

"Most his dogs can't fight," Pup said. "I seen his yardboy give them the needle before they go out and they still lose."

"That's because his dogs are straight off the chain," Knott said. "Ain't been prepped. No exercise, training, diet. They have to go through their keep first. No keep, they lose every time."

"Fuck him," Tink said. "He killed Tep."

Tep Langer was found in a rowboat, spread-eagle and naked, save for a pair of multicolored tube socks. The boat had been set by anchor in the center of the Inner Harbor for all to see from the brick promenade. No one but the tourists were there, seeing a lone black man with a hole in his forehead and a few in his chest, being poked at by seagulls and grackles. Those of the west side, including Knott, heard of their beloved son's death by word of mouth and a blurb on the news. An empire had ended, and the remnants scooped up by Kruk and his crew. The west, and most of the south, disallowed this new empire and no Kruk crew members were ever tolerated on their side by residents or the rising independents—corner boys for Langer who had forged ahead on their own, forming their own crews and laying claim to single corners rather than whole territories. The west side without Langer had armed itself again and shootings rose to new levels of frequency.

RJ said, "Tep was in the game. He knew what the risks were so don't be blaming Kruk."

They moaned some but kept it short. Tink yawned.

"We done?" Tink asked.

"Yeah we done," RJ said, waving him to go on.

The three got up and eventually left. Adrian and Tink went downstairs and Pup went back to the front room, but not before Knott grabbed him and wiped his nose clean.

"You didn't tell them it was the last fight night," Knott said to RJ, once Pup was out of sight.

"We'll tell them when we pay them," RJ said. "Better that way."

19

*T*he basement floor chilled Stevenson's fingertips and the last set of push-ups caused his arms to tremble. Next to him, notes, sketches, open books, and pictures of the Point covered the weight bench. He would rest a minute between sets, looking over it all, scanning chapters he had memorized years ago. Each sentence read like a pull-start rope yanked back, the motor releasing the lessons of another life.

> *Simple pneumonics are to be utilized for planning assaults small and large.*
> *To begin, use METT-T: Mission, Enemy, Terrain, Troops, Time available.*
> *Once detailed reconnaissance is obtained, move to SALUTE:*
> *Size of the enemy, Activity of the enemy, Location, Uniforms of the enemy,*
> *Time, Equipment.*

Field Manual 90-10, Military Operations on Urban Terrain, had been updated with a new title since he had left the military, FM 3-06, Urban Operations. The corner bookstore in Fells Point, with a magic and costume shop on one side and a sports bar on the other, had a tattered copy in the military history section. Stevenson bought this, the US Army Guerrilla Warfare Handbook, and a US Army Ranger Handbook. He visited the costume shop and found more than he needed.

What are we doing?

He held her hand on the way home, wanting to, but also to keep her still. The brown paper bag behind his seat held the cash taken from the safe and he didn't want her poking through it. At home, car idling in front, they held hands for a minute and spoke in short sentences to fill the void. Eventually, they ran out of things to say and just stared at one another. He would have kissed her but the mission had started, and Knott's face flickered like candlelight in the corner of his eye.

A tapping rattled the basement window.

Taren.

"You asleep?" Taren asked, crouched, bookbag on his back.

"I'm up. Give me a minute."

He locked up and waved to Kendra. Her door screeched when she went back in and she had to open and close it twice. He pulled his skull-cap down past his ears and trotted up the street to catch up with Taren.

"Forgot your gym bag," Taren said.

"I'll come back for it."

They rounded the corner, both of them scanning the street.

"Your door broke?" Stevenson asked.

"The hinge came off. Mama said she'll fix it when she gets some time."

"Tell her I can do it."

"Cool. Come over after school. You working?"

"Sort of. I have a few days off but I have errands to run."

They crossed Broadway and Stevenson checked his Timex, taking post. The day workers were assembling at the convenience store, watching traffic, ready to be first up to the window. A few had tool belts on.

Lamb had called, asking for Stevenson to repeat himself after every other sentence. He made a mental note to personally clean the wax out of Lamb's ears when they met up again. Lamb's phone, prepaid and disposable, was his first. He was in the county, on his way to look at the motorcycle Stevenson had found in the classifieds, and was unsure of how to act like he knew what a buyer of a motorcycle should ask. *Fastest Production Motorcycle Ever Made*, the ad said. *Best Offer. Cash Preferred.*

"See you after school?" Taren said. He stayed put, waiting for an answer. He scratched the back of his head.

"You need a haircut," Stevenson said. He reached out to Taren's head but was too slow.

"So do you." Taren crossed his arms. "C'mon, please? You can eat dinner with us."

"Don't you have homework?"

"I always got homework."

The bell rang, the first of two, each five minutes apart. After the second, the doors would be locked.

"I'll do my best."

"You better."

Taren held up a fist and Stevenson met it with his. Two children, a boy and girl the same age as Taren, crossed the street up ahead. The girl, her braided pigtails bobbing as she hopped, was yelling for Taren to hurry up.

"Girlfriend?" Stevenson asked.

"She in my class." Taren walked, then skipped backward. "I told her you was my Pop." He turned around and sprinted, his book bag swinging back and forth across his back.

Swick-swick-swick

Stevenson watched him join his two classmates and they walked together, the girl giving Taren a shove when they all tried to squeeze into the corner entrance at the same time.

His new phone rang, also disposable. A "chuck-it", the clerk called it. A "burner". He took it out and listened.

"Doc?"

"Yeah."

"Found the house. Now what?"

"I should be by that way in an hour. I'll call you when I'm ready. That okay?"

"Yes, sir. I'm in a cab and got plenty of money."

"Remember what we talked about?"

Lamb said he did. Stevenson hung up and walked back the way he came until he came upon a bench. He sat and took a scrap of paper out. He read the international number, dialed it.

"Bonjour, ce signal de la confiture," a woman said.

"Hi. Speak English?"

"Yes, monsieur. How may I assist you?"

"I was interested in the S240 model."

"The mobile unit, yes. Now with 4G jamming capability. What would you like to discuss?"

"I need it shipped overnight."

"Of course. To the states?"

"Yes, madame."

"That will not be a problem. Your name please?"

"Ben. Carson."

Flurries fell scant on the western suburb of Baltimore County as Stevenson watched the parking lot of USA Everyday Surplus. He had ridden to Fiddler's Green and exchanged the BMW for the pickup truck in the garage. After charging the battery, filling the tires, and grabbing the tarp that covered the horse trailer, he saw the registration sticker on the license plate was expired so he peeled the one off Carminda's Honda. He had hoped she wasn't going anywhere but let half the air out of the rear tires to be sure.

The truck revved up and down when in park. The idle valve was dirty, he assumed, but overall it did fine, considering it sat in the garage for years with only the occasional startup to keep the fluids flowing. The heat worked well, too well, and his eyelids were heavy. It was odds and ends now, the core supplies purchased and the motorcycle retrieved. Lamb met the seller at a gas station and made the purchase, then walked away when Stevenson gave him the signal from across the station's lot. The caboose at Stillman Point would be the supply hooch, he had decided. It could be secured with chains and a lock. He would alter the bike there, removing the nonessentials and disconnecting the lights. Spray paint it flat black.

The surplus store, a warehouse on the main drag of Catonsville sandwiched within smaller strip malls, dry cleaners, garages and closed down sno-ball stands, was open until eight. The lot was empty and the streetlamps had yet to come on. Stevenson adjusted his skullcap, put on cheap sunglasses, and checked himself in the rearview mirror. He pulled his lips in, then pursed them, testing the thick mustache he'd purchased at the costume shop in Fells Point. Hideous, but necessary. He got out and shut the door, adjusting the tarp over the motorcycle and blue fuel cans that filled the truck bed.

He checked his Timex.

See you after school?

"Damn."

Taren. It would be after midnight by the time he got home, too late for dinner. He walked across the lot, thinking of apology gifts a surplus store might have.

When he entered, a chime rang. Behind a counter to the immediate left an older gentleman sat on a stool. He was shuffling receipts in his hand like cards. Behind him, an office, the door open and lights out.

"Hey partner," he said, "I'm closing soon so keep it short."

"Roger that."

"What're you looking for? I can save you some time."

"I see what I need right there," Stevenson said. He pointed at the back and kept walking.

The floor was crowded with a sea of inventory and lit with a few rows of warehouse halogens. The aisles were narrow and only a few large enough for the average American to navigate. He passed weight sets, canoes hanging from the ceiling, circular racks of clothes, bows and arrows, tents, camping gear. A stuffed black bear stood in the middle of it all, up on his hind legs, arms high and wide. The pose was unnatural, for the bear showed no teeth and the doll eyes glued in its sockets looked ahead, questioning more than menacing.

Headless mannequins in jumpsuits of all types lined the back wall, each standing on a shelf at eye level. More crowded racks filled with uniforms—mechanics, janitors, delivery men, pilots—stuck out below the mannequins.

"*I can pull those down for you,*" the intercom boomed.

The shopkeep leaned out of the office, waving. He held an old chrome PA microphone and kept his finger on the talk button, his wheezy exhales filling the building. "*If you can't find what you need, let me know.*"

"Will do," Stevenson said.

The last mannequin wore a neon yellow suit festooned with racing patches. Stevenson fished in the rack, flipping collars one by one, checking sizes.

Two Hundred Proof Drag Strip was a few miles away from the surplus store and a brief helicopter ride to downtown. Saint Cat saw the occasional racer from the strip, the ones that weren't medevaced to Maryland Shock Trauma or Hopkins Burn Center. Every year, at least one bypassed all three and was taken the long way with lights off to the county medical examiner's office.

His phone, the old one, buzzed in his shirt pocket. He unzipped and pulled it out, crouching.

"You there?" Zooey asked.

"I'm here."

"I'm getting off early. Are you around?"

"No. I'm getting some chores done for Carminda. I won't be back until late."

"Well, you can call me later if you want."

"I want."

"Hey, I bought you a Minor Threat CD."

"God, I haven't heard—"

"Find everything you need, partner?"

Stevenson dropped the phone and shot up, his arm cocked back. The old shopkeep stumbled, bug-eyed, his foot catching on the leg of a rack. Stevenson grabbed the man before he fell.

"Sorry, sir," Stevenson said. "You scared me."

"My fault," he said. His feet pedaled backward until he stood upright and steady. Stevenson let him go. "My wife blames me for her weak bladder."

"That'll do it." Stevenson picked up the phone and listened, but Zooey was gone. He tucked it away and looked at the suit display.

"They send you over from the strip?"

"Sure."

"What are you looking for?"

"Black Nomex."

"Chest size?"

"48."

He looked Stevenson up and down. "About 6'2"?"

"Yes, sir."

He reached in the rack, the hangers squeaking on the metal bar. He turned sideways, facing Stevenson, biting his lower lip with yellowed dentures. He pulled a suit out and checked the collar.

"It's Nomex and it's your size but it ain't black. Sorry about that. Can you suffer with this?"

"Little loud, but if that's all you have, I'll take it."

He draped it over Stevenson's shoulder and walked back down the aisle.

"Suit's flame resistant so they'll probably be able to identify you afterward. You do have a helmet, right?"

"Yes, sir."

As they passed the bear, Stevenson rubbed his hand over its rump.

"Is there a story with him?" Stevenson asked, waiting for the man to turn around before he stuck his thumb at the bear.

"That's Bubba. Head of security. He got here around the time Carter was elected." The shopkeep leaned in, lowered his head and waved Stevenson to come closer. "I've been telling people for years I tracked him down in the Adirondacks but really, it was the wife that got him. The poor beast wandered into the wrong campsite while I was off doing what bears do in the woods. Bess took care of business with a little .22 shot to the head. I came back and there he was, dead as a doorknob. Sprawled out like a rug. Where'd he come from, I asked her. Know what she said?"

"What?"

Stevenson watched the shopkeep's smile flatten at the edges.

"Can't remember. It'll come to me."

At the counter, the shopkeep took his stool.

"Cash or charge?"

"Cash."

Stevenson took the suit from off his shoulder and rested it on the glass countertop. Military memorabilia filled the case underneath, mostly from World War II. Patches, knives, a few medals, and a Walther P38, the Nazi Army pistol of choice, were on the upper shelf. Stevenson was reaching in his pocket for money when he saw the row of gas masks on the bottom shelf. All were black with clear round eyepieces and a thick metal filter over the mouth. In the corner, under the last mask, was one of a different character.

The shopkeep said, "That suit is slightly used but nobody ever got burnt up in it." He jabbed the buttons on the cash register and the receipt churned out at the top.

"What kind of mask is that?"

He looked at Stevenson, then into the case. "Oh that? Something, huh?" He got off the stool and slid the case's door back. He pulled both out, the black one and the other, and laid them on the jumpsuit. "Found those in Merkers. Snuck them back in my rucksack. You ever heard of Merkers?"

"Northeast of Frankfurt."

"That's right," the shopkeep said. "Paid attention in school, I see."

Stevenson pushed aside the black mask and picked up the other with both hands, holding it close for inspection.

"I don't think they'll let you race with that on."

"How much?"

"Not for sale."

Given the abrupt reply, Stevenson eased off. "Sure is different from the others."

"That it is. Look at those eyepieces. I always assumed it was an officer's mask, considering how much detail went into it. Never seen another like it."

The eyepieces were smaller than the others, oval and slanted downward, the lenses crimson, dark and impenetrable to light. He couldn't see his fingertips on the other side.

"I can't even tell you what it's made of. That ain't rubber or latex, I know that. Some kind of leather maybe? Dyed with food coloring?" The shopkeep reached over and pinched the mask between his index finger and thumb, rubbing them together. "Remember the soap commercial where the Irishman would cut a slice off a bar of soap?"

"Irish Spring."

Stevenson turned it around and around again before coming back to the front. The mouthpiece was copper and rectangular, only slightly raised, unlike the others.

"I think there was a piece that was supposed to attach to the front. Doubt that little filter would do much good against a whiff of poison gas but who knows." The shopkeep jabbed the last of the transaction out. "I got you here at $505.27."

"I'll give you an even grand if you throw this in with a few Ka-Bar knives."

The shopkeep looked at his customer, then the mask. His chest raised, lowered. The PA was still on, buzzing.

"Bess always hated those masks looking up at her. For the longest time she said it reminded her of the man that came back from the war. Been some years since I told somebody their story."

"I'll give it a good home," Stevenson said. He laid a stack of fifties on the counter, his hand over top and waiting for recognition.

"It's a deal."

The shopkeep retrieved three knives from the case and set them next to the mask. He licked his fingertips and pulled a plastic bag from under the register.

"Keep the bag," Stevenson said, scooping everything up. "Take care."

He trotted to the end of the lot, looking around, the parking lot's lamps on now and casting long shadows of him fleeing. He got in the truck and tossed the purchases on the floor.

He had to make another stop before heading to Stillman, to set up. He needed one more tool.

A weapon.

20

RJ stood at the top of the stairwell, counting a brick of bills. There were two others of the same weight in Tink's coat, bound by rubber bands. Numerous dogs barked in both rooms and the noise echoed, even with the doors closed.

"I stopped counting an hour ago," Tink said, looking over the railing at approaching footsteps.

"What?" RJ shouted, still counting. Back and forth he'd go, between the main floor and the stairwell, checking the money.

"I said I stopped counting an hour ago. They just keep coming."

"Adrian got even more," RJ handed the brick back. "Gotta be like two hundred people up in here."

"You going to give me my stool back now?"

RJ ignored him and went back in, opening the door to where the chicken wire pit was. Every cage had a dog and the yardboys had to shout to hear one another. Two sat on the cages of their fighters, waiting for their names to be called. Pup and another boy were next to the chicken wire pit, holding a scrawny pit bull down on its side. The dog, every rib visible under patches of white and brown, gyrated its neck and hind legs under Pup's grip. Darkened scars overlapped crusted new ones.

"Get your knee on it, Pup," RJ said, stepping up. "Damn."

Pup put his knee on the dog's rib cage as the other boy duct-taped its hind legs together. The dog gagged and cleared its throat, then breathed in as deeply as it could. One of the yardboys jumped off his cage and took a leash from around his neck. He opened the cage and a head, chocolate with its fur short and scalp tight against a boulder of a skull, poked out. It looked around, its whole body wagging and shaking the cage. It came out after the yardboy attached the leash and shook front to back, as if stepping out of water.

"Toss him in," RJ said to Pup.

Pup picked the taped dog up and it put up no fight, its head bouncing in Pup's arms. RJ stepped back, losing his breath when the dog looked his way. The eyes were scarred white, treated with battery acid so not to see its attacker.

Pup heaved it over the chicken wire and it landed with a single bounce and lay motionless. They all watched, waiting for it to move. The yardboy straddled his dog, holding it at the chest and neck, its barks screeching, begging.

RJ said, "You killed it, Pup." He leaned over the wire, yanking the dog's taped legs. It didn't resist or move. "This the only bait you got?"

"Yeah. Timmy usually bring some but I ain't seen him."

"Man, fuck Timmy and fuck you. Now what's this shorty going to bump his dog with?"

The yard boy was putting his dog back in the cage. He seemed neither burdened nor delighted.

Pup looked at the floor, then to his partner, an older kid with kinked hair who was looking away from it all. He found a task in the corner and busied himself there, out of RJ's path.

RJ stepped toward Pup and Pup backpedaled, turning as if ready to run. He never liked Pup, never understood why Knott let him hang around.

"Last damn fight and you got to fuck up now," RJ said. He reached for Pup but the side door opened, blocking his grasp.

"Go on, bitch," Knott said. He had one hand on the upper arm of a woman in a red one-piece skirt, the other on the back of her neck. She was wearing a hair net. "Move!"

"What about my weave?" she asked, stumbling in matching heels.

Knott told her to shut the hell up. He moved her out the door and pushed her to the stairwell where Tink took over expulsion. She pulled away from Tink and started a tirade of obscenities. Knott came back in and slammed the door.

"C'mon, yo," Knott said to RJ, heading back to where he'd come from. "They're being weighed in now."

RJ looked in the practice pit, spitting through his upper incisors. If you want it done right, his father would say.

"Go throw it down the chute, Pup." RJ pointed at him, following Knott out the door. "You going to take care of it later."

*　　*　　*

Stevenson sat in the corner of the caboose since sunset, geared up and mask on, humming cadence calls to pass the time and clear his head.

Heeeeey I feel alright now
Feeling good—Feeling Good!
Feeling good—Feeling Good!
Airborne—Airborne!
Airborne—Airborne!

The lenses changed all things to red until darkness finally settled in. The wind off Cherry Cove seeped between the caboose's slates, chilling the inside space and his gloved hands. The bike's gas tank chinked when the temperature dropped another few degrees. When evening settled, shouts called up from the parking lot, someone yelling out where to park and how not to, but the last hour was silence. The building stood far off from the train tracks, too far for his tinnitus to pick up on what was happening inside.

He checked his Timex.

H-hour had arrived.

He stood, smacking the sheathed Ka-Bar knife on his right leg, and the holster inside the suit.

Weapons loose.

He opened the back door and it moved silently on hinges slathered with ball bearing grease. The sky had been clear when he entered but now flurries covered the foliage and melted on the collapsed conveyor belts and scrap metal. He crept down the three steps and got on his stomach, looking through the underbelly of the caboose. Only the lights of the top floor were on, the rest of the building an asymmetric black mass against the gray sky. He stood and turned around, smacking the Ka-Bar once more to reassure himself. The tracks were clear, the water dead.

Almost—Almost!
To the top—To The Top!
Airborne—Airborne!

The side fire door was closed but Stevenson heard someone grunting one-word answers and two-word questions in cell phone vernacular. In the distance, beyond the parked cars, someone stood at the gate by their lonesome.

He passed under the trash chute where it arched like a boot and emptied into the dumpster. On the other side was the concrete landing of the exterior staircase. He reached up and knocked lightly on the bottom of the door.

The door opened and banged against the railing. Then nothing but breathing.

"What the hell?" A man in a cashmere topcoat and wingtips stepped onto the landing and looked over the lot, letting the door close behind him. He walked to the edge of the steps.

Stevenson grabbed him by the ankles and yanked. He fell too rapidly to protect his face and his forehead hit the concrete before the rest of his body. Stevenson dragged him under the railing and sat him up so his back was in the corner of the staircase's block and the building. Blood bloomed from a linear laceration in the center of his forehead and ran down the center of his nose as Stevenson frisked him, finding a snub nose .357. His head rolled but jerked back halfway, his parted bangs falling forward like closing curtains.

"What?" he began, then, swaying a little, slumped to his side.

Stevenson threw the revolver towards the water, then took out the tin cigarette case from inside his suit. He opened it and ran a gloved finger over the inscription, POKE. Six small syringes were capped and full and he removed one and put the case back. He pushed the doorman over and pulled his waistband down just enough to show a strip of upper glutcus. He drove the needle in and slammed the plunger.

"What," the doorman began again, then faded.

Stevenson dragged him around the building and lay him flat under the attached conveyor belts. He started for the stairs, then stopped. He went back and closed the man's coat, then rolled him on his side so he faced the building.

He crept low up the steps and slid in through the door, pulling it tight so it latched and locked. An unprotected light bulb shone above and he unscrewed it and crushed it underfoot. Beyond was another doorway into a darkened open area and he heard moaning coming from somewhere deep within it. People were in there, too preoccupied to notice the doorman's absence.

He took the stairs by two and three, proprioception taking over.
Feeling good—Feeling Good!
Feeling fine—Feeling Fine!

Knott watched Adrian weigh a white pit bull. It dangled in the harness calmly, all of this protocol to it. His owner studied the dial on the scale.

"Eighty-eight," Adrian said, looking at Knott. Protest was coming.

"Naw, naw," the dogman said, waving both hands. "That no right."

"Fuck it ain't," Adrian said. He looked at the arena where an older man stood inside of it, leaning against the iron bars, staring at some women by the port-a-potties. "Hey Georgia, c'mere."

The old man turned around, searching faces until he saw Adrian waving. He yelled *whachu want* over the crowd but Adrian only waved harder. Knott, dressed in the crew's uniform black denim, stood to the side of the scale, watching the dogman. He was Hispanic, sweaty in a crisp wife beater and jean shorts with a white belt. He went back and forth between his posse and the scale. The posse, four men of similar garb standing by the bathrooms, made no hint of emotion, letting the dogman vent to them without saying a word.

RJ walked up, asked Knott what the holdup was.

"Too heavy," Knott said. "He got to forfeit something."

"Ten percent," RJ said. "If he want in."

"They'll want in. They always want in."

Georgia made his way through a small crowd around the scale, buttoning his red blazer as he limped along. He, Adrian, and the Hispanic dogman talked in a huddle briefly before Georgia broke off again, heading through a haze of cigarette smoke toward the bleachers.

The bleachers were mostly vacant, a baker's dozen of bodies seated about, coming and going. On the bottom bench sat a white man in insulated tan coveralls, zipped to the top. A pit bull of the same tan color with a wide chest squatted between his legs and wore a thick collar with a galvanized steel leash attached. The dog panted but was otherwise still, watching people walk to and fro with a wide arc around him. He occasionally had to readjust himself when his back feet slid apart on the concrete.

Georgia leaned over and talked for a bit to the dogman, his left hand occasionally accentuating his words. The dogman's head was shaved and tattoo ink covered his entire neck, stopping abruptly under the chin. As Georgia talked, the dogman nodded with little effort. When Georgia stood straight, the dogman turned around and looked at another white man sitting on the top bench.

"Everybody gots they massa'," Knott said to RJ.

"Got that right. Looks like Kruk got himself a killer now."

"Two of them. You talk at him yet?"

"I will."

The man at the top, Kruk, also had a shaved head and wore gold-rimmed sunglasses with earrings and a chain to match. His white polyester jacket was unzipped halfway and the chain lay in a thicket of red chest hair. He leaned forward and spoke with a smaller version of himself who wore a red warm-up suit and a Kangol flat cap on backward.

"White boys don't look right in Kangols," RJ said.

"Rogo don't look right period."

Rogo scrambled over the bleachers down to the dogman. They conversed, then looked back to Georgia, nodding vehemently.

Georgia hobbled back through the crowd to RJ and Knott.

"Them Mexican's dog is eight pounds over the contract weight but Kruk's cool with a ten percent forfeit."

Knott and RJ looked over to Adrian. The Hispanic dogman was already handing over a roll of bills.

"Whachu got, A?" Knott asked, hands cupped into a bullhorn.

Adrian unwound the rubber band. His thumb flipped the bills to the end of the pile. He nodded once.

"That dog right off the chain," Georgia said, standing next to Knott with his arms crossed. They watched the Hispanic take his dog down from the scale's harness. "Look at him. He ain't ready."

"Nope," Knott said.

"Hoppers and boppers these days, they play dogs like the lottery. Ain't doing the work. Just trying to get lucky."

Knott tuned out. He surveyed the floor, watching small time bets everywhere, people with handfuls of bills in fierce negotiation. A few men were playing a quick game of dice against the far wall, the wait for the next fight taking too long. By the port-a-potties a lone white man stood talking to an apple of a woman, her white jeans tight on wide hips, ending in a sorry pair of muddy boot heels with tassles. Still wearing Saturday night attire to a Tuesday night fight. The white man held up three fingers high and looked across the room to the bleachers. A woman appeared from behind the bleachers, stick thin and faux tanned. The apple woman trotted that direction, her Jheri curl slapping the back of her satin blue jacket, heels clicking above the hum of multiple conversations. The dealer had a gun in his waistband and he readjusted his jacket over it. Behind him, between the port-a-potties, a man's bare brown ass worked like a jackhammer. Knott turned from this, wanting no parts of bouncing that act out the door.

Adrian trotted over to him and Georgia. "Let's do this."

Georgia nodded and walked back to the arena.

"Let me go get with him," RJ said, looking at his watch, then the bleachers.

"I'll be right at the ring," Knott said, pointing straight ahead.

"Yeah?"

"Yeah. What, you worried?"

"About what?"

"What else. That boy crazy."

RJ grunted, spat, and went on, weaving between people. Knott went to the ring, politely making his way to the front. Some began protest when they felt him brush past until they saw who it was. The dogman in coveralls had already dropped his dog in the pit but held it at the chain. The dog was lying down and this seemed to stimulate more betting all around Knott. Georgia stepped through the iron gate and the Hispanic dogman tried to follow.

"Nobody in the ring but dogs and the ref," Georgia shouted. "Drop him behind the scratch line. Unhook when I say go."

The dogman walked over to where the other scratch line was. His dog was barking at the people, pulling against the leash, and everyone spread out. Knott kept his place, eyeing the dogman rather than the dog. The dogman picked his dog up and dropped it in the ring.

Georgia took two bottles of water from his blazer's side pocket. He walked over to the tan pit bull and dumped the bottle from neck to hindquarters and back again. When he was done, the dogman leaned over and rubbed the water off. The dog only panted, tail wagging.

"I just clean him," the other dogman said when Georgia approached. "He got no poison on him."

"All dogs get washed in the pit," Georgia said. "That's the rules."

The dogman nodded with a sigh. Georgia doused the dog and it lunged at him halfheartedly when the water washed over its head but the leash held him back. The dogman rubbed the water off.

"Let's go over the rules right quick," Georgia said at the center of the ring. He walked in a circle, pointing at the Hispanic dogman. "Some new folks up in here."

Knott surveyed the crowd again. People came closer, shoved. RJ sat next to Kruk and they spoke like old friends. Knott's gaze fell lower. A woman with a cell phone stood ringside, holding it up to Georgia, recording. Knott stepped over and ripped it from her hand, dropped and smashed it under his heel. The floor was damp in straight lines, with specks of dirt, and he took brief note of it.

"Get your ass out of here," he said.

Her boyfriend was already backing away and, noticing this, she followed. Knott took their place at the ring, hands on the balustrade.

Georgia said, "When I say drop, unhook your dog. If a turn is called, one of these dogs lost interest and has to be brought back to the scratch line. You going to hear me say 'handle' when that happens. That's when

I'll bring your dog back to you and they'll start again. If a dog jumps out the ring, they lose. If I say pickup, either the fight is over because we got a down dog, it won't stay down, or we got a draw. If I need your help, I'll holler, but I don't ever holler." A club that looked like the leg off a coffee table lay to the side and Georgia picked it up. He smacked it once in his palm. "Y'all ready?"

The crowd yelled in a chorus of *hell yeahs*. Everyone on the bleachers stood but Kruk and RJ continued talking, even more animated.

"Drop!"

The dogmen unhooked their fighters. Both dogs stayed where they were. The Hispanic's dog was still barking, his neck held high, protesting the people and their noise. The other dogman leaned over and yelled a command and Knott saw the dog's calm vanish. It jumped to all fours and stopped panting. Then and there it knew its purpose.

"Oh shit," Knott said.

The white pit bull never saw it coming. In leaps like a gazelle the tan pit pounced, grabbing hold of its opponent's neck like vice grips. It whipped the white pit like a rag, like it weighed a fraction of what the scale said. The tan pit pranced in a circle as it did this, losing its balance and regaining it by ramming the white pit's body against the bars. It pushed up until the white pit's head fell over the railing and dangled. The tan pit stepped back and slammed its opponent down on the carpet.

Berserk energy washed over the crowd. Clapping, screaming, obscenities, everyone trying to outdo each other's bravado. Knott stepped back to the edge of the crowd, aggravated by all the jostling. He looked to the bleachers. RJ was patting Kruk's back. Adrian stood on a milk crate against the wall by the scale, and Knott headed in his direction.

"Oh damn," Adrian said in a pained voice. His face was contorted, as if being forced to watch. "That dog just tore the other one's guts open."

The Hispanic crew in the corner were still stoic, looking at their dogman before them. He only shrugged, his rounded shoulders dropping more. They walked single file past Knott and Adrian without a word, around the corner toward the exit.

Adrian said, "That's just—"

Above it all rose a noise foreign to all the fights Knott had ever attended. Metal grinded in such pitch that everyone stopped, gasped even, at the shrillness of it.

The bleachers were moving backward rapidly, throwing sparks out on either side.

*   *   *

Sal Goddard had never bought an electric hoist, the price never right and the set-up too much of a hassle. He went with the manual hoists to move granite and marble slabs around the shop and the manuals rarely broke or jammed. A good grip on the chain, gloved of course, and anything could be lifted. Or pulled.

On the floor below Stevenson was pulling down on the circular chain hand-over-hand as fast as he could, the grind of metal on concrete overhead. The hoist was attached to an I-beam and a cable ran parallel to the ceiling, out the open door and up to the floor above. The scraping stopped when the resistance was gone.

The upper floor's door came down first, end over end. Then bodies, screaming. The bleachers went by and the hoist's chain reversed direction briefly until the locking mechanism caught. The cable went taut again when the bleachers passed and slammed against the building. The hoist stayed firm on the I-beam.

Stevenson ran through the darkness back to the stairwell, patting the Ka-Bar and the holster. He climbed the stairs with his back against the wall, looking up as he did.

No one was at the open door. Just barking, many dogs barking.

The spectacle was not the pit but the bleachers and bodies below. People peered over the edge of where the sliding door used to be, some lying on their bellies. To the side, RJ sat in the corner, hands flat on the ground, knees to his chest.

"The fuck, yo," Knott said after breaking through the crowd to find RJ. He squatted next to him, putting his hand out. RJ jerked back slightly before recognizing Knott.

"What happened?" RJ asked, smiling nervously.

"I don't know, man. One second I'm watching the fight and the next, your ass is jumping off the bleachers right before they left the building."

"See that shit?" RJ asked. He leaned forward, looking out of the opening. "I could've died."

"You came close. "

Knott stood and went to the opening, poking his head out. The height made his stomach clench and nausea followed. In the snow-covered grass were bodies, none moving. One of them had landed on a conveyor belt.

"Oh damn," Knott mumbled, throat catching on the words. "God...damn."

"Help," someone yelled from below.

Knott leaned forward a little more to see the bleachers dangling against the building. Tangled within the benches was Rogo, hanging upside down with his jacket over his head.

"Help me, goddammit."

Knott went back to RJ. He was standing, arms crossed tight, looking at the floor. There were gouges in the concrete from where the bleachers had been dragged.

"Rogo," Knott said, laughing, because he didn't know what else to do. "He upside down, yo."

"See Kruk?"

"Naw." Knott rubbed the tip of his foot over another strip of damp concrete. It stretched across the room.

RJ leaned into the corner, sliding down to a squat again. "Almost died, yo."

His eyes were glassed, his defenses down. Knott saw the boy from years ago.

"C'mon, man. We got to get these people out of here."

Metal yawned, then rattled. Old pipes overhead that Knott had never noticed jiggled back and forth and bits of rust and dirt fell in straight lines, the particles forming curtains of dust. Georgia, still in the ring, spit the dust from his mouth, then rubbed his eyes. The Hispanic's dog was motionless, disemboweled, and the other lay next to it, watching the surroundings. Adrian stood by the scale. The moneyman always stayed where he was told to stay. Tink came lumbering toward them from the elevators.

Knott yelled, "What the fuck you doing, Tink? You can't leave the door like—"

The lights went out just as fluid spurt from the old pipes, stinking of chemicals Knott knew as fuel. Another odor made itself noticeable to him then.

Cigarette smoke.

Stevenson yanked the power switch sideways and it snapped off.

"Who are you?"

In the doorway leading to the stairwell stood a young boy but Stevenson could not see more than his shape, a darker red amongst red. The only light came from the partial moon through the wire mesh windows. When Stevenson walked toward the boy, he backed up. The dogs barked wildly, their cages rocking.

"Don't run," Stevenson said.

The boy didn't listen. He tried to open the exit door but it was locked at the top and out of reach. He darted into the next room and shut the door. Stevenson kicked it open.

"You can't," the boy started, tripping as he walked backward. When Stevenson was upon him, the boy held his hands up to deflect.

At the end of the room were shadows hanging from the ceiling, and Stevenson stepped past the boy. The shadows were dogs, hanging by the neck from the ropes he saw during recon, each with its tongue sticking out to the side in comic book death. Below each, excrement and urine, emptied out at the time of expiration, and the mask did little to filter the smell. Death row for the losers.

Stevenson turned around and grabbed the boy by the upper arm.

"Where's Knott?"

The boy went limp, refusing to look at Stevenson. When Stevenson asked again, screams erupted from the other side of the wall, both men and women. Flickering light appeared under the side door.

Stevenson dragged the boy to the exit door and unlocked the top lock. He tossed him onto the landing.

"Get out of here," Stevenson said and shut the door. There were keys in some of the deadbolts and he turned all of them and snapped them off.

"What the fuck?" RJ yelled, his voice cracking into a squeal. He and Knott had their backs against the wall, on tiptoes.

It rained fire, and except for them, everyone was aflame. The crowd jumped and wailed like trapped feral cats and smacked themselves in a spastic macabre, too overcome with the pain to think about shelter. Some rolled and a few no longer moved, face down on the concrete as if waiting for the flames to finish ravishing them. The apple woman was running backward, her head engulfed. She spit repeatedly, smacking her face. Knott and RJ watched her take the same path as the bleachers, right out the opening and into the darkness below.

"Stay up on the wall," Knott said. He smacked RJ's chest and they walked sideways.

RJ put a hand on Knott's shoulder.

"Don't leave me," he said.

They passed the doorway. Knott heard Rogo above it all, still yelling for help. A puddle of fire was in their path and Knott hopped over it. The fuel coming out of the pipes had slowed to a trickle and most had put their own flames out while they fled for the elevator. Tink was pushing people in, yelling to RJ and Knott to hurry up.

RJ only looked at the puddle, having no clue what to do with the obstacle. Fear was heavy upon Knott but within, for a moment, disgust.

"Let's *go*," Knott said, grabbing RJ's arm and pulling him around it.

Stevenson opened the door to a stream of burning people. Hair and shoulders mostly, but some had streaks of fire down their backs and he knew they didn't feel the worst of it then, but they would within the hour. He stepped aside as they passed and they left a trail of smoke and burnt hair behind them. They were running for the stairwell exit, most taking no notice of him. They pounded on the exit door, calling for help.

Circular puddles of lit diesel were shrinking in the dips in the floor and he walked through them without caution. Most of the crowd was trying to get in the elevator but some gave up and followed the others to the exit door. The elevator's light was on and smoke hovered around it. The occupants cried and writhed, as if trying to get out of their own skin. Ahead, a tan pit bull ran around where the bleachers once were. It nipped at its backside, trying to get at its burn wounds.

Jaris Knott was on his knees, pulling himself around the entrance of the elevator to where the panel was inside. Another man was next to him who simply dived between people's legs and stayed like this, his feet sticking out, one foot missing a shoe. Knott had a key in his hand and was trying to put it in the elevator's panel.

Stevenson unzipped, pulling Coleman's revolver free from the holster.

The elevator key found its home and Knott got on his feet in a crouch, pushing back against the crowd to make room. As he tried to turn it, he looked out of the elevator.

Someone in a pink jumpsuit was walking toward him, pointing a silver revolver. The tips of their boots had flames caressing upward and drops of fire fell on the floor where they walked.

Knott twisted the key repeatedly, begging it to give way.

"That's him," someone said in the elevator, straining the words. Tink. "There he is."

He wore a teal mask with streaks of black and gray and the copper filter over the mouth shined, reflecting the flames. When the gunman stopped and leveled the revolver, Knott saw the reflection of the scene in the crimson lenses and within it, himself. He could see the bullets in the revolver's cylinder. Hollow points. The gunman's thumb pulled the hammer back and Knott, for the rest of his days, thought that all sound stopped then, so he alone could hear the hammer come down when the trigger was pulled.

"Jody," the man in the mask said, a raspy voice Knott was sure he heard right.

A dry snap followed, then nothing.

The key turned finally and the elevator doors started closing. Some had noticed the gunman and screamed. The gunman stepped forward with his other hand reaching out but the doors shut and the moment was lost.

Stevenson holstered the revolver. The voices and cries faded, the elevator descending into the belly of the building. The people at the exit door had been kicking and pounding it repeatedly and he heard the door finally give way. When they were gone, all that remained was the barking of the abandoned dogs.

A man lay face down by the pit, his blazer blackened and shredded. Inside the pit was the tan dog, feeding on a disemboweled white pit bull, growling as it chewed. The white pit bull was still alive, its tail thumping as it whined, patches of fur burnt off and pink skin exposed.

The center port-a-potty was rocking side to side. The top had melted and fused the door shut. Stevenson minded it while walking over to the opening. Someone was yelling out there, from below.

"Hey, hey yo, what the fuck?"

A scrawny man was tangled in the bleachers and stopped all sound when he saw who answered his calls. On the ground were three bodies, lying in awkward positions not known to the living. There was an urge to help, brief but strong. *Primum Nil Nocere*, a phrase taught on the first day of medical school. First, Do No Harm.

The port-a-potty fell forward and to the side. The door burst open with a kick and a man dressed in black crawled out. Wads of bills fell on the floor and he snatched them up, jamming them inside his jacket.

Knott's friend from the hospital. Adrian.

Swick-swick-swick

"What happened?" Adrian asked, looking around, seeing someone standing at the other end of the room. He walked up to the body, nudging it with his foot "Georgia?" He nudged the body again and, realizing, began to run.

Stevenson sidestepped into Adrian's path and pulled the revolver back out. Adrian then saw what he was actually speaking to.

"We cool, we cool," he said, nodding, putting both hands overhead.

Stevenson reached around and found a small gun in Adrian's waistband, a .380.

"Take it. Money too."

Stevenson pitched the gun out the opening. He holstered his own and Adrian lowered his hands.

"What the fuck you supposed to be?"

Stevenson landed a haymaker and Adrian collapsed, spread-eagle. He took out the cigarette tin and repeated the sedation process. When Adrian's groans stopped, Stevenson stood, looking at the pit. The tan dog was lying on its side, eyes lazily open, its jaw and neck covered in the blood of its opponent.

Stevenson unsheathed the Ka-Bar and crouched next to Adrian. He put his foot on top of Adrian's wrist.

"I wanted to see what all that noise was," Tink said, phone in his hand. "When the power went out and that shit was coming out the ceiling I went back to check on the electrical box. There he was, dragging Pup by the arm to the stairs."

"And you ain't help him?" Knott said, more than asked. People had their phones out but he didn't care who they called now.

"Phone don't work," Tink said, his thumb mashing the buttons. He looked about at the others. "Don't nobody's work."

"Who the fuck you going to call?" Knott asked.

The bottom floor finally arrived and the door opening made them all cry out in relief. Knott stepped out and watched them all run. He reached in and yanked RJ out of the stampede when he saw him pass.

"Let's go, yo," RJ said, trying to pull away. He was limping, missing a shoe.

"I got to get the key," Knott said.

"Fuck that key. Let's go."

In the stairwell, people were running down the steps and Tink held the door open for them. They dipped under his arm.

"Don't none y'all say a damn thing, ya hear?" Tink said as they passed, their shoes crunching the remnants of the broken lightbulb. When Knott and RJ approached, he said, "Pup just went by. They broke the door down up there."

Knott and RJ exited and Tink slammed the door. Cars were all trying to leave at once. Knott grabbed RJ's arm.

"Holdup," he said. "Ain't going nowhere anyway." They stood there, watching over the lot.

"Fuck it," Tink said. "I'm out. Ain't trying to see no po-po tonight."

"They ain't coming out here," Knott said.

Tink ran down the stairs and joined the fleeing masses. On the other side of the dumpster a short man was helping one of identical stature and dress, in a cashmere coat, with long hair hanging over his face. Bing Bing and his cousin.

"Eh Bing," Knott said. "What happened?"

"You tell me, man."

The two men went on drunkenly, dodging the fleeing cars. Knott went down the stairs, looking around, expecting anything. RJ followed, hands on top of his head, hyperventilating.

"My Pops is going to *kill me*, yo."

"No he ain't."

"Yes he is, J. I tol' him we was done with this shit, yo. Ohmigod, he's going to kill me."

RJ threw a spin in as he walked, punching one hand into his palm. He murmured pity for himself, limping about, his sock getting muddy.

Knott said, "We straight?" He stopped walking.

"What?" RJ froze, looking at him bug-eyed. "Straight?"

"You don't know nothing about this?" Knott pointed behind him. "'Cause there some jacked-up folks back there."

"Fuck no I don't know," RJ cried, his voice carrying throughout the lot. "How the—what—how—." He threw his hands down as if whipping a pair of gloves off. "Quit playing with me, yo!"

Knott watched RJ, looking for a break in his delirium. RJ stood there, hands at his sides, mouth down at the corners like he was going to cry.

Knott said, "C'mon, let's bolt."

The Escalade was parked next to the building, nose facing the surrounding fence. Knott held the keychain up and the alarm beeped. They got in and he smacked his hand around on the floor.

"Reach under your seat," Knott said.

RJ did and pulled out a Glock 9mm. Knott produced his Glock .45. He pulled the slide back.

"I didn't think to bring these in," Knott said. "Never needed them before."

"Whachu think happened?"

"The fire? Natural shit, I guess. Electrical fire or something."

"*Natural shit?*"

"I don't know, brother. Can't understand none of it right now." He looked RJ dead-on. "I don't think them people that fell out is alive."

They sat quietly, watching the side door. The last of the cars left. The snow had stopped but gusts whipped up and cut visibility.

RJ said, "Let's go, man. Somebody might've called this in."

Knott saw something from the corner of his eye. Behind them.

"Look," he said in a hiss. He sank low in the seat. "Right there."

The trash chute was moving and snow was falling off of it. A figure appeared for a moment, leaping from the cage of the chute into the dumpster.

The Man in Pink.

Stevenson landed on something soft, organic, but the metal still boomed with his weight. He stayed motionless, listening. Not a car remained that he saw. His shaded vision adjusted in the confines. Everything dark red.

He had landed on a dead dog and his boots sloshed on the innards, moving the aroma with his steps. Stepping aside did not provide escape because he stepped on another. Within the moonlight, under a glowing blanket of red powder, were more dogs, scattered haphazardly.

From the center of it all crawled a miserable thing, announcing its intended path with stuttered growls, its front legs trudging forward, hind legs duct taped crudely. It looked left and right and tilted its head at the other miserable thing in front of it and Stevenson saw the dog really wasn't looking at all. It tried, but its eyes were scarred, white as the snow that sparkled on its fur. It kept on crawling until it was at Stevenson's feet, waiting for Stevenson to move.

There was no thought wasted on picking the dog up, unzipping the fire suit and loading it in rump first opposite the holster. Only its nose, grooved from missing flesh, poked out. It was shivering, gulping air in as if it would be its last, and its cold footpads clutched Stevenson's ribs.

"Look-look-look," Knott said. "There he is again."

The man in pink climbed out of the dumpster and disappeared on the other side. Knott opened his door and the interior light came on. RJ squinted, dropping low in his seat.

"Hold up," RJ said. "Let's wait on this."

"Wait on what?" Knott got back in and shut the door. The interior light went dim, then off.

"He got a gun too, yo."

"So?" Knott said, raising his own. "We ready. C'mon."

"Hold up," RJ said. He put a hand on Knott's wrist, pressing it away toward the windshield. "Listen."

An engine had started around the corner, a low grumble interrupted by spits of revving.

"Motorcycle," Knott said. He opened and closed the door with a slam and reached in his pocket for his keys. "I'm going to block the gate. Take this." He tossed the .45 in RJ's lap and started the truck.

From the other side of the dumpster a black motorcycle appeared with the man in pink riding. He drove a careful pace, enough to dodge the potholes, but it was still a pace of escape. Knott put the truck in reverse and stomped the gas, then put it in drive, whipping it around.

"Get ready," Knott said.

The man in pink saw them and the bike's back wheel spit mud and pebbles briefly before it caught ground. The Escalade had been ahead only a moment before the bike pulled ahead and was at the gate.

"Bitch is quick," Knott said. He worked the window switch on the console. "Shoot his ass."

RJ hopped up on the seat and worked his torso out of the window, sitting on the door's ledge. The motorcycle had passed the gate and was on the street.

"Shoot!" Knott yelled.

RJ raised the .45 just as the Escalade exited the lot. The drop to the street was domed and they took it without slowing down. RJ pulled the trigger as the Escalade dipped and his arm dropped down with the momentum. The bullet passed through the top of the wheel well and out of the headlight. Knott slowed and RJ raised the gun again but the bike was barely visible now, its rider working the gears to full speed.

Powdered snow blew across the expressway and formed brief twisters when Stevenson went through heavier portions but none of it had stuck to the road. He passed a few cabs and a motorist, but no police. He'd seen no blue and white lights strobing behind him or in front, heard no sirens approaching. The dog had repositioned itself inside the suit, hiding from the wind.

A few miles up he took the exit for North Hill Park. Off of the exit lay a gate for emergency vehicles that emptied into the paved running path around the park's lake. He worked the bike through the gap between the gate and sidewalk and rode around the lake at low speed, until they approached a lone pier. He stepped off, put the kickstand down, and stepped back to the center of the running path.

The dog had fallen asleep and only roused when Stevenson scooped him out and set him down on the bare asphalt, on the white center line separating foot traffic. With a hand on the dog's chest, Stevenson pulled the tape off the hind legs as gentle as he could but the dog whimpered, ending this in a squeal of mercy.

Stevenson took the gloves and boots off. He pulled the Ka-Bar from its sheath and unzipped the suit and stepped out of it, then unbuckled the holster and dropped it on the pile. He pulled on the occipital area of the mask and, when all things had their own color again, he thought of his first autopsy, that first cut behind the head ear-to-ear, where the scalp is undermined and pulled until skull is visible and the brow is pushed forward and down, giving the corpse's face a look of severe aggravation. There he stood, sock-footed in a t-shirt and nylon sweatpants. The sweat on his head crackled as it froze. He dropped the mask, studying it.

Never had that in me, to watch such a thing.

His gut clenched, thinking of the bodies he saw on the ground, that he passed when he drove the bike out of the caboose. Steam rose above them, dead but warm still. Three he saw, none of them Knott.

The dog stirred, curling into a tight ball. Stevenson sat next to him and put the boots back on. The dog crawled up into his lap, growling in grunts, and he picked it up and set it on the clothing. Under the bike's seat was a duffel bag with a matching sweatshirt inside and he slipped it on, his trembling becoming vigorous. A clip of bills was in the bag's front pocket and he grabbed it, dropped it, and scooped it up and put it in his pants pocket.

The edge of the pier, ten yards he had measured the week before, had no railing at the end but a 4x4 pressure-treated post was bolted across the last plank. He rode the bike up onto the pier and kept it going but brought his leg around and stood on the foot peg. He stepped off in a run and the bike wobbled slightly but kept straight. It hit the 4x4 and the front wheel arced straight up, then plummeted through the thin sheet of ice surrounding the shoreline. The black water bubbled and steam erupted briefly, then went still.

He flung the Ka-Bar in the lake and balled up everything else, stuffing it into the duffel bag. He cradled the dog under his sweatshirt and they fast-walked the opposite way they came, toward a trail that joined a pedestrian bridge over the expressway. The duffel bag hung on his shoulder, feeling heavier than it was.

This boy here says what you do you become, Bulldog.

"Fuck you, Collins."

CPSIA information can be obtained
at www.ICGtesting.com
Printed in the USA
FFOW02n1055040515
13155FF